A fiendishly wrought labyrinth of tales within tales, opening out from the most intimate horrors into aeons of desolation, wonderfully written and devilishly compelling.
Hal Duncan, author of *Vellum* and *Ink*

Achieves an uncanny and unsettling quality, trailing itself spookily across the tender membrane of the reader's imagination.
Adam Roberts, author of *Twenty Trillion Leagues Under the Sea* and *Jack Glass*

A little like wandering through a library assembled by some insane devotee of fantastic atrocities and excesses.
Robert Maslen, editor of *Mervyn Peake: Collected Poems*

From a satanic Punch and Judy show staged in the catacombs beneath London, to a ruined city stalked by warring immortals at the ends of the Earth, and maybe even beyond, Timothy J. Jarvis's debut novel draws together London horrors familiar and fresh, retold and reinvented, to thrilling effect. *The Wanderer* is a grimoire, filled with stories about stories, stories within stories, legends, folktales, histories and foretellings. It's a book you'll stay up all night reading – both to find out what happens next, and to forfend the nightmares it will surely inspire.
Neil D. A. Stewart, author of *The Glasgow Coma Scale*

The
Wanderer

The Wanderer

Timothy J. Jarvis

PERFECT
EDGE
BOOKS

Winchester, UK
Washington, USA

First published by Perfect Edge Books, 2014
Perfect Edge Books is an imprint of John Hunt Publishing Ltd., Laurel House, Station Approach,
Alresford, Hants, SO24 9JH, UK
office1@jhpbooks.net
www.johnhuntpublishing.com
www.perfectedgebooks.com

For distributor details and how to order please visit the 'Ordering' section on our website.

Text copyright: Timothy J. Jarvis 2013

ISBN: 978 1 78279 069 3

A CIP catalogue record for this book is available from the British Library.

Design: Stuart Davies
www.stuartdaviesart.com

Printed and bound by CPI Group (UK) Ltd, Croydon, CR0 4YY

We operate a distinctive and ethical publishing philosophy in all
areas of our business, from our global network of authors to
production and worldwide distribution.

CONTENTS

Then van Worden took, from his satchel, a bundle of yellowing mildewed papers tied up with twine, put it on the table. From what Mr Letherbotham could see, the sheets were covered in dense scrawl, mostly in English, but with passages of Latin, Greek, Hebrew, and some other languages he didn't recognize. He peered closer, over the top of his glasses.

'Found this yesterday,' van Worden said. 'Clearing out the cellar of the new premises.'

'What is it?'

'An old manuscript. Much of it is hard to make out, but...'

Mr Letherbotham cut in.

'What? That worn-out old Gothic trope?'

He rolled his eyes.

Simon Peterkin, 'The Taw'

Foreword

On the 18th December 2010, Simon Peterkin, a British Library archivist and writer of weird tales with a small, if cultic, following, disappeared from his Highgate flat. The event wasn't widely reported in the popular media at the time, for, though the circumstances were bizarre, it was not deemed newsworthy: there was no human angle, no one left behind – Peterkin, who was sixty-three years old at the time of his disappearance, was a man of lonely habits, was estranged from his family, had few friends. It did, however, attract the notice of some horror and strange fiction journals, including *The Shambles*, for which I'd written a number of articles. The editors asked me to investigate and write up Peterkin's vanishing; being intrigued, I readily agreed.

The residents of the mansion block where Peterkin lived gave strange accounts. At about seven in the evening, not long after he was seen entering his apartment for the last time, the sounds of a struggle and a high-pitched nasal yawping were heard from within. The building's porter was alerted. When this elderly Scotsman entered, he found the flat empty, no sign of violence. The only things obviously untoward were a lit cigarette, burnt down almost to the filter, extending a withered finger of ash, reeking in an old tortoiseshell Bakelite ashtray on the desk in the study (Peterkin had never smoked; the ashtray had been used to hold the boiled sweets he sucked on while writing). And a revolting stink.

A short while later, two police officers, whom, as they happened to be walking past the block, the porter had hailed from a window, entered the flat. Tracking the stench to its source, they opened the door of the wardrobe in Peterkin's bedroom to find the shoes and belts heaped untidily on its floor spattered with vomit and diarrhoea. The toilet in the bathroom was also in a state, and there were empty packets of laxatives and emetics in the bin.

The wardrobe was large enough to hold a man, and the initial conclusions of the police investigation were that Peterkin had hidden inside while the porter made his quick search of the flat, then somehow stolen out. As to his subsequent whereabouts, it was suggested he might have taken his own life; friends and colleagues testified he'd been stricken by bouts of misery in the months preceding his disappearance. No attempt was made to explain the more antic features of the case.

To my mind, this interpretation of events is lacking. First, the porter, who seemed to me highly reliable, claimed he had remained outside the door to Peterkin's flat till the police officers arrived, had only turned his back for a few brief moments while he called out to them. Besides, even if he had, for some reason, lied, Peterkin couldn't have passed through the mansion block without one of its other residents, many of whom, curious, were either milling about in the lobby, or standing in the doorways of their flats, spotting him, and all swore they didn't see him leave. Second, the idea he left the apartment through a window can be discounted; they were all fastened on the inside by security bolts. In any case, the flat is on the fourth floor, and there is no external fire escape, or anything of the like. It has been proposed by some that Peterkin might have shinned down a drainpipe, but that's absurd; the climb would have been arduous enough for someone young and fit, and he had long suffered stiff and painful joints.

It seems, then, Peterkin simply ceased to be, slipped out of existence, or passed into some other realm of being. Uncannily, certain of his macabre tales describe similar disappearances.[1]

Here my researches reached an impasse. Then, a month or so after Peterkin vanished, I was attending a horror convention and got talking to an acquaintance, Fiona G. Ment, the editor of the magazine *Gore*. Our conversation turned to the Peterkin case, and it emerged that Ment and Peterkin had been good friends, had met following Ment's favourable review of Peterkin's novel, *Ilona Joo* (1998), and subsequently collaborated on a novella, 'In the Teeth of Winter' (2002).

Like me, Ment felt the official account of the disappearance unsatisfactory, that the investigating officers must have missed something. She did, however, share their belief Peterkin had committed suicide. She related to me how, about a year before, while in Glasgow, visiting an old university friend and researching a short story,[2] Peterkin had undergone some harrowing experience. He'd refused to talk about it, but Ment had gathered, from details let slip, it was in some manner eldritch. Whatever it was, it blighted Peterkin's cast of mind, turned him morose and suspicious; afterwards, he'd even been seized, on occasion, when drunk, by episodes during which he turned delusive and strange, ranted that he was being persecuted, then, with a cunning look in his eye, mumbled low about how he'd best his tormentor.

When I explained I was looking into the disappearance for an article, Ment told me she'd been trusted with a spare key to Peterkin's. And so it was I found myself, six weeks after he'd vanished, inside that eerie flat. It was much as I'd expected, as the dwellings of lonely fastidious men often are. Still, Ment and I searched it thoroughly. We were rewarded, discovering, in a box file, inside a suitcase, on top of the wardrobe in Peterkin's bedroom – placed there, we supposed, for concealment – a bundle of papers bound up with string. It was a typescript, of some length; we presumed it to be something Peterkin was working on at the time of his disappearance. I was, of course, anxious to examine it. But Ment persuaded me we ought to appeal to the appropriate authorities first.

It took some weeks, but eventually word came back that the typescript had been looked at by the coroner and deemed of no relevance to the inquest,[3] and that Maureen Peterkin, Simon's sister, as executor, had approved our request. It was sent to me.

I opened the parcel, untied the knots securing the string, then settled down to look over the document. The machine on which it had been typed was presumably well-worn; many of the characters are blurred, partial, or faint. It is in a very poor condition: mouldering, water-stained, most of its sheets crumpled, some marked by darkish smears. A title on the first page identifies the text as *The Wanderer: A True Narrative*. On the next there is an epigraph, taken from the North American folktune, 'Going Down the Road Feeling Bad', and a dedication, the first of many addresses to a hypothetical, but fervently desired reader. On the page following that, the narrative begins. I skim read it first, skipping those sections that are difficult to make out, due to the bad state of the typescript. Then I called Ment up to tell her I thought it an unpublished novel written by Peterkin, perhaps his last work. She expressed interest in putting it into print, if it had any merit, but said I could hold onto it for a time, if I wished.[4] I then settled down to peruse it more carefully. It took me a fortnight or so to read it through; many of the pages had to be scanned and digitally enhanced, so obscured was much of the text. During this time, I became less and less sure about its status. There are a number of things that intimate it is not the fiction I first took it for: first, there is the matter of its prose style, which is very different from that Peterkin usually wrote in; second, there is a general air of it being more *account* than *story*; third, is the fact that there are things stated in the text which resonate with the strange manner of Peterkin's disappearance; fourth, there is the condition of the typescript in places, which accords with things told in the narrative; fifth, and perhaps most compelling, is a text I discovered, while looking over the typescript that second time, which appears independent confirmation of some of the things described in it (I've given this text, in this volume, in an appendix). Of course, all of these apparent validations could simply be coincidences, or otherwise rationally explained; perhaps Peterkin planned the whole thing as an obscure hoax. But I can't simply reason them away.

I leave it up to the reader, then, to decide what nature of thing *The Wanderer* really is.[5] Even merely taking story as *story*, there are certain thrills to be had from it, for all that its style is somewhat rebarbative. And it is my belief its depths will intrigue those with an interest in the weird. It is for these reasons I present it here.[6] I should warn, however, I've rarely been able to banish it from my brain since that second read-through and no longer often sleep easy.

Timothy J. Jarvis

1   See 'The Brass Ferrule' and 'The Glass Eye of the Stuffed and Mounted Bream that Hangs Over the Mantelpiece in the Old Stainer Place', both collected in *The Seven Circles* (1994), and 'Loathstone' from *The Black Arts* (1999).

2   'Necropolis', which appeared in the Summer 2010 issue of *Hauntology*.

3   It must have been a fairly cursory examination.

4   As, very sadly, Fi Ment died in the summer of 2011, it fell to me to seek *The Wanderer*'s publication.

5   Some will find it reassuring that certain events described in the typescript do not accord with historical fact, but I find the concluding pages offer an explanation as to why this does not preclude its being a true account. Another element which may be taken as pointing to *The Wanderer*'s being a fiction is the title's apparent reference to Charles Robert Maturin's Gothic novel of 1820, *Melmoth the Wanderer*, a work that was an avowed favourite of Peterkin's. The influence of *Melmoth* would seem, certainly, to reverberate throughout *The Wanderer*: in its narrative structure, its prose, its depiction of diabolically prolonged lifespans, and its denouncements of the mechanisms by which institutions compel belief. But, for me, this is too flimsy a circumstance

to ward off my disquiet.

6   And also because, if *The Wanderer* is a true tale, to publish it might aid in thwarting an evil. I am indebted to Maureen Peterkin for permitting me to offer the work to the public in its entirety.

A Note on the Text

Producing a 'clean text' from the typescript frequently required the use of software to enhance digital copies of pages, but only very rarely guesswork. Throughout, the spelling is aberrant, and this has been standardized. Obvious solecisms have also been corrected, but the many instances of tortuous syntax, left unaltered, since they do seem to be part of the design of the work. They are also an aspect of the prose which renders it very different from Peterkin's general style; he tended to favour terse well-constructed sentences. Another way in which *The Wanderer*'s idiom differs from the one Peterkin generally wrote in, and another feature that might pose some difficultly to the reader, is the occasional use of archaic vocabulary. Underlining has been switched for italics throughout.

The Wanderer

A True Narrative

Goin' down the road feelin' bad,
Well, I'm goin' down the road feelin' bad,
Oh, I'm goin' down the road feelin' bad, Lord, Lord,
And I ain't gonna be treated this a-way.
Traditional

To the hoped for, though doubtless chimeric, reader

Prologue

Dusk is gathering, but the grey canopy overhead is breaking up, and I hope to be able to begin my labours by the light of the moon that's soon to rise. I'm sitting on the deck of the rusting hulk I've made my home, a cargo freighter, named, many ages ago, exactly why or by whom I cannot guess at, the Ark, that, long since wrecked or scuttled, now moulders, canted, keel buried in the silt flats of a broad estuary, the mouth of a river known in earlier times as the Thames.

I turn to look west. In the past few years the skies have been rife with baleful hues; tonight the sunset is violet and bile. Silhouetted stark against it is the picked carcass of a vast city; its colossal edifices, sun-bleached, time-worn, scoured by dust-gyres, seem monstrous tidewrack or the strewed bones of a race of giants.

The light of civilization has long since departed that place. It was once known as London: a name whose origins are lost to the roiled past; a name not merely said, but incanted, a word from a black rite; a name that must still haunt the dreams of the degenerate local tribes. Before rootlessness was forced upon me, it was my home. In the midst of its ruins, I found, preserved in a glass case, in what appeared to be a museum of antique curiosities, the typewriter on which I'm producing this account. When I recognized the letters on its keys I was overjoyed; my native tongue hasn't been spoken for millennia, has long been dead and forgotten. Pondering this, I realize I'm not sure for whom I write. Perhaps only for myself; save the demon who stalks me, I doubt there is another living who could make sense of these words. Still, I will write as if there were: to admit there's no one left able to read this account, aside from that devil and myself, would make the needful exertions unendurable. So, since I feel sore swollen, gravid with the spawn that is my tale, I'll pretend; I'll address you often and cordially, my reader, less to ingratiate my pitiful efforts, than to evoke you by incantation. I'd also beg tolerance of my lack of facility, for my ungainly prose; I haven't written for an age and must grope my way.

My harried and woeful immortality began millennia ago, when I was but twenty-nine years old. Since then I've travelled the world over. But, as the Earth, which has completed countless circuits of the sun since the things I wish to tell of occurred, always returns to the place it set out from, my wanderings, despite imponderable distances travelled, have brought me back again to the scene of the events I mean to recount.

Though I know it will be a tiresome, enervating task, I've decided to embark on the composition of this memoir now because I've become convinced, in recent years, history is drawing to a close. The tainted aether, the weird colours in the sky, is just one of a number of harbingers of the world's demise. And, though I know I've placed myself in danger, it felt only meet to return here to London to set down my tale. Besides, it's my birthplace and has been crying out to me, calling me home.

For thousands of years, I hid among the remnants of the Tibetan civilization, the impregnable Himalayas my ramparts. My life was, for the most part, that of an anchorite. Still, while other peoples I've encountered, suspicious of my ceaseless youth, have driven me away, the natives of that region treated me with kindness. I became adept at their language, a harsh, if poetic, tongue, punctuated by sibilance and guttural clicking, often traded goods, and twice, near crushed by accreted loneliness, spent some years living in one of their communities.

Those mountain dwellers practice beliefs recognisable as a decayed form of Buddhism and still hold with a doctrine of eternal return, which, given the many auguries of the apocalypse, would seem absurd. Though the most horrific omens – seething seas turgid with dead fish, howling dust storms, caustic rains which defoliate forests and ulcerate the skin – aren't seen there,

there are still portents – the mountain climate has not proved impervious to change: once-freak winter thaws, which cause devastating avalanches, are now common, and the shades of the air are perhaps even more garish there than elsewhere. It would seem mere obduracy, even in that haven, to deny history is at a close and claim the principle governing existence is cyclical. The creed, though, is less foolish, I have to own, than that of the age I was born in. It held sacred, against all evidence, the notion of ineluctable advancement, for nature, for organisms, for human knowledge; I can testify history does not move towards one great goal – from time to time things start over, and it's back to square one. But the notion perpetual return governs existence is, while less idiotic than the teleological attitude, still entirely implausible.

The main reason, I suspect, the Himalayan faith has proved tenacious, where others have faltered, is that it doesn't require a belief in a benevolent Omnipotence – life is too cruel for such a conviction. Indeed, now the world has waxed so desolate, so quiet, it seems to me, were there a deity, or pantheon of such beings, it would be possible to hear breathing in the void. It is not, so I can only assume either the Earth has been abandoned, or void was all there ever was.

The sun sets, and the sky grows dim. Looking out over the river, I see it glows like tarnished gold still, as if it has enticed and drowned straggling rays of daylight. I watch the corpses of rats, and feral cats and dogs float past, for a moment, before the water too darkens. Night lugs its bulk into the firmament and squats there, blotting all out. Then slowly opens its myriad eyes. A short while later the moon rises – waning gibbous, bloated, wan, and mottled, sickly. But bright enough to work by, so I set up the typewriter on my makeshift desk, a piece of driftwood resting on two oil drums, pull up my chair, an actual chair, plastic, that I found in the corner of a shipping container on board this hulk, and settle down to compose this prologue.

And now I can't put it off any longer. I prevaricate only because I've no desire to relive the events about which I feel bound to write. But I must now send beaters into the brakes of my brain, flush out cowering memories. These fragments I will shore against my ruins. And so I begin.

That's the Way to Do It!

As it had been a long and tiresome day, I went for a pint in the Saracen's Head after work. The evening was cold and the breath of the few pedestrians fogged in the air. In the pub's grate, a fire crackled; I was glad of its warmth. A quiz programme was showing on the television in the corner of the room, sound low, but just audible. The presenter, a clean-shaven, jowly old man, wearing a suit in a sheeny fabric, fired questions at a chubby young woman hanging upside down by her ankles from a contraption that looked like something the Inquisition might have used to torture heretics. Distracted by efforts to keep the hem of her floral dress clamped between her knees, she was struggling to answer the simple riddles the gamesmaster posed. Then the image cut to a shot of an audience member: a scrawny young woman, crying with laughter. Catching sight of herself on the studio monitors she shrieked, 'She ain't got no knickers on!' A close-up on the contestant's face, now flushed, followed.

While I sat sipping my lager and gawping at the screen, a bearded old man sidled up and perched next to me, in one gnarled fist, a pewter tankard of ale, in the other, an unlit cigarette, loosely rolled, shedding tobacco all over the table-top.

'The wolves are coming back,' he said, in a hoarse voice, knitting his brow.

'Ah,' I replied, noncommittal.

'Mark my words, they're coming back. You can count on it.'

In those days I hated to be accosted if it was a quiet drink I sought (now, of course, I pine for company, any company), so turned, meaning to rebuff him. But this, I saw, was unnecessary; he then seemed barely aware of me, ran his fingers through his hair, stared into his glass like a crone scrying in the leaves at the bottom of a teacup. Reaching under my seat, I took the novel I was reading, *At the Mountains of Madness*,[1] from my bag, found my place, settled back in my chair.

I'd read six pages of the fastidious, yet overwrought prose, when I noticed an awed hush. Glancing about me, I found all gazes were fixed on the television set. The volume had been turned up, but not loud. Most of the patrons were motionless, their faces drawn and tense, though a couple of younger men at the bar mouthed, 'Take the money,' over and over, as if it were a petition in a litany. Looking up, I saw, on the screen, a young man standing before two plate-steel doors, supplicating the audience for help making a decision, while, at his side, the oily host grinned, rubbed his hands together.

At that instant, the reverent hush in the alehouse was broken by a loud shout. It was a colleague of mine, perhaps a little drunk, who had seen me through the open door. I turned, gestured, frantic, for her to be quiet, but she was unaware.

'What're you doing here?' she called out. 'We thought you'd gone home.'

Rapt piety disturbed, the regulars turned to glare. Out of the corner of my eye, I could see the television screen; the male contestant, face twisted, bitter, was being strapped into what looked a dentist's chair, by two lab-coated molls. I shook my head, then, pressing my lips firmly together, pointed at my mouth and raised my eyebrows. But to no avail.

'We're all just over the road in the Sheaves. Come on, join us.'

'Why don't you?' the publican growled, from behind the teak bar. 'Clear off.'

Abashed, I got up, crossed over to the young woman. Her name was Rachel. She took my hand in hers and looked up at me through dark lashes. Her greenish-grey eyes were startling. My chagrin waned, I bent down in mock gallantry to kiss her knuckles, was rewarded with a pert grin (when I think of that moment in these desolate surroundings, I am truly heartsick).

I followed Rachel across the street. We entered the Sheaves, a lively, noisy bar, with film and concert posters on the walls, and speakers in every corner playing loud music. I joined my co-workers. They were sat on sofas round a long table that looked as if it had been bought at a sale of second-hand school furniture: initials and expletives written on or carved into the timber. Rachel, who'd left the gathering to get money from a cash-machine, explained to the others how she'd seen me drinking in the Saracen's Head. I greeted everyone, and they seemed glad to have me there. They shuffled up. Rachel motioned for me to sit by her.

We drank late into the night, increasingly soused, a binge. Rachel flirted with me, sitting close enough for her thigh to brush mine. Then, after the pub closed, the gathering dispersed. I escorted Rachel to the overground rail, we walked with our fingers interlaced. At the entrance to the station we parted, and she kissed me lightly on the cheek.

I didn't have to wait long at my stop before a bus arrived, but it broke down before getting very far, on Mildmay Park. I was tired, very drunk, had the start of a headache, and longed to be in bed, so, in spite of the chill and the driver's vow he'd have the engine fixed in no time, I decided to walk to Highbury Corner where several routes converged. The night had got even colder and now the air was heavy with damp; the streetlamps were hazed. Then, perhaps three or four minutes after I'd alighted, the bus passed by. A couple of teenagers leant out of a window to jeer. I swore bitterly. A moment later, I saw the sight that was to curse me.

On a Saturday afternoon, six weeks, or so, earlier, out shopping in central London, I was walking by way of Covent Garden from Neal Street to the Strand. On James Street, I was forced to weave through crowds of tourists queuing for cheap theatre tickets and watching street-performers bedizened as aliens, robots, classical statuary. Entering the Piazza itself, I heard, over the bustle, the harsh stridulation of a Punch and Judy man's swazzle. It was some moments before I saw the booth itself, hunched in one corner of the square. Its chipboard surround was painted to mimic an ornate proscenium, two ivy-twined columns supporting an arch, keystone ornamented with a carving of Punchinello's head, three cherubs, each cradling a lyre, perched atop, smirking down at the stage. The drapes around the fit-up were blue, not striped red and white as they usually are. A small group had gathered, elderly for the most part. There wasn't a single child among them, which struck me as odd. I crossed over for a closer look.

The play was part-way through. Punch meted out blows to a portly man carrying a black doctor's case.

'I the medic now!' screamed Punch, striking the other with his stick. 'A littel of your own physic will do you a power of good.'

'No more, I pray, Mister Punch,' the good doctor pleaded. 'I am quite cured now, I swear to it!'

'Oh, but you still look peaky, you bad still. Physic! Physic! Physic! Physic!'

With each repetition of the word, Punch laid a blow on the leech's cranium.

'Mister Punch, no more. One pill of that physic is a dose, I tell thee.'

'Quacky, quacky, quack, quack,' screamed Punch, a berserk mallard, chasing the physician around the stage, administering a vicious pummelling.

'A few more and you'll not want curing again, quacky, quack, quack. Maybe you don't feel the medicine inside?'

And with this, the hook-nosed hunchback poked the doctor, hard, in his vat of guts, and the man fell down dead.

'Hee, hee, hee,' laughed Punch, casting the body over the front of the stage. 'Heal thyself now, if you can!'

The antic capering continued, the bloodless, but brutal cudgelling, as Punch beat to death: a horse, a rich man's servant, a ghost, and a milk maid and her cow, a glum beast with dangling udders, which yielded to fate with a doleful low and a slow shake of its massive skull. Finally two lawmen, dressed in tricorner hats, frock coats, and pantaloons, entered, and, managing to dodge Punches swipes, seized hold of him and took him to court.

The play was violent and bawdy, the drubbings savage, the puns lewd – in court, the judge, a puppet with a sagging face, wearing the full-length wig, described the hunchback's mistress, Pretty Poll, as having, 'on many occasions, suffered a good length of rod.' It definitely wasn't suitable for children, it was good there were none in the audience. I was surprised no one complained, but all just gawped on, listless.

Following the trial, a guilty verdict was delivered. Punch, sentenced to death, was strung up on a gibbet by a hooded hangman, kicking and screaming to the last.

'Surely some mistake. I no bad man. I was just having a littel fun!'

After Punch's burial, the curtains closed. The rest who'd been watching shuffled off, but I hung around, intrigued to see the puppeteer behind the bizarre, archaic show. After five minutes, when no one had emerged from the fit-up, I walked round to the rear; the curtain there was drawn back, the booth empty; it seemed he or she had somehow slipped away without my noticing.

Over the next few weeks I saw the booth on a number of occasions, in various places around town. Mostly I ignored it, walked straight past, but occasionally I'd a moment to spare and stayed to watch the buffoonery. It appeared the puppeteer was following a script, not improvising; there were minor changes to the dialogue at each performance, but the order of events remained the same. I never saw the Punch and Judy man, he never came out from the fit up to take applause, of which anyway, there was only a smattering, never passed round a cap. The audience was always, aged, and I recognized many of the same faces each time. It was all odd, passing odd, but I never suspected malignancy (perhaps because I was preoccupied by work: it was busy at the office then). It wasn't till the evening I, lacking patience, got off the bus, broken down but soon fixed, I realized a weird evil was at work.

As I strode, irked, through London's night-quiet, heading for Highbury Corner, I saw a primly-attired old woman coming towards me down the centre of the road. She was walking along the broken white line like it were a tightrope: feet splayed, painstaking, arms flung out as if for balance. From time to time, she stumbled. Overhead, in a clear sky, hung a moon like a dollop of bacon grease in a black pan. I crossed over and, drawing closer, saw the old woman was in a stupor. She threw her head back, jaws agape, and screeched, in a tone that possetted my blood, 'That's the way to do it!' It was then I recognized her as one of the wonted spectators of the Punch and Judy show.

Letting her go on ahead, I followed after, allowing myself to believe I acted out of kindness: not rousing her, lest the abruptness of her waking caused distress, but keeping an eye on her, ensuring she didn't come to harm. Thinking back on things now, I realize my true motivation was less noble: curiosity.

The old woman walked on, south, back the way I'd come, her progress slow, halting. Due to the lateness of the hour, there were not many vehicles about, and the drivers of the few cars and vans that passed spotted her in time to slow, skirt round. As the warmth, if not the whirl, of the drink wore off, I began to shiver, my headache worsened. Looking at my watch, I saw it was half past midnight, heart of the witching hour. On Kingsland Road, I kept to the shadows, wary lest anyone see me creeping in the woman's wake and presume my intentions were ill. Under the railway bridge near the junction with Old Street, a powerfully built man with close-cropped hair, dressed in a well-tailored suit, staggered out of a club. Sighting the old woman, he slurred a hail in an Estuary accent. Getting no response, he reached into his jacket, took out a gun. I stopped. Calling out again, he loosed off a round. The bullet caromed off the tarmac near the old lady's feet. When she still did not react, he snorted, went back inside the seedy bar. My pent-up breath escaped me in a rush, and I ran to catch up with the woman.

She continued walking down Shoreditch High Street, turned onto Commercial Street, then stopped before Christ Church Spitalfields, stood looking vacantly up at the heathen obelisk that served as its spire. I also turned my gaze on it. It towered skyward to rend the veil of cloud shrouding the moon. Before, I'd remarked it seemed to bear down on an observer as if poised to topple; that night this caprice of perspective struck me as an ill augury (would that I'd listened to that mantic tremble and not followed the woman further). I concealed myself in one of the entrances to Spitalfields Market and watched the woman. She was motionless some time, then, with an agility and strength belying her seeming stiffness and frailty, hauled herself up and over the gate, dropped down, darted off, and disappeared out of view behind the church.

Running over, I too scaled the fence, though with greater difficulty than my quarry, and caught sight of her ducking into a mausoleum at the rear of the boneyard. I crossed the small cemetery plot, but paused, uneasy, if intrigued, on the threshold of the sepulchre. I stared up at the firmament hoping to compose and nerve myself by tracing patterns in the strewn disarray of the stars, but the sky was silted by the city lights, and only the very brightest of them were visible. But I found the mettle anyway, went in. Inside there were several memorial tablets and a marble sculpture on a granite plinth: a female angel in prayer, wings outflung, face raised to heaven. Water stains lined the statue's cheeks, imparting a melancholy air to her devotions. In one corner of the sepulchre, there was an archway giving on to stairs going down into the dark. I descended and passed through a narrow entrance into a crypt. There was a sputtering taper set in a wall sconce that gave out a wan light, a large sarcophagus, whose stone surface was covered with intricately carved designs, and, in an alcove at the rear of the tomb, a pile of human bones, stacked neatly according to type: mandible with mandible, femur with femur, skull with skull... This arrangement struck me as antic, disquieting; some bones had fallen from the shelf and lay heaped on the floor – their confusion did not perturb half so much as the harmonious disposition of those in the nook.

And there was no sign of the woman. I was perplexed. I could almost believe she'd lain down to rest on the jumbled bones piled on the floor, and, undergoing the processes of putrefaction and decay in an instant, been reduced to a tawny skeleton and lost among the other relics.

In all likelihood, I would have quit that place and returned home, had a rat not drawn my attention to a place of concealment so obtrusive, and so macabre, I'd not considered it. The rodent emerged, squealing, from a small crevice at the base of the sarcophagus. Upon closer inspection, I found a slight draught to emanate from the fissure and decided to try opening the stone coffin's lid. I tried it, but it was too heavy to lift by hand. Realizing a tool of some kind was needed, I cast about and discovered, in a gloomy niche I'd previously overlooked, a crowbar. I supposed the elderly woman had moved the lid aside just enough to allow her to climb inside, chucked the crowbar into the nook, and, once lying prone, slid the lid back into place; a feat, though one she'd shown she'd the strength for, vaulting the churchyard gate.

Taking up the crowbar, I set to prising up the lid. Misjudging its weight, I was too forceful, and the slab overtipped, fell to the ground. There was a violent report, and the clay floor tiles crazed where it hit.

The sight confronting me when I leant over to look into the box confounded: a flight of stone stairs descended into abysmal darkness. At the centre of each step a shallow trough had been worn by the passage of many feet; they looked hands cupped to catch alms.

I can't explain what I did next, save to say, intrigued, nerve bolstered by the drink still roiling my blood, I found it easy to deny my misgivings a voice; there was fanned within me a blaze of awe and curiosity that left fear and reason in ashes. Clambering over the side of the casket, I began to descend the staircase.

Once I'd left the light of the taper behind me, it was black as pitch, and I was forced to grope my way. Then, after a while, I saw a glimmer beneath me. The steps came to an end, and I found myself in a tunnel lit by guttering cressets. It sloped sharply downwards ahead. The floor was packed earth, but the walls and ceiling were regular stone blocks. I went on. The masonry soon yielded to stark rock, and several times I was forced to scramble over piles of rubble where the roof had caved in. Soon the last vestiges, bar the torches, of man's attempt to tame this dread olden place were far behind me. A slick of filth coated everything. I felt I'd wandered into the burrow of some predacious beast. The tunnel forked a number of times, but I was guided on by the trail of burning grease, like someone following will-o'-the-wisps into the heart of a mire.

After passing through a stretch so strait, so low, I had to squirm in the muck on my belly, I felt a faint breeze. Carried on it was a droning; pausing a moment, hand cupped to my ear, I made out what it was: the hushed voices of a large crowd. Reaching the top of a steep incline, I began, cautiously, to edge forwards. A few steps further on, the rock beneath my feet gave way to scree and my legs went from under me. After sliding a short way, flailing, I managed to seize hold of an outcrop, check my descent. By a faint, flickering light, I saw I'd entered a vast cavern. The atmosphere was dank, the dark granite walls, piebald with pallid fungi. Something cold and glairy dripped into my hair from the roof far above, ran down my nape. Stinking water pooled in hollows underfoot.

A large number of people were gathered on the far side of the cave, but I'd not attracted their notice; they were quite a way off, I was shrouded in shadow, and the pattering cascade of grit I'd started went unheard. Nearer at hand, several mineral deposits rose from the floor like the gnarled, grasping fingers of some monstrous buried crone. I clambered down to the foot of the slope, then, crossing over, hid myself amid them.

A large crucible of burning liquid, source of the fitful glow, limned the faces of the crowd with red. They were many, at least two hundred, all elderly, all attired in Sunday best, all staring straight ahead. I craned my neck to see what transfixed them, but my sight of it was blocked by a man head and shoulders taller than the rest. Cowled and robed figures walked through the throng swinging fuming thuribles. Then, the tall man, nudged by someone behind him, shifted, and I saw what held the throng rapt: the weird Punch and Judy man's blue fit-up. I stared aghast.

Then the mutterings of the crowd were silenced by an eerie, drawn out, 'That's the way to do it!', the sound of the swazzle keen and strident, and the play began.

Ritual mayhem, brutalizations and murders, the throng replying to Punch's asides solemnly and with one voice – a dire litany. Under open sky, the play had seemed merely grotesque; now, beneath ground, by a baleful glimmer, under an acrid pall, it seethed with dread.

But was familiar. The same script. Till the end, when, after being hauled kicking and wailing to the scaffold, Punch did not submit to the noose, but began to chaff his hooded executioner.

'Mister Jack Ketch, if you please, what must I do?'

'Mister Punch, it's simple enough, place your head,' here he knocked his knuckles against the hunchback's skull, 'through this loop.'

'What for? I don't know how!'

'Now, Mister Punch, no more delay! It's very easy.'

'Alright. Let me see. Is *this* the way to do it?'

Here Punch jutted his head forward to one side of the noose.

'No, no! Here!'

'Like *so*, then?'

Punch thrust his chin out on the other side of the halter.

The hangman threw his hands up in frustration.

'Not so, fool.'

'Mind who you is calling fool. It's tricksome. See if you can do it yourself. Only show me how and I'll do it directly.'

'Very well, I will.' The hangman poked his head through the hempen collar. '*There*. You see, it's easy.'

'And then pull on it, *so*!' yelled Punch, with glee, grabbing the free end of the rope and hauling the hangman into the air, kicking and howling. He threshed a while, then hung lifeless, swinging to and fro.

'Huzza, huzza!' Punch crowed.

He cut the body down, laid it in a coffin dragged from the wings. Before nailing the lid shut, he took the hangman's hood, put it on. Two pallbearers entered, picked up the box, and toted it off on their shoulders, performing an antic jig as they did so.

'There they go. They think they have got Mister Punch safe enough.'

The hook-nose took off the hood, threw it into the crowd, then whirled about like a dervish, trolling in a cracked and strident tone.

They're off! They're off! I've done the trick!
Jack Ketch is dead: I'm free,
I do not care, now, if Old Nick
Himself should come for me.

The curtain fell. When it rose again the backdrop had changed to a moonlit London street, St Paul's looming behind. Punch stood singing and beating time on the setts with his stick.

Right foll de riddle loll,
I'm the boy to do 'em all.
Here's a stick,
To thump Old Nick,
If he by chance upon me call.

A head peered around the drapes at the edge of the proscenium then. I glimpsed bloated features, malevolent eyes, a forked tongue, crooked ram's horns, stifled a gasp; the other puppets' faces were fixed, this one was hideously expressive. Gripped by convulsive shivers, Punch retreated.

'Oh dear!' he quavered. 'Talk of the Devil and he pops up his horns. That is the old gentleman, sure enough.'

The dread thing emerged from behind the curtains, approached Punch, walking with a strange scuttering gait. It was arrayed in a gore-daubed suit of plate, cuirass chased with fine renderings of vile deeds, and held, two-handed, a broadsword. Its torso and arms were human, legs, a goat's, and it had a lizard's tail. I could have held it in the palm of my hand, but was stricken with terror, for it seemed alive.

'Good, kind Mister Satan,' Punch wheedled, bowing low. 'Lord and master, most remorseless and most cruel, I never did you any harm, but all the good in my power.'

The fiend stopped, darted out its serpent's tongue to taste the air, then started towards Punch again.

'There, there, don't come any nearer. How are you, good sir? I trust you and your respectable family are well. Much obliged for this visit, but I'd be sorry to keep you, I know you must have much pressing business in London town this night.'

The thing snickered, continued to cross the stage.

'Oh, what *will* become of me!' wailed Punch.

Closing with Punch, the thing swung its sword; the

crookback, leaping aside, narrowly avoided having his head cleaved from his body. Once he'd recovered his balance, he lashed out with his stick, but failed to land the blow. The thing backed away, and Punch followed, flailing wildly. But the fiend was the fleeter and more agile of the two, and, after a bit of business in which it laid its head down on the boards, and moved it rapidly from side to side to dodge Punch's swipes, it darted into the wings.

'Hee, hee, hee,' laughed Punch. 'That's the way to do it!'

'Oh no, it isn't,' the audience intoned.

'Oh yes, it is,' Punch retorted. 'He's off. He knew what was good for him, what side his bread was buttered. He knew not to fool with Mister Punch.'

A heartsnatching yawp followed. Punch flung himself to his knees, whimpering.

'Oh, forgive my arrogance, Mister Devil, sir. I won't ever be bad again.'

The thing came back out from behind the drapery and stalked towards the pitiful, cowering Punch. It beat the air with its tail and breathed fire; I was no longer in any doubt the miniature demon was quickened by some malignant occult force. Standing facing the audience, it unbuckled and removed its breastplate, then plunged its sword into its scabrous bulging belly, gouging a long rent. Ichor spurted. It drew out its blade, leant on it as a weary greybeard leans on a cane. Then there was a movement within the wound, and some gore-slick thing slopped forth. The demon lifted this spawn to one swaying pocked dug. It suckled, swelled, then dropped from the teat. Its rough form was that of a mastiff, but it was a dread chimera, a freakish hash, with a tapir's snout, a hagfish's grisly gape, a fox's mealy muzzle, a goat's grizzled beard, a sea devil's lure, a vulture's ruff and tonsure, a platypus's venomous spur, a lobster's claw, a toad's throat sac, an armadillo's plated back, the mandibles of a stag beetle, a turkey's snood, carbuncle, and wattle, a hog's bristles and wild eye, a warthog's tusks, a narwhal's braided horn, a rat's tail, a man o' war's scourges, a weasel's sneer, an echidna's spines. It was covered with sores. Slaver dripped from its maw. It was fetid; I gagged on its stench, far off though I was.

It whined like a hyena, whooped like a gibbon, yowled like a mandrake, growled like a bear, then loped across the stage, pounced on Punch. The wind was knocked out of him, his stick flew from his grasp. But he quickly got his breath back, fought back. He and the hellhound rolled about the stage, a welter of teeth, fists, tusks, talons. The hellhound got Punch's nose between its jaws, worried at it. Punch howled, went to his knees, eyes rolled back in his head. But then he sneezed, blasting the hellhound across the stage, stunning it. After snatching up his stick, Punch ran over, pulped its skull. A lurid matter dripped down the front of the fit-up, staining the drapes.

'Hee, hee,' he giggled. 'It'll take more than *that* to bring me low.'

Then, holding his arms stiffly, as if clasping a partner, he began to waltz, crooning the while.

I am the famous Mister Punch,
I am no damn beginner.
I'll eat that curséd hound for lunch,
Its master for my dinner.

During the scuffle the demon's injury had healed and, while Punch cavorted, it donned the cuirass it had removed to birth the hound. Then it spewed flames at the whirling hunchback. Punch's pointed hat and ruff caught ablaze, and he lurched about, moaning. Then he threw himself down, rolled, and put out the flames. Then leapt to his feet, charged, but the demon whacked him round the head with the flat of its sword, knocking him over. He stood again, this time unsteadily, clutching his skull and whimpering. The demon didn't press its advantage, but stood pointing and cackling. Then, once Punch had recovered from his daze, rage seemed to get the better of fear.

'Why, you must be one very stupid Devil not to know your best friend when you see him. It seems we will have to try who is the best man, Punch or the Devil!'

With that they fell on one another, reeled about the stage, a frenzied gyre. Recalling my mobile's camera, I got it out of my bag, took some pictures. Of course they didn't come out, and not because it was too dark; indeed, the crucible had flared up. No, the images were warped, blurred, smeary moils.

Punch had the worst of things; the demon laid him open in several places, and the front row of the watching crowd was spattered with his blood. Eventually he collapsed and lay prone. The demon stood over him, prodded him in the ribs with a cloven hoof. But the trickster was only feigning. He tripped the demon with his stick, got to his feet, and rained down blows – blows so savage his staff shivered. Before the demon had time to recover from this assault, Punch drove the splinter he still held into its chin. It thrashed about. Blood welled from its gaping jaws, and soon the drapes round the fit-up were steeped in it. Finally the diabolic light faded from the demon's eyes, and it fell still.

'*That's* the way to do it!' cried Punch.

'Oh yes, it is,' the crowd responded.

Punch rolled the demon's body over the front of the stage with his foot, frolicked insanely.

'Huzza, huzza, the Devil's dead,' he screeched.

Then he grew sombre.

'Friends, we have a problem. Hidden somewhere near at hand, there's a snoop, a busybody, a meddler, a cheapskate who's watched the show without paying. He didn't ought to've done that. Oh, no, no, no. What do we do to fuckers like that?'

There was silence.

'Don't you know? Tear them limb from limb! Get him!'

The elderly folk began casting about, snuffling, scenting the air. I stayed stock-still. Then one old woman pointed at the stand of stalagmites.

I fled, ran back across the cavern to the mouth of the tunnel, turning my ankle a couple of times on the uneven rocks. Scrabbling up the slope of loose gravel, I looked back, saw the horde scuttling after me in a ruck. They scuffled, each frantic to be the first to lay hold of me.

I did not slacken my pace till I reached outer air. My heart was a flaring coal, I rasped for breath, shuddered. But I'd outpaced the frenzied pack. I gulped air. After climbing over the graveyard fence, I began to walk north on Commercial Street. It was just gone three in the morning. Though the streets were fairly empty, as was to be expected at that hour, it seemed the ordinary night-time round went on. A bus filled with dishevelled revellers went by me, and I passed a young woman smoking out the window of a first-floor flat, sounds of a raucous party behind her. She waved at me. I began to question what I'd undergone. Had it all been a figment? Brought on my stress? Recent pressures at work had strained my nerves, and I'd been sleeping badly for some months. Had I been drugged? But then, looking down, I saw my clothes were smeared with filth from the tunnels, stank.

At that moment, I heard a low moan behind. Turning, I saw the mob of old folk coming down the road after me. They walked with a strange jerky gait. I bolted.

Turning on to Shoreditch High Street, I saw a gap beneath a hoarding put up to hide an empty plot – a derelict warehouse had been torn down in preparation for the redevelopment of the land. I lay on my belly, wriggled under before any of the horde rounded the corner. Hunkering down, a bit back from the boards, I watched my pursuers' feet pass. I thought myself safe, they kept on by, but then there was a howl; I believe one of them got wind of me. They began pounding on the hoarding. I turned and ran, stumbling on the uneven, rubble-strewn ground.

Reaching the wall on the other side, I looked back, saw one of the chipboard panels splinter, give way. The pack swarmed through the breach. Frantic to rend me in sunder, they jostled each other, brawled. I gawped, aghast, as one man, neat, lank moustache, hobbling with the aid of a stick, punched a woman, grey hair scraped back into a bun, to the ground. She rose again, grappled with her assailant, bit into his upper arm. He clubbed her with his cane, splitting her skull, and she crumpled, was trampled. Though his arm bled heavily, the man came on, not even pausing to pluck out the woman's false teeth, still fixed in his stringy muscle.

Turning away, I clambered over the wall and found myself on Boundary Street. I ran north. I'd not got far, just crossed the junction with Calvert Avenue, when I heard the rumbling plaint of a worn engine and that wonted call of the night-time city, 'Minicab?' Turning, I saw a battered saloon had drawn up alongside me. The driver, an aging Rastafarian, with a heavily lined faced, grinned at me across the passenger seat. His teeth were overlarge, stained, carious. A sour haze of smoke roiled inside the car. Stuffed with the wound locks of his dreaded hair, the traditional red, green, and yellow tam he wore, girded his head like a motley halo.

He looked me over, took in the state of my clothes, my face, drawn and wan, the jittery looks I darted over my shoulder, and his grin waned.

'Wh'appen? Mon, you look like you seen obeah badness.'

'What?'

Very slowly, enunciating, he said, 'Evil science. Devilry. You shaking like a leaf.'

Not knowing what to say, I began to stammer something about knife-wielding youths, after my wallet.

The driver cut in.

'Rass. Dem rude bwoy teifs is choble. Dey vex me up. No worries tho, we step.'

'Sorry?'

With great patience, 'I can get you out of here. Fast. Jump in.'

I wavered a moment, but only a moment, opened the door, got in.

'Where you wanna go?' the driver asked.

'Highgate?'

'Sure ting.'

As we pulled away from the kerb, I caught a glimpse, through the rear window, of a liver-spotted claw seizing the top of the wall behind. I paled, shuddered.

The Rastafarian turned to look at me.

'Wha' dat? Everyting fine, no?'

'Sure, I'm fine, really.'

After we had driven a little way, he lit up a large joint, which he toked on furiously. He offered it, but I shook my head: it was fogged enough with fear.

'Mon, you still look scared,' he said. 'You sure you is alright?'

'Oh, I'm just tired, that's all.'

'Sure.'

He shifted gear then, and, glancing down at his left hand on the stick, I saw it was missing the ring finger. Catching my look, he turned to me again; I feigned interest in the buildings we passed by. He grinned.

'You wanna know about my hand? Nuh true?'

I frowned, shook my head. He chuckled.

'Don't be 'shamed. I tell you, pass de time.'

And so the Rastafarian, whose name, it emerged, was Clifton, told me his strange tale. He kept glancing asquint – whenever I was bewildered by his Rasta patois he'd offer a gloss. He'd come to London as a young man in the mid '70s fleeing the gang violence sweeping Kingston. But low kinsmen had, by threatening family in Jamaica, dragged him back into the turmoil. At first his part was minor; he held down a regular job as a doorman at a central London hotel and was only occasionally called on for intimidation or debt collection. He kept trying to get out, but, as he explained with a wry smile, his reliability, diligence, and honesty were like balloons and stones in his pockets: the top-ranking badmen trusted him more than his Yardie brethren, who were, for the most part, grasping, crooked, so he rose in the order, even as he sank in crime. So when a boss known to all as the Count needed muscle for a big cocaine deal, he asked Clifton. Planning had been painstaking, and the first part of the under-taking, gone without a hitch. The coke had been flown into Heathrow from Jamaica, hidden in guitar cases, delivered to the Count. He'd had it cooked up and was ready to sell it on to the dealers. A night-time meet, at an isolated, abandoned church in rural North Bedfordshire, was set up.

When, on the evening of the sale, the Count pulled up outside Clifton's Harlesden flat, in a blue van, with, as cover, the name of a glazier's firm on the side, Clifton felt dread, fear greater than fitted the risks of the deal, almost hid or ran. But he did not, went out, got in the van.

The drive out of the city, passed uneventful, in smoking ganja, talking about music. Then, several miles after they'd come off the M1, on a narrow, winding country lane, bordered by high verges, a badger darted out in front of them, froze in the glare of the headlights. It was too late to swerve or brake – there was a thud, then two jolts, as they rolled over the thickset beast.

The Count got out to look over the damage. It wasn't too bad: a headlight smashed and the front grille dented, that was all.

'Rahtid! Surprise we not broke a axle, dread,' he said, scratching his head.

Sheepish, pointing back down the road with his thumb, Clifton asked if he could go, check on the badger.

'Fool!' the Count barked, slapping his forehead. 'We dey pon haste, mon!'

'Is choble, is crosses,' Clifton said, kissed his teeth, turned away.

The Count smirked. Anyone else he would have beaten down, but he was fond of Clifton and his do-gooding ways. He bowed low, so low his forehead almost scraped the ground.

'Alright, I ease up. Gwan, if you must, Saint Clifton.'

'Saint Clifton' was the epithet the other gang members mocked him with. He pretended to hate it, but in truth, prided in it, a little.

After going back down the road a short way, Clifton came across a smear of blood on the tarmac. But there was no sign of the badger. He paused, cast about him. Overhead, the moon shone brightly behind a winding sheet of cloud; the hawthorns lining the verges cast twisted shadows. He returned to the van and they drove on.

It wasn't long afterwards they arrived at the assigned meeting place. Their contacts were already there, awaited them in a nondescript brown saloon. When the Count parked up on the grass, two men got out of the car. One, fairly old, short, wrinkled, hard-faced, flint-eyed, with slicked-back grey hair, dressed smartly in a black suit, camel coat, and paisley scarf, and carelessly toting a revolver, was the very image of an East End gangland boss. Age had not withered, but toughened him. The second man, who also wore a suit – his a grey pinstripe, which, though in cut and material less fine than his companion's, was still of good quality, if ruined by stains, dark splashes up the trouser leg as far as the knee – whose coat was a pea jacket, collar turned up against the cold, and who'd a pumpkin-shaped head and broken nose, was a thug, there for heft and thew.

The Yardies got out of the van, stretched, stood, shivering, wrapped their arms about them for warmth. To Clifton the country night seemed eerily quiet – there was no noise save the purling of a nearby rill.

The breath of the four men plumed in the cold, damp air, as if their spirits had been loosed from fleshly bonds. There was awkward silence a while, then the two gangsters approached the

Yardies. The man in the camel coat held out his hand to the Count, they shook, and he introduced himself and his companion. He spoke as if a damp rag had been stuffed down his throat. His name was Peterkin,[2] the brute's, Haines.

'Let's have a look at the gear then,' he went on.

'Where de cash?' asked the Count.

'In the boot of the car, mate. I wanner see the product first.'

'Nah,' the Count said, shaking his head.

'Look, I tell you what,' Peterkin went on, aping a smile. 'To demonstrate me good faith, right, I'll put me gun away...'

He dropped it into his jacket pocket. The Count kissed his teeth.

'Let me finish. I'll get my pal to show you the money, which is in the car, right, then ask him to stay over there, where he can't cause no trouble. Which he'll be happy to do, 'cause I'll ask him nicely. Awright?'

The Count muttered, 'Aks 'im nicely,' sighed, but then nodded.

Turning to Haines, Peterkin sent him off. He crossed to the car, unlocked and lifted the boot, took out, opened, and held up a suitcase full of banknotes. The Count relaxed. Haines closed the case, put it away, shut the boot, then leant against it, took a paperback from his jacket pocket, a Jane Austen, and, after finding his place, by a dog-eared page, began reading.

The Count went round to the rear of the van, opened up the doors. Peterkin and Clifton followed him.

'An' you can tell your bloke to clear off an' all,' Peterkin said. 'I don't want no funny business.'

The Count nodded at Clifton.

'Gwan over there, dread.'

Clifton walked to the edge of the graveyard, to where the hillside sloped away, took the end of a joint from his pocket, lit it, stood toking, looking out over prospect: fields of scorched wheat stubble, hedgerows, a small, tree-girt lake. Having finished his smoke, flicked the butt to the ground, Clifton looked over to see how the deal was going down. It seemed Peterkin had asked for a trial of the wares, for the Count had filled a small glass pipe with a little of the freebased coke, was offering it to the Cockney. He put the stem to his lips, took out a lighter.

From somewhere near at hand, there was a horrid shriek. Glancing over his shoulder, Clifton saw it was only an owl stooping on a fieldmouse. But then he heard a half-strangled cry from the Count.

'Pussy clot!'

Turning back, Clifton saw Haines had crept up on the Count, had him by the throat. Clifton broke into a run. The Count got free, elbowed Haines in the gut, thumped Peterkin, who was struggling with his gun, which had snagged on the lining of his pocket. The older man staggered backwards. Then hurled the crack pipe at the Count's head. He missed. Then came loudening reports, awkwards echoes, followed by a roar. A fireball engulfed the van. The blast threw Clifton to the ground.

Later he'd realize some ethanol, which is used in freebasing, must have spilled; perhaps, when the van ran over the badger, a flask had been juddered, fallen, cracked, leaked. The alcohol, touched off by the fallen pipe, then ignited the petrol tank. But at the time, lying prone, stunned, he thought maybe it was a bolt from Jah. Then a lump of twisted metal hit his head, and all went black.

Here Clifton broke off to peer through the dirty windscreen at the road ahead. Looking out the window, I was stunned to see Pentonville Prison leering down at me in the moonlight; enthralled by the story's unfolding, I'd not been aware of the passing of time (though, setting down Clifton's tale here, I'm confounded so much was told in what can only have been a short drive). I gazed into the fug pouring from the jail's chimneys, seeing weird forms.

'Rahtid! Gwan!'

I looked up. An elderly couple stood in the road, looked vacant. Clifton crossed the centre line to avoid them. As we passed by, they glared and pointed, suddenly animated, and the old man darted forward, clawed at the car. His hand struck the wing-mirror.

'Rass! I tink I hit dat tata,' Clifton said, putting his foot on the brake.

'What?'

'That old man. I's worried I hit him.'

The car came to a stop. Clifton put it into reverse. I blenched.

'No, don't.'

Clifton took his foot off the accelerator, looked at me.

'What's up, mon?'

I turned to look over my shoulder. The old couple stalked toward the cab, glaring baleful, the man shaking his balled fist. I fought to get my breath.

'Just keep going,' I pleaded. 'I can't explain, but I'm in danger...'

Clifton too turned to look back down the road. The old folk feigned meekness then; the old man switched his gesture to a wave.

'Alright, the old man seem fine. You scared though, no?'

'I am, but I don't want to talk about it, not now.'

'Sure ting. We get going then.'

'Thank you.'

We went on our way.

'So, did you lose your finger in the explosion?' I asked, once my heart had ceased drubbing.

Clifton shook his head.

'Uh uh, mi have more fi tell,' he replied, with an enigmatic grimace.

When Clifton roused, that night of the drug deal turned sour, he was lying on his side facing the burnt-out van. It still smoked; its paint was blistered, peeling, its tyres were cankered. Clifton realized he'd been out some time, for, though darkest night persisted in the west, a faint greying of the sky in the east augured dawn. There were three blackened figures lying on the ground by the van's rear doors, and the reek of charred flesh was in the air. Clifton retched. It began to mizzle; the droplets seethed as they fell on the smouldering husk. Clifton's skull throbbed; he put his hand to his dreads and it came away slick with blood. He passed out again.

When he came round once more, he lay on his back, staring up at the sky. It was day, though overcast. He'd turned to torpor, was able to move only his eyes. The dark stink of ordure, and a high cloying fetor choked him. Somewhere close by, a cracked clamour. Looking askance, Clifton saw, to his left, a man ringing a hand-bell. He wore a sacking robe and cowl, and his face was in shadow save his eyes – pupils, the pale grey of winter rain, rheumy, and whites, bloodshot. He had posies pinned all over his robe, sprays of spring flowers: daffodils, primroses, bluebells, and snowdrops.

We had to take a detour due to roadworks outside Holloway Prison, but I didn't mind; Clifton's yarn held me rapt. After he'd described the sinister cowled figure, he took his left hand off the wheel, slapped the dash for emphasis.

'It a duppy-man, I's sure!'

'Duppy?' I asked.

'It's what you call a ghost, an evil spectre.'

Rolling his eyes in their sockets, Clifton looked about him. He lay on a tumbril heaped with corpses, with ashen lesions, hectic cheeks. To his right, he could see the graveyard and beyond it the church. The van was gone. A flock of crows wheeled cawing overhead. To his left was a cluster of low, thatched, wattle-and-daub buildings, desolated. Aside from the duppy-man, and the dead on the cart, there was no one in sight.

After stilling his bell, putting it in a pouch with a leather strap, he wore over his shoulder, the duppy-man took up the handles of the barrow, pushed it before him, trudged across a miry field, to the edge of a carcass-filled pit. Then he began peering at the bodies on the cart. He took in Clifton's seventies garb and dreadlocks without reaction, but started on sighting the signet ring the Rastafarian wore on his left hand. He eyed the ring, tried to pull it from Clifton's finger. But it would not slide over the knuckle.

Reaching into his poke, the duppy-man pulled out a knife. He began hacking at Clifton's finger. Though inert, unable to resist or cry out, the Rasta was not benumbed. The edge of the blade was dull, the cutting, agony. Once he'd sawn through the bone, the duppy-man tore the finger free, put it in his bag, wiped his knife on Clifton's shirt.

Clifton closed his eyes. He felt the duppy-man take hold of him, lug him from the corpse heap, let him fall into the mass grave. On striking the mounded carrion, he opened his eyes again, found himself lying on the dank earth in the graveyard of the church once more, the sun rising in the east, the burnt-out van a little way off. The duppy-man, corpse cart, plague pit, village, were all gone. But so was the ring-finger of his left hand, a raw and bloody stump in its place.

He held that hand up.

'See?' he said.

I nodded. I asked him what he did after.

'I step out, mon. The Cockneys'd left keys in the ignition, so I took their car, drove back to London.'

'Do you think it true? All that?'

'I don't know what I think. Most of mi friends reckon there was some obeah, some bad science, in that place. Puttin' away the special sister I live with. She says to mi there was no duppy-man. She says I is pure bobo, a fool to think so. Maybe she's right.'

Clifton explained his 'special sister', by which I gathered he meant his lover, thought metal blasted from the van had loped his finger, that his dread vision had been caused by vapours from the burning narcotics. Then he shrugged.

Clifton's story had solaced me; I felt it true, felt he, like me, had somehow strayed over the bourn between the everyday and the eldritch – the truth of the old saw about the burden shared struck me then. Later, reflecting on the consolation his tale had afforded, I placed classifieds in several newspapers seeking folk who'd undergone similar horrors, proposing a gathering to relate dread accounts, and, in doing so, lessen their grip. I'd hoped Clifton might respond, but he did not: perhaps he never saw the adver-tisement, or perhaps he'd been, by that time, convinced by his lover's rationalization.

On finishing his tale, Clifton leant down, put a cassette into the tape-player. He grinned as the first strains of an orchestra filled the car.

'What you tink?' he asked. 'Know it?'

I confessed my ignorance of classical music.

'Ah shame, is irie.'

He told me it was a piece by an Estonian composer, Arvo Pärt. I found it soothing.

When we arrived outside my flat. I took out my wallet, but Clifton shook his head.

'Everyting's good. I enjoyed to talk wit you so there's no charge.'

'No, really, thank you, but...'

'No arguments. You keep yourself good.'

With that he smiled and fell to rolling another spliff.

'Thanks. That's kind of you.'

'Is nuh ting.'

I got out of the car, rummaged in my satchel for my keys.
Clifton leant over, wound down the passenger window.

'Likkle more,' he said, then waved, lit his spliff, drove off.

I went inside, got straight into bed. In spite of all I'd
undergone, I slept soundly till my alarm went off. On being
roused, though, after a few moments oblivion, the night's terrors
crowded back. At first, I thought them residues of nightmares;
once fully awake, I sat stark upright and cried out.

I spent the following few months struggling to maintain a
seeming calm, while my brain seethed. In the office, I was
diligent, finding respite in my work. Outside of work, I was no
longer taciturn, reclusive, but outgoing, spent many of my
evenings in pubs and bars: I found succour in both companionship and drink. All those who knew me were shocked and
pleased by the change; I believe I've never been liked as much,
before or since, as I was at that time. My flirtation with Rachel
grew into romance. We were well suited, similar in character,
though she didn't share my tendency to gloom, we had many
interests in common and went together to art galleries, concerts,
plays, and films. While with her, I found I could forget gnawing
fears.

However, despite these distractions, memories of the hellish
night remained; a splinter, left unattended, begun to fester. There
was one evening, when, at the end of a meal I'd enjoyed with
Rachel, at a cheap, but good, French restaurant, I became
distressed by a turn the conversation took and nearly drove her
away. We'd eaten well and drunk a bottle of wine. After dessert,
while we awaited coffees, Rachel took my hands in hers.

'Strange. I've worked with you for a long while, but I've only
got to know you in the last few weeks,' she mused.

I grimaced, partly mocking, partly in earnest. 'You're not

regretting it, are you?'

'Shut up! I just mean we wasted a lot of time.'

At this moment our coffees arrived. I spooned sugar into mine, stirring vacantly.

'I guess we have,' I said, staring down at the scum whorling on the surface of my espresso. 'It's just, I didn't think you liked me, not in that way.'

Rachel pursed her lips, wrinkled her nose, petulant.

'Well I did. Would've thought it fairly obvious.'

'Not to me.' I sipped my coffee.

'That's because you're an idiot,' she said, grinning.

'Fair enough. Still, things have happened at the right time.'

'I suppose.'

Rachel looked away, bit a fingernail, said, 'Are you keeping something from me?'

'What?'

'Not maliciously,' she went on, 'but because, I don't know, you're scared of my reaction.'

'There's nothing. Really.'

'But I might be able to help,' she sighed, staring up at the light fixture. Then, looking down, 'Your hands. You've got to be careful.'

I glanced down at them. They were dry and cracked, boiled-ham pink. I'd been scouring them often.

'They're fine. Just get like that when the weather turns cold,' I lied.

She winced. 'Look after yourself. I worry.'

'Well don't,' I said, vehement.

'What?' She sounded hurt.

I almost raged then, but damped my ire.

'I just mean there's no need,' I said. 'I'm fine.'

Rachel nodded, turned the conversation to a less fraught topic.

After the meal, Rachel stayed at my flat. We spent nights

together often, which I was glad of; when alone awful thoughts kept me from sleep.

(Soon it will be dark; the moon is setting out to sea, casting a wavering grey path on the water. Would that I could walk down it into eternity's repose. Instead, I will sleep fitfully on the grease-stained blankets I've laid out in the wheelhouse of this ship. The moon was waning gibbous when I began this account, now it is in its first quarter; it seems a fortnight has gone by, though, due to listlessness and the unvarying routine of my labours, I've not been aware of the passage of time – I'm grateful to that wan satellite for alerting me to it.

In fact, I'm thankful for more than that. All my writing has been done by moonlight: I'm wary lest the devil seeking me be close at hand, so lie low during the day, in the wheelhouse. It is always in murk, its windows are filth-caked, and I've no means of making light, bar an electric torch, whose batteries I wish to save, and flame, and one of my reeky hog-fat and bulrush tapers would soon choke the place with smoke; and when it's been too dark to work outside, during the new moon and on overcast nights, I've been loath to show, on deck, a light that might be seen for miles around.

During the time I've been writing this account, little has happened, save in my head and on the page, but perhaps I should give a brief portrait of my day-to-day life. The barbarians round about avoid me, perhaps suspicious of my pallor and stature: their skin is a healthy dusk due to constant exposure to the torrid sun – I burn, but do not tan; and, as men no longer attain the height they did in the past, I'm head and shoulders above even the tallest of their race. I have several times been ashore to forage for roots and tubers, or to hunt down and kill, with a spear bodged by binding a carving knife to a sturdy branch with twine, one of the small reddish pigs that wander abroad. In a clearing, a little distance from the hulk, I have a fire pit. There I'm able to boil water dipped from the river, make it safe for drinking, and cook my food, hopefully without drawing my enemy's notice: the rising smoke is lost among the sooty streaks of the local natives' many fires. In some ways, I'm glad life's dull; every evening I continue my narrative from where I left off the previous morning, and nothing distracts me from my task. But, though things are quiet, they are fraught – I am sore afraid of being found. Indeed, I believe the last truly restful night's slumber I had was in Rachel's arms, long ago. Our relationship was a time of calm, of blithe forgetting. But it was soon at an end: a buried evil will always claw its way to the surface.)

While I enjoyed that lull, London was harrowed by some random cruel assaults. Victims were badly beaten, by a cudgel or similar weapon; few survived, and those that did couldn't describe their assailant, having been struck down from behind. Witnesses were appealed for, but none came forth. Despite an increased police presence on the streets, the spate went on. People were afraid to walk the streets after dark.

One evening, I'd been out drinking in Soho with an old university friend. We left the pub at closing time. Drunk and less cowed by the attacks than most, the terror kindled by the demonic Punch and Judy show dulling other fears, I decided to walk to Trafalgar Square, from where I could catch a bus to Rachel's house south of the river. My friend was travelling in the opposite direction, and, more wary than I, hailed a taxi. We made our farewells, then I set out, threading my way through the labyrinth east of Carnaby Street. There were a few other brave or foolhardy folk on the streets: a suited man, on the way home, I supposed, from a late night at the office; a Chinese restaurateur carrying a brace of ducks; a hot-dog vendor; and a group of American tourists.

Then, on Wardour Street, I heard, raucous and baleful, Punch's traditional brag. It came from a dark alley on my left. I peered into the gloom, but could make nothing out. I called out, and, overhead, a curtain was drawn, and light spilled down. Sprawled, face down, on a heap of black plastic bags beside a large kitchen bin, was a man wearing chefs' whites. His skull had been staved. A clear fluid ran from his ears and nostrils, pooled, nacred, in the folds of the refuse sacks. He convulsed, mewled low. By his outflung right hand, which held a smouldering cigarette, was a ram's skull, with involute horns. Swagged with fruit and vegetable peelings, it looked some pagan fetish. Then the jerky rise and fall of man's shoulders petered, and he fell still and silent, slumped. Matter glugged from the head wound. I staggered back, stumbled, fell, scrabbled away.

After lying, retching and gasping, on the pavement a while, I called the emergency services from my mobile. I explained what I'd seen to the operator. Two uniformed officers arrived only a couple of minutes or so later. While one went to look at the corpse, the other questioned me. She was young, younger than me, yet composed, efficient. I gave an account, in response to her prompting, of what I'd heard and seen. She glared at me when I described the hoarse yell. After I'd told all, she walked off, to talk into her radio, then returned, stayed with me. At some point, I began shivering with shock and cold, and, escorting me to a nearby bench, she sat me down, fetched a blanket.

Not long afterwards, a senior officer drew up in an unmarked car. He was middle-aged, slightly balding, had a neatly trimmed moustache. After briefly looking at the body, he asked me to get in the car, drove me to a nearby police station. I sat in the passenger seat next to him. On arriving at the station, he took me through the reception, along a series of corridors, resembling those of any modern office building, drab carpet, thin partition walls, grainy fluorescent lighting, and into a small interview room. It was sparsely furnished: a plain wooden table, on which a cassette recorder sat, three plastic chairs, a filing cabinet.

'Take a seat,' he said. 'Can I get you anything? Cup of tea, coffee?'

I rarely drank tea, but felt like one then. I nodded.

'Which?'

'Sorry, tea.'

'Milk, sugar?' he asked, glancing down at my trembling hands.

'Yes, both, please.'

'One or two?'

'One or two what?'

He smiled.

'Sugars.'

'Oh. Two please.'

He nodded, left the room. Awaiting his return, I sat, mused, decided to say nothing of the horrors of the dire Punch and Judy show. After a few minutes, the officer came back into the room with a woman who was slightly older than him, had wiry grey hair, wore glasses.

'Sorry, forgot to introduce myself before,' the man said. 'Oliver Hardy.' He grinned. 'Eccentric parents. This is my colleague Amanda Hayworth. What's your name?'

I told him, he nodded, they sat down, and Amanda pressed record on the tape machine. They questioned me at length about my discovery of the victim, and my whereabouts earlier in the evening. They were official, but kindly. Then, when they had nothing further to ask, they left me alone for a few minutes.

On their return, they sat down at the table again, without a word, pensive. Amanda rubbed her eyes under the lenses of her glasses, then looked intently at me.

'Your notice was drawn to the alley by a cry of "That's the way to do it!" Is that right?'

I nodded.

'Any guess as to the meaning of those words?'

I shuffled uncomfortably in my chair under her scrutiny.

'Don't know. But it's Punch's refrain in the traditional puppet shows.'

'Do those shows have any particular significance for you?'

'No.'

Oliver grunted, scraped back his chair, got up, left the room without a word.

Amanda frowned, then smiled a thin smile. When Oliver returned a minute later, he was clutching my satchel; I realized then I'd left it with the uniformed police woman, forgotten it.

'Is this your bag?' he asked.

'Yes.'

Reaching into it, he took out a slim paperback. It was *That's the Way to Do It!: A History of the Punch Tradition.*

'Well?' Oliver demanded, brandishing the book.

I blurted everything. The detectives heard me out, sceptical grimaces on their faces. Then they asked me to wait a moment, left the room. I sat waiting, listening to the tape recorder's low whirr, regretting, bitterly, my outburst.

When they came back in, Amanda sat down, fixed me with a glare, while Oliver remained standing, at her shoulder. They'd clearly been wrangling, my guess was Oliver had been urging good sense, while Jane insisted on following protocol.

'We've discussed your statement,' she began. 'Do you think you could show us the crypt you talked about?'

'Yes.'

'Are you aware hindering a police investigation is an offence?'

'Yes, I am.'

Amanda nodded, removed her glasses, pinched her nose between the thumb and forefinger of her right hand.

'Alright, then. Shall we go?'

The short drive to Spitalfields passed in silence. I was sat in the back of the car, separated from the detectives in the front by a metal grille. When we arrived at Christ Church, my companions took a bolt-cutter to the padlock securing the gate. We entered the graveyard, I led them to the mausoleum, we entered, went down to the burial chamber. Oliver and Amanda probed the thick darkness with torch beams. The place was as I remembered it: the bones stacked in an alcove, tumbled on the floor, the sarcophagus. There was nothing in the crypt with which to prise up the lid, so Oliver went back to the car to get a jemmy. Once he'd levered it off, set it on the floor, Amanda shone her torch into the stone coffin. Inside lay a yellowed skeleton wrapped in a mouldering shroud, with, in its ribcage, two rats feeding on the carcass of a third. After shooing the rodents and moving the bones, Oliver groped for a secret entrance, but found nothing.

Both detectives were now convinced I was delusional, but still Amanda insisted on following correct procedure. She called out a team to dig beneath the crypt. Their van arrived soon after, and they trooped into the mausoleum carrying picks, shovels, a pneumatic drill. I waited in the car, nervous and exhausted, fell in an out of a doze, dreamt of a formal ball in a vast, richly appointed hall – chandeliers, armchairs, *chaise longues*, plush upholstery, gilt-framed mirrors – at which elderly folk waltzed with dread olden things. It was a while before Amanda came out, looking haggard, to tell me they'd found no stairs, no underground passageway. I began to bawl.

The detectives drove me home. Oliver walked me to the door of my flat, gave me a leaflet listing the telephone numbers of several counselling services. He said they wouldn't be pressing charges, but that I was required to seek some kind of help, that they'd check up. As soon as I'd locked my front door behind me, I screwed the leaflet into a ball, threw it into a wastepaper basket. I then went through to my living-room, flung myself down on the couch, fell into a stupor.

Sunlight, spilling through a gap in the curtains, woke me, the following morning, from a bad dream. In it I wandered the aisles of a huge deserted library, looking at the titles on the spines of the volumes on its shelves, unable to make out a single word.

Once fully roused, I went to the front door, stood rattling it; it was several minutes before I could convince myself it was securely bolted. Then I walked round the flat, pulling all the curtains closed and putting on all the lights. I turned up the heating, switched on my television and both my radios, unplugged my telephone from its wall socket, then found some parcel tape to muffle the doorbell's clapper, seal up the letterbox, and cover all the flat's ventilation grilles with. Afterwards, I stripped, had a scalding bath, scrubbing myself till my skin was an angry red, bleeding here and there, then I dried myself, got dressed, went through to the kitchen, poured out a mug of whisky, drank it at a single draught.

Of the two days that followed, I remember little, just fleeting impressions. I do know I didn't leave my flat, not once. I contacted no one. I allowed myself only snatches of sleep, drank whisky to dull my brain, coffee to sharpen it, ate little, just handfuls of dry cereal from the packet, toast, soup from the carton, cold, and watched television, fleeting through channels with the remote, hoping to forget in the drift of that cut-up.

On the second evening, Rachel came to my door, called out, 'Where are you? Everyone's worried! Are you there?'

I stayed quiet and still. After a while, she gave up, went away.

On the morning of the third day, I went into the hall, found a local rag jutting from my letterbox, the tape I'd stuck over the slot torn free. I dug out some matches, set fire to the newspaper, went into my room, cowered beneath the bedclothes.

Later, I learnt that the paint on the front door, which dated to the building's conversion into flats, nearly twenty years before, was not fire-retardant. It went up straight away. Burning smuts spread the blaze, fluttered through the air, lighted on my coatrack and the old sofa I kept in the hallway. Fumes swiftly overcame me.

A neighbour called the emergency services. They responded quickly, the fire was put out, and I was carried out, still out, by the paramedics. When I came round in the ambulance, I babbled, struggled, and they had to sedate me. At hospital, my raving continued, and, following treatment for smoke inhalation, I was transferred to a mental health unit. Rachel, my parents, and some friends came to see me. So I gathered afterwards, I knew no one. I fixed visitors with a glare, grabbed their hands, spoke to them in a low, desperate tone, claiming the brutal murders in the capital were my doing, that devils had possessed me, made me kill. This was reported to the police, and Amanda Hayworth came to speak with my doctors. She told them what I'd found in the Soho alleyway, explained I wasn't held under any suspicion. When, after some weeks, I was still deranged, the psychiatrists treating me recommended that my parents give permission for me to be committed a time. They reluctantly agreed.

For six months, I was confined to a sanatorium on the Kent coast, the Fairchild Institute: a foursquare Georgian country residence, atop the cliffs, staring blankly out to sea, a place of light-grey stone blocks, ivied gable ends, a gently pitched roof, myriad chimney stacks. My room on the third floor, in the former servants' quarters, was cramped, but otherwise comfortable, well-appointed; it contained a double bed, a wardrobe and writing desk, and had a small en-suite bathroom with a shower, toilet, and wash basin. From the window I could see the edge of the bluff and, beyond, the Channel. On days when the sun was out and light glittered on the water, the sea looked thin-beaten gold agitated by faerie hands.

The routine of the sanatorium was unvarying; I soon lost track of the days. We inmates were awoken at seven in the morning. After we'd washed and dressed, some with the nurses' aid, we were herded downstairs to the refectory, fed breakfast, sometimes cereal, sometimes porridge, often burnt and virtually inedible, occasionally eggs, bacon, and toast, given our medications. Mornings were taken up with compulsory therapeutic activities. On days when the weather was inclement, these took place indoors, we were set to perhaps bread-making or sewing (our handling of the needles carefully supervised); and when it was fine we were taken outside to play croquet or badminton (our handling of the mallets and rackets, likewise). After a light lunch of soup or sandwiches, we were allowed to occupy ourselves till the evening meal, to read in our rooms or wander the Institute's grounds. As these were on the landward side, to the rear of the main building, where the terrain sloped sharply away, they'd been landscaped, three terraces cut into them. Immediately behind the house was a paved area with a row of benches it was possible to sit and enjoy the prospect of undulating fields of wheat beyond the outer wall from; then, below that, was a kitchen garden, with beds of herbs and aromatic flowering plants; and, on the lowest level, a large, immaculate lawn, surrounded by shrubbery, with, at the far end, a shade-dappled copse, with a murmuring rill running through. But, lest you think this idyllic, surrounding the grounds was a high wall topped with coils of razor-wire – I was put in mind of the thorny thickets growing round the cursed castle in 'Briar Rose'. Dinner was always served early, at six, and usually consisted of chunks of grey meat and vegetables cooked in simmering water for hours till reduced to an insipid slop. Afterwards we were free to either play board games or watch television, till nine, when we were sent up to bed.

Within three weeks, or so, I was mostly sane once more. But, sure what I'd undergone hadn't been delusion, the cause, rather than effect, of my frenzy, and, therefore, grateful for the sanctuary the lonely and secure spot afforded me, I feigned continued aberration. After all, the grey food and the wall aside, it was a pleasant enough place.

Thinking it possible one or more of the other inmates had, like me, been deranged by an uncanny experience, I began turning the subject of conversation to the bizarre during the evening games of scrabble, chess, or draughts. I learnt the bulk of my fellows were mundane neurotics, obsessives, depressives, but that there were a few with stranger afflictions: a man so appalled by, what he called, 'the sinister half-life of plants,' he'd broken into his local garden centre one night and torched the place; an ex-soldier who, convinced his testicles had been possessed by an ancient demon in the Iraqi desert, masturbated compulsively to rid himself of 'cursed seed'; a woman who felt she was harried by an evil horde of miniature squirrels; and an old man, a former ventriloquist, who said his dummy had come to life one night on stage and turned against him, that he'd been forced to dismember it to save himself. These tales, in particular the latter, intrigued me at first, but, over time, I realized they were mere delusions.

I, though, had, I was sure, been afforded a glimpse of some cankerous truth about the world. My certainty of this led me to regard those who came to visit me as fools. I was incensed by their complaisant prattle. Most of my friends were repulsed by my disdainful, nasty manner and didn't return after their first few visits. Rachel suffered my anger and derision for some months, coming to see me often, no matter how badly I treated her. In the end, though, she also found it too much. I can still recall our final conversation, a painful and poignant memory.

We were sitting, side by side, on the Institute lawn. It was a clear day, the wind coming off the sea a little chilly, but the sun's rays warm, a caress. I was staring off into the distance; Rachel was looking at me with concern, stroking my arm.

I pushed her away, roughly.

'I didn't ask you to come here again,' I said, not even turning to look at her. 'Why won't you leave me alone?'

'Why are you being so cruel?' she replied, gnawing on her fingernails. 'I'm trying to help you.'

'I'm trying to help you,' I mimicked. 'Stop biting your nails. It's pathetic.'

She began crying, silently. Her indrawn breaths seemed to rack her.

(I can't be sure, even with so much hindsight, why I drove her away; my motives are murky to me. I know I still felt a great deal for her then. But I'd grown wary and bitter.)

Her sobs ceased, she seemed to calm.

'Don't you want me there for you when you're well again?'

I turned to her. She wiped the tears from her cheeks with the back of her right hand, gave me a piercing look, grinned, a cold grin that haunts me still. I shrugged.

'Well,' she said.

And that was the last word to pass between us. She stood, walked away, left me sitting there on the lawn. I saw her only once more, a year or so later, walking down Tottenham Court Road. She was laughing, hand in hand with a man a few years older, who looked to dote on her. I ducked into a shop and watched them go by through the window.

I scarcely treated my family any better than I did Rachel, but they stuck by me.

During my time at the Institute, I strove to remain distant from the other inmates – I couldn't be sure who I could trust. But even the most leery may blunder into the toils of friendship, and so it was with me; there was one whose company I fell into often: Colin Elton, middle-aged, a former lecturer in Medieval History at a red-brick university. He'd suffered a breakdown when research he'd been engaged in for many years was copied and published by a trusted colleague. Few believed Colin's claim, he was thought resentful, his reputation was ruined, the thesis was forever linked with the plagiarist's name. It had to do with the way the Black Death spread its contagion; it was abstruse, and I couldn't quite grasp it.

Colin's was a fascinating mind, and we had many long conversations ranging over divers subjects. The Middle Ages were, of course, his particular area of interest, but he could discourse on everything from architecture to the Eleatic paradoxes. In truth, our chats were less dialogues, more lectures:

for the most part, I was attentive merely, just from time to time prompting him with queries (then I knew little; now, now I wish I knew less). Colin was generally quite well, but so afraid of his ideas being thieved, he was mute with most people. I don't know why he chose to trust me.

One evening, about six months after my committal and confinement to the asylum, I was playing my, by then habitual, evening game with Colin – mostly we played chess, but that evening it was draughts – when he interrupted a disquisition on the court of Louis XIV to look about him nervously.

'You can't ever be sure someone isn't listening in,' he said, leaning close, lowering his voice, tapping the side of his nose with the forefinger of his right hand. 'They've got people everywhere. It's not safe, even here. Any of these lunatics could be one of them.'

'How can you be sure I'm not?' I asked, impish.

He scowled, cocked his head. Then picked up two counters from the board, one of each colour, pressed them into his eyesockets, squinted to hold them in place.

'What are you doing?' I asked, irritated.

He grinned.

'Do you know why the dead in Ancient Greece were buried with coins in their mouths?'

'No. Can we get back to the game?'

Colin took the pieces from his orbits, pocketed one, or seemed to, then put both hands behind his back. A moment later, he held out his fists to me.

'Choose.'

'Stop it,' I said gently, shaking my head.

He opened his fingers. There was a counter cupped in each palm. He returned one to the board, flipped the other into the air with his thumb. It arced, tumbling slow. He caught it with his right hand, slapped it down on the back of his left, kept it covered.

'Heads or tails?'

'Colin,' I groaned.

He grimaced, got up from the table, walked away, taking the piece with him. Reaching the door, he turned, held up the piece, called to me.

'To pay Charon's fare.'

'What?'

'The boatman. Ferried the dead over the River Styx.'

He was shouting now, his voice hoarse, breaking, his eyes wild.

'Did you know, photography, at first, was used mainly for filth, as it is again now, I suppose, and memorializing the dear departed? Mothers holding their just-dead infants up for the camera as rigor set in. Dead wives propped up by rods hidden beneath their skirts. Think of that. And remember me like *this*!'

'Don't be so morbid, Colin.'

He put the counter in his mouth, under his tongue, turned, and left. His outburst had distressed some inmates; an old woman who sat in a wicker chair by the window, puckered up her face, began to hoot like an owl, thrash about, and a young man clutched his head, howled, soiled himself. Nurses rushed over to restrain them, another hurried after Colin to ensure he'd not swallowed the draughts piece.

That night, he somehow crept past staff on duty, found a way over the wall, threw himself off the cliff. At least that's what was assumed to have happened; there were smears of his blood on rocks at its foot, but his body was never found, perhaps swept out to sea by the undertow.

Pangs of remorse goaded me from listless stagnation; I felt my confinement, was seized by an urge to get out, even if it meant putting myself in danger. I called my parents, and the following day they came to see me. They saw me well and, that afternoon, signed the papers rescinding my committal.

I returned to London. In the asylum I'd been denied news of the outside world, deemed too troubling; it wasn't till after my release, then, I learnt the chef whose body I'd discovered had been the last victim of the beatings, that no one had been convicted of the attacks, that there were no suspects or leads.

My parents had organized for the major repairs to my flat to be carried out, but there was still much to be done; I spent my first few weeks at home redecorating. Sooted walls needed stripping, a fresh coat of paint; curtains had to be washed and aired; scorched, mouldering carpets taken up, replaced, though in the hall and lounge, I found the boards in good condition, left them bare. The work done I revelled in the results: the place felt new, purged of dread associations.

My life returned to seeming normality. I found temporary work, it didn't pay well, but enough to get by on; I was thrifty. After a few weeks, I felt settled enough to contact some old friends, sent text messages saying, simply, 'I'm back. Get in touch.' I went out drinking with them. They all said how well I looked, awkwardly skirted mention of my sickness. I did not, though, attempt to contact Rachel; there seemed no way I could make amends, and I thought seeing her might cut me to the bone.

And that's the end of this tale; a return to an ordinary, if slightly hollow, existence. At least till the day, frantic to share my woes with any who might understand, I placed the classifieds.

Or almost the end. There's an uncanny epilogue to relate. One evening, perhaps six weeks after I was released from the Fairchild Institute, while walking past Smithfields Market in a stupor, listening to music – I distinctly remember the song playing was Blind Willie Johnson's 'It's Nobody's Fault But Mine' – a harrowing gospel-blues, I felt someone tap me on the shoulder. I turned, taking out my earphones. An old man stood there, smiling a thin-lipped smile.

'Don't remember me, eh?' he said.

I shook my head.

'Well. I was the one warned you about them wolves.'

Then I recognized him: the man who'd accosted me in the Saracen's Head all those months ago. Thinking him a phantasm, I shook my head to clear my senses. But he was real.

'Seems you didn't take heed,' he said, took a roll-up from his shirt pocket, lit it with a match struck on a filthy thumbnail. He cupped his hand round the flame, drew on the fag, got it smouldering.

'You'd've done well to've listened to me,' he went on, without taking the roll-up from his mouth, letting it dangle from his bottom lip.

But I'd turned away. I put my earphones back in, set off briskly, not once looking back, Blind Willie's hoarse zeal drowning out anything further he might have said.

I

I'd had an eternity to brood over the writing of this memoir, to order my impressions, to consider by what alchemy to turn incident into prose; yet, when I came to set down the first words, to begin, I faltered. Baffled by its convolutions, I'd no idea at what point to open my story.

Perhaps the proper way to have started would have been to introduce myself, give my name, but that's something I couldn't do. My memory's no better than that allotted any common man, is entirely unsuited to immortality. The events I've written of, and those I've still to tell, seared, burnt, blistered, scarred my brain, but I've forgotten much else. My recall of names is especially poor; mine was lost to me long ago, as were those of the others I will write of: I've made up those used in this account.

Deprived of this gambit of name-giving, that brazen alloy of brag and cozen, that feigns a laying bare, while claiming sway, it took me many hours of staring up at the wheeling constellations and ruminating before I hit on an opening. I knew I'd need to plunge in, write swiftly, allow myself to be swept along by the currents of my tale, or else I'd founder. I decided simply to begin at the beginning, cast my mind back to that time, long ago, when I saw the eldritch skull beneath the skin of the wonted world and my life was changed forever. But what happened to me on that dreadful night is only part of what I wish to set down here; I must, lest I lose the momentum I've built up, press on.

II

Having found out the world I'd known was merely a bright painted scrim, and glimpsed the vile shambles on stage behind, I shambled through life, staggered, listless. My brain had baulked at what I'd seen, yet I was sure it was no delusion. The ground beneath my feet had been undermined; I felt it might at any instant give way, and I fall through into some dread cavern. The next year and a half passed in routine and tedium; my seared nerves took solace in the bland and dull. After a while, though, I began to gag on that pap life. I wished no longer to cower from, but rather to confront my fears, and in so doing perhaps put them to rout. I grew frantic to talk with others who'd suffered as I had, to share my tale with people who wouldn't sneer or doubt my reason.

It was then I conceived my plan of placing classifieds in national newspapers, advertisements seeking those who'd seen, as I had, dread things. Sifting through replies was frustrating; I had many, lots mocking, several clearly deranged. In the end, I winnowed them down to just six, the only ones, I believed, in good faith and showing sound mind. I contacted these respondents, arranged a meeting.

The day set soon came round. It was midwinter, less than a week before Christmas, but though it was cold, and blustery, it was sunny. After lunch, I took a walk across to Hampstead Heath. On top of Parliament Hill, a number of people flew kites, a colourful flock against the clear blue sky. I spent some time gazing out over the city from that spot, seeking landmarks, my eyes returning again and again to the dome of St Paul's, which looked the top of some bald giant's head, some bald giant buried to his brows in the silt of the floodplain. Then I went home, continued work on a critical essay on *The Lost World* I was writing for a journal of Conan Doyle studies. I managed a few paragraphs, but, when the light began to wane, I grew agitated, unable to concentrate.

Though I'd managed to keep most friends, in spite of the impassivity that was my bulwark against the quailing of my mind, I'd been feeling, sometimes, alone, since I knew all would have met my telling of the diabolical Punch and Judy show with concern or scorn, but not belief. I'd been, then, in previous weeks, filled with joy at the thought of meeting others who might hear and give credence to my tale. But, as the time of the gathering approached, I grew apprehensive, anxious lest the evening be filled with horror. I fought to quell these misgivings. Would that I had not.

I still, though, had nearly two hours before I needed to leave. So I put on the radio, listened to the tail end of an interesting programme about the Delta blues. But it was followed by a comedy panel show, and the forced drollery twanged my nerves, and I got up to change the station. Turning the tuner knob at haphazard, I happened upon some loud yowling, perhaps a radio play, which startled me, set my heart hammering in my chest. I switched off the radio, went through to the bathroom to splash my face at the sink.

My flat was on the top floor of a mansion block about halfway up Highgate Hill,[3] a little uphill of the spot where, in the folk tale, Dick Whittington (why is it I can recall this name and not my own?) heard the bells of Bow Church calling him and turned back, and just by the place where, or so the tale goes, William Powell, the Highgate Prophet, passed on, one sunny morning, in April 1798. Powell's tale is strikingly bizarre. He'd been a parsimonious Treasury clerk till he'd won a sum on a lottery and grown spendthrift, lazy and insolent at work. He'd been sacked from his position, the money had soon run out, and he'd ended up destitute. It was after his fall he became known as the Highgate Prophet; he'd a strange ritual: early every morning, in all seasons, all weathers, he'd walk from the Sloane Street poorhouse he lived in, to the foot of Highgate Hill, stand a moment in contemplation, raise up his arms to the sky, then run up the hill. If he was spoken to by a passer-by, or stopped, or looked back, he'd return to the bottom, start again, would keep on till he managed to dash all the way up in one go. He'd explain, should he be asked about his odd behaviour, his conviction the world would end if ever he failed in his rite. Well, that fine spring morning in 1798, he did, dropped dead, heart burst. Of course, the world did not end then, or so, anyhow, it would seem.[4]

Being high up, my flat commanded good views, and the bathroom window, which faced south-east, afforded a prospect of the river basin, from the City to the Isle of Dogs, and, on a clear day, even of far-off Shooter's Hill. That evening, though it wasn't late, six o'clock by the chimes of a nearby church, it was already quite dark, and all I could see were strewn lights below and, above, in the east, glimmering, the first faint stars of the evening. The sky was clear, and I hoped it would remain so; the following morning saw a celestial event, a total eclipse of the moon, apparently the first Winter Solstice eclipse since the seventeenth century, which I wanted to see.[5]

Returning to the living room, I poured myself a whisky, settled into my armchair to read from my collected works of Edgar Allan Poe. I find Poe's prose, with its bizarre mixture of the punctilious, the arid, the droll, and the macabre, a calming influence. His idiosyncratic genius lies not only in the narratives themselves, but in the way they crystallise some abstract notion. I began with 'The Angel of the Odd', superficially the most frivolous story he ever penned, though a close reading reveals it to be a poignant account of the havoc alcohol can wreak on the mind. I found myself distressed by the eerie tale that followed 'The Angel of the Odd' in my anthology, 'MS. Found in a Bottle', so flipped to 'The Sphinx', a story I had, since my return from the Fairchild Institute, found absolutely invaluable as a means of staving off madness. Under its influence, all that seems grotesque admits of a rational interpretation. It helped calm my perturbation.

When it was time, I dressed warmly to spite the cold, in coat, scarf, and gloves, then left my flat, locking the door behind me. Little did I realize I should never return.

For the meeting place of the gathering, I'd settled on a pub in Borough, the Nightingale. It was a convivial old boozer, and I'd chosen it in part because I thought its friendly air would mitigate the horrors we were there to tell of. I also knew that there'd be a lock-in, a tradition of the landlord's in the weeks running up to Christmas, which would allow ample time for the unfolding of our tales.

Walking down Highgate Hill, the festive decorations everywhere struck me, jarred with my mood: Christmas trees, tinsel, fairy lights. I headed for the stop at the hill's foot, where I could catch a bus to take me all the way to London Bridge. It would have been quicker to travel by tube, but I'd, of course, conceived an acute loathing of the chthonic. When the bus came, I got on, went upstairs; I always preferred to travel on the top deck for the view it afforded. The bus drove down Holloway Road, almost deserted at that time, to Highbury Corner, where an altercation started up between the driver and a youth who'd boarded without paying. The engine, at idle, juddered. Finally, the youth was intimidated into getting off by other passengers, who were annoyed at being held up, and we were on our way once more. When I next paid attention to where we were, the vehicle had just turned onto City Road. A row of shabby Georgian terraces there recalled Mildmay Park, filled me with dread. I stared down at my feet till the bus reached Finsbury Square.

Then, raising my head to look out, I saw office buildings, constructed, according to some strange panoptic rationale, almost entirely of glass. The road was congested and progress was slow. A few minutes later, passing Moorgate, I glimpsed 30

St Mary Axe through a gap between buildings; its tessellating windows reminded me of an insect's compound eye.

Finally, the bus crossed London Bridge, the lights of waterfront buildings reflected in the river below, gemstones strewn on a jeweller's blackcloth.

When the double-decker pulled into the terminus, I alighted, struck out for the Nightingale. On the way, I passed a man in the entrance to a pharmacy, lying on his side, back to me, knees drawn up to his chest, swaddled in a frayed blanket, half a beer can, jagged torn edge, with a few coins in, by his head. In the glass of the chemist's door, I could see his face reflected. He was youngish, had short, brown hair, a full, matted, reddish beard. Though his eyes were half open, I was sure, from the sedate, regular rise-and-fall of his chest, he slumbered. On his nape was a crude tattoo in blue ink, pigment bled, hard to make out. I leant in to peer. It seemed a sword, straight crossguards, blade hanging down. Just then he snorted, twitched, and, thinking he was, after all, awake, to cover my gawking, I scrabbled in my pocket, drew out a pound, tossed it into the makeshift alms cup. But when the coin hit with a loud chink, he stirred, opened his eyes, blinked, looked dazed. Turning, he squinted at me, then pulled out, from beneath his bedding, a pair of glasses, black plastic frames held together with gaffer tape, put them on.

'Sorry. Didn't mean to wake you.'

Grunting, he rubbed his eyes under the thick lenses.

'Just got to sleep.'

'Well... Sorry.'

I backed away.

'Arsehole.'

I went on, pace brisk.

On reaching the Nightingale, I saw fitful flickering behind the frosted panes; a fire was burning in its hearth, and I was glad, because of the cold, the gusting wind, and because it would make the place even snugger. The pub's board, a painting of the songbird it was named for, squalled as it swung restlessly back and forth. I went inside, looked about. Many of the pub's appointments dated back to when it first opened, the late-Victorian period. The space was partitioned, by wooden screens inset with panels of etched glass, into a public bar and saloon at the rear; the island bar was mahogany with a pine counter, and had a canopy carved with a row of leering heads, Green Men, foliage sprouting from their mouths, wreathing their faces; and the walls were decorated with a lapis-tile dado and hung with fly-spotted mirrors in tarnished gilt frames. Apart from the wavering glow of the fire, the only source of light was a motley array of standard and table lamps, dim bulbs, but the effect was cosy, not dismal. There were Christmas decorations up: paper chains, swags of ivy, sprigs of mistletoe, and a tree hung with silver baubles and clumps of angel hair, but they were muted, sparse, didn't irk me.

I'd told the others to carry a copy of *The Sphinx of the Ice-Fields*,[6] as if we were a book group meeting to discuss it; I knew them, by this token, by the volumes laid out on the table. They sat in slightly strained silence, by the fireplace, in the saloon. I'd meant to be early, but the truculent youth at Highbury Corner and the traffic in the City had delayed me, and it was already five past the hour, and, seemingly, I was the last but one to arrive. I joined them.

We began by, in turn, giving our names and occupations, that ritual of first gatherings. As I'd stipulated replies to my classified should be anonymous, provide no identifying personal details, it was the first time I learnt anything about those I'd invited to attend. A young man wearing jeans, a T-shirt, and a suit jacket introduced himself first. He was William Adams, a graphic designer. A woman in her late twenties, strikingly pretty, dark complexioned, long dark hair, spoke up next; Rashmi Natarajan, a legal secretary hailing from Edinburgh. Then came Elliot Wainwright, a pensioner from Norwich, with a cheery lined face, shock of white hair, and white tufty eyebrows. The stylishly dressed middle-aged woman sat next to him seemed familiar to me. Her name was Jane Ellis. She described herself as a single mother of two from Blackheath, but, as she was speaking, recognizing her brittle accents, I realized why I knew her: she was the author of a number of historical romances, one of which, *The Feminine Monarchie*, a fictionalization of a love affair early in the life of Charles Butler, the, till the book's publication, relatively obscure seventeenth-century musician, grammarian, and apiarist, the 'Father of English Beekeeping', had sold very well and been adapted into a Hollywood film. Jane had been quite a bit in the public eye till about four years before, when it had been announced she was retiring from writing. She was followed by Duncan Wolfe, a butcher from Glasgow, a sullen man whom I judged to be in his mid-twenties. His mien suggested one who'd seen and endured much: he'd a wearied air, sallow skin, drained blue eyes, his long, tangled beard and close-cropped hair were dredged with grey, and he was missing an arm, the right, severed quite high, near the shoulder, the sleeve of the old-fashioned, worsted suit he wore was pinned across his chest. I was the last to give my name, tell of my job.

Once this rite was over, and I'd told how there was one still to come and that I felt we should wait a bit, at least, I offered to get a round of drinks in. There were nods and thanks. Noting we'd no spare seats, Elliot offered to grab another for the latecomer. I, after taking orders, went up to the counter; William and I wanted lagers, Elliot, a light ale, Rashmi, a vodka and lemonade, Jane, a gin and tonic, Duncan, a porter. Once the bartender had poured the drinks, William came up, tapped me on the shoulder, asked if I needed a hand with carrying. I nodded, smiled.

We took the drinks back over, set them down. All supped. Duncan asked if anyone minded if he smoked. No one objected, so he took a briar and tobacco pouch from his shirt pocket, set about filling the pipe's bowl, a deft feat one-handed, got it lit. Once the flames had died, and the tobacco smouldered dully, he took a long draw, roiled the smoke in his mouth, let it spill from his lips, gave a satisfied sigh.[7]

At first, conversation was stilted. We were, after all, complete strangers, brought together solely by the weird things we'd undergone. As we sipped our drinks, however, it grew easier. We exchanged inanities, details of our daily lives, chattered, largely without awkwardness, till a fraught moment came, when Duncan, in what seemed a rare spell of volubility, began talking about his trade and the handling of meat, subjects clearly near to his heart, not noticing that Rashmi, who'd already announced she was vegetarian, looked sickened. Jane diffused the tension by gently interrupting the dour Glaswegian to enquire about the last member of the group, the person whose arrival we awaited. I explained that, I knew almost nothing about him or her, that all I could say for sure was that he or she wrote in a crabbed scrawl and probably, based on the postmark on the envelope the response came in, lived in north London. Jane nodded.

Talk then turned to a scandal that had recently provoked the outrage of the tabloids: a well-known television host, thought a paragon, had been involved in an orgy in a London hotel room during which a prostitute had died of an overdose.

'I think he's pure stupit,' Rashmi said, after we'd been discussing the issue for some time.

Taking a paper out of her bag, she opened it to an article discussing the affair.

'Says here, was a set-up gone wrong. The hookers paid for by one of the other red tops. Imagine falling for that! I don't feel any sympathy.'

Jane, her head canted to one side, frowned.

'Why not?' she said. 'Think about it. His life is ruined. And due to a tragic accident, something not really his fault. And the journalists behind it all won't suffer, though they're also partly to blame. I feel sorriest for the wife, though. Imagine being married to someone for years and then... But it must be hard to be scrutinized all the time.'

'I still think he's an idiot, but.'

William drummed his fingers on the table.

'It just sickens me that such sordid ephemera displaces war, famine, and genocide from the front pages.'

Elliot pinched the bridge of his nose between thumb and forefinger.

'In my day you could look up to stars. They were decent, moral people.'

'No they weren't,' William snapped back. 'Their indiscretions were mostly kept secret or ignored is all. Everyone colluded in that. Today's celebrity culture may be cruel, but it is more honest.' He paused, then said, in a tone more contemplative, 'Except stars are now adept at manipulating their own disgrace for gain. There may be something more disconcerting... Perhaps it's that nothing's really at stake anymore, everything's such a sham.'

During the discussion, Duncan and I sat in silence, but, while I followed it with lively interest, seeking insights into my companions' characters, he sat staring down at his pint, grimacing. But he interjected then, saying solemnly, shaking his head, 'Aye. All's going to Hell, right enough.'

'Oh, come on,' William came back. 'I didn't mean that. I don't think people are actually any worse now than they've ever been.'

'That's not what I mean, really. Something else. What you said afore...' Duncan trailed off, shrugged.

'Things are worse,' Elliot mused, after a moment's silence. 'When I was a boy you could leave your front door unlocked and not worry yourself about it.'

'But people had less money, and less access to medical care, education, and so on,' Jane replied.

'Aye right,' Rashmi said. 'This country's going tae shite.'

Jane frowned. Elliot grimaced. Then nodded.

'I don't like your language, but you *are* right. Too many foreigners, too many scroungers...'

Groaning, William slammed down his pint glass, reached into his pocket, took out a pack of cigarettes, lit one, drawing the smoke deep into his lungs. The tobacco glowed, ireful.

'Too many old fucking pricks...' he muttered, under his breath, but not quite quiet enough.

Rashmi turned to Elliot.

'Foreigners,' she said, glaring. 'You mean like me?'

'No, indeed, young lady. I mean this new influx, not the good old colonials. These Romanians and what have you.'

Rashmi gave him a look, wrinkled her nose.

'No, no,' Duncan said, pulling on his pipe. 'You've all misunderstood. It's newspapers, television, and such. Not an ethical decline. To do with language, things.'

He exhaled a plume of fragrant smoke.

William reached out and, with two fingers, slid a glass ashtray towards him across the table, looking through it at the grain of the wood beneath, jerking it from side to side, as if it were a ouija board's planchette, and he, feigning it moving according to the whims of a spirit. Then, he put down his cigarette, looked up at the butcher.

'Hmm. Language, things,' he said. 'I think you're right. It's to do with the way the self-appointed guardians of morality abuse their power, the way the cultural images we're surrounded by work to subjugate us. No one is free, not even in their leisure time.'

'I don't mean to be rude,' Jane said, leaning forwards, 'but what sort of graphic designer are you? Aren't those images your stock in trade?'

'Well...' William began, then shrugged, drank a draught of his beer, took up his cigarette again.

I turned to him, spoke up.

'I don't think you're getting what Duncan means. It's got nothing to do with ethics or politics. With ideology. Or only tangentially.'

'No? Then what?' William demanded.

'Like he said, it's to do with language, things. Simulation and abstraction. The proliferation of dissolute signs.'

'What does that mean?' Rashmi asked, squinting at me.

'Increasingly representation doesn't refer to anything. Reality is being hollowed out from the inside. The fabric of the world has been rent, and through these tears creep things that come from some alterior, some other place.'

Elliot smiled. 'Cuckoo,' he said, tapping his head with a forefinger.

Jane fixed me with a glare.

'Nonsense,' she snapped.

'Is it?' I replied. 'We've all seen that other place, haven't we?'

'Aye, pal,' said Duncan, patting his stump with his left hand. 'That we have.'

We chatted a little while longer, then Jane, glancing down at her watch, interrupted to remark we were in danger of losing sight of why we'd gathered. The other respondent had clearly decided against coming, she said, and there was no point delaying longer. A murmur of assent from the rest. Elliot argued, though, that we should hold on to the empty seat, just in case. Jane proposed, that I, as the organizer of the meeting, tell my story first. I protested, but the others gently insisted, and, looking round at their expectant faces, I realized I'd no choice.

'This all happened about two and a half years ago, now,' I began. 'As it had been a long and tiresome day, I went for a pint in the Saracen's Head after work. The evening was cold...'

III

As I type this, I can hear wheezing breaths and the odd low moan from the Ark's wheelhouse. I have solitude no longer. I've propped the wheelhouse door open, and inside, in the gloom, I can just make her out, slumbering fitfully on my pallet.

I will tell all. But now I feel it's time for a brief sketch of the ways I've spent my diuturnity.

At first, for a short time after I learnt of my fate, though in hiding, I attempted, so far as possible, to live in company, as I had before, forming friendships, taking lovers, staying in contact with my family, and so forth. But it proved too difficult. After a while, people would find it suspect I didn't age, and the deaths of the very few I could take into my confidence caused great heartache; it's hard to know you'll outlive everyone you love. Finally, I resolved my life should be solitary and sought solace in learning, skills. But given endless life there's no sense of accomplishment in mastery. Still, reading and playing musical instruments went on affording me some distraction. For a time, I was also still quickened by wallowing in the fleshly, and, wary of forming any attachments, took my pleasures with prostitutes. In the end, though, even this no longer enticed me. I felt I'd exhausted all life's possibilities, well, those I could morally countenance, and, truth be told, quite a few I could not, and listlessness set in.

Apprehension of death, as ineluctable and imminent, is vital to being; deprived of a looming end, I ceased to be fully human (though I knew I'd be found eventually, I also thought, as my pursuer had others to seek and seemed to wish for a cruel protraction of the chase, to torment with tedium, the dark day could be eluded, perhaps even till aeon's end if I was canny, which has, of course, proved true). I also found it wretched I didn't age; it's from observing their own decay people derive their sense there is change in the world; I, staying the same, see only stagnation.

For centuries, I drifted from place to place, earning enough through casual labour to pay for necessities: food, clothing, accommodation. Reclusive, I spent most of my spare hours buried in books. Though I read diversely, my tastes favoured texts written before my cursing, which, perused still by scholars, could be acquired from museums and libraries. Later on, this inclination of mine was reinforced; after the torches of civilization burnt out, and the power went down, once and for all, I could read nothing but printed books, which, having ceded to various electronic formats around the time I learnt of my fate, mostly predated it. It was still possible to obtain them, for many places of learning had housed the large part of their catalogues in underground depositories. These stores had been built to protect their contents against the depredations of time and, having entrances that were difficult to force and often concealed beneath the rubble of the buildings, torn down by suspicious barbarians, that had once stood above them, were safe from sack.

During my relative youth (my flesh does not wither, but I still feel the years score me) there was much talk of travel to far-flung planets, something that would have provided escape from the mundane. But it never came to pass. Neither have beings from alien worlds visited Earth. Either this sphere is alone in being able to support life, or the societies of all populated worlds have, as those of this, always fallen into decadence before attaining the technologies that would enable venturing into the void. (As an aside, I now feel sure humankind had aspired and failed, but nearly, to kick loose of the Earth in eras prior to that of my birth, that some myths of the age, such as my own native culture's tale of the death of Bladud, or the stories of the confounding of the builders of Nimrod's great tower, the crash of Kay Kāvus's flying throne, and Phaëton's and Icarus's falls, were weak, distorted recollections of foundered space flight. Indeed, I'm now convinced all legends are faint memories of violent events of previous epochs.)

In the end, the entire globe fell into darkness, once and for all, or so it would seem; there do not appear to be any embers of civilization still smouldering from which it could be rekindled. Folk went back to a nomadic life, and the cities, which, till then, had afforded me throngs to lose myself in, were abandoned. I travelled to the Himalayas, hoping to find refuge in loneliness and harsh steeps instead.

As I've already described, my existence there, aside from some years spent living with natives, was that of a hermit. But it was ascetic in its externals merely: thought is a great and complex pleasure, and I surrendered myself to it. I also had my books, of course; I replenished their stock when needful through trips to archives located in former seats of culture, fraught, but worth it. I was sore drouthy after knowledge, but not just knowledge, for stories too. Aside from my eyes, that gulped the words, and my hands, that turned the pages, my body, at times, seemed an encumbrance: an old nag which, despite its usefulness having passed, must still be sheltered, fed, and watered. On occasion, though, a shock would restore me to the world of things; my days were not solely spent in contemplation and reading. Once I'd got used to the thin air, I spent some time climbing in the mountains. Not till I finally die (should that release ever be afforded me) will the memory of the prospects to be had from the higher peaks cease to inspire awe. But the place is calm, too. If I felt agitated, I could go and sit by a mountain lake, gaze at the reflections of the green firs lining its shores, which danced on days when wind stirred the branches and roiled the waters, or, if it was overcast, I could climb above the clouds, feel the sun on my face, look down on the vapours, a seeming plain of ice and snow. Though I did little during my age-long stay, I never felt tedium; strange, since I'd always preferred the bustle of a city.

I'd just completed my account of the gathering of the party on that fateful night in the Nightingale, when I fell ill. For two days, I lay on my blankets in the dark, agued, delusional, aching in marrow and muscle. I soiled myself in my torment, guts clenching, finally shat blood, hawked up grumous dark matter, could not get my breath. I was tormented by febrile visions: Rachel knelt by my pallet, but, when I reached out to her, recoiled and spat; I heard, again and again, the screech of a swazzle, saw Punch gyring, beating his stick in time to an off-key dirge; Colin Elton stood before me, dug in his eyesockets with his fingers, plucked out the glaucous balls, proffered them, cupped in his palms; and a figure, swathed in shadow, leered over me, bellowed, 'The others are dead, you're the only one left. I'm coming for you, remorseless cruel.'

I thrashed, writhed, moaned, sweated, then, this morning, the sickness loosed its grip. I sprawled, fatigued, on a bed become a sty. The first thing I did, when enough strength returned to me, was stagger down the Ark's gangplank and across the estuary mud to the river's edge, hauling my bedding, to wash some of the filth from it and from my clothes. But first, I wished to bathe. I stripped, waded out a little distance, crouched down; the water was cool, I ducked my head. The sun, low in the sky, diffused by a haze, was ochre, the sky, pale blue, wholesome colours, rare these days, the Earth's last. I began to feel myself again, traces of the sickness waned. I turned my back to the shore, looked out across the broad reach, cupped brine to my face, sluiced away the bile dried in my beard.

Then, turning to look over my shoulder, I saw someone coming toward me, at a run, across the flats. Assuming I was discovered at last, and, wishing not to meet death naked, I stood to retrieve my clothes. But, as I did so, I saw it was actually a local tribeswoman, and modesty forced me back down into the shallows, covering my groin with my hands. Reaching my piled bedding, trousers, shirt, the tribeswoman halted, and, fixing me with her eyes, unabashed, began to gesticulate and jabber in the ugly speech of the folk of the region. I realized that, for her to have overcome the fear of me her people seem to have conceived, her situation was certainly desperate. However, I felt incapable of empathy, gazed at her listless, before waving her away.

She stood her ground, continued to remonstrate in her gibberish tongue. I splashed water at her. She began to cry; tears beaded her lashes. She was young, comely, the petulant curl of her mouth, endearing, her skin soft, dusk, her frame lithe, and the long dark tresses that wreathed it, thick, lustrous. After the custom of her race, the tribeswoman wore a scanty shift of animal hide. I've been chaste an age, and, long denied, my lust has withered, but I'm still drawn to beauty; I felt my resolve weaken. Also, I'd the strange impression I'd seen her somewhere before, which lulled me; though I realized, on later reflection, this was likely because she'd been one of a native hunting party, which, a few days before, cowering behind the bulwarks, I'd watched pass close by the Ark. Doubtless her streaming pennant of hair had caught my eye then, even if I'd not been entirely aware of it. Then she pointed between her legs, stabbed at the air with a flat hand. Thinking she was offering sex in return for whatever she was after, I looked away in disgust. But perhaps I misread the gesture. Whatever, she barked in anger, dredged up a handful of mud, slung it in my face. By the time I'd wiped my eyes, she'd reached the reed beds, was soon hidden from view.

After scrubbing myself, and washing my clothes and bedding as best I could, I got out of the brackish water, feeling better, and returned to the boat, laid out my things to dry off in the sun. Later, sore hungry, I dressed, my clothes by then only slightly damp, and strolled to the clearing where I have my firepit. I fried, in a skillet I'd found in the ruins of London, and gorged on strips of smoked pork and drop scones made from oatmeal. After, I returned to the boat, spent the rest of the day reading over and correcting my recent writing, the incident of the morning forgotten.

With dusk's approach, I stopped work, went again to the firepit, kindled, then smothered a fire, and roasted some vegetables in the embers. After this supper, I returned to the Ark, took up my banjo, went to sit on the bowsprit. I'd found the instrument in the same museum, in the abandoned metropolis to the west, I'd got my typewriter from, likewise sealed in a case. I sat, with my feet dangling over the water, the banjo in my lap, picking the melody to the migrant farm workers' lament, 'Going Down the Road, Feeling Bad', an old plaint of the indigent and persecuted against hardship, closed hearts, the dust of the trail. In a canebreak, across the mudflats from the hulk, croaking toads accompanied me.

As I played, my hands began aching, a lingering weakness, and I put the banjo down. I pondered the sickness; I doubted I'd caught it by contagion, as I'd not been close to another person in months; perhaps it was given to me by one of the midges that harry me at dusk, or maybe I drank or ate contaminated water or victuals. Whatever the case, it was among the worst ailments I've ever endured; I suspect, ordinarily, a mortal one. If only I could have died, rather than remaining shackled to a life that's long ceased to offer anything other than tedium and suffering. It might seem these two states are opposed, that my trials must at least offer respite from boredom, but unfortunately they do not. I've already told how aeonian life renders many joys meaningless, friendships cannot endure, achievements are hollow; it also saps extremity's vigour, for adversity merely stretches days, misery bloats nights. Time, for me, has no wings. There's an early twentieth-century gospel song, whose lyrics I still recall, a song of laying one's burden at the feet of the Lord. I find the notion keenly poignant; if only I believed there was a God who could relieve me of my burden of undying flesh.

I was lost in reflection a time. Then an angry hubbub, carried on the breeze to my ears, roused me, and, looking in its direction, behind me, I saw a rabble careering through the marsh weeds, a little distance up river. Standing, shielding my eyes against the dying sunlight, I tried to make things out. As the rabble drew nearer, I saw there was one out in front, chased by the others. Stones were thrown. Then I saw the quarry was the young woman who'd come up to me that morning. Terror contorted her features. As I watched, a rock struck the side of her head, cut her scalp. Blood welled, ran down her neck. Then she was running past the Ark, the pack at her heels. I recalled a similar scene I'd seen just after settling on board the hulk, which ended with a bloodied and broken corpse on the slob, surmised the tribe punished offenders against their codes with a brutal death.

Such are the customs of the last-days folk, the end-of-the-world folk.

Tripping, the young woman stumbled, fell, and the mob were on her, pummelling, kicking. Amid the ruck, I saw a tribesman's snarling face, gore-spattered. The woman wailed, a pitiful cry that roused my long torpid compassion.

I climbed on the gunwale, teetered there, yowled.

All heads turned. I spread my arms, yawped again.

The beating paused a moment, then went on; the tribesfolk were not cowed. I felt useless, knew I needed to act quickly, or the woman would die. So, with little deliberation, yammering, I threw myself off, tumbled, plummeted. It was a death drop, but, though when I struck it was agony, and I sank deep into the mud, I was able to recover myself fairly swift, clamber from the pit, charge the natives. Aghast on seeing I'd survived the impact, they broke, ran howling. The young woman sprawled on a patch of silt darkened with her blood and piss.

I carried her limp, broken, gory, and stinking body on board the Ark, laid her on my bedding, tended to her injuries, swabbed her cuts clean. Then, leaving her to slumber, I came out on deck to write up the recent, violent events.

It is now the evening of the following day. On waking, the young woman tussled and wailed, her brow very hot. I sat by, nursing her, moistening her lips with fresh water. I thought she would die. She clawed at the bedding, arched her back. After some hours, though, the agony seemed to pass, and she fell into a deep sleep. I came out on deck to prepare myself a frugal repast. I think it best I leave her now to rest. I will press on with my account.

IV

On the evening of the gathering in the Nightingale, once I'd finished telling my tale, I sat back, took a sip from my pint, glanced round at the company. Elliot looked concerned, Jane nodded, her expression serious, Duncan scowled, Rashmi seemed bemused, and William tried to cover a smirk by feigning to fish for something in his eye. Rashmi spoke first.

'Who's Blind Willy Johnson?'

'A blues musician, but that isn't important,' I said, impatient.

I turned to William.

'What's funny?' I asked, irked, but striving to hide it.

'Nothing. Really.'

But he snickered.

'Don't you believe me?'

'I believe you,' he said.

Then lit a cigarette. His face was set. But the corners of his mouth twitched still.

'Haven't you experienced something like it? Or, if not, why are you here?'

'Hey, calm down.'

I grimaced, looked away.

'Don't tell me to calm down,' I muttered.

'Have you ever seen the Punch and Judy show again?' Jane, asked me, gently.

I swigged at my drink.

'No, I haven't, thank fuck, otherwise I'd be back in an institution. But, look, I want to know what he,' I pointed at William, 'found so amusing.'

William sighed, ran his hand through his hair.

'You know. Blind Willy?'

'Prick! So childish. I've just told you how my life was destroyed, and you snigger at that?'

'I know, I know. I'm sorry. My life's over too.'

'Alright. Tell us about it.'

He'd smoked his cigarette to the filter, lit another from the stub.

'Fine.'

Then Elliot spoke up.

'My son was killed in those attacks.'

He slumped, head in hands, began sobbing.

Rashmi stared open-mouthed, Duncan tugged at his beard, William smoked, and I threw back another draught of my pint. Only Jane made to comfort the old man, reaching out, putting her hand on his shoulder.

'I'm so sorry,' she said.

'I'm sorry too,' I broke in. 'I didn't mean to...'

'Don't be silly, lad,' through his tears. 'How could you know?'

'Yes, but...'

'The police never could tell me anything,' he went on. 'Now I know why.'

He sat back, wiped his eyes. Looking over his shoulder, I was disconcerted to notice the cover of an old issue of Punch hanging in a frame on the wall, the hooknose grinning out at me, impish.

Just then a man approached our table, asked to borrow one of our ashtrays, broke the taut silence. He was middle-aged, wore a three-piece, pinstriped suit, and a pink tie; I took him to be a solicitor or city banker. William told him, go ahead. As he reached over, his sleeve rode up, revealing an ostentatious gold watch and a tattoo I recognized, with a shock, as identical to the one inked on the neck of the young homeless man I'd inadvertently woken earlier. William blenched when he saw it, let his cigarette fall to the table.

Once the man had gone, Jane addressed Elliot.

'Do you want to talk about it?'

'I don't really, no. It's got no bearing on the events I want to tell you all about.'

While this exchange took place, Rashmi pulled a compact from her purse and, looking in its mirror, which threw a patch of faerie light on her face, reapplied her lipstick. I stared, incredulous.

William spoke up.

'Elliot, do you want to tell us your story?'

The pensioner smiled.

'Why don't you go ahead with yours?'

'Well,' William stammered, seemingly afraid.

Then he appeared to recover his composure. Turning, I saw the suited man leave; it seemed he'd only been fetching the ashtray for a friend on the way out.

'Alright,' William continued. 'This all happened about a year and a half ago now,' he began.

Then he stopped, took a swallow of his beer.

'In former times,' he said, fretting at a beer mat, 'the void was a stage and the sidereal throng players on it. Now things are utterly otherwise.'

'What?' said Rashmi.

William sighed.

'Nothing, doesn't matter. Anyhow, that evening I'd been out drinking with a friend and, a little drunk, decided to walk home across the Heath...'

The Lamia

It was one of those rare nights in late May when, after several weeks of warm weather, the North Wind rallies for one last desperate assault, and there is ice in the air. But it had been a pleasant day, and evening, and William and his friend had been drinking outside, in the garden of the Spaniards, an old inn on Hampstead Heath, in bygone days a haunt of highway robbers. There was still a little light in the sky when they left the pub, and thinking himself in no danger, and having a scarf and jumper with him to ward against the chill, William decided to cut across the Heath to Gospel Oak Lido, then walk on through Dartmouth Park to his flat on Junction Road. It would sober him up a little before he got home to his girlfriend, Catherine, who was probably working late, waiting up for him. William's friend was going to catch the Northern Line back to his flat in Tooting, south of the river. They walked together a little way, towards the underground, then parted company by Whitestone Pond, on the edge of Hampstead Village, exchanging childish feints, taking their leave with curt valedictions.

'Fuck off, then.'

'You fuck off.'

His friend headed off, but William stood a moment in contemplation of the pond. In earlier times, it had been a watering hole. He pictured a team of horses, weary, sweat-drenched, having drawn a carriage from Cambridge or Northampton, slaking their thirst with long swallows, breath ghosting in the cold air.

On his way to the Heath, William passed a butcher's van parked up. Its rear doors stood ajar; inside William glimpsed hanging carcasses, a mottle of red muscle, white fat. Holding his breath against the reek (here Duncan shook his head, muttered something), he went on by. Then the butcher came out of a door from which the clamour of a restaurant kitchen could be heard. He was handsome, had a harelip, wore a white cap on his head and a blood-smeared apron. Crossing to the back of the van, he clambered in, lifted down a side of pork, hefted it onto his shoulder. Turning to tote it into the kitchen, he smiled, nodded, friendly, at William. There was, on the back of the hand the butcher held the meat with, a blue tattoo, blurred, looked like a knife. There was a red provenance mark printed on the meat, also difficult to make out, perhaps the rough outline of a watermill.

Then William cut down a short mews, cobbles underfoot, Georgian buildings, wrought-iron lamp posts. A few steps in, he was hailed by an old woman wearing nightdress, hairnet, and curlers, who leant out of the ground-floor window of an incongruous '70s block of flats.

'Excuse me,' she called out. 'Have you seen a black cat?'

William looked over at her. 'What, ever?'

'No,' the woman snapped. 'Tonight, near here.'

'Can't say I have.'

'She's quite fat. But I don't overfeed her. Has a mark on her chest like a lower-case 'r'.'

William shook his head.

'Definitely haven't seen her.'

'Oh. She always comes in for supper around nine, but not this evening. I don't know where she could have got to.'

'Oh,' William said. 'Sorry to hear that. I hope she turns up.'

He idly pushed a chocolate wrapper toward the gutter with his toe.

'That's not your rubbish, is it?' the woman barked.

'Er, no.'

'Well, perhaps you'd be good enough to find a bin for it.'

Thrown off guard, William bent down, picked up the litter.

'Thank you, young man.'

As he turned to go, the old lady mused aloud, 'Where can that cat have got to?'

'I don't know,' William replied, though not sure an answer was looked for. 'Perhaps she's out hunting birds.'

'Oh no, she wouldn't do that. Jemima's a good cat.'

'Right you are.' William mimed tugging a forelock. 'Anyhow, best be off.'

He went on, leaving the old woman babbling and tutting to herself. Once out of sight, he threw the wrapper down.

Reaching the Heath, he walked through a sandy dell and a stand of trees, and came out into a clearing, with, at its heart, a marshy slade, which a sign told him was the Hampstead Heath sphagnum bog. As he walked by, he heard, a low gurgling coming off the mire that, though he didn't quite know why, struck him as loathsome, foreboding, and he quickened his pace.

Following a footpath headed towards the Lido, William reached a gate, passed through it, and came into a meadow. He skirted it, kept to the track, which ran along the treeline. Crows roosted in the branches overhead, their harsh clamour filling the air. The way then led into another spinney. Under the interlaced branches of the trees – oak, elm, birch, and other varieties William didn't recognize – it was gloomy, the fading light of the evening, filtering through the interstices, just enough to see by, but not to dispel bugbears. The path here was less trodden, in places overgrown. He was almost through to the other side, when he saw, just ahead, red eyes glaring at him, baleful. Blood beat in his ears. He saw a wolf leaping for his throat; a mad, brutal killer, butcher and ghoul, wearing a necklace of cured genitals and a skin cloak, a patchwork of flayed faces, rushing him, brandishing a meat cleaver; a roused corpse lumbering toward him, keening from between worm-eaten lips. Then a coarse laugh broke the hex, one of the 'eyes' arced through the air, blinked out, and he smelled cigarette smoke. A woman, naked from the waist down, stood up, stretched, scratched her crotch. Sighting William, she gasped, dropped to her haunches, hands to her groin. A thickset bald man stood up beside her, hastily zipping his fly.

'Oi, fucker!'

William broke into a run, didn't slow or look round till he was back under open sky. His lungs ached. Glancing over his shoulder, he saw he'd not been followed. He still trembled, but was able to laugh at his own foolishness. Then he went on his way, pace brisk.

Darkness was encroaching, and the first stars came out, early arrivals into the theatre, impatient for the drama to begin.

A little further on, William emerged from a copse to see, ahead of him, atop Parliament Hill, beneath a just-risen new moon like a nail paring, silhouetted against the darkening sky, a throng, with, at its heart, three riders, holding burning brands aloft. Thinking it safest to skirt this gathering, William struck out from the path.

In the gloaming, he didn't notice a fallen branch, tripped, stumbled, fell, landed awkwardly, twisting his wrist. His cry drew the attention of the party on the rise, and a drawn-out, 'Halloo!' was sounded. The men on horseback rowelled their mounts and charged at him, those on foot running to keep up. Before he could rise again, William was beset. The horses were big, had wild rolling eyes, pitchy coats. Awful nearness of sharp hooves, rank stench of horseflesh. The horses were clad in heavy barding; skittish, twitching, tossing their heads, pawing at the ground, they sounded a carillon. The riders also wore full plate; their faces were hidden behind the lowered visors of their helms. Sputtering, reeking, the torches cast a fitful light.

"Tis not our quarry,' one of the riders cried, the leader, William thought, for, while his companions' suits of armour were plain, his was ornate: black enamelled, chased with scrollwork, a wyvern, wings outflung, graved on the cuirass, a sable ostrich-feather plume adorning the helm. His steed's armour was also black tinted.

He turned to William.

'Something direful is abroad this night. Seek refuge, while you can.'

William could only catch odd glimpses, through the chargers' moiling shanks and hocks, of the rabble following the knights, but, from what he could see, they seemed a disparate company: teenagers with facial piercings; suited businessmen and women; construction workers, still wearing overalls, hard hats, reflective jackets; a gaggle of young women in short skirts, barefoot, heels in their hands, all wearing either Devil's horns or rabbit ears, save one in a tiara, who wore a sash with, 'A right to wear white (honest)', written on it, a hen party; a few couples in evening dress; white-haired pensioners; vagrants, unwashed, unkempt, wearing shabby cast-offs, the men with matted beards. All in contemporary dress. William was bemused.

The knights backed, turned their mounts, rode a little distance off. It seemed they were holding council. One of the mob neared William, helped him to his feet. It was the butcher he'd passed earlier.

'What's all this?' William asked.

'You'd best stick with us,' was the reply. Actually, it came out a little like, 'You'd betht thtick with uth,' he had a slight lisp, his cleft lip. 'For your own safety.'

'Is this a film shoot? A historical re-enactment?'

The butcher waved his hand, dismissed the enquiry.

'Will you join the hunt?' he asked. 'In numbers we can't come to harm.'

William shook his head, squinted at the butcher.

'What? What do you mean?'

'There's a thing. A monster. Its lair's on the Heath. Children. It preys on children. But it'll eat any flesh. It's hungry. Ravening. It'll eat animals, anything, but... It's got a taste, you know? It's already taken ten.'

He paused to draw breath, and William broke in.

'What are you on about?'

'Hear me out. Ten. Six kids, three young women, an infirm old man. It's strong, but goes after the weak. We mean to stop it before it kills again.'

The throng had clustered round, peered at William. A young woman in scraps of gaudy, one of the hens, screeched, 'It'll tear your 'eart out.'

She clawed at her sternum. She'd a tattoo the same as the butcher's, but more distinct, below her left collarbone. The blade hung down. He now saw the marking was a medieval broadsword.

An older man, suave, wearing a dinner suit, pointed, chuckled, 'Here. I think he's getting rather an eyeful.'

The hens all cackled.

'So 'e is, cheeky fucker. Looking at me tits, yeah? Like what yer see?'

'Leave him alone,' the butcher said. 'He's alright. He's one of us now.'

An old man dressed, absurdly, in a tweed suit and deerstalker, spoke up, tremulous, 'Look here, I think they've bally well reached a decision.'

The knights approached at a slow trot. All turned to face them. Drawing near, the riders reined in their mounts, and the knight in black armour raised a gauntleted hand. Looking about him at the band, who gawped up at the knight, William realized all bore the sword tattoo. The knight began to bellow.

'My friends, the thing we hunt is not one of God's creatures, but a demon!'

A wood pigeon cooed.

'Born in a lake of fire and spewed forth from the abyss to wreak havoc on the world. It must be stopped!'

There was clapping, and a shout went up.

'It is vile. Predacious, cruel. Knows no pity, has all the dread strength Perdition could gift it.'

William looked about at the party. All cowered in fear.

'But we fight for the Lamb! And this will be our talisman!'

He drew a broadsword from the scabbard that hung at his waist, raised it over his head, grasping the blade, pommel to the sky, then, lifting his brand aloft, held it behind; a crucifix, stark against the flames. The gaggle cheered. William, discomfited, sidled through the press to its edge.

The leader sheathed his weapon, spread his arms.

'We must be as a light to chase away the shadows from this land,' he went on.

At that moment, an anguished howl was carried to them on the breeze. There was tumult. William saw his chance, legged it.

But he didn't get far, only about halfway up Parliament Hill; one of the knights vaulted into the saddle, rode him down.

'You will bide with us till this thing is done. You cannot evade your charge.'

'What? What are you on about? Let me go!'

The knight took out his blade, jabbed at William's chest.

'Nay,' he growled. 'And we will brook no refusal.'

William pleaded, but the rider herded him back to the group. When he was in the fold once more, the Black Knight went on.

'The hell-spawn will feel the bite of steel this night.'

He cupped his hand to the side of the helmet, cocked his head.

'Hark! That blood-curdling yawp was the last cry of a victim, I warrant it. We must make haste if we are to catch the accursed creature. Let us sally!'

Then, with the flats of their blades, the knights began to drive the rabble on. William was caught up in the stampede.

The hunt rushed pell-mell on, back the way William had come. Drunk, and, in any case, unfit, it wasn't long before he was struggling for breath, and in spite of the chill air, lathered. His brain panged. Sore weary, he hung his head, kept on. It was some time, then, before he became aware the butcher was scurrying at his side, furtively attempting to attract his attention.

'What?' William gasped.

'You shouldn't've pissed them off.'

William placed his foot clumsily, turned his ankle, stumbled, almost fell. Grabbing his arm, the butcher steadied him. The ruck had continued to hurtle, and, had he fallen, he'd have been trampled.

'They're pledged to protect mankind,' the butcher went on, after a moment.

'Really?' William spat. 'What are you on about?'

But, just then, they passed by a tree he knew, by the shape of its leaves, to be a horse chestnut, and a vivid memory came to him.

As a young boy, conker season had always been William's favourite time of year. Every autumn, he set aside a Saturday afternoon, which he'd spend throwing a stick again and again into the foliage of a chestnut tree down the road from his childhood home, knocking the seeds from its branches. Sitting, cross-legged, on the ground, he would split the spiny casings, plucking from their corpse-white flesh the prized, glossy nuts. Then he'd return home with the small handful that most nearly resembled the ideal conker he held in his brain. He'd temper the seeds, by roasting, pickling, an esoteric ritual. The pickling took ages, and William found the waiting drear, a strain, spent long stretches gazing at the conkers floating, like specimens in phials, in old jam jars, on shelves in the garden shed. When, finally, the conkers were ready, he'd take great care boring holes in them, then tie them onto lengths of twine. He won all his battles, was, while conker season lasted, undisputed lord of the playground, pestered for his lore, though it was known he'd never reveal it.

What William recalled that night on the Heath, was the season he was finally bested, the year he was cast down, smashed all his jars. That autumn, a new boy had started at his school. Short for his age, shy, named Carol, which the other children thought a girl's name, a lisper, he was often set on. Though William wasn't one of the main bullies, he sometimes stood by, chanting taunts, jeering.

Then, one cold morning in October, William arrived at school to find a huddle outside the gates. He could hear shouts, Carol's, supposed he'd been ganged up on again. But, drawing nearer, he realized the cries were of glee, not anguish. He joined the throng. They watched, avid, a game of conkers. Carol had been pitted against Steve, the roughest of the school's bullies, but strangely all the cheering was for the new boy. William soon realized why: Carol's aim was sure, his blows, stout, his conker, tough. After two strikes the husk of Steve's nut split, exposing the soft, pale innards. A third smashed it to pieces.

The onlookers cheered, the bully slunk off, shamefaced. Then a girl standing by William called out to Carol, issued a challenge.

'Bet you can't beat Will, though. He's the best conkerer ever.'

Cowed by what he'd seen, William tried to wriggle out of it; with him, he'd only the best conker the tree had yielded that year, a lustrous slogger he'd called Achilles – he was reading a book of simple retellings of Greek myth – and he didn't want to risk it. But the gang took up the chant, 'William the Conkerer', and, sighing, he put down his satchel, took Achilles out, and went up to Carol, feinting. Before beginning, they worked out who'd go first; Achilles was a seasoned veteran of six battles, while Carol's conker, Paris – a city his family had taken him to that summer – only a two-er, so William was given first go. Carol dangled his chestnut, easy, while William flailed away at it overarm. He struck three clean blows, began to grin, enjoy himself, but then made a bad mistake, missed, got the strings tangled up.

'Snags,' Carol piped, gaining the attack.

William's spirits sagged as Carol's conker whacked over and over into Achilles, setting it jigging at the end of its string. By the time he got control of the match back, its husk was crackled. On the first attack, Achilles hammered square into Paris, but suffered the worse, then, on the second, glanced off and flew from its string into the watching mob.

'Stompsies,' went up the cry.

Picking up his bag, William walked away, briskly, before anyone could see his tears.

(William had strayed, or so we thought; I remember bemused grimaces round the table. It almost seemed like he was taunting, mocking us. It was boring. Rashmi even took the gossip magazine from of her bag again, began openly to read it.

'Was the butcher Carol?' Jane asked. 'You recognized him then?'

William shook his head. 'No.' Surly.

Duncan tutted.

William glared.

'It was so lucid. And it's part of my tale, picked up later. You'll see.'

The Scotsman shrugged.

'I swear! My horror was eerily fitted to me.'

William drew deep on his cigarette, seemed near to tears. Duncan looked away, down at the table, drummed with his fingers on it.

I urged William to go on.

He sniffed, put out his cigarette, resumed.

'I was lost a moment, and, when I came back to myself, saw the butcher looking oddly at me. I asked him again what he was on about, and he narrowed his eyes, seemed, of a sudden, cagey...')

'We're forbidden from revealing the secrets of our order.'

On hearing the trite stock phrase, William sneered.

(Reflecting on this cagey response of that butcher's now, I wonder if it was the exploitation of the human desire to be privileged with secret lore that lay behind the power of culture's institutions. Faith exacted as the price of aped disclosure; mysteries like will-o'-the-wisps enticing the unwary.

When the recondite knowledge was held true by the powerful, as in times of superstition, this was bad enough. But when, as in so-called Enlightened eras, the secrets were fictions thought up solely to compel belief, and the elect, having concocted the age's truths, scorned them, void and meaninglessness pullulated.)

'Since I'm here under duress, you know, against my will, the least you could do is tell me what's going on.'

The butcher frowned.

'I don't know any more than you. Some evil thing is loose, and we must kill it.'

The pack, now climbing a hill, had slowed. Breathing a little easier, and headache eased, William felt a throb of sympathy.

'What are you lot anyway? A cult?'

By way of answer, the butcher gave his name, 'Thaul', Saul, told his story.

He'd been a thief, a burglar. Was limber, could swarm up a pipe, climb a trellis, wriggle through a small window, even a dogflap, was, though lowly in the gang, prized by his mates. One day, the gang were tipped off, by their fence, about a haul to be had at a certain church in north London: solid-silver, gemstone-studded chalice, paten, crucifixes. They went to break in, on a moonless night. Spotting a lattice window ajar high above, the gang sent Saul shinning up a drainpipe. He'd nearly reached the open casement when the pipe's rusted bolts sheared. Falling, Saul grabbed at a gargoyle, but the mossy stone was slick. He struck down on a marble slab, a Victorian philanthropist's stone. With a wet thud and crack. A few months before, he'd dropped a sack, holding a fur coat, a stoneware ewer, and several bottles of wine, onto a patio. The same noise. Blood and matter spattered his pals.

'Lads, I'm done,' he tried to say, but he couldn't speak.

His mates scarpered. Staring up at the night sky, he lay there, a long while, unable to move, in agony, seeking solace in the constellations. They offered none, those faint gleams. Then the pain ebbed, and he knew he didn't have long. He was very cold.

But then, as the first daylight gilded the spire looming above him, a gaunt figure, dressed like a monk, wearing a habit, face sunk in the gloomy folds of a cowl, approached, knelt down by him. Reaching out, this stranger laid a cold hand on Saul's forehead, and, in a deep, hoarse voice, urged him to confess. Though he thought the stranger a figment, born of his dying brain, Saul, who'd been brought up Catholic, finding he could talk again, got his sins off his chest. Signing the cross, the stranger absolved him, and warmth and feeling returned to his frame. He got to his feet.

The stranger clasped Saul's shoulder, asked him his name. On learning it – there was only a little confusion due to Saul's lisp – the stranger pronounced it a sign. He went on to tell of a fellowship of men and women pledged to ridding London of fiends. Saul butted in, said that, though he'd not return to crime, neither would he turn on old friends.

'My son. They left you here to die. But, in any case, you misdeem my sense. I do not mean human wrongdoers, but true abominations of the foul Pit.'

'What?'

'Demons, son.'

Saul scoffed.

'But,' the stranger pressed, 'you now know the healing power of God's forgiveness. The malignance of the Enemy does not equal it, but is strong and must be resisted.'

Finally, Saul caved, agreed to attend the next gathering of the defenders.

'I was convinced by what I saw that night,' Saul then said. 'Everyone here has a similar tale.'

Shrugging, William turned away, peered ahead. The rabble had entered a thicket of firs, bracken, brambles, had to pick their way. Underfoot was spongy moss. Small creatures scurried out of their path, and they crossed trampled tracks, signs of larger animals, perhaps badgers and foxes. Now in the van, the riders hacked at the underbrush with their swords.

William didn't know exactly where they were, but thought probably not far from Kenwood House. He recalled then, with a shudder, the false bridge in grounds of the house, painted wood shamming engraved stone. As a child, he'd often thought there must be a fantastic realm lying on the other side of that bridge, that, if the magic words were said, it'd become solid, and he'd be able to go there.

Saul, angry William was again lost in reverie, prodded his shoulder.

'The order has had a long, hidden, but lofty history. Its knights have waged war on evil for centuries. This place would've long since yielded to darkness if it weren't for their vigilance.'

'Bollocks.'

'You'll see.'

Just then, the mob entered a glade. One of the knights gave a cry, mingling revulsion and triumph, dismounted.

'Mark this!'

All gathered round. Two bodies sprawled side by side on the grass. William recognized the lovers he'd come across earlier. The place reeked of slaughter. The man's clothes had been torn from him, his belly had been slashed, entrails worried, and his hand, pale, tallow, had been torn from his wrist, lay on the grass a short distance off. The woman, aside from the mortal wound, her throat torn out, was untouched. It seemed the kill was fresh, that they'd disturbed the beast, run it off, but William couldn't shake the feeling it'd simply lost interest, wandered away.

The knights cast about, seeking spoor; one, sighting a print, crowed.

'Clear sign!'

Then the paladin in black turned to address the pack. At first he couldn't be heard over the ruckus, the panic, but a cry of, 'the Black Knight wishes to speak,' went round, and all fell silent.

'The demon, knowing it's hunted, will have gone to ground,' he said. 'If we do not tarry, we can track it to its lair.'

The other horsemen circled behind, began to drive the mob forward once more, but the Black Knight rode on ahead. At first, William kept glancing down at the ground as he ran, looking for the trail the hunt followed, but he'd fallen to the rear, couldn't make anything out amid the welter of prints of those before him. They came out into the open once more, charged across a swathe of grassland, then came to a halt in a hollow before a low granite escarpment, a miry place. William, done in, went down on hunkers.

'There!' the leader bellowed, pointing to a crevice in the rock.

William saw a sallow pitted skull, human, lying, canted, in the mud before it, a hole smashed in the brain pan. The Black Knight ranted. Weary, filled with dread, William paid scant attention, but grasped the pith – the demon would be cowering, afraid, a brave stealthy man or woman might steal up, volunteers were urged to speak up, there was glory in it. There was a clamouring, pleading, many wished to be selected. Saul was chosen, and a sigh went up from those disappointed.

The butcher was handed a short dagger by the Black Knight, sent into the tunnel. At the mouth, he paused a moment, breathed deep, then went in.

An uneasy hush fell.

A crow came wheeling out of the darkness, alighted on the skull, and perched there, hopping foot to foot. Nothing stirred else. Then, just when William thought he couldn't endure the racking tension longer, there came a moan and a wild, gleeful howl. The whimper was soon choked, but the yawping went on and on, before faltering, stifled by sobs, as if the revel had been soured by regret, as if two tempers warred in one frame. The hunt stood, hushed. Then there was cracking and rending, a wet crunch, slurping. A gory gobbet was tossed from the lair. Saul's head. By some vagary of fate, it came to rest bloodied stump down, so it seemed the butcher was entire, just buried to the neck. The eyes held a look which mingled appeal and reproach. William felt it was directed at him.

The stars stared down, unblinking, entranced.

Grisly noises came from the lair; William retched. The Black Knight crossed over to the severed head, leant down from the saddle, snatched it up by the hair. Turning it over in his hands, he peered at it. The cranium had been staved. A little matter glooped from the ragged hole. Then the knight addressed the hunt.

'Saul was a good, courageous man. His death must be avenged. We will dye this quag red with demon's blood before this night is out.'

Quelling nerves, William spoke up, 'But you sent him in there, to his death.'

The pack turned to glower.

'Yes,' came the Black Knight's response. 'A glorious death, he was well prepared for and sought.'

'Glorious? Death? Absurd.'

'The Lord has a place thet by at hith right hand on high for thothe who fall fighting in hith name.'

It was subtle, but the knight was lisping, mocking.

William raged. 'You fucker! Why did you send him? Not go yourself? Fucking coward!'

Those standing nearest William shied away, and the Black Knight drew his sword, levelled it at him.

'No Knight of the Order should be exposed to such contumely! Smite him!'

Forcing a path through the crowd, one of the other knights ambled his charger over to William, thumped him with a gauntleted fist. He fell to his knees, blood running from a gash to his brow, head pounding.

During William's stand, a large black cat had come prowling from the cave mouth, then, sighting the crow perched on the skull, slunk towards it, dragging its belly in the mud. Just as the horseman raised his fist to strike William again, the Black Knight's mount, skittishly backing, trod on the cat's tail. Hissing, the cat arched its back, then dug its claws into the horse's fetlock. Rearing, the charger threw its rider.

The Black Knight landed hard on his back; Saul's head flew from his grasp and rolled into a nearby bramble thicket.

Mewling, the cat ran back into the tunnel.

The mob looked on silent, aghast. William's beating was stayed; the other knights went to their leader's aid. He lay whining. 'Ah, fuck, that hurt. Stupid fucking cat.'

He lay, weighed down by cumbersome plate, flailing his arms and legs, like a beetle turned on its back. His two companions dismounted to help, grabbed him under his arms, lifted him. Once on his feet, it was still a little while before he could stand on his own, needed the other knights to hold him, prop him up for a bit. Then, when he was recovered, he clambering back into the saddle, gestured toward the dark fissure.

'We must smoke out the monster. Go, collect wood, bring it back. Bring greenwood, which we need for its reek, as well as dry.'

The pack split up, dispersed. William, bloodied, still reeling, cowed, did not baulk, but went along with one of the parties, made up of the hens, as it turned out. They went into a small copse of spruce, beech, elm. A knight rode hither and yon nearby, keeping vigilance. One of the young women, taking a large clasp knife from her handbag, set about hacking limbs from the living firs. The woman who'd earlier jibed William, pinched his arse, winked at him, was vexed when he didn't even flinch, spat, slapped him, setting his head throbbing again. Then she turned to her friend who was hewing the pines, asked what she was doing.

'The needles are really smoky when you burn them,' came the reply, followed by a snort of laughter. 'I once set fire to me mum's Xmas tree with a fag.'

She glared at William.

'What you looking at, dozy fucker? Why don't you take these,' she pointed at the branches already cut down, 'back over?'

William did so, without a murmur.

When enough wood had been gathered, it was heaped before the crevice, and a teenager, wearing a hooded top with a band name, 'Swine Grinder', printed on it in a Gothic font, came forward to kindle the tinder with his cigarette lighter. It caught, then the logs went up. The fire limned the leering faces of the mob with a hell light. They revelled, and the spindly shadows they threw cavorted jerkily behind them, a rabble of charred wraiths lured, by the flames, to cross into this world from some dread other place, a place of ash. The fire smoked, and the light wind blew the billows into the cave mouth.

The pack gathered round the blaze, sat on coats spread on the damp ground, or squatted on haunches, bided awhile. Sandwiches, flasks of tea, whisky, or brandy, packets of cigarettes, a pipe or two, were taken from satchels, rucksacks, pockets. But they'd barely got settled, taken only one or two bites, sips, puffs, before the waiting was at an end.

A monster writhed from out of the roiling smoke. A big serpent, withered arms, brimstone eyes, needle teeth, set askew in perished rubber gums, wings, ragged, like broken umbrellas, flapping frantic. It gyred in the dirt, opening and closing its mouth, but was penned. A groan of disgust, horror went up. William retched, turned away. Riding over, the Black Knight drove his brand into the demon's face. Wailing, it cringed back. One of the other knights crept up behind it, pinned its tail with his blade. Shuddering, it heaved, brought up a mess of offal.

The serpent squirmed, impaled, unable, it seemed, to shed its tail and flee, as some lizards can.

'See the ease with which men of pure heart best a creature of darkness!' the Black Knight hollered. 'Now we need only someone to come forward, dispatch it.'

The throng roared, clamoured to be chosen.

'I hear your petitions, but I'm afraid I must disappoint. It is my will the newest member of our order should seal his loyalty by finishing this. Come forward.'

The Black Knight, peering into the pack, sought William out, then pointed. Struggling, William was hauled, pushed forward, left standing, swaying slightly, in front of the demon, which moaned, squirmed in the dirt. He was hardly aware of the sword thrust into his hand.

The crowd started to chant, 'Off with its head!' over and over.

The demon stared up at William, a pleading look in its eyes, then spoke, in a weak sibilant hiss, 's's drawn out.

'Pleassse, ssspare me. You know not what it isss you do.'

Its struggles had torn a long gash, but the sword held. A yellow ichor welled, pooled, seething. Mostly, William felt revulsion, but there was grain of pity there too.

'I won't do it,' he said, to the Black Knight. 'Choose someone else.'

'No. It must be you. What is it they call you, my son?'

William didn't reply.

The Black Knight rode over, drew his sword, held its keen edge to William's throat.

'Pray, tell me, what is your name?'

William spat it out.

'Auspicious.' He raised his voice, 'Friends, this young man is William. We will ken him as the Conqueror.'

He clapped his hand to his chest, and the cuirass knelled as if hollow.

'Now, cut off the thing's head, make an end of it.'

The demon darted out its forked tongue, looked up at

William, imploring. 'I just wish to be left in peace. I mean no harm.'

'But,' William said, in a low voice, wiping the sweat beading his brow with his left forearm, 'haven't you killed tonight?'

The sword was so heavy he could hardly lift it. He tried to let it go, but could not, the hide-bound handle cleaved unpleasantly. He didn't dare look down at his hand. Dull aches ran up his arm.

'I must eat. I cannot quell my craving for flesh.'

It began to weep

William groaned.

'I'm no killer,' he shouted up at the stars, before backing away from the demon.

'Yes,' the Black Knight said. 'Yes you are.'

He began repeating, 'William the Conqueror,' over and over, and the rabble took it up, yelled it. William was flustered by the din. He was shoved back toward the serpent. His pleas were smothered by the chanting.

Then the demon puked once more. William saw something glinting in the spew, a ring, unusual design, three bands of silver braided. He picked it up, wiped it on his shirt, then peered at it, holding it to the moonlight, frantic not to see a certain inscription. It was there, though, the words he'd spent much time mulling, before giving to the jeweller, a week or so before Catherine's last birthday.

The demon gawked on, aghast, as a wail tore from William's throat, and, finding strength in pain and rage, he swung the sword.

The pack fell silent. The demon started speaking, but got no further than, 'It's not...,' before the blade cleaved its neck. The head arced through the air, still jawing, but soundlessly, eyes rolling, life's dying embers. Thumping into the mud, it fell still, eyes clouded. The body slumped, rank, acrid ichor spouting from the neck stump. The wings fluttered, then fell limp. William took several paces back. Finding the sword no longer fast to his hand he let it fall. Its blade was corroding, smoked. A cheer went up from the mob. The black cat, a screeching ball of fur, came out of the cave mouth, scampered across to the demon's severed head, pounced on it, clawed at the sightless eyes.

Then the carcass's hide began to boil, giving the impression of a myriad life beneath the surface. Scales were shed. William stood agape as the naked, decapitated body of a woman was revealed piecemeal. When a pale mole-strewn belly was exposed, he ran over, roughly grabbed the cat by the scruff of its neck, tore it away. Taking up the severed head, he stared down at its features, saw, mauled, twisted by fear, Catherine's face. The cat, clawing at his shins, raised a cry, which, beginning muffled, like the sobbing of a child, rapidly swelled into a banshee wail, a mandrake shriek. Looking down at the creature, William saw a white marking on its belly, a rough outline of a gallows. He kicked the cat from him, fell to his knees in the mire, raged at the firmament.

When, anguish spent, he wiped his eyes, looked about him, the dell before the bluff was deserted. He'd not heard the others leave, and there was no trace they'd ever been there at all, no tracks in the dirt, no sandwich wrappers or cigarette ends. He was alone, entirely alone, clutching his girlfriend's bloody sundered head.

Overhead, the lights went up, slowly, and the stars, appetite for tragedy sated, left the theatre, one by one.

V

Today, it's blustery and the sky, lowering – thickset clouds stampede by, a frenzied herd. Yet it's still close; the gusts do not freshen, the rack doesn't baffle the heat. The sun, glimpsed through gaps, is now directly overhead, and it's stifling. I reckon there'll be a storm before dusk.

This morning I did little: prepared breakfast, porridge, for the young woman and myself; ate my bowlful; collected firewood. The rest of the time, I stood in the prow of the ship, looking out over the estuary, lost in thought, watching the scudding billows, odd rays of sunlight scintillating on the chop, a gull dropping mussels onto a concrete slipway a little distance downstream.

I took a break from writing, for I finished my account of William's tale last night. I was only a few days in setting it down, as I've been able to work undisturbed; all's been quiet, little's happened. The tribeswoman's got much better, is now able to feed herself, and, though still weak, seems out of danger. She spends most of the time resting on the pallet in the wheelhouse. I've given this up to her, and, since the weather's held fair, at least till today, have been sleeping on the deck, the night sky, my canopy, the constellations, its embroidery. Apart from writing, I've done little, spent one afternoon foraging for edible tubers and grasses and another fishing with my makeshift spear, stood, stock-still, waist-deep in the river, till the fish, no longer wary, thinking me perhaps only a piece of flotsam entangled in river weeds, swam close enough to strike at.

I'd be soothed by this calm, were it not that I feel sure it merely a lull, fleeting, that my enemy now comes for me, and soon. As I've written, I'm sure I've evaded him so long only because he wished to prolong the hunt; I know, in my guts, in my bones, he doesn't track by sign, but by unerring instinct (and so have given up, as needless, my tiresome strictures about hiding during daylight hours, living only at night, and not lighting fires or tapers on the deck of the hulk – one good in this).

In fact, I wish something would happen, even something bad, even the thing I most fear, for waiting harrows me.

It's now early evening. The threatened storm hasn't come, though the wind has got up even more, is now howling off the sea, and I've been forced to move my desk into the lee of the cabin. The young woman sleeps inside. My head is swathed in torn strips of linen; I've just finished cleansing, swabbing, and bandaging a hack to my brow. Though I've no mirror, I know the wound, from what I could tell from the crazed, hazy reflection of my face in the river's roiled waters, from nervous fingertips, and from the tribeswoman's reaction, to be severe.

It's as if the hankering I set down this morning invoked the tumult that came after. I could almost believe this typewriter cursed. I'll certainly be wary what I type from now on.

Having, for millennia, spent most of the time sedentary, reading, lost in contemplation, I'm easily wearied; my earlier exertions have exhausted me, I'd like to rest. But, as I fear my enemy closes in, I feel I must write this night, tired though I am. Later, I promise to tell, in full, of the events of the turbulent afternoon just past, but first I reckon it needful, for my tale, the shape of it, that I describe all that's happened to me in the last year or so, since I left the Himalayas, my aeon-long refuge. Besides, my brain throbs, my hands shake; I doubt I'm yet equal to the task of telling of the violence that took place a mere hour or so ago.

Every city and town is now girded by heaps of junked tech; after the power went down, once and for good, their folk processed out to edgelands, lugging dead machines, dumped them there. These midden are like wen, festering metal and plastic, seething chemicals, or barrows, haunted by wights of rampant code. I considered scavenging vehicles from them, but doubted there were any that still went, knew I didn't have the know-how to fix one up, and was, besides, in fear of the places, the murmuring of the weird artefacts, the miasma, the strange thin glow at night. I was also anxious about the notice I might draw – a worry made worse by reports I'd heard from mountain dwellers of a man, with pale skin like mine, wandering the region – and decided travelling unobtrusively the safest course. So I walked the most part of the distance and rode the rest on beasts caught and tamed, or thieved (I'd nothing to trade) from settlements lining my route. It was a wearying trek, and fraught, for I had to stay watchful against attacks by wild folk and beasts. At first, I went unarmed; most were cowed by the yowling I made as they closed (I'd learnt to make loud unearthly noises in my throat) and my freakish looks – I was garbed in loose robes, as is the custom of the Himalayan peoples, but also, as protection from the sun's relentless blaze (which is more intense these days, than ever before), wore a sackcloth cowl and ancient ski-mask. Then, a few weeks into my journey, while crossing a large tract of dried-up lake bed, I was set on by a horde who, clad in feather cloaks, teeth filed to jags, faces daubed with bright pigment, hair slicked with grease, brandishing bones, came howling over the salt flats, out of the haze. They clubbed me down, hog-tied me, toted me back to a cavern under a large rock, once, I'd hazard, an island of the lake, their dwelling place, beat me some more, left me, thinking me dead, or nearly so, with only a young couple to watch over me, went out to seek more prey. There was no cruelty in it; they were starved, I was food. After a short time, my guards began groping each other, breathing hard, I struggled free of my bonds, overwhelmed them, staggered off. After that I armed myself with a tapering steel spar wrested from what looked like an old telecommunications rig, wielded it like a spear, used it to drive off foes. I'd been sore hurt by the cannibal tribe, was some days mending. Of course, I'm not ever in any real danger (save for from the fiend who hunts me), but wounds still cause me pain. Another time, a few weeks after, as I was crossing a range of cragged peaks, a mountain lion padded up to me while I slept, no fear of the fire I'd set in the mouth of the cave where I'd laid down, and tore a gobbet from my thigh. I woke, in agony, and it went for my neck. We wrestled a time, but then I punched it repeatedly in the throat, buckled its windpipe, left it gasping, ran. I limped on the injured leg for days, and it festered, though finally it healed, as all my wounds, no matter how severe, do in time.

I also used my makeshift spear for hunting; mainly goats and swine, though occasionally other beasts. When I made a kill, which wasn't that often, I'd feast till replete on the choicest cuts and offal, in revel, then cure the rest, by smoking, to carry with me. Once I brought down a small elephant, which gave me meat for some weeks. But it was rank and greasy, and I gagged on it as I forced it down. Most of the time though, I subsisted on roots, berries, nuts, and mushrooms, though I gave up eating these last somewhere in, what was, at one time, Eastern Europe, when I ate a toadstool and was in a bad way for several days after: shaking, sweating, guts aching, puking, bowels loose, and, the worst of it, dogged by vile gibbous forms, seen askance, that fleeted when I turned to look full on them. Perhaps these were mere figments, but I think the bane somehow gave me sight of the realm of horrors that lies alongside our world, but is wontedly mercifully occulted, that place I'd been forced to look on in the cavern beneath Spitalfields, that William had glimpsed on Hampstead Heath, and of which I'll tell more as my tale unravels.

Crossing the plains of erstwhile Central Europe, I found that place, which had once been strewn with cities thronging with folk, but had been left a concrete, steel, and glass desert with civilization's end, again teemed with life, had been overrun by plants and animals that had busted out of the parks and zoological gardens where they'd been penned, or had returned from elsewhere. Herds of fierce aurochs and wall-eyed wisents roamed, grazing vast tracts of grassland, hunted by tribes of burly simple folk who rode swine and slept in hide tents; thickset rodents swam in lakes and rivers, flashing orange incisors; boars crashed through the thickets of forested swathes; beetles blundered through the grass underfoot, flowering bushes thrummed with wasps, bees, and hummingmoths, and midges harried at dusk. And the skies were also flocked with life. Geese, swans, crows, starlings, thrushes, hawks, buzzards, finches, gulls, magpies, and shrikes. And stranger kinds too. Once, though, when passing by a dead oak at sunset, I heard a loud 'oop-oop-oop' and, looking over, saw a hoopoe perched on one black bough, sickle beak darting this way and that, vivid crest lost against the lurid glow in the western sky. Another time a bearded vulture kept pace with me a stretch, wheeling overhead, till, feeling it an ill omen and a sign that might give me away, I killed a sheep and laid out its carcass; last I saw of that carrion bird, it soared on an updraft, dropping mutton bones on to a pitted concrete slab, remnant of a road or runway, to crack them open, get at the marrow.

One evening, while making a fire to dry my clothes after crossing a wide river, once, I think, the Rhine, wading and swimming, I looked to the east and saw a man on horseback stark against the waning light there. I broke camp, pressed on, into the sunset and through the night, garments wet and clammy, risking a chill, ensuring I left as few tokens of my passage as I could, seeking a place of refuge. Hazard favoured, and, the following morning, as a red stain spread across the sky at my back, I came across, and nearly tumbled into, a shaft sunk into the ground. A ladder, rungs still holding firm, was bolted to one concrete wall. I clambered into the pit, reached the foot of the ladder. A little of the dawn light filtered down through ventilation ducts, and, once my eyes were accustomed to the gloom, I explored the place. It was dank, cramped, empty, bar a few metal chairs, and, strewn about, food tins long since bloated by the rot

of contents. I climbed out, tore down a knot of ivy and briar from
a tree that stood near, dragged it back, and, descending the
ladder again, pulled this tangle over the hole after me. I was four
days hiding in the bunker. On the second, hooves drummed by
overhead, and, listening at one of the grilles, I was sure I scented
pipe smoke. I stood with my ear pressed to the vent, seized by
dread, many hours, but the rider did not return.

I reached the English Channel without further event, waded
into the water. Sad at heart, it had served me well, I abandoned
my lance. After a long wearying swim, I saw, looming out of the
sea mist ahead, hoary cliffs and recalled, with sorrow, Colin
Elton's fate. I found a cove, pulled myself up on the beach, and
lay a while, getting my breath back. Then I made for the place
once known as London, drawn there because I couldn't conceive
beginning this memoir elsewhere, and by a feeling that, if there
was to be a final fray, the spirit of the place might give me an
edge. And I wished to see how it had changed. Perhaps, too, my
compulsion to return was influenced by the cosmology of the
peoples of the Himalayas among whom I'd lived so long.

My first sight of the city since I'd fled, aeons before, was from
a hill just to the south-east. Though, doubtless, it had been razed
and rebuilt, again and again, in the ages between my leaving and
its eventual desolation, the place I knew could still be discerned
in it. The river wended west to east, as in my day, though its
meanders had shifted, I could no longer read its scrawl, and I
doubted any had called it the Thames for a long, long time. The
tallest structures were, as then, mostly to the east, foundations
sunk into the marshland there, though they dwarfed even the
skyscrapers of my era, actually scraped the sky, gored the soft
underbelly of the mass of cloud that hunkered over the city.
Under the pall of that lowering smother, a vast glass dome near
the centre of the place looked a whited blister. Around the central
core, the husks of the great edifices, low dwellings clustered, the
suburbs, scavengers about carrion, or ring within ring of wizard

stones circling a place of sacrifice, the whole one grey temple of an awful rite. Then, with shock, I sighted a building I knew in the midst of the place: St Paul's, just as I recalled it, but with dome staved. As the masonry of the original would have long been dust, I supposed this to be the ruin of a later replica.

I'd reckoned on a throb in my chest, seeing that place again, after so long, but I felt nothing; my heart's calcified.

As I've written, civilization has fallen and risen again, many times over, but this time it seems the cities have been abandoned for good. Why, I don't know. It was neither dire cataclysm nor scourging plague, and the weapons of humankind's darkest invention remain on their launchpads, listing, mouldering. Perhaps the call of the wild – a lure ever since humankind first, weary of wandering, of hunting and foraging, settled the land, penned and raised beasts for slaughter, tilled the soil – finally grew too loud. Though, for centuries after the final desolation, folk were still drawn to the cities now and again, to wonder, to scavenge, to loot, and, finally, merely to lay waste, in the end, even the vandals stayed away; for the last few millennia the former founts of civilization have been left alone to the ravages of time and the elements.

I walked down into the ruins. The streets of the place once known as London were as the streets of the Earth's other derelict cities: littered with dross, strewn with debris, and vacant save scurrying rats.

As I wished to see again the region I'd once lived in, I headed north. I walked residential streets a long time, then through a slum, then an industrial district, shadows of chimneys and cooling towers striping the roadway. I couldn't make out any of the writing I saw, on signs, fascia, and the ilk; it only vaguely resembled Latin script.

Then, after passing through an alley running between scarps of riven masonry, with rubble underfoot, so that, eyes narrowed, I could believe myself not in the city at all, but in the mountains, walking a dry gorge, I reached the river. I sought a place to cross, but the bridges that had once spanned it had fallen, the only remnants, piers, jutting up like bones of giant folk buried too shallow and part disinterred by heavy rain; I had to swim. The river was frigid, I shivered as I waded in. Halfway across, treading water a moment to get my breath back, I looked down, saw beneath me a shoal of sprat scattering before a pike.

Arriving at what had once been known as Highgate Hill, I discovered it was girded by a high wall. I walked along it till I came to an opening, went in. The entrance hall of some attraction, a row of ticket booths, most windows gone, two still in their frames, clouded with age, sightless eyes. Dust lay so thick, I was slowed to a trudge. After clambering over the wreck of a turnstile, going outside again, I went on, found myself on a cobbled street that climbed the hill. I walked up it, thought of Dick Whittington, fairy-tale hero and thrice Lord Mayor, and William Powell, early lottery casualty and pauper visionary, walked past: a roundhouse, wattle-and-daub walls, thatched roof; a half-timbered dwelling, jettied upper-floors beetling; a geodesic dome, dark, glassy obsidian; a foursquare townhouse, pale masonry, portico with fluted columns; and a stark tower block, dingy concrete. Entering this high-rise, I found it choked with mouldering draff, its dank walls daubed with graffiti, gaudy hues, armoured vehicles, folk in strange garb, fierce chimera, crude filth, excessive twisted acts, twisted excessive anatomies, priapic voluptuous monstrous contortions, jagged scrawl.

At the top of the hill, I came across a museum housed in a subterranean complex. It was pitchy inside; I was only able to explore as I found, just inside the entrance, an old electric torch that weirdly still worked. Most of the display cabinets had been smashed, contents taken or wrecked, but there were some smaller chambers further below ground that hadn't been plundered. In these, I discovered, in sealed cases, along with many artefacts whose use I couldn't fathom, my typewriter, a spare ribbon spool, two reams of paper, a ballpoint pen, and my banjo. And, in a store room of some kind, I found a cupboard, also shut tight, holding staff uniforms, dust sheets, a little mildewed, but otherwise fine, which I pilfered to replace my ragged clothing and linen, and, beside the cupboard, a hand-barrow, once used, I supposed, for moving exhibition pieces, that, made from plastic, had survived intact. This I took to cart my things in.

Then I returned to the centre of the derelict city to seek out the site where, in my day, the British Library had stood. I hoped a place of learning might have endured there, that mining might unearth riches. The area had been laid waste, but, delving in the ruins, found I'd not hoped in vain, discovered a hatch from which, once the seal was broken, a musty redolence of old paper, ink, and leather bindings wafted. Underground stacks; lodes of lore, seams of stories. I spent a short while wandering the shelves reading titles by the light of my torch. In the end, I took only one sole volume with me, The Narrative of Arthur Gordon Pym of Nantucket;[8] for I was tired and hungry then, intended to return the following day, rested, sated, to spend more time browsing, carry off as many volumes as I could pile into the barrow, leaving just room for my meagre few things.

After, I entered the vast glass dome, found a shopping district inside. I explored, seeking retailers where I could outfit myself for the weeks ahead. Beneath the vault it was stifling: in former times, huge fans would have circulated the air. I wandered the arcades, foraging, seeking supplies. But it was a dispiriting and profitless endeavour; sacked millennia before, the place was miserable testament to folk's urge to mar. Most lasting items had been wrecked. Had they been thieved to make use of, I could have understood, but they'd simply been rent, smashed, crushed, shivered, and left. Amid the junk, though, in a cookware shop, I did find a carving knife, a steel, to bring it to keenness with, and a skillet.

All perishable goods had long since mouldered, but their rot had spored a fetid riotous life. A stinking mess lay deep in the aisles of the victuallers', and strange flora grew in it: gaudy orchids, giant pitcher-plants, and creepers, which twined about the struts of the shelving, and whose white flowers reeked cloying, charnel.

Surrounded by this evidence of the wanton vandalism of folk (and the lush wantonness of nature), my thoughts turned to those social contracts that, for all their seeming permanence, are always torn up at the first hint of threat. Thinkers have proposed divers theories of civilization: some have been positive, argued it's the apotheosis of humankind's condition, a waypoint on the journey to enlightenment, or the foundation stone of a divine city; others, neutral, mechanistic, claimed it's simply one stage in the cycle of history, or the most natural response to folk's being in the world; and a few have flayed it, called it malign, an institution enabling oppression and exploitation, or a decadent way of living, a fall from an innate state of grace and innocence. I'm perhaps better placed to speculate than any philosopher, due to my diuturnity; it troubles me to offer my theory, though, for it's bleak. Civilization seems to me only a filmy shroud laid over the seething rot that's the true way of things.

Strange to relate, but while thinking these dark thoughts I felt loneliness more keenly than I'd done for an age. I tried to envision the precinct as it would have been on a busy Saturday, before the exodus, but my imagination failed me. Then, overwhelmed by the heat and stench, I ran to find an exit. Outside, I hunkered down and retched.

Once recovered from my bout of nausea, I got to my feet. I'd fled the dome without securing any provisions, save the knife and skillet, which I still clutched, but nothing could have induced me to re-enter that place.

Standing there, feeling lorn, in the sun, in the empty dead air of that street, which would have once been noisy, bustling, I conceived a wayward need to return to the place where I'd been damned.

Deciding to wait till the next day, I spent the night in the lobby of a dilapidated hotel in the central part of the city. After a frugal repast, I slept fitfully on a mildewed couch.

I set out just after sunrise. To cross the Thames, I was again forced to swim. Reaching the south bank, I stretched myself out on the stony beach there – the tide was at low ebb – to rest, steam in the sun. Lying down, I disturbed a small crab, and it scuttled away across the shingle, clacking its claws as it fled.

Once I'd my breath back and had dried off a bit, I got to my feet, entered the warren of streets south of the river, headed roughly in the direction of the place I sought. Dun concrete warehouses wreathed in sallow mist loomed overhead. The only living things were rats; they scurried after me.

After wandering lost a while, I came across a block of masonry in a glass case. Knapped flint and chequered stonework; I couldn't, of course, read the label, but recognized the exhibit as a chunk from the tower of Southwark Cathedral. I was stunned, time which antiquates antiquities, and has an art to making dust of all things, had yet spared this fragment. I presumed it must have been excavated from the ground somewhere nearby, and that I was close to the site on which the church had stood. The Nightingale had lain only a short distance to the south-east of the cathedral, so I pressed on into the dawn glow.

A few moments later, I came out into a large square. Once, perhaps, it had been a bright, airy place of restaurants, cafés, bars, but now was a gloomy grove of yews, the first perhaps sprouted from a seed carried there in the guts of a bird, or in mud caked in the tread of boot or frog of a hoof. I knew, somehow, it was the site on which the Nightingale had stood.

I went down some steps, entered the murk beneath the writhen boughs. Every sinew of my body resisted, but I felt compelled. Ten paces or so in, I saw a dark form on the ground.

Standing stock still, holding my breath, I waited for my eyes to adjust. Once they had, I saw a corpse laid out on the flagstones.

I knelt down, put my hand to his cheek, felt a faint warmth; he was but recently dead. He lay on his back, dressed in a dishevelled, threadbare suit, shirt torn open, feet bare. He was wan, starveling; shadows pooled in his hollowed cheeks, dark as bruises against his pale skin. He'd been hobbled with duct tape; his arms were outflung, but red marks on his wrists showed they'd been likewise bound; the remainder of the roll of tape, whose origins I couldn't guess at, and several used scraps, lay on the ground beside his body; traces of glue adhering to the skin around his mouth and nose, and a patchiness to the beard growth there, told the use the scraps had been put to. His torso was pocked with small burn lesions, and many cigarette butts haloed his head, painstakingly arranged. Round his neck had been knotted a serpent, still alive, if sluggish, with a pair of tiny diaphanous wings, taken, perhaps, from a child's toy, tied on, just behind its head, with ribbon. The snake, it seemed, had been striking repeatedly at the dead man's face; his cheeks and forehead were lacerated and flecked with venom. Most grisly of all, in each eye a cigarette had been stubbed; slow, the heat of the ember boring a hole through cornea, aqueous humour, iris, and lens, and into the vitreous body, end left jutting.

I choked a howl, anguish born in part of what had been inflicted, and in part of the fate it foreshadowed for me; the dead man was William Adams.

There was a deep wound to the region of the heart – the death blow. As far as I knew, there was only one weapon on Earth that could have dealt it, and it was held by the evil being who'd cursed William, and myself, and others, with immortality in the first place. Once I'd ceased to reel, I crushed the snake's head with my boot heel, walked away, left poor William's carcass to rot in the dismal spinney. In a way, I envied him his death, if not the manner of it.

I headed back toward the hotel, where I'd left my possessions. Knowing the demon who hunted me was close at hand, I intended to quit London that afternoon, but I lost my way, and it was only after several frantic hours that I finally found the place. By then dusk approached, and I thought it probably safer to spend the night holed up, that my enemy might steal up on me in the dark were I to set out then.

Over a grim supper of the last of some smoked mutton, grey, a fur of mould to scrape off, I thought about what I'd seen that day. It was all too easy to reconstruct what had happened to William; I quailed, realized what foul glee a victim who feels pain but cannot die offered cruel evil. Only one aspect puzzled me at first: that William's mouth and nose had been taped up. After all, there was no one to hear him cry out, no one who could help him if they did. It was not till later, lying awake between snatches of sleep on the damp sofa, I understood. To me it seems the most repellent aspect of the brutalization, a worse outrage even than what was done to his eyes. He'd been made to pull deeply on cigarettes, then his lips and nostrils had been sealed, preventing him from exhaling the acrid smoke till his persecutor willed it. How many times this was repeated, and how long William was left to suffer each time, I did not wish to contemplate. But there were a lot of cigarettes arrayed about his head.

The following morning I rose before sunrise, went outside. I'd slept poorly, woken twice in terror, sure I'd see Punch leering down at me. During the night there'd been a heavy downpour, and, as the drains were blocked with dead leaves and rubbish, there was standing water in the street. Under the hotel's portico, though, the ground was still dry, and I hunkered down there to breathe deep, dispel the lingering wraiths of my nightmares. But then, just as I was starting to calm, a small rodent scurried past and, following it with my eyes, I saw something that set my heart fluttering against my ribs like a trapped bird. On the paving, not far from where I sat, was a scattering of ash and a clump of dottle.

Possibly these were left there to intimidate me, though I think it more likely it was mere chance the spot had been chosen to shelter from the storm and have a smoke; I doubt, otherwise, I'd have been let escape. Afraid, I packed my few things and set out, pushing my cart before me, walking east. I chose the heading pretty much on a whim; the rising sun seemed to betoken sanctuary is all.

(Reader, you may be wondering why I, whose life hangs heavy about my neck (in truth, I'm unsure the condition that's my lot should be termed life: my state's nebulous, liminal, like that of the fabled undead), fled the beast who means to kill me. Well, though I'd gratefully yield to almost any death, I want to put off the remorseless torture of a death at his hands as long as I can, and won't stop running, even if it means toting my burden further.)

It was full day by the time I'd left the city's outerlying regions behind. Cresting a rise I came upon the Thames meandering sedately through meadowland studded with poppies and buttercups and decided to follow its course.

As evening came on, sore weary, feet blistered, I realized, from the broadening of the channel and the salt tang in the air, I'd come to the sea reach. A vast tenebrous mass loomed out of the mist and the dusk on the other side of the river. It was a hulk, this battered vessel on whose deck I now sit, writing. I was shocked by its size; it was far too large a vessel for these waters. Drawing closer, I saw, stencilled on its transom, in paint somehow hardy enough to have survived the weathering of millennia, and still a deep red, 'Ark'. Why this name was written in Latin characters, though it would have been chosen, I think, after that script was dead, who chose it, and whether or not they knew the significance of their choice, I've no idea. Whatever, it seemed auspicious; I felt it a sign this was the place to await the coming end of things.

So I decided to swim across the broad estuary and assess whether the wreck would make a fit dwelling place. At first I worried about getting my things across, but then found, luckily, that, even laden, my barrow floated.

The crossing further exhausted me, and, on reaching the far bank, I had to rest a while to get my strength back. Then, looking for a way to gain the Ark's deck, I made a circuit. I came across no sign of how the vessel came to its pass: whether, caught in rough seas, its crew sought shelter in the calmer river mouth, without a pilot aboard who knew the shallows; or, for some reason, was purposefully sunk, at a time when the area was all underwater (from time to time, when the Earth's balance has been clouted awry by folk's ransack, the sea levels have risen cataclysmically; this has happened again and again, for, though memories of such floods have been held in the minds of descendants of survivors, they've always been shifted into myth (as I've mentioned, I'm sure all legends are buried folk memories of such turmoils), recalled as the vengeance of wrathful gods, not the result of overweening greed). Whatever, the anchor had been dropped before wreck or scuttling; half sunk in sludge, a little aft of the ship, it looked the skull of one of the massive beasts that walked abroad during the Earth's infancy (and haven't, for some reason, again). I clambered up its massy chain. Moss grew in the hollows of the links, making climbing treacherous, and several times I nearly slipped and fell; I'd not have taken the risk as a mortal.

Reaching the hawsehole, I stretched up, seized the gunwale, hauled myself on board. I slumped down, sat leaning against the bulwarks, looked about. Scavengers (perhaps aided by the elements) had stripped the aft-deck; it was marked with brownish-red mottles, rust stains about the corroded stubs of bolts that once secured fittings; the only things that remained were a few metal containers for the stowage of freight, scattered haphazard. I went to each in turn. The doors had been forced;

they were empty, save webs swagged in corners, and, underfoot, the muddled bones of small creatures, that, seen but dimly in the halflight, looked dainty ploughs, harrows, scythes, sickles, and flails, the tools of faerie tillers, reapers, and threshers.

There was a cabin of riveted steel plate amidships. I crossed to it. It had windows fore and aft, but, salt-rimed, grimy, they could no longer be seen through. Trying the door and finding it unlocked, I went inside, prodded the gloom with my torch. In one corner was what looked a clumped heap of polished nautili shells, a machine of some kind, probably the helm controls. It had been set about; a wreck made of its nacred whorls.

Back outside, I explored the foredeck. It had also been plundered; the only features that remained were a winch and a hatch cover. This latter, I surmised, gave access to the companionway. I examined it closely. The seal was filth crusted. In the centre was a keypad, keys marked with strange sigils. I pressed a few at random. Nothing happened. I tried a few more combinations, then gave up. I doubted the ancient mechanism still worked, but, even if it did, it would probably take an age to find the correct combination. Besides, the air below decks was almost certainly fetid and unwholesome, and the wheelhouse was a good-enough hiding place.

Then I crossed to the winch. Turning the handle on an idle whim, I found it extended a primitive gangway from just below the level of the deck on the landward side of the ship; a mechanical backup, I supposed. I kept cranking till the ramp's far end settled on the estuary mud.

After fetching the barrow, I set about cleaning the cabin, making it habitable.

While writing the foregoing account, I saw the sun set and rise ten times; composition took much longer than I thought it would, for early on the day after my wounding, the portended storm broke. Its violence kept the tribeswoman and me to the cabin for two days. A welter of thunderheads choked the sky, the wind raged, the rain welted down. The waters of the estuary were roiled and knouted. The wheelhouse was battered; I feared the wind might blow in the windows. We had, laid in, provisions enough to ward against hunger, but, still, it was a fretful time; the storms at the end of days are brutal, and the whole time I fear it's the last, the final cataclysm. So, though I was able to do a bit of writing, I could not fully concentrate: it was too noisy, and I, too anxious.

At noon, on the third day, calm came. I went out on deck, stood at the taffrail looking out over the river. The Thames was turbid, swollen. Green wood, stout fallen branches, even trees felled entire, and bloated carrion, rats, boars, sheep, cats, and dogs, drifted by. After a while, I saw the body of a child, a little boy, amid the flotsam; he floated past, so close I could see the sulky look on his face. I abandoned my watch then.

Since the storm abated, it's remained still. A light drizzle has persisted, though, and, so I might have somewhere to work while the tribeswoman sleeps, I spent the best part of a morning building a lean-to shelter, of driftwood with a thatched roof of rushes, beside the cabin.

It's now time to tell of the events of the afternoon my forehead was laid open. After lunch that day, I left the Ark, went hunting, spent a while stalking a herd of the reddish, hairy swine that forage round about, but the mugginess sapped me, I wasn't quick enough, a kill eluded me. Returning to the boat, weary, filthy, dishevelled, I heard a scream, broke into a run. I flew through a brake of bulrushes, brittle stems slashing at my face, reached the edge of the flats, and saw, at the Ark's taffrail, the tribeswoman, looking down, agape, at a pack on the mud, some of her old tribe, hostile, armed with slings, cudgels, and large knives, brandished blades' burnish blazing. As I watched, the tribeswoman snatched up several branches from a pile of firewood I'd collected, hurled them, one by one, at the natives. Cringing from these missiles, they took cover behind two steel lobes that jutted from the ooze like a sounding leviathan's flukes from the brine, blades of the Ark's massive propeller. They launched stones at the young woman with their slings, but she was far above, and their shots went awry, some striking the plate-steel bluff of the ship's transom, sounding cracked knells. Then the tribeswoman, having strewed the pile of firewood, had to crouch, scrabble on the deck for sticks of the right heft, and a burly man ran out from behind the propeller blades, neared the ship, threw up a rope and grapnel, tried to hook the bulwarks. Sighting this, I saw the tribeswoman had had the foresight to winch in the gangway at the posse's approach.

Wielding my flimsy spear, I charged. Several stones were slung at me as I ran, one hitting me in the chest, cracking a rib, but though I bellowed, I didn't slow, and the tribespeople scattered as I closed. Then, realizing the weapon I was armed with was a pitiful improvisation, they crowded, set upon me. I tried to block, but a blow shattered the haft of my spear, and I was clubbed to the ground. My assailants backed away a few paces. Lying in the mud, too weak to stand, I groped in the silt, laid hold of my knife, my makeshift spearhead, still lashed to a short section of splintered pole. Then a tribeswomen approached me, knife held over her head. Her air of authority, and the rich purple cotton shift she wore, which stood out from the plain linen robes of the others, marked her out as a leader of some kind. She hacked at me, her blade struck my brow, a fierce blow, and though the edge was dull, I felt it bite bone. Up above, the tribeswoman wailed, her shriek echoed by the cry of a seagull circling overhead, perhaps the same bird I'd seen that morning. The richly arrayed tribeswoman raised her face to the sky, crowed. Slashing blind – blood poured into my eyes – with my carver, I opened her belly. Her guts slithered forth, slopped over me. Keening low, she crumpled to her haunches, shook, then keeled over. I stabbed her in the heart to stop her mewling.

Baring my teeth, I snarled, spat, and writhed on the ground. I was gore- and shit-slathered, tangled in loops of intestine. The natives ran wailing. I managed, crawling, to make it to the water's edge, before passing out.

When I came to, I dragged myself into the river, allowed the brackish water to wash over me, wash me. Then I groaned to my feet and stood tottering a moment, before staggering back towards the Ark, calling for the tribeswoman. It was a short while before she heard me and came, snivelling, chary, to the railing. Seeing me alive and the natives gone, she cried out in relief, extended the gangplank once more, ran down it, ran to me, flung her arms around me. Then, seeing the extent of my injuries, she backed away and, smiling, wan, took my hand, led me up the ramp, to the bed in the wheelhouse, gestured for me to lie down. I did, slept for hours.

On waking, I found the woman had torn some rags into strips for bandages, left them on the deck by a pan of water simmering over a small fire. I stood up, a bit unsteady, to look about for her, saw her swimming in the river, a short way out from shore. As I watched, she pulled herself up onto a sandbank, and seeing she was naked, I craned, gawked – my carnality may be jaded, but I still have a cool eye for a nude. Water glistened on her skin, dazzled as a ray of sunlight thrust through the clouds. Then I saw her turning towards me and averted my gaze – I'd no wish to appear sleazy. My gaze fell on my typewriter. I saw it had been used while I slumbered; there was a sheaf of paper, fluttering in the breeze, held in its carriage. Crossing over, I saw my scrawled amendments to William's tale had been typed up. I looked briefly over the transcribed sections, thought them faithful. I was puzzled, but too weary and in too much pain to ponder long, so sat down to tend to my wounds, to cleanse and swathe them.

The tribespeople have not returned in the time it has taken me to narrate the forgoing accounts of my journey and the afternoon they attacked, perhaps daunted by my strange resistance, or simply deterred by the violent weather. I'm thankful for this: I'm still weak and would have had difficulty running them off. Other than work on this typescript, I've done little. On the morning of the second day after the storm had blown itself out I scented a foul stench; it was the corpse of the tribeswoman I'd killed, begun to rot. The tribeswoman and I constructed a bier from driftwood, sent the body floating down the Thames, out to sea, on the ebb tide. After we'd conducted these mute obsequies, I saw, lying on the mud, a rope and grappling iron, left behind by the tribe in their flight. I picked them up, took them back on board the Ark.

Today I've corrected the drafts of everything I've written since completing William's tale, and passed them to the young woman. It seems she is able, and happy, to type up my changes. I'm glad to have discovered this aptitude of hers, she'll act as my amanuensis, make my task easier, and, moreover, the work seems to please her, she hands me finished pages with a proud grin. She seems kind, good-natured, so it comes as no surprise she wishes to help, but that she is able to in this way puzzles me. All I can think is that she has some faint inborn memory of my tongue, that spoken, albeit a long, long time ago, by her forebears. However, I've since tried communicating with her, both verbally, and in writing, and it is clear she comprehends nothing, is able only to copy out the characters before her, I suppose the hereditary knowledge of English, watered with each successive generation, is weak in her.

This morning there was another rain shower, but afterwards the rack broke up, and, for the first time in days, the sun shone. It's now night. Occasionally, from overhead I hear a strangled screech; the gull has once more returned, looking up, from time to time, I glimpse a bird-shaped void wheeling in the star-spattered sky.

I feel I should now press on with my account of the evening in the Nightingale pub; I've neglected that strand of my story too long.

VI

After unfolding the grisly end to his tale, which, though I'd seen it coming, as had most round the table, still shocked deeply, William broke down, and, shoulders hunched, head in hands, began to weep. The rest of us, harrowed, stupefied, sat gawping while he weathered his distress.

When, at last, his tears spent, he lifted his head, he looked about the table, then put a cigarette in his mouth, went to light it. His hands shook badly, and he had to fight to hold the flame of his lighter still, but he got the tobacco smouldering in the end, pulled fiercely, and, leaving the cigarette dangling from the corner of his mouth, wincing as smoke drifted into his eyes, smoked it to the filter, stubbed it. Then he was racked by coughs.

'Never touched a cigarette before that night,' he said, grimacing, once the fit had passed. 'Now can't do without them.'

And he lit up another.

Duncan, refilling his pipe, glanced up, mumbled something into his beard.

Jane reached out, put her hand on William's shoulder.

'I'm so sorry. It must have been...'

She trailed off, frowned, smiled sadly, shrugged.

'Just dreadful, William,' Elliot said. He shook his head.

'Aye, right awful what happened,' Duncan agreed, having got back his voice.

Turning to me, William said, 'I'm sorry about before. Nervous, not mocking laughter.'

'I can see that now,' I replied. 'And I'm sorry I was so defensive.'

He nodded. Then, with sudden savagery, crushed out his cigarette.

'I truly loved her.'

Sniffing, he wiped his eyes with the back of his hand.

Duncan then offered to buy another round. Only Jane, who'd moved to orange juice after her gin and tonic, declined. William in hollow frolic, suggested we get a drink for the empty chair, said the sixth person invited to the gathering had, in truth, turned up, was sat there, but had been turned to a wraith by what they'd gone through, was invisible, incorporeal.

'Look,' he said, gesturing at air. 'They're trying to attract our attention. Definitely thirsty!'

There was a smattering of chuckles from all but Rashmi, who, narrowing her eyes, seemed about to say something, only choking it when Jane glared sharply.

I went up to the bar with Duncan to help carry the drinks. It seemed he was, perhaps due to his accent, misheard, for he ended up with an additional lager. Weird, given William's jest. Duncan queried it with the publican, who apologised, said we could have the extra drink, no charge, rather than he chuck it away.

After taking his change, Duncan deftly picked up three pint glasses in his one hand. I'm ashamed to own I looked at him, stunned. He saw, grinned.

'Takes a bit of practice, but it's not really that tricky. I won't be useless.'

I stammered an apology.

'Nae bother,' he said, grinning.

Then he flinched.

'What is it?' I asked.

'Oh, nothing. A twinge, that's all. The arm I lost.'

I looked at him, scratched the stubble on my chin. Guessing what I'd been on the brink of asking, he nodded.

'You'll find out what happened, soon enough.'

He smiled, went back to our table. Scooping up the remaining glasses with both hands, I followed him over.

We handed out the drinks, setting the spare pint down before the empty seat. William frowned at me, and I explained the landlord's mistake. He paled.

'Uncanny...'

'These things happen,' I said, making light.

'They do,' he said, pointedly.

'Dead creepy,' Rashmi put in.

I felt bad, felt I should have left the pint, that it should have occurred to me it would upset William. So, hoping to dispel the disquiet, I attempted a witticism.

'I'm not sure lager's the first pick of drink for a wraith, but tough, boggarts can't be choosers.'

There were groans, not laughs, but the mood did turn less fraught.

Rashmi then asked William about the investigation into his girlfriend's death, how he'd avoided blame, why he wasn't wasting in jail.

'There was no investigation,' he said.

'How?'

'There was no death,' William replied. 'At least, not till later.'

We all peered at him. He described how he'd returned to his flat, in a daze, after the horrors of the night on the Heath, having left the beheaded corpse where it lay, to find Catherine waiting up for him, worried. While he fought to quell the shock of seeing her living, she stared, anxious, at his, stinking, gore- and ichor-smirched shirt. He'd been set on by a gang of youths on his way home, he lied. He'd not been badly hurt, the blood wasn't his, he'd hit one of the thugs in the face with a wildly flailing elbow, started a nosebleed, they'd thrown him to the ground, pissed on him.

'Jesus!'

She sniffed.

'Smells worse even than blood and piss only. Like bile and rot too. What happened? Did you antagonise them?'

William hissed.

'Of course not! Just a random attack. Fuck! Some sympathy wouldn't go amiss.'

'I'm sorry! So sorry. Horrible!'

She put his clothes on to wash, sent him to bathe.

After that night, at first, if anything, they were closer than before. But things turned sour. Havoc loosed in his brain, William grew morose. Catherine had her own anxieties, it seemed, and likewise sank into despondency. At first they bickered a lot, then, after a while, aside from curt exchanges about bills, other mundanities, ceased speaking altogether.

One night, Catherine, hoping to cheer them both, mend some of the hurt, suggested they go out for a meal. They agreed to put grudges aside. While waiting to order, and eating starters, they chatted, and their talk, if small, was civil, even pleasant. Then, once they'd finished the first course and were waiting for their mains, Catherine, perhaps starting to feel the effects of the red wine, talked about the upset William's recent callousness had caused her.

'You've been pretty cold yourself,' he came back, a touch rankled.

'I have, I'm sorry. But, look, since the night you were attacked, you've been different,' she said, gently.

'Not really.'

'Yes, you have. What did happen that night?'

'I've told you everything.'

He spat out the words like fish bones.

'Do you not love me anymore?' she asked.

'Catherine, doll, I'm sorry. I do, of course. But you've not been yourself, either.'

She squinted, smiled melancholic.

Just then, their waiter came over, apologised. There was a problem in the kitchen. Service would be slow. Would they like another bottle of wine, no charge? Yes, they said. That was fine, they were happy to wait.

They'd soon finished the first bottle and begun on the second. They held hands over the table, laughed together for the first time in months. Things were going far better than William had thought they ever could; he was glad the filthy wrappings had been taken off the festering canker, felt he might even be able to salve it, unburden himself, tell Catherine the truth. Then, she leaned forward, stroked his face.

'Will, there's something I haven't told you. I thought you'd find it too strange. I don't think we should keep things from each other anymore, though.'

'What is it?'

Catherine stared up at the dim bulb glowing in the storm-lantern hanging low over the table, a sibyl consulting a caged sprite.

'I've told you before about the imaginary friend I had growing up, haven't I? Jessie.'

'Yes, yes of course.'

'How she looked just like me? Longer hair, paler skin, but otherwise just like me?'

'Yes.'

'Spirit of my stillborn twin. That's what I think.'

She broke off, looked up.

'You know?'

William smiled. But beneath the table he fretted at his paper napkin.

'I know.'

She tore a shred from a fingernail with her teeth.

'What I've never told you, have never told anyone, except my parents, is that, though I stopped seeing Jessie in my early teens, I had the feeling she was there with me still, watching over me.'

Pausing, she smiled to herself.

'Recently that feeling has left me. I think she's abandoned me. For a few months, I've felt alone.'

She shook her head as if to clear it, blinked slow.

'You probably think I'm mad. But that's why I've been preoc-cupied... a bit down these last weeks.'

William stared at her.

'So,' Catherine said. 'What's upset you? Why have you not been yourself?'

She looked at him, waited. He took a big gulp of wine. Then the waiter brought their plates over, set them down. Catherine took up her knife and fork, but William sat, hands still in his lap, tearing at the napkin.

'If you won't tell me what's wrong, at least eat,' she said, irked.

'Did you ever misplace your ring?' he asked, jabbing with his finger.

'What?'

He pressed the heels of his hands into his eyes.

'Did you ever lose it, leave it anywhere, anything like that?'

'I left it at my parents' house once. Mum found it, sent it back to me, remember?'

'No.'

He slumped in his chair. Shreds of napkin fluttered to the floor. The soft lighting and low murmuring of couples, now seemed gloom and muttering. Catherine's hand trembled, her lips twitched, she paled, and the dark suspicion William had been gravid with since the night on the Heath slopped forth.

'What did you do?' Jane was eager to know.

William sniffed, winced.

'I got up from the table, without a word, accidentally knocking my plate to the floor. It smashed on the tiles, and gravy flowed, slow and heavy as blood, along the grout lines. Leaving the restaurant, choosing a direction on a whim, I began walking. I'd not gone far when I heard Catherine calling, turned. She'd chased after me. Without looking, she stepped off a kerb.'

Trembling, William reached out, took up his drink, downed half of it at one draught.

'There was a bus. The driver braked, but couldn't stop in time. She was in a coma for six months, died without regaining consciousness.'

'Oh God,' Jane exclaimed. 'I'm so sorry.'

William stared at her, vacant. As though reliving the events of that night.

'Son, are you alright?' Duncan asked.

William shuddered, came back to us.

'This is the first time I've told anyone the whole…'

He trailed off, looked down at his drink, then, after a few moments, raised his eyes again.

'After the funeral I spent months holed up in my flat, avoiding people, going out as little as possible. Recently I've returned to work, started socializing again, but it's been hard.'

Rashmi, who'd been distractedly stirring her vodka and lemonade with her straw, took a sip, then asked William what he thought the truth of all that had happened to him was.

'I don't know. I try not to think about it. I also can't talk about it anymore. Perhaps someone else could tell their tale?'

A brief exchange followed; the upshot was that Jane offered to relate her story, after she'd gone to the toilet. Getting to her feet, she left the table. I looked round the pub. Though it was still quite early, the Nightingale had begun to empty out; it was a week night after all. A large party still caroused, noisily, in a corner at the far side of the saloon, though; from the cards and scraps of wrapping paper strewn over their table, I guessed it to be a birthday celebration. The other remaining patrons sat in pairs and threes, conversing quietly.

While we awaited Jane's return, I told William of the sword tattoos I'd seen that evening. The one inked onto the businessman's wrist he had, of course, remarked himself. He said he had, in the preceding months, noticed more and more of the markings, something that disconcerted him, reminded of his ordeal, filled him with fear one of the strange fellowship might recognize him, again enmesh him in occult horror. We began discussing the possible meaning of the tattoos; Duncan, Elliot, and Rashmi joined in.

I've already described that the Nightingale was divided by a wooden partition, inset with etched glass panes, into a public bar, at the front, and a secluded saloon, at the rear, where we sat. What I haven't explained, though, was that some of the panes, if narrow, were almost the full height of the partition and had designs only round their margins, were clear in the centre, and that through one of these I had a good view, if a little distorted, of the pub's entrance. As we were talking, I saw a man open the door, stand on the threshold a brief instant, then stagger in a few paces, leaving the door ajar behind. Sleet had begun falling; a swirl blew in and settled on the carpet (today it's blustery, the wind roils the waters of the estuary, thrashes up spray, and a goatskin the tribeswoman has laid out on the deck of the Ark is flecked with spindrift, glistens in the sun; the sleet on the carpet in the Nightingale that night glistered the same way). The man wore an ill-fitting rumpled pinstriped suit, an unkempt, very fake wig, had sunken dulled eyes, raw sagging skin, and a puffy nose. He hopped from foot to foot, wringing his hands. The patrons nearest him feigned unconcern, though some glared at the open door. I watched him, warped by the lumpy pane of glass, cast about, then, catching sight of our gathering, or, rather, of Duncan's back, through that same pane, begin cackling silently, reel, stumble, fall against a table, upset a pint. After getting his footing back, he untied the length of twine he was using as a belt, dropped his trousers, kicked free of them, began to gyre, arms outstretched. His pants were threadbare, stained. The landlord opened the counter hatch, came out from behind the bar, crossed over to the drunk, seized him by his collar, and hauled him to the door, kicking, bellowing, and threw him bodily out, threw his trousers out after him. Just before the door was slammed on him, he bawled, in a cracked reedy voice, 'You fucks! You're cursed to a living hell!' Though I couldn't say quite why, I felt his outburst was aimed at my companions and me.

The shout had finally drawn the notice of the others (no one, apart from me, faced the public bar), and they turned to look over. I don't, though, think any of them caught more than a glimpse of the crackbrain.

'What was that? What did that mean?' Duncan asked, clearly rattled.

'I don't really know,' I replied. 'Some drunk. The landlord threw him out.'

Duncan frowned, looked as if he were about to say something further, but, at that moment, Jane returned.

'See the freak?' she asked.

Elliot nodded.

'Lots of them about, bedlam on the streets,' he said, winking.

Jane sat, took a sip of her juice.

'Shall I begin?'

'Go ahead,' I said.

'Alright. Have any of you been through the foot tunnel under the Thames at Woolwich?'

We all shook our heads, though I told her I'd used the one at Greenwich.

'Yes. They were built at the same time to similar designs, but, while the Greenwich tunnel's been kept up, the one at Woolwich has fallen into disrepair. One hot summer's day, about four and a half years ago, I'd taken my two boys to have a picnic and play in the fountains in Barrier Park. As a treat I decided to take them back by way of the tunnel. We'd been through it a few times, they liked to pretend it was the secret passage to a superhero's lair...'

Jane paused a moment, looked down at the table, bit her lip.

'First, though, I need to tell you something that happened a few years before that,' she went on, a break in her voice. 'It bears on my tale...'

One Moment Knelled the Woe of Years

Though it wasn't till the bizarre and dread afternoon she wished to tell of, that Jane strayed from the path of the ordinary and everyday, and into weird regions (actually, less straying, than having that path wander from beneath her feet), the terrible foundations of that dark hour were laid four years before, on a muggy evening in early summer.

That night, her husband, Roderick, was late getting back from work. She'd had to put their boys, Jeremy and Peter, then aged six and four, to bed, and she knew he'd be sorry to have missed them. But she'd not been concerned about his tardiness; he was a university lecturer, English Literature, Victorian poetry his field, and was sometimes held up at work by unscheduled meetings, panicked students, and so on. When he'd finally arrived home, though, and she'd heard his key in the door and gone to greet him, she'd felt a vague foreboding; he was by nature dark-skinned and by temperament calm, but stood on the threshold, framed in the doorway, wan, twitching, his eyes darting this way and that. Yet, when she'd asked how things were, he'd said all was well.

During dinner he was quieter than usual, ate seemingly without relish, but otherwise seemed fine. They chatted. Then Roderick asked how the boys were, what they'd done at school that day. Jane, whose head was, just then, full of the charred ruins of London after the Great Fire, the setting of the book she was writing, had paid scant attention to their gabbling earlier, couldn't tell him.

He was put out.

'I wish it were the other way about.'

'What?'

'I mean, I wish I could stay here, that it was my job could be done from home, that I could look after them.'

Jane swigged her wine.

'That's not fair.'

'It is fair. You know it is.'

'Are you trying to start an argument?'

'No, look, I'm sorry…' Roderick began.

But Jane cut him off.

'You've met my mother. It's hardly surprising I don't have the keenest maternal instincts, now is it? But I try, God knows I try.'

He reached out, took her hand in his.

'You're great with them. I'm sorry. I didn't mean it. Those boys… They really love you.'

Jane scowled, then, shaking her head, smiled wan.

'Thanks, you. But I suppose I can be a bit distant…' She hung in thought a moment. 'Distracted. I wish I was as good with them as you are.'

Later after they'd finished dessert, Roderick shuddered, downed his wine at a draught. But Jane thought it was just exhaustion or the onset of a cold, sent him through to the living room.

'I hope you're not coming down with something. Go on, relax, I'll tidy up here.'

He slouched off, without a word. Once she'd cleared the table, put the crockery, cutlery, and pans in the dishwasher, she went through to join him. She found him sitting in an armchair, rocking back and forth, eyes glazed, mumbling. Running to him, she then went down on haunches beside the chair, threw her arms round him. For a moment he sat, unstirring, tensed, hissing, then abruptly grinned, thumped Jane to the floor, stood, and stalked out of the room. When he returned, before she could get back on her feet, he had a large kitchen knife in his fist. Raving, snarling, he lunged at her. She'd just time to snatch up the heavy iron poker which hung on a stand in the grate, then he was on her.

Terror tempered and whetted, and, in spite of his greater heft and thew, Jane, flailing with the poker, fended off Roderick's frantic slash and stab and struck him a blow on the temple, knocked him to his knees. Then she fled the corner he'd penned her into, fleeted up the staircase, going to her sons. He tore after. Reaching the landing, she turned, swung the poker, caught him in the throat, sent him sprawling down the stairs. At their foot, he pitched forward, landed awkwardly, falling on the knife, driving it into his sternum. He grunted, then rolled onto his back. The knife was sunk to the haft, and blood welled, soaking into the rug he lay on and flowing sluggish along the grout lines of the tiled floor. He wallowed in his gore, then lay still. Jane howled. The poker fell from her hand, thudded down the stairs, spinning, end over end, struck the tiles, clanged.

Then she heard the door of the boy's bedroom, along the corridor, opening, and, turning, saw Peter in the doorway.

'Mummy, what's happening?'

'Peter, go back into your room, shut the door,' she barked, wild. 'Don't come out till I tell you to.'

'Why?'

'Just do as I say!'

Sensing his mother's panic, shaken, Peter did as told.

Jane turned back, then gasped. Roderick was gone. Bloody footprints crossed to the front door, which now stood open. She sank down on the stairs, sat with her chin on her knees, fell into a trance fit. She didn't rouse from it till ten minutes or so later, when two police constables, a man and a woman, came into the house, called up to her.

Then she startled. Edging round the blood, the PCs crossed the hall, began climbing the stairs. The WPC said, sternly, 'What happened here?'

Jane gawped. The WPC told her a man, bleeding heavily, a knife handle jutting from his chest, had rattled drinkers outside a pub on the banks of the Thames, then thrown himself into the river, been swept downstream. A trail of blood had led them back.

'You need to tell us everything.'

Jane sat in a daze, shaking her head.

'Look,' the WPC went on. 'You're not under suspicion of murder. Some of your neighbours are outside. They saw everything. We know you were just defending yourself. But you still need to tell us everything that happened.'

'Why didn't they help me!' Jane yowled.

'Who?'

Jane stared.

'Oh, sorry,' the WPC said. 'Well, they were scared. They're an elderly couple.'

Then there was the sound of muffled sobbing. Turning, Jane flew to the boy's bedroom, opened the door. Peter and Jeremy flung themselves at her.

'Mummy, Mummy, what's going on?' Jeremy asked, tearful.

Jane looked down at her sons bewildered. She turned to the PCs, shrugged. Then frowned, blinked, crumpled to the carpet, and lay there on her side, curled up, moaning low. Peter and Jeremy crouched down beside her, put their arms around her, held her as she wept. The PCs hung back, shuffled, uncomfortable.

Then Peter asked, 'Has Daddy gone?'

Jane, howled, tore up fistfuls of the carpet's thick pile.

'Mummy. It's alright. It'll be alright.'

'No, my love. No it won't. I'm sorry.'

'It will, Mummy. Who is she?'

Jane was thrown into confusion.

'Who?'

Peter took her hand, puckered his face.

'The other woman.'

Then Jane understood. The father of one of Peter's schoolfriends had recently left his wife, run off with the family nanny. Jane seized on this with relief; the ordinary sorrow of a broken home would be easier on her sons for the time being. When they were older they would be better able to cope. She choked her grief, began spinning her lie, then, remembering the PCs, turned. They'd come up behind her. She caught their eyes; they frowned, but nodded tacit agreement.

That night, Jane, with the PCs' help, got the boys out without their seeing the blood, pretending they were playing a game, blindfolding them. The three of them then stayed in a local bed and breakfast while the forensic team were examining the house. When they were done, Jane went back and finished cleaning up, while the boys stayed with friends. It only took her a couple of days. Afterwards they moved back in.

The witness statements and evidence all backing up Jane's account, no charges were brought against her. Roderick's body was never recovered, so she was denied the end a funeral gives. But life, a kind of life, if a blasted life, went on. Though she came close, a number of times, to telling her sons the awful truth, she never did. The lie, as with all swaddling lies, became harder, not easier, to expose as the years passed. At first, Peter and Jeremy asked often whether they might be allowed to see their father. She told them he'd moved abroad, that she didn't know how to reach him. Whether or not they believed this, she wasn't sure, but, eventually, they stopped asking. Jane feared, though, that Peter bore silent resentment.

At first, Jane spent her days dozing, fuddled by booze and sleeping pills, and her nights, stark awake, cramming caffeine tablets down her gullet, in dread of dreams in which she relived every racking instant of that evening. But, finally, the raw fear lessened, and the nightmares abated, though they didn't cease altogether.

When she woke on the morning of the day of her tale, however, it was from a less harrowing, if weirder dream. She stood, at dusk, amid a clinkered plain, before a squat turret, a stump of dun masonry, set between two humped knolls and a craggy peak. Ranged on the hillsides, a host of riders. In her hand, a horn of some kind, brass tubing, a battered whorl. Taking a deep breath, she set it to her lips...

Then she was sitting up in bed, shaking, sweating. It was light outside. She strove, recollected herself. It was the first day of the school holidays, and she'd resolved to spend the next few weeks in fun with Peter and Jeremy, then aged ten and eight. She'd been a bit absent the previous months, slogging away at a novel; it wasn't quite finished, but nearly so, and she felt she could take a break from it. She thought it the best work she'd ever done. As, about two years before, her novel, *The Feminine Monarchie*, had been optioned for a film, she'd been able, for the first time in her life, to ditch pecuniary aims and write with a solely aesthetic rationale; she'd abandoned the shallow seam of fool's gold, trite historical romance, she'd been mining, passing off as the real thing, bored deeper, seeking rarer ores. She'd thrown herself into the work.

The book, in common with her other titles, had a historical setting, but was otherwise entirely distinct: strange, dark, nimble and clunking by turns. Its subject was Wenceslaus, the tenth-century Bohemian martyr.

It was the novel's last chapter Jane was most pleased with. She'd been inspired by an ancient legend, of a cave beneath Blaník Mountain and a knightly host sleeping, enchanted, till the Czech motherland be beset by enemies and need defending. In this exhausted coda, Wenceslaus, roused from millennial sleep in 1939 by the tumult of an advancing Panzerdivision, wakes his page and rides, with the young lad following behind on foot, to Blaník's summit, dismounts, surveys the hostile forces. Then the page asks, of the tanks in the van, 'Sire, what nature of beasts are those?'

After peering at the war machines a while, Wenceslaus says,

'Those, my son, are the dragons of yore. I reckoned the last of them slain, but it cannot be so. It seems they lived on in some wild places. Plainly a blackheart has done what only the evilest of men would, having happened on a clutch of eggs, he has dug them up, reared them from hatchlings. The brood will, then, be fiercely loyal. Dragons are devilish foe even without armour and these creatures, look, wear plate-steel barding. We cannot ride 'gainst them, 'twould go badly for us, 'twould be a slaughter. I rede we leave the knights slumbering, wash our hands of these wicked times.'

But the page, shamed by his master's cowardice, leaps astride the saint's white horse, charges the enemy troops. In the novel's melancholy final passage, he is cut down by German machine guns, and Wenceslaus walks back down to the entrance to the cavern beneath the mountain, goes inside, intones a formula to seal, once more, the stone gate behind him, returns to sleep.

Jane had titled the novel, *His Master's Steps*.

(I'd read one of her novels some years before, and, while decidedly popular, it was artful, tangled. When she'd retired, the press had cited the pressures of raising two children as a single parent; I felt we were about to learn the real reason.

His Master's Steps had never, as far as I knew, been published. I asked her if this was the case.

'Yes,' she answered, regretfully. 'My agent didn't like it, and after what happened, I hadn't the heart or energy to seek other representation for it.')

Jane got out of bed, showered. Dressing, she wondered how to spend the day ahead. She'd lots of nice trips planned for the boys' holiday, but that day didn't want to go too far from home. She'd been tired out by work on the book, and had been drinking more heavily the previous few weeks, around the anniversary of Roderick's death. So she thought she'd take advantage of the fine weather, have a picnic in nearby Barrier Park. She went downstairs, proposed the idea to the boys, who'd been up for a little while watching cartoons on television.

'Sounds nice,' said Peter, briefly turning from the antics of an anthropomorphic sea urchin. 'Glad you've some free time.'

It was not said reproachfully, but still Jane felt a smart.

Barrier Park was in Silvertown, on the north bank of the river, by the Thames Barrier, part of attempts to regenerate an area that, once a thriving industrial region, was, by then, run down. It was a spot Jane knew well, having based a novel, *Tonight Nelly, Tonight*, around a 1917 blast at a munitions factory there.

When Jane, Peter, and Jeremy got there that day, they first ate a picnic sitting on the grass by the riverbank, watching yachts and tugs sail past. Peter said he thought the Barrier looked, 'a crash-landed spaceship,' so Jane made up a story about its alien pilot, a good-natured, if bad-smelling, gas cloud, from a far-flung star system, who, having survived the crash, freed himself from the wreckage of the craft, wafted to shore, and floated through London, recording impressions of the city and literally getting up people's noses. The boys laughed at the idea the alien thought St Paul's Cathedral housed a huge boiled egg, and that the tourists queuing up outside were waiting their turn to dunk a toast soldier or two.

After lunch, Peter and Jeremy changed into swimming costumes in the toilets of the park's coffee shop. Then they ran, excited, to the paved area near the entrance, where there was an open fountain, children scurrying about, getting drenched, squealing. Peter and Jeremy went off to join them. Jane, stood by, watching, soon soaked by spray. She grinned, filled with simple cheer, her hipflask of vodka, if not quite forgotten, fingers straying to it from time to time, at least remaining in her handbag.

A bit later, when the boys were tired out, the three of them went to sit on the grass, in the sun. Once they'd dried off, they went back to the café, Peter and Jeremy got dressed again, and

Jane bought them ice creams, and a coffee for herself, into which, for all she felt happy in that moment, she couldn't resist dashing a slug from her flask. They walked back over to the bank, sat looking out over the water. Sunlight, frittered to motes on the chop, dazzled, joyed, hid that the river was, really, a filthy gruel.

Then it was time to head home. At first the boys didn't want to leave, but, when Jane promised to take them through the Woolwich Foot Tunnel on the way back, grew eager to be off.

It was only two stops on the Docklands Light Railway from Pontoon Dock, by the park, to King George V station, not far from the north entrance to the foot tunnel. Jane took her sons' hands, and they all climbed up to the eastbound platform. The track, elevated on a concrete viaduct, resembled something from the set of a dark science-fiction film, even in bright sunlight.

(I've seen first-hand that none of that era's bleak futures came to pass, nor any of its utopias. In fact, till the power went out, the same cycle repeated itself, over and over. Civilizations rose, gained ascendancy, fell into decadence, decayed, were ravaged by pestilence, destroyed by war. Then, from charnel pits, ruins, corpse-manured, scorched soil new societies sprouted. Perhaps certain thinkers of the ancient world, who believed the universe was periodically destroyed by purging fire, reborn from ashes to experience the same history, were close to the truth. Indeed, on reflection, perhaps my scorn for the cosmology of the Himalayans in the early pages of this text told more of my fears than its claims; for those of finite span, time as a wheel consoles, offers a life force that persists beyond death, transcendent flight to aspire to, but for the immortal it's intolerable, a vertiginous meaningless swarm; but maybe it is the true way of things: these harbingers of the end of days could, after all, be signs of the imminent catastrophic rebirth of the universe. I suppose, though, that doesn't have to imply strict recurrence; the cycle of time could begin again, but take a different path, the deck could be shuffled; in fact, I feel that more likely (or is this merely a fervent hope on my part?))

At King George V, Jane, Peter, and Jeremy got off the train, headed towards the river, and, after a short walk, arrived at the subway's north entrance, a structure reminiscent of a mausoleum. They went inside, called the lift. When the doors opened, they stepped into the wood-panelled interior, and, after the attendant had pushed a button, a rattling descent began. Gaze fixed on a picture of a topless model in his tabloid, the attendant didn't acknowledge Jane and her sons, or even glance up. She, to keep the boys from seeing the photograph, distracted them by offering sweets from a packet she took out of her handbag.

The attendant seemed vaguely threatening, and, when the lift shuddered to a halt, the doors opened, and she, Peter, and Jeremy could step out into the tunnel, Jane was glad.

The only sources of illumination down there were fluorescent tubes fixed to the ceiling at intervals; the light they gave out was harsh, grainy, and it took Jane's eyes a moment to adjust.

The tunnel was lined with glazed white tiles, save the floor, which was laid with tattered linoleum, dirty, a welter of shoe and bootprints. The boys ran on ahead and Jane jogged at their heels, pouncing on them from time to time. Her roars and their spooked cries dinned from the walls. The subway was almost deserted, wonted for a weekday afternoon. They could see only one other person, walking ahead of them, whistling, doleful tune eerily resounding, but he or she strode briskly away, was soon lost to sight. The mournful air could be heard a few moments longer, but then faded.

After Jane and her sons had been dawdling along a short time, they turned, saw the lift behind had been swallowed by the tunnel's arc, its dip to scoop under the river. That before them was still hidden. Jane pointed this out to the boys, then to scare, told them they'd fallen through some weird crack into a terrible place where the tunnel was without end, and haunted by a dread beast, with pincers, stalk-eyes, a mottled warty carapace, a toothy maw, that scuttled on spindly legs, seeking children, who'd misbehaved, to devour. The boys shuddered, yelled, ran in circles round Jane, then tore ahead.

Then Jeremy cried out in real fear, frantically gesturing at the tunnel wall.

Jane ran up. There was a dull-red stain on the tiles.

'Mum, what's that?'

Jane bent down, peered at it.

'It's a patch of rust. Come on, let's get going, otherwise we won't be home in time for tea.'

But Jeremy wouldn't be consoled, screamed, 'It's blood! It's blood!'

Jane, tutting, ignored him, walked on. Peter followed, but Jeremy remained behind, staring at the stain.

'Mum!'

'Come on, Jeremy, stop being silly!' Jane barked, without turning round, rattled, unsure why.

Then her youngest ran to catch up, wailing, and, gaining them, grabbed Jane's skirt, tugged.

'Mum! It oozed!'

She tried to pull away. He squeezed her hand tight, grinding the second knuckle of her little finger against her wedding band.

She pulled her hand away, scolded him.

'Jeremy! Stop being such a baby!'

And his shoulders began, jerkily, to rise and fall; he blinked back tears. Jane softened then, knelt down beside him.

'Sorry, didn't mean to be angry. It's just you hurt my hand. And I promise the mark you saw was only rust. Nothing else.'

'Sorry, Mummy,' he said, wiping his eyes. Then, brightening, 'You're right, it was nothing. Oh, I love you, Mummy!'

Smiling, she got to her feet, took hold of his and Peter's hands. They pressed on.

They went on, hand in hand, Jane between the two boys, all

happy. It, therefore, took longer for her to heed the gnawing at her guts. They'd surely walked at least the tunnel's length; where, then, was the end? She broke into a stride, almost dragging her sons along, jarring their shoulder joints. But still there was no sign of the far end of the tunnel.

Then, when she was sure they'd gone far enough to be somewhere out under the centre of Woolwich, Jane stopped, breathing hard, tremoring.

'Mummy, you okay?' Peter asked.

She fought to quell her jitters.

'I'm fine, really. Just worried it's getting late.'

She calmed. Of course, her brain was awry; content, she'd not boozed much or taken any pills that day... Yet, she couldn't walk on, couldn't make herself; they'd have to turn around. She told Jeremy and Peter she thought it would be fun to return to the lift they'd come down in, go back up, take the ferry across the river. They loved boats, were excited. They all headed back down the tunnel, the way they'd come.

Jane's heart slowed, but, then, after they'd been walking a time, she realized they should have come again on the rust stain that had so disconcerted Jeremy, but hadn't, and she panicked once more. She wanted to hasten, suggested a race to her sons. Shrieking, blithe, they flew ahead. She careered behind.

They'd been running along for what seemed an age, no sight of the tunnel's end ahead, when Jane's mettle failed her, and she stumbled to a halt, leaned against the wall, winded, took out her hipflask, gulped from it. The boys, realizing she was no longer running behind them, stopped, went back to see what was wrong.

'Mummy, what's that?' Jeremy asked, indicating the flask, which Jane, absently, passed hand to hand.

She started, nearly dropped it, then, feigning unconcern, returned it to her bag.

'Oh, nothing, Jeremy. Something for my head.'

Peter eyed her askance.

'Don't lie. What is it?'

'I'm not lying. My head's just started really hurting. It's a remedy, that's all.'

'No it isn't! Smells horrid. You're drinking, aren't you? You're a drunk!'

Jane cringed back.

'Peter! How dare...'

She trailed off. Her head did pang then. She reeled.

'That's why Daddy left for someone else, isn't it?'

She smacked him on the ear. He cowered back. She stared aghast at her hand, leant against the wall, slumped down, began to weep.

Just then, a faint call echoed down the passage from somewhere ahead.

The boys started. Jane choked her sobs, stood.

'That voice,' Jeremy said. 'I recognize it.'

'Just the wind,' Jane said. 'Playing tricks.'

'The wind?' Peter shook his head. He held up his hand, 'There's no wind.'

The call came again, clearer this time.

'Peter. Jeremy.'

'Who is it?' Jeremy asked.

'It's Dad,' Peter replied.

'No,' Jane said. She bit her lip, hard enough that blood beaded. 'No, it isn't.'

Jeremy peered up at her.

'Can't we go to him?'

She whimpered.

'No. There's no one there.'

'What are you talking about?' Peter said. 'It's Dad. Dad's there.'

'No, Peter, he's not. He can't be.'

'Why not?'

'He's dead,' she blurted.

Jeremy started to cry. Peter sneered.

'He didn't run off,' Jane went on. 'He killed himself.'

She squeezed her eyes tight shut. Moaned.

'So painful, oh God, I wanted to keep it from you. But I shouldn't have, I shouldn't have done that. It's going to go badly for us, I know it.'

Peter stamped his feet. Snarled.

'Liar!'

He balled little fists, flailed at Jane.

'Why can't we ever see him? It's not fair!'

Jane hugged him to her. He thrashed, wailed, tried to get away, but she held him tight.

'You're hurting!' he howled.

As if seared, she let him go then. She looked down at her sons. Peter had cringed back, stood, wary of her, glaring. Jeremy looked confused, had also backed off, sucked his thumb. Jane approached Peter. He flinched, but didn't shrink away. She got down on hunkers before him.

'I'm sorry I hurt you,' imploring. 'I'm frightened. Something ghastly...'

But she was cut off by Roderick calling again, louder this time.

Peter made as if to run, and Jane seized his arm. He struggled, could not get loose.

'I hate you!'

Then Jeremy turned, took off. Letting go of Peter, Jane started after him, ran him down, went to grab his collar, but slipped, skidded into him, brought them both down. Then Peter tore past. Jane grasped at his leg, got hold of his trouser cuff, but it tore off in her hand. Jeremy got to his feet, fled after Peter. Groaning, Jane got up, tried to give chase, but she'd turned her ankle when falling. And she felt as if her tendons had been unhooked. She stumbled along, fell behind. She begged, but her sons ran faster.

Soon they were lost to sight, hidden by the bow of the tunnel. Their footfalls were heard a short while longer, then waned away. Silence smothered her, then darkness, as, overcome, she blacked out.

When she roused, it was from a febrile vision of murky corridors stinking of brine and decay. Midden of slops. Human carrion. Machines in alcoves burbling like simpletons. Otherwise, her brain was void. She knew only a throbbing in her ankle. She sat there shuddering. Then her memory returned to her, slowly, piecemeal.

She looked about. Amid the shoe and boot marks in the dirt on the floor, she saw hoofprints and another, strange, spoor, skittering scratches. Staggering to her feet, she stood tottering, head cocked, listening. A faint clanking drifted down the tunnel to her. It waxed, then she saw, in the distance, a withered old hunchback, matted grey beard, shrunken head, sparse white hair, wearing a filthy torn robe, sackcloth, shambling, leaning on a crutch tipped with an iron ferrule.

(I didn't realize at the time, but the next section of Jane's tale cleaves closely to Robert Browning's fevered poem of 1855, 'Childe Roland to the Dark Tower Came'. I've often mused on the meaning of this.)

Jane started towards the old man, thinking to ask if he'd seen her sons. Nearing, she called out, but he ignored or didn't hear her, didn't even glance up at her hail, continued walking, with his slow, awkward gait, toward her, looking at the ground, and, from time to time, fretfully shaking his head. A starling, spangled breast, flitted hither and yon above him, now and again alighting on his shrivelled skull to rest a moment.

Jane closed the distance. The old man, eyes fixed on shuffling feet, did not, or feigned to not, note her till she was right before him. Then he started, cringed back. The bird, which was, at that moment, perched on his crown, flew off. He stopped, and, leaning on his stick, peered up at Jane. Rheumy eyes, mouth hanging slack, strands of spittle strung over the gape. Then, after working his lower jaw from side to side, he spoke.

'What're you doing here?' he croaked

'Looking for my sons. You haven't seen them, have you? Two young boys?'

'Young,' he said, leering. 'How young?'

He spat on his free hand, tried to smooth down his wispy hair.

She backed away.

'What?'

The old man started chuckling, then choked, took several wheezing breaths, hawked, spat a dark clot. Then, squinting at Jane, he said, 'A symmetry in that. I'm seeking me old mum, see. Well, at least I think I am.'

'So you've not seen my sons?'

He shook his staff at her, lost his balance, fetched up sitting on the floor, cursing.

'Now hold on,' he groaned. 'I never said that, did I?'

Jane reached down, helped him back to his feet.

'If you know anything, anything at all, please tell me.'

He puckered his leathery lips.

'You'll find them through there,' he said, pointing out a service hatch in the tunnel wall, metal, painted a dull green. Jane turned. She'd not noticed the hatch before. Thanking the old man, who doffed a figmental cap and grinned sly, she turned the handle, swung the hatch open, and stepped through. Turning her ankle again, on uneven ground the other side, she fell to her knees.

All was dim. After getting to her feet once more, she stood still, waiting for her eyes to adjust. But, before they did, her surrounds were lit up. She saw she was somehow above ground once more, on a barren heath, desolate scrubland to the horizon's bound. The hatch, the tunnel, gone. Overhead, an overcast sky.

Gloaming, night gaining the upper hand in the endless war in the firmament. But the dying sun had rallied and flung a spear through the clouds. Then all fell dark once more, the light again occulted.

'Jeremy, Peter,' Jane called out, but feebly. She despaired; it was a forlorn hope; the cripple had lied in every word.

Then, rummaging in her handbag, she found her mobile phone, took it out. She'd never upgraded; it was an old model, a brick. She knew the tired horror trope, expected to see she'd no signal. She did not expect to see, on the screen, a pixelated, but finely detailed picture of a dead and scorched oak trunk, with a cleft in it like a mouth awry. She gawped, and that mouth gaped to show, within, a chubby pinkish infant stuck with a spear, its own mouth a puckered 'O'. She dropped the phone. It lay there on the ground, screen up, showing a staring eye. She kicked it from her into the dark that beset her.

At that moment, light stabbed through the clouds again, and Jane saw a swathe of the wretched quitch grass, gorse, ragged thistle, dock, and heather had been trampled, sign that a rout had crossed the plain. She set off, followed this trail a time. Before long, she grew used to the crepuscular, cloud-blotted light, and, while it lasted, found she could see, but dimly, but enough.

Then the sun fell though, the hordes of night overran the sky, and it was as if her eyes had been tarred. She then kept on a way in the dark, but, hearing the gush of a swift stream, wanting not to blunder in, stopped, and sat on the damp sod to bide till dawn.

But she didn't have to wait that long, for, by and by, the cloud cover broke up, and a reddish moon cast its light on the plain. Jane, tilting her head back, gazed up at the stars. Usually she saw only chaos, murk in the night sky, for she'd never learnt to pick out the constellations, never learnt their shapes, their names; but the engraving on that strange welkin had been chased by an apt, if devilish hand, and she saw its lurid scenes clearly: bloody battles, torture and torment, bizarre beasts locked together in brutal strife or grotesque lust.

She walked on, the rush of water growing louder, and soon came to a foul-stinking brook; it was in spate and, seen by the unwholesome light of the bloodmoon, seemed a torrent of gore. Gnarled alders and forlorn sallow lined its bank. She broke a branch from one of these lorn trees, then, shuddering, forded the stream, using her stick to probe for rocks and hollows, picking her way, tentative, in dread, at every step, of setting her foot on a dead man's cheek. Once, as she thrust the branch out, she struck something living, and it gave a horrid shriek, too close to a baby's wail, before thrashing away. On gaining the other side, Jane then had to struggle through a briar patch, thorns rending her clothes, and, tearing free of the thicket, found herself on the edge of a churned field strewn with bodies, men hacked to hash, horses with bellies slashed, guts spilled, strange blooms. The shambles reek stifled.

Not far from her, on the edge of the battleground, a gaunt nag skittishly pawed the ground, rolled its eyes. Its quivering flanks were spattered with mud and cruor.

In the distance, across the field, a dark tower loomed, its many turrets clawing at the stars, its flanks warty with bastions. Jane felt drawn to it. She trudged on, over that awful plain, wary of the scattered blades and caltrops, hardening herself to the stench and terrible sights. It was eerily quiet: the crows made no cawing squabbling over morsels, the blowflies barely thrummed. She passed many war engines, gory travesties of farming implements. There were harrows and ploughs for raking and furrowing flesh, not soil, bladed wheels and flails for reaping and threshing men, not crops.

That morning, feeling summery, Jane had put on a pretty floral-print pleated skirt, that, knee-length, left her calves bare. Then, she stumbled over a severed hand, looked down to find her footing, and saw her shins were flecked with gore. Something broke within her; she pressed the heels of her palms into her eyes, moaned, low.

When she took her hands from her eyes again, her surroundings had changed utterly. She now stood amid a parched waste, with, overhead, a moon like a pitted and tarnished coin, and, underfoot, coarse grey sand. The battlefield and its horrors were gone, but that desert was too a place of death, strewn with crosses botched from planks; with horse, pony, and mule carcasses, hides turned to leather and part-flayed by dust storms, ribs jutting like the timbers of wrecked coracles; with covered wagons, canted, warped, and sun-bleached; and with the bones of men, women, and children, gnawed, scattered by scavengers.

A little way before her, set between two humped knolls and a craggy peak, was a squat keep of drab stone. There was but a single oak door, with iron battens, in sight, no windows or loopholes. The merlons of the parapet, eroded to stumps, looked like rotten teeth.

Jane made for the tower, raising, as she walked, ashen familiars that scampered in her wake.

She stood a moment, before the door, then tried the handle. But the door was shut fast. She reached out, chary, took hold of the brass knocker, a ring hanging from the jaws of a crocodile's head, knocked. After waiting for the echoes of that one knock to die, she hammered away, bellowing her sons' names.

Inside the tower, all was still.

(At this point, I interrupted to ask Jane how she knew Peter and Jeremy were within.

'I just knew,' she replied. 'A mother knows.')

Jane walked round the tower, seeking another way in, but found none, no other doors, no windows or loopholes at all. Coming on the door once more, she kicked it. She jarred her bad ankle, but the door swung open, had been unlocked while she circled the turret.

The hinges wailed, another tired horror trope. Jane heeded

them not.

She found herself stood in the hallway of her own house. Fear faded away. As if she'd drunk a draught of nepenthes. She looked about her, saw nothing unwonted, though the rug spread out on the tiles at her feet put up her hackles. She'd a memory of throwing it on a bonfire in the back garden, years before, but that memory was dim, seemed merely a figment. Of course, the rug hadn't been burnt; it'd never been blood-matted, gruesome.

Then she heard chattering from the dining room. Peter and Jeremy larking. Crossing over, heart light, she opened the door, looked through, saw her sons sitting at the table, which was set for dinner, draped with the checked cloth, laid with four places. An open, half-empty bottle of red wine in the centre. Beyond, seen through the kitchen door, a man, stood with his back to Jane, wearing an apron, stirring something in a pan on a stove. The smell of frying onions, their sizzle.

Peter smiled.

'Mum. Come in. Dad's cooking.'

The man turned. Roderick. He smiled.

'Have a seat. And some wine. Won't be long.'

Jane sat, poured herself a glass, sipped. It was good.

'What're we having?'

'Risotto,' Peter said.

'Lovely.'

She felt buoyant, yet calm.

'Mum,' Peter said. 'Are you ill? You look it.'

'Well, I don't feel great, Peter. Writing's been tough these last weeks. I haven't been sleeping well, either. But don't worry, I'm definitely on the mend now. I'll be fine, especially with my boys to look after me.'

'But you need to see a doctor, Mummy,' Jeremy said, near to tears.

'No. I'll be right as rain. Soon as I've had some rest.'

But, just then, she heard, faint, a squeal. Reeling, clutching at the table, she saw, in her mind's eye, a blood-mad, lorn horse on a carrion field. She blinked, shook her head, swigged her wine. Peter and Jeremy stared, worried. Wind in the old horse chestnut in the garden, she thought. A shot from a film watched long ago, forgotten save that bleak image.

Roderick put a lid on the pot, crossed over to join them.

'Nearly there,' he said, raising his eyebrows, rubbing his hands together. 'Think I might have some wine myself, you know.'

He glugged out a glass, draining the bottle, raised it.

'Here's to us.'

The others echoed the toast; glasses of wine and cups of squash were clinked.

Then Jane heard scrabbling, and, turning, saw a scrawny-necked vulture at the garden window, perched on the sill. She started, gasped. The carrion bird leered at her, wicked, then flapped off. Then she noticed Roderick's faint reflection in the glass, hanging, caught in the branches of the briar out there. His apron was gore-smeared, there was something wrong with his face...

She moaned, squinched her eyes. Then felt Roderick's hand on her shoulder, blenched.

'What is it, my love?' he asked, gently. 'Not feeling right?'

She turned to look up at him. There was no blood on his apron, his face was handsome, as it ever was.

'I don't know what's wrong.' She shuddered. 'Mind playing tricks.'

'Stress,' Roderick said. 'You've nothing to worry about. Not with the three of us looking after you.'

'Yes, don't worry, Mum,' Peter put in.

Jeremy gripped her hand.

'I'll try not to. Thanks so much, all of you. What a loving family. I'm so lucky.'

Roderick smiled, bent down, kissed her. There was a putrid

waft, a greasy feel. Only her frazzled brain. Then Roderick cleared his throat, mimed tapping with a pen on a pad.

'Are you ready to order?'

Peter and Jeremy giggled.

Jane pretended to mull over a menu.

'Difficult choice. What would you recommend?'

'Well, the chief's special today is Isle of Divels Crab Risotto, Madame.'

'Sounds great. I think we'll all have it.'

'Excellent choice, Madame.'

Roderick returned to the kitchen, came back bearing a tray laden with four steaming bowls, set it down, passed out the dishes.

'Right, tuck in,' he said. 'I'll just open another bottle of wine, won't be a moment.'

Closing her eyes, smiling, Jane leaned over her bowl, breathed deep. Then retched, choked by fetor. Squinting down, she saw a welter of grubs. Looking about, frantic, she saw Jeremy with a writhing forkful halfway to his mouth. She leapt to her feet, slapped the fork from his hand. It clattered to the floor.

The boys stared, shrank from her. Looking again at the bowls, Jane saw they held only creamy grains of rice. She broke down. As did the others.

Roderick appeared in the doorway.

'What's wrong?'

'Sorry,' Jane said, shaking herself, blinking back tears. 'I'm not myself. Need some fresh air. Can you get Jeremy another fork, my love? I won't be long.'

She got to her feet, went out into the hall. Roderick started towards her, then, grimacing, stopped. Her heart juddered. She gritted her teeth, fought for calm. Then, she opened the front door, went outside, slumped down on the doorstep, breathed. The cool night air did her a little good.

But then all lurched, reeled; the moon shone down, not on a

terrace of Georgian townhouses, but on a barren plain, strewn with broken-down covered wagons and carts, horse, pony, and mule carcasses, graves, bones. Vultures wheeled overhead.

She whimpered, then retched. Spewed bile. Her boys! Oh fuck, her boys! She bit her cheek hard, blood filled her mouth, tottered to her feet, went back inside the tower.

A dark dank chamber. Ceiling beams so low she was stooped. Moonlight from outside, but weak, unable to burrow far. Her eyes adjusted to the gloom, then she looked about. It was not her entrance hall.

Hunkering down, she stroked the rug on the floor, the same that had disconcerted her before, even when the glamour was on her. It was roughly like the one she now recalled, clearly, carrying out into the garden, retching at its shambles stink, then burning. A breeze had blown the foul smoke back towards the house. It had been a warm day, and all the windows had been open, and she'd had to run inside to shut them, crumpled, breathless, sobbing, once she had. The rug in the dark tower had a similar pattern, of muted blotches, a similar deep pile. But it was antic somehow, shabby, matted, patchy. Bending down to peer closer, she gagged on a gore reek, realized what she was looking at: a patchwork of human scalps. Cringing back, she staggered, hit her head on the hard stone wall.

As she stood, rubbing the knock, she saw, hanging to her left, a scrap of animal hide with a crude painting on it, a horrid mockery of a photograph she, Roderick, and Peter had sat for, when Peter was just a baby.

It was not her entrance hall. But it *was* an awful apery of it. The dining and living room doors were here just chalk outlines on the wall, though. Where then were her boys? Jane peered about, noticed a wall-hanging that had no counterpart in her house, walked over to it. It was threadbare, its colours dulled, but she could still just make out its design. In the foreground, a company of armoured men, on foot, cowered, a winged beast, with black hide, leathery pinions, long jaws, and snaggle-teeth, stooping on them. And, in the top right of the picture, smaller, three mounted knights, one clad in swart armour, herding a rabble of peasants, in sackcloth, towards a narrow fissure in a rocky escarpment. There was an eerie sense of residual energy about all the figures, as if they'd been moving the instant before.

(When Jane finished describing the tapestry, Duncan, Elliot, and I turned to William to see his response. But, though he was listening attentively, nothing in his expression suggested he'd noted the resonance with his tale. Jane also seemed unaware of it. At the time, I wondered if this was feigned, if she'd deliberately evoked William's story, though I couldn't fathom why. Revelations later that evening suggested, however, that all our experiences had been wrought by a sole malevolence, and that, just as it is thought all mankind's dreams come from a collective oneiric pool, all dark experiences are drawn from a single well of horror, into which, from time to time, a poor unfortunate unwittingly lowers his pail.)[9]

Putting out her hand, Jane touched the tapestry. It gave slightly under her fingers. She reached out, took hold of the cloth, drew it aside. A wild writhen thing leered out at her from the passage the arras concealed. Cowering back, letting the wall-hanging fall, she tripped on the warped boards, staggered, fell down heavily. Throwing out an arm to steady herself, she felt, beneath her hand, the gruesome rug. And it too yielded, sagged into a hidden opening.

Some beast beneath was disturbed; a scuttling started up. Leaping to her feet, Jane backed away, breathing hard. The rug was abruptly seized, pulled down into a ragged hole. The scratching waxed louder, more frantic. Edging closer and looking down through the hole, Jane saw a dingy pit, floor strewn with gnawed bones, some with gobbets of flesh still clinging to them. Then she glimpsed a mottled carapace and a brutal pincer, shrank away.

Dread giving her grit, she tore down the tapestry, ready to fight her way past the horrid creature, but found merely a tarnished, cracked, fly-spotted, and warped mirror in a nook. She had a fit of giggles, then, controlling herself, looked about her again. There must be some other way out of the chamber. Where were her boys else? Then she saw, on the far side of the room, in the deepest shadows, a ladder. She crossed to it, climbed up, groping for the rungs, and found there was a trapdoor in the ceiling. Pushing it open, she clambered through.

The upper chamber was lit by sputtering rush torches in wall sconces, was bodged up into a grisly sham of the dining room in her house. The chairs and table were rickety, with rusty nails jutting, and covered in tallowy fungal growths. Peter and Jeremy sat, on the chairs, at the table, eating squirming filth by the forkful. And behind them stood a ghoul, yellowed bone, swagged with shreds of grey muscle and scraps of leathery hide, clad in rags and a blood-spattered apron. Dried-up eyes sunk into a shrunken skull; mouth a raw rent, twisted into a grisly smile.

Jane moaned, retched.

'Are you alright?' the thing Roderick had become asked, tenderly.

Struggling to compose herself, sore afraid of what the horror might do if it realized she was no longer cozened, Jane breathed slow.

'Sorry. I'm fine, really. Just feeling on edge.'

The thing looked leery at her. Strained smile without, turmoil within, she clubbed her brains, but all seemed hopeless.

Then Jeremy, looking up at the thing, seemed to see something of its true, its loathsome, aspect, blenched. She tried to catch his eye, but was too late.

'What's that!' he wailed, pointing.

The thing made to move toward him, and he jumped out of his chair, ran, weeping, to Jane. She squatted, took him in her arms.

'Don't cry, Jeremy,' she said. 'I'll not let any harm come to you.'

Then, feigning mettle, she called out, 'Peter! Come here. We're leaving.'

Peter thumped the table, stood, took one of the thing's withered hands in his.

'Only if Dad comes with us,' he said.

'Peter, my love,' wheedling, 'that's not your dad. Your father is dead.'

'Of course I'm not dead!' the thing barked. 'What's wrong with you?'

'Jeremy,' said Jane, desperate, 'tell Peter.'

Jeremy looked out from behind her legs, where he quailed.

'Peter, it's true. That's some kind of a monster. It's not Dad.'

'Why are you being so hateful?' the thing said, doleful look on its ravaged face.

'Peter, please,' Jane begged.

Scowling, he shook his head.

Frantic, Jane, started toward him. The thing sneered, reached into the pocket of its apron, took out the kitchen knife he'd fallen on years before, now tarnished, but kept keen-honed, brandished it behind Peter's back. Jane stopped. Sweat pooled in the hollows of her collar bones, despite the chill. The thing grinned at her.

Then she rallied her routed wits. She needed to get Peter outside somehow; the sight of the desert waste might shiver the illusion for him, as it had with her. Taking Jeremy's hand, she led him over to the ladder.

'Climb down,' she whispered. 'Wait for me at the bottom. Don't be scared. And don't budge from the foot of the ladder.'

'Okay,' Jeremy said, through tears. 'We're not leaving Peter, though, are we?'

'No, of course not. Now, be brave for me.'

He nodded, then placed his foot gingerly on the first rung, started down. Glancing over her shoulder, Jane saw the thing make to approach, then stall, stand grimacing. She followed Jeremy down, slow, grabbling for each rung. The door was shut again, and it was very dark. The dread chitinous scratching still rose from the pit beneath.

After Jane had stepped down off the last rung onto the floorboards, she groped about in the dark, found Jeremy. He flinched away, whimpered.

'It's me! It's me. Don't fret.'

'Mum. That noise... It's horrible.'

'Jeremy, stay here, against the wall. Don't move. Do you understand?'

'Yes, Mum.'

'Okay. I'm going to go up there again now. When I come back down Peter'll be with me. And we'll leave.'

Then she reached into her bag, took out her hipflask, raised it to her lips to swig, put some of the fire in her she was bluffing, but, as the vodka swilled into her mouth, she felt disgusted, cast the flask from her, to clatter to the floor, spat.

'What's that?' Jeremy yowled.

'Don't worry, sweetheart. Just wait for me here.'

She climbed back up the ladder, clambered through the trapdoor. In the sham dining room, Peter and the thing stood much as she'd left them.

'Do you think you can both forgive me?'

The thing narrowed its eyes.

'It's the strain of this book,' she went on. 'Writing's so difficult just now, has made me bad tempered. But I promise I'll make it up to you. In fact, I've just bought Jeremy an ice cream. Peter, would you like one? The van's waiting outside.'

The boy bit his lip.

'Jeremy's had one?'

'Yes.'

He squinted down at his feet.

Louring at Jane, the thing again waved the blade.

'Can I have a flake *and* hundreds-and-thousands?' Peter asked.

'Of course you can.'

He started for Jane, but the thing held fast his hand.

'Peter, can't you see she's trying to trick you? There's no ice-cream van. It's too late for that.'

Peter turned, looked up at the thing, frowned.

Then came a faint cracked air. An ice-cream van's carillon. Jane's mouth dropped open. The thing flinched as if struck.

A scurry. Peter darted forwards, the thing tried to hold him back. Sinews snapped, gristle grated, the thing's pale and mottled hand was wrested from its wrist. It howled, wept. Peter screamed, struck at the hand. It loosed its grip, fell to the floor, but, as he ran wailing to Jane, scuttled across the boards after. Peter hid behind Jane, and she stepped forward, kicked the hand. It flipped, then lay on its back, waggling its fingers, unable to right itself.

The thing, tears running down its tattered cheeks, said, 'I just wanted for us to be a family again. Why take my sons from me?'

Jane turned to Peter.

'Climb down the ladder. Quick. I'll be right behind.'

Peter, then Jane, began scrambling down the ladder. Bellowing, the thing lurched at them, hacking with the knife. When they reached the bottom, Jane cast her eyes upward, saw it, haloed by the light spilling through the hatch, clambering down.

She started herding her sons towards the chinks of moonlight seeping round the edges of the door, keeping them to the wall. Then the thing missed its footing, dropped, thudded to the boards. Rot spores drifted up, gyred in the light from the trapdoor. After lying prone a moment, the thing struggled to its feet. One of its eyesockets was shattered, the shrivelled ball dangled by a purple and nacre chord, and its jawbone hung askew, its black tongue, a slug in brine, lolled. Then, staggering towards Jane and the boys, the thing that had once been Roderick blundered into the pit. There was a splintering and a crunch, then a chittering, scrabbling, rending, shrieking.

Jane, reaching the door, threw it wide, and she and her sons flung themselves through...

...and stumbled, gasping, into a wood-panelled lift, one of the foot tunnel's. The operator, an elderly woman, glanced up at them, smiled, nodded, pressed the button. Perhaps she thought they'd been playing at 'it'.

When they were out in the open air again, in the waning light of late afternoon, on the south bank of the Thames, they walked to the river's edge, looked out across it. Then Jeremy shuddered, put his hand to his mouth, pointed down at the shingle beach. A dead swan lay on the pebbles, wings spread, plumage muddied, long neck crooked. A thin smear of blood on its beak.

VII

I write this in a cramped compartment in the hold of the Ark, far from sunlight and moonlight and rain and wind... I fear I'll never know these things again (I shudder, am wretched to think how, when I first saw, in dark red, stark against the drab steel of its hull, this hulk's name, I thought it a sign the vessel was to be a refuge). This room was, I'm sure, an office once; it's furnished with a desk, a chair, and a filing cabinet, empty, save some scraps of paper with meaningless squiggles on and, in the bottom drawer, a pentacle made of five paper clips, bent and twisted together. The tribeswoman and I are confined here, unable to leave, to return to the companion hatch, even if we did feel it worth, to feel the warmth of the sun on our skins again and to gulp our lungs full of fresh air, giving ourselves up to those waiting without.

With no sight of the sky, it's hard to gauge the passing of time, but I'd hazard we've been down here at least a fortnight. Our supply of food has dwindled, and I fear will all soon be eaten up, and that the tribeswoman will starve, even though we've been sparing, and I've often gone without, knowing hunger can only cause me pain, not kill.

Thankfully, we'd more water, and I've not had to go without. That cannot kill me either, but I know, of old, the searing of a parched throat is worse than an empty stomach's pangs. I'm glad, too, not to have to watch the tribeswoman die of thirst, it's a bad end, worse than wasting away, belly empty.

I blame myself for our dire pass; we were safe, but I wanted to return for my typescript and typewriter, would not be deterred, was frantic to finish my tale. As it is, I doubt I'll now be able to; I reckon my age-old adversary behind the attack that led to our being trapped, and await his bursting in, soon, to torture and make an end of me (and, and this wrings me, throw the tribeswoman, if she's not by then succumbed to hunger, to her former tribe, as a hunter might throw scraps to his hounds). I must press on, with all haste, if I'm to have any chance of setting down all I wish to tell.

Having just looked over the corrected proofs of my account of Jane's tale and the conversation and events that preceded it, which the tribeswoman finished typing up earlier this morning, it occurs to me that, for you, no matter whether you barely read, merely skimmed, pored over, or struggled with those pages, only a short time has passed since the afternoon my forehead was laid open and I put the posse from the tribe to rout by killing their chieftain; for even the most painstaking or sluggardly, it can't have been more than an hour's reading. But it's not so for me; it's actually been many weeks since then; my wound has long healed, and things have happened to the tribeswoman and me to entirely overshadow that afternoon's violence.

My work has been halting, hampered by turmoil.

Forgive this digression, but, now death looms, time, which once hung so heavy, again seems rare, and I feel compelled to hold it in my hands, examine its facets, as a jeweller, loupe screwed into one eye, would a gemstone.

But, with these musings on time, I'm squandering the handful of it remaining to me; I must return to my tale. But I felt the need to make clear that, though for you, my reader, a short time will have passed since the skirmish, really, in my reckoning, it's been over two months. Wanting to avoid diminishing the dread atmosphere Jane's tale builds, and to give you, my reader, a tolerably straight way, I've resisted breaking it up. But I have, while setting it down, been battered by squally fate.

While I was working on the melancholy epilogue to William's tale, the tribeswoman and I were granted a lull of a week and a half or so. I was writing the large part of that time, and she, having taken on the burden of meeting most of our wants, spent her days collecting firewood, hunting, fishing, and foraging. She was adept at these things, far more skilled than I, and seemed to pleasure in them. I did, though, take responsibility for the daily chores, such as cleaning, cooking, washing, and so forth, but these tasks were done fairly quickly, didn't take me away from my tale for long. On a couple of occasions, though, as I wished to learn some of the tribeswoman's wilderness lore, I did go with her on an excursion. She imparted to me a few of her skills; showed me how bulrush stems, dampened and pulped between stones, yielded long fibres that, once dry, could be stranded into strong, flexible twine for snares; taught me that mushrooms, roots, berries, and nuts could be found by watching the wildlife, that birds flocking to a particular tree told it was in fruit, that boars digging in the earth was a sign of tubers that were good to eat beneath the sod; demonstrated how to drowse bees' nests with smoke, shake out the stupored bees, plunder the honeycomb.

She and I communicate solely through gestures. Not since our first encounter has she addressed me in her own tongue, and she doesn't try to convey anything by means of expressive noises, which I find strange, as it's something that it's natural to do; I'd think she'd been struck mute by her beating at the hands of the natives, but that I've heard her cry out in her sleep, and that she sometimes lilts quietly to herself.

Those peaceful days were marred only by the pricks of my conscience, by my remorse over the tribal leader slain. I won't claim it was the first death at my hand; in a life as long as mine has been, well... But I don't believe I'd ever snuffed a simple, innocent life before; till then, my killings had been, more or less, just. I cursed myself for not being shrewd enough to hit on some way of putting her and her minions to flight without bloodshed. I often dreamt of her final throes, was wakened.

But, otherwise, that period was calm, happy. The tribeswoman and I grew close.

On the afternoon of the tenth or eleventh day, while trying to recall the exact words of the bewigged drunk's weird curse, I heard the tribeswoman scream. Dashing to the gunwale, I looked downriver, to the swathe of estuary mud laid bare by the low tide, where she'd gone seeking razor clams for our supper. She was stood atop a rock jutting from the flats, fending off, with the stick she'd taken with her to help her walk in the quag silt, a pair of swine, boar and sow. They'd yellowed teeth, wild rolling eyes, the boar larger and with a ruff of coarse bristles and reddish tufts ridging its spine. The beasts grunted, snorted, shook their heads, circled the outcrop, churned up mud. As I watched, the boar backed off a little way, then rushed at the tribeswoman and up the steep sides of the rock. Its hooves clattered, scrabbled, and it fell back, but, as it flailed, it thrust forward its head, gored her thigh with a tusk. She yowled, staggered, almost fell. I ran down the gangplank, ran towards her.

But she'd no need of a shining knight; as I made for her, feet sinking with each stride, she feinted at the sow with her stick, then lunged at the boar, put out one of its eyes. Squealing, it turned, fled. The sow stood its ground a moment, snarling, but then the tribeswoman whacked it on the snout, and it too bolted.

After clambering down from the rock, the tribeswoman hobbled towards me, grimacing. Nearing, she stopped, hiked up the hem of her shift, showed me where the boar had gashed her. It was high on her thigh, and I felt a tremble of longing, such as I'd not had in a long, long time, and I looked away, shamed.

The wound was fairly deep, and we went back to the Ark to swab and bandage it.

Much of the rest of the afternoon we spent together, collecting our evening meal, wandering the flats, eyes open for tell-tale dints, delving gingerly in the mud if we sighted one, hoping to grab the clam, without disturbing it, before it could dig deeper, and haul it out. Then we'd heft our catch, and either place it in the sack we toted, or chuck it back if it seemed scanty of flesh. When we'd gathered plenty, we returned to the Ark, and I continued marking up draft pages, while the tribeswoman went off again. Just after sunset, she came back with a bundle of samphire to go with the clams. I put down my pen, and we cooked up the shellfish in the raked ashes of a fire. Then feasted till juices ran down our chins.

That evening, after eating, we were both strangely elated; I wonder if it was the rich clamflesh made us so. We sat together in the prow of the Ark and I taught the tribeswoman to pick out some simple tunes on the banjo. Afterwards, I played and sang for her. At first, she sat quiet, just listening, then she began singing wordlessly along, harmonizing with my melody lines. Once I'd tired, the pads of my fingers were sore, we lay back on the deck, looked up at the sky. It was cloudless, dark, dark blue, daubed with a bright, full moon, spattered with stars. I thought to point out to the tribeswoman the constellations I'd learnt as a child, but found I couldn't recall any, if indeed they could still be seen in the sky, if the stellar clutter hadn't shifted too much over the long ages. I'd not picked up any of the intervening epoch's sidereal ragtags, either. So, I made up fit-seeming names for shapes I saw instead. There was the courtesan, shielding her face with her fan; her suitor, the beggar boy, cap in hand; the snail; the sail-fin shark; the death's head hawkmoth; and the spider monkey. I was hushed, not afraid of my voice betraying us, but awed by the beauty in the welkin, sleepy, and content. Finally, we retired, the tribeswoman to the pallet in the cabin, me to blankets spread out under my lean-to. I felt really happy. However, something happened that night to dispel my good mood. I wrote an account of it the following morning, perhaps it's best I give you that version, composed when it was still raw.

Last night, the tribeswoman came to me in my shelter as I slumbered, woke me, traced, with her finger, the healing scar slashing across my brow. Opening my eyes, I saw her, by the moon's light, crouched on haunches beside me. Naked. She gazed at me hard, with her soft brown eyes, her dark hair, hanging straight down, framing her face. I felt lust for the first time in many ages, sat up, throwing off my blanket, lapped at her breasts, thrust my hand between her thighs, groping in the warm dark cleft. Closing her eyes, biting her lower lip, she seized me by the nape, pulled me to her, then straddled me, took hold my cock, sought to stick herself with it. But I was limp, have been chaste too long. Grimacing, shamed, I pushed the woman aside. She looked at me, bewildered, hurt. I noticed she'd removed the bandage from her wound, that it was healing very well. I was about to mention it, to cover my embarrassment, but she padded away. For some time, I lay awake, staring up at the thatched roof of the lean-to.

This morning, when I roused the tribeswoman, she acted as if nothing had happened; I doubt anything will happen between us now, and that saddens me, if in a muted way; I've grown to find her enthralling.

I was wrong about this, we've fucked since, though in delirium, not desire, a frenzied, bane-freaked rutting that's soured all lust now. But our mute friendship has continued to grow, and I'm glad of that.

Our tempers are well matched, and hardship has also tempered our bond, for, since the night of my chagrin, we've known no peace.

The following morning, I woke early, brain throbbing. The sky was cloudless, still blue-black impasto, though there was a faint scumble out over the sea. Leaning over the bowrail, looking down on my reflection in the river, a long way below, I saw it clear; the air was still, there wasn't even the faintest of breezes to rumple the image. It was chill, my breath ghosted in the air, but all augured the day would turn warm and that it would be another of sane shades in the sky, there were no sick tints in the dawn haze, only rose. I roused the tribeswoman. She also seemed a bit blear and sore-headed; she winced, clutched her skull. I supposed the odd, if pleasant, fuddlement we'd felt after eating the shellfish to have been the result of some mild toxin, and that we were now feeling its after-effects. Once we'd eaten breakfast, the tribeswoman returned to the cabin, went back to sleep. I sat down at my typewriter to briefly set down the previous day's and night's events before they faded.

I'd only been working a short time, when, looking upriver, I saw charcoal smudges on the flats in the faint, if waxing, light. I crossed to the bowrail, peered; seals, as many as a hundred, and a few larger beasts, walruses and seacows, hitching themselves across the ooze, making for the water. Just then, rising clear of the horizon, the sun set the sloblands blazing. Squinching my eyes against the glare, I watched the animals cross a lake of fire, slip into the river, swim out to sea.

I knuckled my eyes, grinned, stood stunned a short while. But my reverie was soon disturbed by shouts and the beating of drums from upstream. I went to the stern. A mob came our way, crossing the mud: the tribe, come to avenge the death of its leader, come for a reckoning.

Horrored, I looked on the throng. They were many, almost the entire tribe, I guessed, men, women, and children, all who could walk, even some who couldn't, infants in slings across mothers' chests, a crone with withered legs who rode on the back of a burly man, all armed, save the babies and the very youngest children, wielding slings, clubs, knives, blowpipes. It seemed they'd picked a new leader, for a young man wearing purple robes walked alone, slightly ahead of the pack, bearing haughty then hunched by turns, looking over his shoulder often, as if he feared some prank, the tribe, sniggering, running off, abandoning him. Not far behind him came the drummers, thickset men with animal-hide tabors on which they thumped out a driving rhythm. Amid the throng was a frame lashed from pine trunks, which the tribe crowded, clamoured, fought to tote.

It bore some large thing. It was cloth draped, and I couldn't tell what it was, only that it was heavy, going by the stoutness of the frame and the many hands needed to carry it.

I called out to the tribeswoman, my voice shaking. She came out of the cabin, blinking in the now bright light, came to the taffrail, saw the rabble, turned to me, biting her lip. It was too late to take flight, we'd be seen and run down. I crossed to the foredeck, winched up the gangplank. Then I went back to stand by the tribeswoman. We watched the tribe approach.

The mob stopped a little way from the ship. The drums fell silent, and the strange burden was set down. Several of the tribe began to untie the thongs holding down the cloth that covered it. I clambered onto one of the shipping containers, boosted up by the tribeswoman, and yowled, loud, drawn out. But the rabble were not cowed, just loosed a few slingstones at me. I jumped back down off the container and took shelter behind the bulwarks with the tribeswoman. A few moments passed, then the clatter of slingstones petered out, and I raised my head, peered over the gunwale, gasped.

The unwieldy thing the tribe had brought with them lay, uncovered, on the mud. A catapult, an arm with a sling dangling from the end, a rope skein. Several of the tribe bustled about it, twisting the skein, even at that distance the creaking of the ropes could be heard. A rough ball of some dark stuff was then loaded into the sling. The chieftain, who had before stood at a distance, crossed over, while the rest took a step back. A flaming brand was put into his hand, and he set light to the projectile. He waited till it was well aflame, sending up a thick rope of black smoke, then knelt down, released the trigger.

The flaring missile arced over the Ark, reeky tail a sooty daub on the blue. I turned, dashed to the prow. The missile came down on a sandbank, out in the middle of the estuary, burst apart in a storm of burning smuts.

Looking back over my shoulder, I saw the tribeswoman

waving frantically at me, ran back to the stern. The tribe swarmed round the catapult, readying it again, adjusting; I feared they now had their aim and distance.

I cudgelled my brains for a flight, frantic, fretting for the tribeswoman's life, and for mine also, for, though the bombs couldn't kill me, one might leave me sore burned, unable to flee or defend myself should the din and smoke draw my enemy, as I feared it would, for to him chaos is what carrion is to crows.

Then I recalled the grappling iron and rope. Beckoning the tribeswoman to follow, I ran to the cabin, and, rummaging around in our pile of things, laid hold of them, a bag of dried provisions, my knife, and my torch. The tribeswoman and I then crossed over to the river side of the hulk, away from the natives, hooked the grapnel to a ring fixed to the deck, and threw the rope over the bulwarks. I gestured to the tribeswoman to go, and she vaulted the rail, swarmed down, hand over hand. While I waited, I looked about, and my heart jolted as I caught sight of, on my makeshift desk, this typescript, and, on top, weighting its piled pages against gusts, my typewriter. I wanted to save these things, to at least try, I'd set down too much by then and had too much still to tell, to *purge*, of this *tale*, this *account*. So I leant over the gunwale, waved to the tribeswoman, signalled she should wait, then ran over to the table, cast about for twine, I didn't want to leave the pages of my narrative loose, saw a skein on the deck a short way off, darted over, picked it up, then, returning, saw the spare ream I kept under my desk, so took it, tied it up with my tale, then gathered up, in my arms, the bundle of paper and the typewriter, took them over to one of the metal shipping containers, went inside, swept away, with my feet, the draff from a dingy corner, and left them there. A wrench.

I came forth, blinking, from the container, turned to look at the natives of the flats, saw the catapult kick like an ass, fling a missile into the air, slew, break a tribesman's forearm in a lash of blood. The flaring lump of pitch groaned out of the sky, struck the corner of one of the containers, rained fire down on the foredeck. Our stack of firewood and some bundles of reeds the tribeswoman was planning to work into twine for fishing lines were soon alight. Burning smuts gyred in the air, spread the flames to the lean-to's thatched roof, a pile of laundry we'd left out, and meal from oats I'd ground, which I kept in an old metal barrel the tribeswoman had found, buried in mud, a little way down the estuary. From the blazing lean-to, I heard twanging, the strings of my banjo, and was sorry. Some embers, falling on me, kindled my clothes, and throwing myself down, I rolled on the boards to put out the flames. Then I got to my feet, darted to the prow, hurdled the rail, grabbed hold the rope, and slid down it, flaying the skin from my palms. As I dropped, I heard a blast, the oatmeal, saw the barrel spin through the air overhead, splash down in the river, float downstream, trailing steam billows. I splattered down, sank, to my knees, into the sludge. The tribeswoman, who crouched a little distance off, waiting for me, crossed over, took my hand, hauled me out. A noise like a toad's croak. I lay gasping. Then another report rolled on our ears, a third projectile had struck the Ark.

The tribeswoman and I loped across the mud toward the river, waded in, began swimming for the far bank. We strove to keep the freighter's bulk between us and the rabble, but the current was backing with the rising tide and we drifted upstream into plain view. Still, we were not sighted till, midstream, we were forced to clamber over a sandbank. Then one of the tribe hollered, pointed us out. But the catapult needed to be turned to aim at us, and by the time the tribe had done so, and reloaded, we'd gained the far bank and begun running, bent, to stay hid, through the reeds there. The shot was loosed, but struck the bank at the place where we'd clambered from the river, by then far behind us.

Reaching higher ground, the other side of the reed bed, we halted, gulping air, peered back over the canes at the Ark. Dense black smoke rose from it, roiled. As we watched, the lean-to collapsed, sparks and ash puffing up. Some of the tribe, who'd climbed on board using grapnels, darted hither and yon, scouring the deck, ragged forms stark before the flames, roisterers at some dark revel. They weren't long searching – I suppose, as I had, they tried the companion hatch, found it wouldn't open – then shinned back down to the flats, crossed over to where the remainder of the tribe awaited them. A small group broke away, walked a little distance off, sat in a circle. The clan elders, I surmised, conferring. After a short while, council over, they rose, rejoined the rest. The chieftain began gesticulating, giving orders. The tribeswoman and I didn't wait longer, but turned, stole off.

We fled north through a land of weald and sward; of woods of oak, maple, birch, alder, elm, beech, and ash, where finches twittered, pheasants strutted, woodpeckers drummed, and swine rooted; and of pastures where rabbits frolicked, hares loped, grasshoppers chirred, sheep and goats bleated, and cattle grazed, their lowing the region's only sorrowful note. Not that, running scared, we'd time for the country's gentle charms.

But the land had a dark side, portended the dread place we were soon after to come upon. On the second night of our flight, a howl woke me. Against the full moon, just kicked loose of the earth, its big round face like a ball of tallow moulded by sooty fingers, was, stark, the shade of a wolf, muzzle to the sky. The tribeswoman, also roused by the noise, sat up, rubbed her eyes. I pointed out the beast to her, but it had slunk off. She fell back into slumbers, but they were troubled, going by the whimpering she made. I couldn't sleep, lay awake watching the moon cross the sky on its rod, ears straining for the whirr of gears.

We broke camp early the following morning and, after walking only a short way, came to a brook. Turning, we saw smoke furrowing the sky to the south: the tribe were on our trail. At first, I was bewildered, we'd covered our tracks well, but then

I heard the hounds. We stood there, stricken, harking to the frenzied yapping. Then the tribeswoman let her pent breath out in a rush and pointed at the watercourse, walked her fingers through the air. I was bemused a moment, then realized what she meant; we could perhaps throw off the dogs, baffle their noses, by wading in the stream a way. I nodded, she removed her sandals, hitched up her skirt, I took off my boots, rolled up my trousers. Then we entered the water. It was shallow, came only to my knees, but was bitingly cold, my toes went numb almost straight away. We headed upstream, where briar thickets hid the stream from view. After trudging against the coursing water till fatigued, till breathing ragged, we clambered out onto the north bank, lay down to rest. The sky was clear, the morning had waxed warm, and, worn out and careworn we fell into a doze. On stirring, looking up, I saw the sun had reached its zenith. At first I was held rapt by the weird bands of vermilion, puce, viridian, and mallow shimmering in the sky, then I cursed the lapse; we'd doubtless lost any lead our ruse had gained us. I shook the tribeswoman awake, and we hurried on our way.

Mid-afternoon we sighted a forest of gloomy firs up ahead, tall, close-seeded, dark. I thought it a grim enough place, but the tribeswoman seemed in terrible fear, shuddered whenever her eyes fell on it. I supposed it a place of fabled evil for her folk. By dusk we'd reached the treeline. We spent the night there, the pines looming over us.

The next day, rising before sunup, we saw, not far off, the fitful glow of a fire, and had to press on into the forest. The tribeswoman shook her head, shivered, but I cajoled, brought her round. Knarled boles rose stark till far above, where twined black boughs and sprays of dark needles all but blotted out the sky, leaving only flecks of light, strewing the canopy with false stars; it was as if the place had seen a battle between the forces of night and day, and night had won a decisive victory, routed day's troops, and the land had been forever ceded to it. The undergrowth was dense, if sickly, tangles of wan ferns, clumps of sere nettles, snares of brittle bramble, and crawled with stagbeetles, cockroaches, ants, spiders, writhed with worms and grubs. Of higher creatures, we saw none, no birds, not even a rat or snake, though in places the brake was trampled, and we heard, from time to time, in the distance, the noise of a large animal crashing through the scrub.

We pressed on into that wretched forest, where I hoped the tribe would be loath to follow. By nicking the trees with my knife, small blazes low on the trunks, I marked our path. After a few hours, afraid to go on lest we lose our way, we halted, made camp, bodging a shelter from thicker fallen boughs and wadded moss.

Stuck as to how to go on, I've been musing abstractly on my tale a short time. It's occurred to me I am, at this moment, and have been many times in the writing of it, in three different places at once. It's uncanny. Just now, I'm huddled with the tribeswoman in our makeshift hut, peering wary into the gloomy pines, but I also sit gawping at Jane, in the Nightingale pub, and at this battered rusty iron desk, in a cabin in the ravelled guts of this hulk, rhapsodizing all these affairs. It's disconcerting; I hope, by the end of my tale, I'll have collected myself. But, now, I'd better press on.

I must return, then, to that drear forest, that place so dismal, so apart from the quick world. The writhen limbs overhead, needle rank, clot the sky. We felt oppressed by them, though were glad of their thick shroud on the second day when we heard thunder, wind threshing the treetops, saw rain running in rivulets down the trunks, realized another storm had broken over the region.

Foraging in that place yielded little, just some bland mushrooms with dun caps, a few grouse and pheasant carcasses, maggot-ridden, but edible, though barely, only if we choked our gags. The supplies I'd grabbed before fleeing the Ark dwindled and, within a fortnight, were used up. I realized we'd have to return to the rich land we'd left behind, or else the tribeswoman would starve. I just hoped the natives wouldn't be lying in wait for us on the edge of the forest (I was almost certain they'd not have followed us in, sure, from the tribeswoman's reaction, the place was a haunt of boggarts for them).

Early one morning, we set out, following my blazes. But then we came to a place where patches of bark had been stripped from many of the trunks, perhaps by beasts whetting horns, antlers, tusks, and too many of my notches were lost, and so was the trail. Given that I've spent millennia poring over books, it might be supposed my brain is crammed with lore. The truth is, though, as I've previously written, my memory's unfitted to the aeons; I couldn't then dredge up any learning to aid us in getting our bearings. Had I been alone I might have wandered that cursed place for weeks, even months, but the tribeswoman had some survival know-how, discovered where south lay by peering at the dull green and orange mottles of lichen on the bark of the tree boles, and, by dusk, had led us to the edge of the forest.

By certain landmarks I saw we were close to the spot where we'd spent our last night before entering the gloomy pines. The tribe had clearly camped there, bided for us, for scattered ashes and cinders, cornhusks, apple cores, and the picked carcasses of sheep and fowl, strewed the meadow. But it seemed they'd given up their watch. They'd left behind some parcels of nuts, berries, and dried fruit wrapped up in spinach leaves; we supposed, at the time, they'd just been missed when the camp was packed up. Famishing, the young woman and I fell to eating these sweet-meats.

They were poisoned. The bane coursing through our wasted frames, maddened us. Though it was cold, we tore off our garments, cavorted, clinched, danced a grotesque shuffle, then, stumbling, fell to the floor. I groped the tribeswoman, kneaded her breasts, pinched her dark nipples, fumbled between her thighs. She arched her back, parted her legs, groaned. I was hard, the first time in many ages. She pulled me to her, and I drove into her, pounded, animal, abandoned, lost. Then she retched, spewed bile from the corner of mouth, her eyes rolled back, she shuddered, squirmed, but I held her tight. Then, howling, she elbowed me, hard, in the face. Tears blurred my vision, blood gushed from nose, she wriggled free, got to her feet, stood a little way off, trembling, glaring, arms wrapped about her. Holding my broken face in one hand, I staggered to my feet, yelled something nasty at her, advanced on her, priapic, enraged. She turned, ran naked and wailing past a holly bush growing on the forest's edge, its bright berries red gouts against the firs, yelped, she'd passed too close, the prickles of the dark green leaves had scratched her, then entered the gloom. I made to follow, but gripes flared, and I went to the floor, clutching my gut, passed out.

I've pledged to write only what is true; wondering how most faithfully to relate the time that came after my poisoning, I find myself facing a crux. Things took place that were so gruesome I believe them most likely bred out of the venom's delirium, but I've suffered strange horrors in the past, and they could have been only the simple truth. Equally, I can't be sure that, of the entirely mundane happenings, some were not delusive, indeed, one of them, though not eldritch, many may find hard to credit: an act of genuine altruism.

But now I muse on truth, I realize, having listened in my long, long life to many, many conceptions of it, spouted by wizened philosophers, mystic crones, foolish striplings, mendacious tyrants, &c., &c., I've lost all faith in the idea. Born and raised during the Age of Reason's dotage, in the city, which, though not its cradle, had been the beating heart of the nation that spawned its most fervent torch-bearers, my youthful education was based on its central tenet, the idea truth could be approached through the painstaking observation of phenomena, a second-hand idea taken from antiquity, first proposed by a scholar who wished to refute his teacher's mystical idealism, just a taunt in a squabble, or so the legend goes. After attaining adulthood, though, I was disabused of the notion; by the late twentieth century, empiricism was discredited, little more than a pedagogical tool, a fable for children. As a way of understanding the world it had proved untenable. After its ruin, folk, frantic to make some sense of their lives, sought solace in myriad wayward metaphysics whose divers assertions about the nature of knowledge and truth led to an epoch of warring systems, and the silent and apparently immobile soil of the Enlightenment era was suddenly riven with flaws, and the ground once again stirred under humankind's feet.

Since that time, I've realized history is rife with disparate ways of making sense of things, each with its own definition of truth, that it's only the brief span of mortal life that gives it the appearance of stasis, stability... Well, perhaps I can best explain by giving examples.

I once spent many years in Naufana, a place that lay amid sun-seared tracts of red sand. Just east of it, on the other side of a long dried-up river, was another city, Ghadis. They'd both once been thriving stops on the Silk Road, famed for their wealth and the richness of their cultures. But Ghadis had been laid waste by pestilence centuries before I first saw its ruined minarets and cupolas fretted from the rising sun, was then desolate save small lizards, with electric blue markings, basking on its roof terraces and in its public squares. And though Naufana still thrived, it was no longer rich, in wealth or culture; its fine skyline of spires, copper domes, azure-tiled roofs, belied the peril, filth, and wantonness of its streets. The city's rulers adhered to a doctrine, established at the time disease stalked Ghadis, which proclaimed all illusory and nothing true; therefore, everything was permitted.

At another time, I lived a while in a city sprawled along one bank of a broad river delta, a city whose name I cannot recall, a place also infamous for vice, though its obscene carnality arose perversely, not due to the permissiveness of the regime, but to spite the diktats of despotic leaders, who, in thrall to a school of philosophers that proclaimed the truth of all things, in terror of that fullness, and intent on maintaining the submissive ignorance of the populace, prohibited everything. When the tyrants fell following a popular libertarian coup, and were hung, along with their associates, senior military personnel, and members of the secret police, from the city's famous green, fluted lampposts, all descended into sheer turmoil and licence, and the place, formerly so gross, so solid, waned to a wraith. A few, perhaps a lucky few, were struck down by a wasting sickness; their innards putrefied, they aware, in great pain the while. A sallow smother of fog settled like a pall on the city; it was hardly possible to see your own hand in front of your face. Then came the sleeping plague; swathes were struck down. I fled.

Though its name is lost to me, my recollections of that place are perhaps starker than those of any other I've ever lived in, save London. I think of it, and the memories come glaring, clamouring, jostling, reeking, tanging.

The Olde Market, with its colonnade, its roof, panes of grimy glass, the bustle of the crowds, the babel of the butchers, grocers, fishmongers, and spice vendors crying their wares, the pungent scents and garish colours of the produce. The frieze over its entrance, of a horse floundering in a mire, flies pouring, in droning mass, from its gaping throat, an incident from the city's foundation myth, whose meaning no one ever managed to make clear to me.

The rooming house I stayed in, which was on the edge of the city, in the gloom of a stark bluff, Promontory Wall, its ramshackle Carpenter Gothic, turrets, steep gables, leaded windows, warped cladding, flaking discoloured whitewash. Inside, the air was stale, there was a film of dust over everything. My room was shabby and drab, the bedclothes were tattered, the sash window, filth-rimed, bulb, bare and dim, carpet, threadbare, the soft furnishings, reeking of tobacco smoke, the maple wardrobe and bedstead, stained the shade of old bone, the dressing table's veneer, badly chipped, the mirror, dark-specked. The sole ornament, an icon of St Christopher, the dog-headed St Christopher, hid a peephole, a squint into the squalid bathroom next door. The ancient landlady, whose shrunken head and wisps of stark white hair brought to mind a dandelion clock, gambled away all her savings, all the rent she was paid, playing rummy with a bizarre antiquarian, couldn't afford to keep the place up. The sole other long-term tenant of the place, the rest of the rooms were let by the hour, and then but rarely, was a leech of some kind, who carried his doctor's bag, black scuffed leather, always, and looked always forlorn.

A ramshackle warehouse, empire of a surly rag-and-bone man, paths leading to it barricaded with broken garden furniture, wrecked statuary, and rusting lawnmowers. A sign over the entrance read, 'Flea Circus'. Inside, beneath a gyring fan, were shelves heaped with bric-a-brac.

A bar, the Anaconda, worn linoleum, filled with chess players hunched over their boards, haruspices worrying at entrails, and opera music, coming from the jukebox.

A library, in a grand building that had once, long, long before, been a ducal palace, which had a few shelves of rare occult texts tucked away, and a phantasmagoria in the old wine cellars. One time, that same antiquarian who was always besting my landlady at cards, took me down there and showed me some weird scenes. Among them a barren plain strewn with animal bones and girded by sawtooth mountains; giants, human frames, but beast heads, fox, magpie, raven, rat, pike, and blowfly, stalking a city, bleak, beset by wastes, streets choked with sand drifts; and a photocopier, a common piece of office equipment from the era of my long-ago youth, for producing facsimiles of documents and images, but this one containing wetly pulsing viscera, seen through an open hatch in its side, and standing on a plinth, in a temple, a place of sacrifice.

I also recall, in that city whose name I can't remember, a massive dome under a louring sky, a former railroad museum, long before closed, standing empty.

And a masked orgy (towards the end, after mores had been abandoned for abandon) in a foursquare town house, gluttony, heavy drinking, drugging, and, later, a snarl of sweat-slick flesh, beastly rutting, a farmyard pungency, laced with acrid reeks, groans and yowls, antique furniture tumbled about.

And (and this is the last thing I saw before my flight) row upon row of the seats of a cinema in the red light district filled the dreaming afflicted, snoring, snorting gurgling, whickering, awash in the kaleidoscopic light of the porn movie playing, in silence, on the screen. These victims of the sleeping plague had glucose IVs in their arms, and their urine, soaking into the upholstery, pooling under the seats, gave off a high cloying stench.

The philosophies which held sway in Naufana and the city whose name I can't remember, are, of course, extremes on a spectrum; in my life, my long weary life, I've lived in countless other places, each with their own metaphysics of truth. In many of them, it was unstable, in flux; these places are the weirdest of all my experience: Tainaron, the City of Insects; Ambergris, the City of Saints and Madmen; Ashamoil, the Etched City; Uroconium, the City in the Waste.

But I must go on, indeed, find I must again apologise for a lengthy digression; it's my hope, though, that it's not been pointless, that I've shown how, if you live long enough, it becomes clear there is no single truth, only a proliferation of divers ones, all merely convenient constructs. Therefore, I think it best I set down my memories of the time I was bane-racked without trying to thresh fact from figment.

A heavy downpour roused me from stupor. It was night and pitch black, neither the moon nor a star could be seen through the heavy clouds. Parched, I lay with my mouth open to the deluge while it lasted. That wasn't long, though, not long enough, and I was still thirsty when it stopped. I was glad, then, to see, by faint gleams, rain had pooled in hollows. I dragged myself over to one of these puddles, lowered my mouth to the water, gulped it down, slaked my dry gullet. I could see, very dim, my face in the puddle – beard matted with blood and bile, nose and the flesh around it, puffy, turning dark. I splashed it with water, but gingerly. Then lay on my back a time, weak, gut sore. Then blacked out again.

When I came to after that, it was late in the day, the sun a faint reddish stain on the clouds still wadding the sky. I'd been roused by the cawing of some crows that had settled on the turf near me. I felt, if anything, worse than before, was frail, too weak to move much. My feeble efforts to scare off the birds, faint hissing, stirring the fingers, was met with croaks that seemed almost derisive, and I was terrified they, thinking me dead, meant to tear at me with their jetty beaks. But they just strutted, preened their feathers. Then one took flight, flapped, wheeled, alighted on my belly, and, wings outspread, throat juddering, kecked up a seed, sowed it, with its beak, in my navel. The flock then took wing, all at once, flew off.

I lay there while the seed sprouted, put forth a shoot. The shoot grew into a midget apple sapling, swift. Then its roots delved into my innards. I groaned, strained, but could do no more than flutter my hands weakly at the end of my arms, couldn't pluck it out. Growing, aging, the tiny tree clad itself in foliage, blossomed, fruited, shed its leaves, fleet, many, many times over. The sun, sinking to the horizon, found a break in the cloud cover, and the tree cast a shadow that crept up over my abdomen and ribs. Then, when the tree's crown, no bigger than my head, occulted the dull red orb, it was blighted. At the beginning of one of its hectic springs. The buds it put forth withered. Its bark split. Lurid, tallowy growths groped forth from the living wood. Foul galls swelled blasted limbs, then burst in a hail of pale grubs, which fell on my belly, burrowed beneath my skin. I closed my eyes, howled, passed out a third time.

More heavy rain woke me. It was night again. The eerie midget apple tree was gone, my belly, though paunchy with the bloating of the poison, was unriddled. I felt a little better, could just stagger to my feet. Though my face throbbed, was swollen tender. My clothes lay where I'd cast them off, and I struggled into them, soaking though they were. Then I shambled into the forest, about where I'd seen the tribeswoman enter it. I felt sure she was dead, it was a fell bane, but wanted to find her body, bury it, keep the scavengers from glutting on her flesh. I searched a short time, but then weakness overcame me once more and, oppressed by the gloom, I left the forest as fast as I could stagger. I'd thought the tribeswoman wouldn't have got far before succumbing, but it seemed she was tougher than I'd supposed.

Out in the open once more, I found the rain had eased off, though a fine drizzle still fell. The blackcloth of night was slightly washed out, but this didn't cheer me much, it would be a dismal day, the cloud too thick for the sun to burn through. Then, looking to the south, I saw black shapes moiling against the grey; the clan returning to see whether their scheme had worked, and, if it had, to gloat.

At first I thought of flight, but I was too, too weary, and reasoned the tribe, not finding our bodies, would figure their scheme had failed, that we'd not eaten the poisoned food, and maintain their pursuit. I decided, then, to stay, feign death; though it burns, I can hold my breath for hours before my body finally sucks in a lungful unwilled. And my black and bulgy face would help with the impression. It would be fraught, but I thought worth trying, for if they were cozened, then, I'd be left alone. And, I perhaps had a little fight left in me, if it came to it. So I lay down, sprawled on the sodden ground, gazing vacantly at the clouds racking by overhead, waited.

I lay there some time, seeing the forms of strange beasts in the clouds. A skein of geese passed by. Then I heard footsteps a little way off, took a deep breath, stilled the rise and fall of my chest. A short while later, grim snarling faces were hung before my bleary dull fixed stare, jerked away. I was peered at, prodded, spat on, beaten with fists, kicked, but did not flinch. Then the tribe turned away. Askance, I glimpsed them gathering the brown-capped mushrooms that had sprouted from the dank earth overnight. Only the leader remained stood over me, staring down, grimacing. Then, as I lay there, under his gaze, a large beetle blundered into my neck, clambered up, over my chin, scuttled, on spindly legs, over my filth-caked beard, and across my cheek. Its feelers tickled the insides of my nostrils, its mandibles raked my skin. Then, cresting the ridge of my cheekbone, it crawled down into my right eyesocket, and stopped in that sheltered spot, the chitinous plates of its abdomen scraping my cornea.

I couldn't suppress a shudder. Paling, breathing in sharply, the chieftain hunkered down at my side. I was on the point of struggling to my feet, staggering off, as fast as my weak legs could carry me, though I feared I'd not make it far, when the leader put his hand on my shoulder, mouthed something. The workings of his jaws and lips were, of course, meaningless to me, but his kindly expression made his meaning clear enough. I don't know why, but I felt I could trust him, made no move to flee. And he reached out, plucked the insect from my eye, cast it away. Then he got to his feet, turned, addressed the tribe. They stopped picking mushrooms, listened. He spoke at length in that strange tongue, which sounds, to my ears, like the low rumble of a distant snowslide, like a capercaillie's jeers and taunts, the clucking in the crop, the clacking of the beak, like children throwing stones at the windows of an abandoned house. After his address was concluded, the tribe struck out south, left me alone. I lay there a while, stock still, before falling into an uneasy sleep.

Some time later, night came swaggering in from the east, and day, faded and frail, turned tail and fled. I tried to crawl to the shelter of the trees, but, drained, couldn't make it, resigned myself to sleeping out in the open. But, though I was enervated, my brain was feverish, and my repose was fitful – sporadic bursts of slumber, long stretches of hectic wakefulness. I was roused from a bit of snatched sleep by an owl's screech, woken from a dream of London, as it was in my youth, but clinker and ash, folk, with charred flesh sloughing from their bones, stumbling in the streets. I shook my head to clear it of this nightmare, then looked up at the sky, saw a meteor shower in the east.

The following morning a hand on my cheek woke me. Peering about blearily, I saw there was someone crouched down by me. I blenched, but then, rubbing my eyes, saw it was the tribeswoman. The feeling of having known her sometime in the past, which I'd remarked when she first accosted me, but forgotten since, returned, this time stronger, more disquieting. But then, recalling I'd thought her dead, gladness chased that uncanny tremor from my brain (I wonder now whether, perhaps, she bears a resemblance, in certain lights, to a long-ago acquaintance). Then I felt another moment's wariness, lest she was a figment or devil, but she seemed real and truly herself, and so she's proved to be. I can only assume she spewed the poisoned food soon after fleeing into the forest, and that this saved her. She'd found and put on her clothes, so I knew she'd recovered her wits. She smiled at me, then reached out, took my hand. I was relieved she'd forgiven me the brute way I'd acted when deranged by the bane.

The poison lingered in our blood, and it was only after resting several days that we felt strong enough to move on from that place. I was then seized by an urgent need to recover this document, this typewriter. I sought to convey this to the tribeswoman by means of gestures, pointed to the south, sketched the outline of the Ark in the air with my forefinger, mimed typing. A look of fear came into her face, and she shook her head; frantic, I got down on my knees, looked up at her in mute appeal. She still shuddered, but I went on with my mummed pleas, beseeching, and finally she cast her eyes down; I'd won (thinking of this now, I am filled with anger at my folly, and guilt over wearing her down). Rightly chary, though, she insisted we ensure we'd food and water to last a while, before setting out. As that land abounded in good things, this was easy enough. We snared rabbits and hares, shot birds down out of the trees with a sling made from a leather thong, cured the meat by smoking it; spent many hours digging up tubers we knew were good to eat; collected and dried mushrooms; picked nuts and berries; and made several waterskins, sacs stitched from deerhide, then proofed with a mix of tallow and beeswax, which we filled from a stream.

Full provisioned, we set out, headed for this hulk, this monstrous, rusting carcass. On reaching the north bank of the estuary, early in the morning of the fourth day, a day cloudless and bright, we concealed ourselves in the same brake of rushes we'd before hidden in, watched the ship. We watched for hours, saw no signs of life, save a cormorant that flapped up from the river, alighted on the portrail, and perched there a little while before flying off, wings outspread to dry in the warm sun, shuffling now and again. Sometime after the sun had passed the zenith, we swam across the river, went aboard the Ark by means of the gangway, which had been lowered. The deck was strewn with char and ash; everything we'd gathered to make the place a home was burnt up.

I crossed to the shipping container I'd concealed my typescript and typewriter in, entered, saw them where I'd left them, in the corner, went over, took them up. The tribeswoman, who'd followed, but waited outside the container, picked up a clinkered long bone and idly clanked it against the ridged metal walls of the container. Lifting the typewriter, I saw, which I'd not noticed before, a number of symbols scored into the floor beneath. They were vaguely familiar, but meant nothing to me.

As I turned, typewriter under one arm, bundle of paper under the other, a blast shook the ship. The tribeswoman yelled. At first I heard, 'Cunt!' But then realized it must have been some guttural exclamation in her tongue. I ran outside, saw we'd been gulled; I'd led us into a trap. A fiery missile had struck the twisted wreck of the wheelhouse; a billow of smoke rose from it, as black, writhen, ravelled as an ancient yew. The tribe, it seemed, had been hiding, watching; some moiled about, readying again the catapult, which they'd set on a hill amid the reeds, a little distance off, and the rest were crossing the flats headed for us. I turned to the tribeswoman, was unable to meet her eyes. But she'd choked her rage, merely shrugged her shoulders, smiled wan. I don't know whether she's truly forgiven me, but she's given me no looks of reproach these last weeks, even as inanition has racked her. I, though, have cursed my rashness again and again. I've also wondered often how the natives guessed we'd be likely to return to the Ark – why they were lying in wait for us. All musings lead me to one dread conclusion. Even assuming the chieftain betrayed me, the tribe would have had no reason to assume I'd return to the Ark; only someone who discovered my tale, and was able to read this long-dead language, would have realized I'd risk all to get it back.

While the tribeswoman and I havered, another fiery missile struck the bulwarks, not far from us, burst apart, spraying the deck with flaring tar. As if my memory had been kindled by a burning smut, I recalled where I'd seen the sigils scratched into the container's floor before – they matched those on some of the buttons of the companion hatch's keypad. I knew, of course, the graving was far more likely to be some reckoning or random phrase, a gambling debt toted up or a crass insult, than the scuttle's code, but anything was worth hazarding. Having gone back into the container and scored the sigils on my brain, I went back outside again, signalled the tribeswoman to follow me, and dashed for the foredeck, typescript and typewriter in my arms. As we ran, a third missile struck. Then I heard one of the tribe cry out in anguish and turned to see a seagull, perhaps the same I'd descried a few times before, stooping on those gathered about the catapult, stabbing with its keen beak, hindering them, gaining us some time. We flung ourselves down by the trapdoor. I, letting drop my things without a thought for the mechanisms of the typewriter, too afraid, too frantic, crouched, tapped the sequence of symbols I'd memorized into the keypad. But nothing happened. I cursed, thumped the hatch, bloodied my hands. The tribeswoman, who knelt beside me, bit her lip, shook her head.

Looking over at those huddled about the catapult again, I saw one stood jabbing aloft at the bird with his sword. Then the blade grazed the gull's wing and, squawking, it wheeled away, rising into the blue of the sky. The bird driven off, the tribesfolk turned back to loading the weapon. They'd their range and loft, even scurrying hither and yon we'd soon be struck, and the rest of the tribe had the hulk encircled – we were not simply able to run as before. I groaned. But then the tribeswoman grabbed my shoulder, shook me, jerked me round to look at the scuttle. It was revolving slowly, lifting, the filth clogging its seal was shed in strips, like peeled orange rind. Once above the level of the deck, there was a crunch of gears meshing, and it began to move to one side. Metal shrieked. Taking out my torch, I shone it into the gloom through the widening aperture. Steps descended into darkness. Dust motes, agitated by the air soughing in through the opening, gyred in the beam of light. I stared. Then the end of the gangway began to jounce, and I heard the noise of drubbing feet. I thrust the tribeswoman towards the hatch, followed her inside.

There, I hewed at the murk with the beam of my torch. Sighting a button on the underside of the deck, I reached up, pressed it. The hatch began to eclipse the opening once more. Dazed, relieved, it wasn't till only a sliver of sky remained that I recalled my document and typewriter. Thrusting out my hands in a panic, I grabbed those things, dragged them through the fast-waning crescent.

Had my stupor lasted a moment longer, the gap would have been too narrow and this document, this typewriter would have been lost.

As soon as the hatch had settled into place once more, a roar from above told of a missile striking the foredeck over our heads. Searing heat forced us down the stairs. We soon reached their foot, found ourselves at one end of a long narrow corridor.

I'll write, in time, of the horrors of the hold. But, for now, I feel I'd best press on with that strand of my tale, the crucial one in truth, which concerns the evening I and the others learnt of our curse, the night we spent drinking and relating our stories in the Nightingale. Before I do, though, I must, lest my narrative be too confused, tortuous, briefly explain how the tribeswoman and I came to be in the straits I told of at the beginning of this chapter: confined to a cabin, far below decks. It's not that there's any gross clog preventing our leaving this place, the doorway's not blocked outside by crates fallen from a precarious pile we knocked against on entering, the door is not plate steel, did not swing shut behind us and seal us in, is but flimsy plywood, locked only with a bolt we pushed home ourselves, and obstructed only on the inside, by the filing cabinet I've pushed up against it as a barricade. It's simply that the batteries of my torch have given out. We've illumination in here, as we found, in one corner of the room, an oil-burning generator, with a full reservoir of fuel. By the flickering light of the fading torch, the tribeswoman managed to get it working, hook it up to the bare bulb dangling by a long cable from the ceiling. It runs with a slight whirring noise. It's fixed down, cannot be moved, and, therefore, we're stuck here, in this office; were we to attempt to find our way back to the companion or set out to search the hold for provisions, for anything of use, we'd soon become lost in the dark, mazy, horror-ridden ways and rave.

I don't understand why my dread foe, who I believe now has the tribe under his dominion, hasn't sent them in to capture or bolt us yet. Perhaps he means to rack me by leaving me to moulder here. And it does distress me sorely to see the tribeswoman wasting. But he doesn't know of the light source, without which we'd have been crazed long ago, nor that I am, in some ways, glad of the reprieve, glad of time to write, to set down as much as possible of what remains of my tale. With this task to inspirit me, my dire situation, and looming agonizing death, harry me less than they might.

VIII

While Jane told her story, the rest of us sat appalled, but in thrall, hardly aware of the Nightingale's saloon, of the pub's other patrons. Then, after her tale was done, she slumped, elbows on the table, head cradled in hands, and we others sat staring, morose, into our drinks. So none of us saw the pint, the pint I'd set before the empty chair, fall, hit the floor, shatter. Lager splashed across the boards, a dark spatter; we all blenched.

'Fuck!' William winced, rubbed his eyes. He'd paled.

'Strange,' I said. 'It wasn't anywhere near the edge.'

Duncan pointed to a pool of beer on the table.

'It must just've skited on that. Aye, that'll be it.'

Jane shook her head, eyes wide with terror.

I went up to the bar. The publican had heard the glass smash, offered to help clear up, but I thanked him, said it was fine, really. So he gave me a cloth, a bucket, a dustpan and brush, and I returned to the table, hunkered down, swept up the shards, mopped up the spill, wringing the cloth out into the bucket. My hands shook. The others sat in fraught silence the while.

After returning the cleaning things to the bar, I sat back down at the table, made a vain attempt to rouse the others from their stupors with a witticism I don't now recall, but received no response, well none bar a grimace from Rashmi. Elliot tugged on each of his fingers in turn, till the knuckles cracked, making William cringe. Then Jane began to sob, quietly, into the sleeve of her jumper, while the rest of us looked on, awkward.

And so we remained for a time. Rashmi was the first to offer Jane consolation. Getting to her feet, she crossed over, and put an arm around the older woman's shoulders.

'There, there,' she said, as if she were comforting a child.

Jane stopped crying, looked up at her, grateful, but perplexed. I was also baffled. Clearly I'd been awry about Rashmi; I'd thought her obtuse, callous, judged her for misguided opinions, rudeness. This impression of her was confounded by the sensitivity and consideration now shown. I thought myself acute, but I'd been dull this time, dull for thinking I could so swiftly grasp someone's whole nature.

Reaching into her pocket, Jane brought out a handkerchief, dried her eyes, blew her nose.

'Why did you give up writing?' I asked, gently.

'How did you know about that?'

'It was in the papers.'

'Of course. Well, I just couldn't bear to make things up any more.'

William sighed, rubbed his eyes, smiled wan, lit a cigarette.

'What about your sons?' he asked. 'Are they alright?'

'I don't know. I've only once brought up what happened that afternoon. It wasn't long after. They were reluctant to talk, but when pressed said we'd played a game, I'd pretended to be a monster, chased them, that was all.'

She paused, fished for the wedge of lime in her drink, squeezed it.

William peered at her.

In response to his unspoken question, she nodded.

'They have changed though. Jeremy's been shy, nervous ever since, Peter, taciturn, sullen. Sometimes I catch them whispering together, maybe scared, maybe plotting. They won't talk to me, won't open up to me.'

She began again to weep. The rest of us tried to solace her, save Elliot, who seemed tired and a little distant, but she waved aside our feeble, if sincere, words of comfort. Then, stemming her tears, looked round at us, forcing a grin.

'I lost more than just my faith in the appearance of things, back then. A lot more.'

'Jane, listen...' I began.

But she interrupted me. 'Sorry, I don't want to talk about it anymore, at least not for now.'

Rashmi then suggested that someone else go ahead and tell their tale.

Duncan spoke up, 'I'll go next.'

Then, slightly shamefaced, added, looking to Rashmi and Elliot, 'That is, if the two of you don't mind, like.'

Rashmi shook her head, 'Sure, go on.'

Elliot was staring up at an oak beam overhead, solid, age-stained, worm-eaten, seemed lost in his thoughts. Duncan reached out, waved a hand in front of his face.

'What is it?' Elliot asked, turning to the Glaswegian, scowling.

Duncan frowned, then said, 'I was just wondering if it was alright if I told my tale next.'

'Oh right. Yes, go on, fine by me.'

'Well, if you're sure.'

'Duncan,' I broke in. 'Do you mind waiting a moment? I'm just...'

I gestured at the men's toilet.

'Go ahead.'

I got to my feet, a whit unsteady, drunker than I'd thought. There was a dull ache behind my eyes, and I knuckled them. Rashmi also excused herself, got up, headed for the women's toilet. Walking over to the 'Gents', stark outline of a man's form on the door, a sigil or fetish, I passed a couple sitting with hands clasped across the table, recalled Rachel with a pang. Going into the lavatory, I was dazzled by the harsh light of a fluorescent tube glaring from white tiles and mirrors, narrowed my eyes. I walked over to the metal urinal. The acrid perfume of bilious disinfectant cakes failed to mask the sour stench of stale urine. I unzipped my fly, began pissing.

'Oi!'

I startled, almost sprayed my shoes, and, looking over my shoulder, saw, at the toilet's small window, open just a crack, the red bloated face of the crazed drunk. He took off his wig, pushed it through the small gap, and dangled it from forefinger and thumb, made it dance, herky jerky. His bald scalp was scabrous, lumpy.

'Do you know the parallax poetry of piss?'

I stared.

'No? It's simple enough. Look down at your stream, close first one eye, then the other, and... That's it. Simple. But truly magical.'

'What? What the...'

But he was gone, snatching his wig back through the opening.

After, as I was washing my hands in the sink, I heard a bolt being drawn back, and, turning, saw an old man, lank moustache, lined face, coming out of the cubicle. My heart scrabbled against my ribs; he was one of the elderly fiends, the man I'd seen staving the skull of another of the mob. Yet now there was no scent of blood on him. He held my gaze, but there was no sign he knew me. I fled the toilet, crossed the saloon, sat back down. My hands trembled, my breathing was ragged. I turned to Duncan, and said, fighting for calm, 'Sorry to keep you waiting. Go ahead.'

'Nae bother,' he said. 'Still holding on for Rashmi.'

Then he peered at me.

'What's wrong?'

The others also looked concerned. Just then Rashmi returned, sat down.

'Hey,' she said to me. 'You look white as a sheet.'

I explained about the old man.

Duncan nodded, sage, patted his stump.

'This missing limb of mine is a constant reminder of what happened to me. Long ago, I learnt to see the good in it. It's proof, don't you see, that what I underwent was no delusion. Wouldn't you rather know yourself sane, but afflicted, than mad? There are other things that tell me that too, as you'll hear. Still, it's a dreadful thing to have to face horrors again. You're sure you're alright?'

'Yes, I'm fine. Another strange thing though...' And I told about the bewigged drunk, how he'd appeared at the window, what he'd said.

'Oh shite. Oh fucking hell.'

Duncan went white, whiter than his already pale complexion, white as tripe.

'What?'

'Well... Look I'm just going to tell my tale. You'll see.'

He had several swigs of his porter, then tapped the ash from his pipe, refilled it from his pouch. Once he had it lit, he sat back in his chair, cleared his throat.

'There's something I want to ask of everyone before I begin. The experiences we've all undergone have been strange... unco, like. But though you're prepared for the bizarre, what I'm going to tell you will be hard to believe. There's one aspect, in particular, you'll find tough to credit. I'll explain all at the end, but, please, I'd like you not to ask me anything till I'm finished. I just want to tell it as it happened, get it straight in my head, tell it true. Understand?'

He looked round the group, plumes of pungent pipe smoke seeping from between his clenched teeth.

Everyone gave their assent.

'Thanks. Well, I'd better start. I was born in Glasgow, spent my early childhood in a tenement flat in the Gorbals. My family was right poor, real kirk mice. My father worked in the shipyards, shipbuilding, you know, down on the Clyde, but what he earned wasn't really enough to keep life and limb together...'

A Treatise on Dust

Therefore, to keep his family fed and warm, Duncan's father had to take stale bread from bins behind bakeries and fill his pockets with lumps of clinkered coke from the heaps by the smelting furnaces down at the yards. Then, when Duncan was five, his mother found work as a maidservant, worn-out clothes and shoes were replaced, and, while the work lasted, the larder was well stocked, and coals crackled and spat cheerily in the grate each evening. But it didn't last long; one evening, only five months after she'd got the job, her employer, a lawyer, came across her alone, below stairs. He'd been drinking, was lusty, used her roughly. The next day, when serving breakfast, a long rent in the skirts of her maid's clothes, hastily, badly sewn up, fired the suspicions of the lady of the house, and she was sacked. Duncan's father said he'd kill the lawyer, but he never did anything about it.

After that, things just got worse and worse: the shipbuilding industry grew rapidly, but, as it did, wages fell and conditions deteriorated; the slum landlords raised rents; and there was a run of very cold winters, putting coal at a premium, and several wet summers in a row, leading to poor harvests that pushed up the price of bread.

Then, one day, a few weeks after his ninth birthday, Duncan came home from the laundry where he'd been put to work, found the door forced, left hanging off its hinges. His father, who'd been introduced to the writings of Marx and Engels by students who drank in the whisky shop he patronized, had been agitating fellow workers, advocating a suspension of labour in protest over low pay, long hours. Thugs in the pay of the owners had broken in, made, of the flat, a shambles: Duncan's parents sprawled in pools of slowly clotting blood in the living-room, face down, skulls pulped – a sturdy pick-handle, one end grisly with hair,

184

bone, blood, and matter, split halfway along its length, had been thrown down on the bodies; his older sister, who'd been bathing in their tin tub, had been brutally raped, beaten, then drowned – Duncan gazed down at her once beautiful face, now swollen, livid, through the water, through drifting ribbons of blood and filth; his younger brother, only one year old, lay where he'd been sleeping in his cot, belly opened with a long knife, guts hanging like streamers from the mobile Duncan's father had rigged up from battered pewter scraps and twine – finally Duncan broke, howled.

(Looking about me, I realized the rest were, if harrowed, rapt, also bemused, curious, as I was; well all except Elliot anyhow, who, lapping distractedly at his ale, seemed barely to be listening at all. Now I understood the butcher's strange preamble.)

Duncan joined a gang of homeless street urchins who slept in an abandoned hotel, the Great Eastern, a building whose respectable, foursquare exterior hid a riot of squalid life. They ran errands for petty criminals, snatched purses on Sauchiehall Street and in George Square, sold their bodies. Life was a terrible weight. Most, it crushed. Duncan proved tougher, bore it up. Though it nearly broke him many times and would have in the end.

Then, around the time of his fourteenth birthday, he'd forgotten the exact date, but knew the month he was born in, one of the other urchins gave him a stolen pack of playing cards. He decided to teach himself a few simple tricks. He found he'd the knack for it. After some weeks practicing his sleight of hand, his act was good enough to take onto the streets. He set up his stall, a packing crate draped with an old blanket, on St Enoch Square, next to the colourful tents of the fortune tellers. He rigged games of Blackjack and Find the Lady, fleecing drunks and gullible yokels in town for market day, and performed conjuring tricks for small change. He did well, his income soon enough to allow him to pay rent on a tiny bedsit in Maryhill, and buy a booth and a costume of top hat and tails. By his twenty-third birthday, he was a well-known figure on Glasgow's streets, always surrounded by a throng making fevered and ill-advised bets on the turn of the cards, and was living in relative comfort in newly prosperous Kelvinbridge. He enjoyed many of the pleasures a modicum of wealth could buy, including some that were more or less illicit, opium, gambling, and the rarer types of bawd.

Finally, though, his renown proved his undoing; the gamers began to shun him. Soon he was struggling to pay the bills of his various creditors, some of whom were low types, and was in fear of being dragged into a dark close, having his legs broken, or worse. He realized he'd have to find another way to make money, decided he'd turn his hand to spirit channelling; it was potentially lucrative, and something for which his showmanship and sleight-of-hand skills suited him well. He sold some of his furniture and part of his wardrobe, he was foppish, had a lot of clothes, and put the money to buying the tools of that profession: a spirit cabinet with velvet drapes, which he had specially constructed for him; a mechanism for tilting tables; and a complicated contraption of spring-loaded rods, fishing wire, and hooks, that strapped to the forearm, was concealed by the shirtsleeve till extended, and would, in an ill-lit room, allow him to give the impression certain objects were floating in the air; among sundry other things. He also had a craftsman, who made props for the theatre, fashion for him a cunning Cartesian devil in the form of a goblin bobbing in a carboy of dusky spirit, blinking its sorrowful eyes.

In his spare time, he practiced those skills he knew would be essential, but which he didn't already have: mimicry, ventriloquism, and escapology, this last for use in spirit-cabinet channellings.

The most enjoyable of his preparations was that of choosing a spirit guide. He decided to invoke Jean-Paul Marat, physician turned seditionist and hero of the French Revolution, who'd actually visited Scotland in 1774. Marat's death had been appropriately bizarre and brutal. He'd contracted a virulent skin disease hiding in the sewers of Paris, the worsening torment of which finally forced him, in June 1793, to retire from the Convention, spend his days at home soaking in a medicinal bath, swaddled in bandages steeped in soothing calamine, the only course he had found to bring any relief. Then, on the 13th July, he was visited by a young woman, Charlotte Corday, who claimed to have information regarding the whereabouts of a group of Girondins who'd fled to Normandy. Marat agreed to an audience and Corday was brought to where he lay in his tub. But Corday, who'd Girondin sympathies, and was a little awry, after a fifteen-minute interview drew a kitchen knife from her corset, stabbed Marat in the heart. Duncan spent many hours perfecting the nasal accent he'd employ.

It occurred to him that what could be offered to the senses, especially what could be seen, as sight was generally thought the most trustworthy of them, was more likely to be believed, and that some external manifestation of the supposed ectenic force, as a kind of plasma, would help snag the sceptical. He tried different substances, rejected cheesecloth and butter-muslin as unconvincing, finally settled on having a vial of Scarab Dust, a sweet effervescent powder for children, concealed in his shirt-cuff, and to pour it into his mouth, at a moment when attention was averted, stir up, with his tongue, lots of white froth, slobber it, snort it from his nose. Of course, it couldn't be moulded, form shapes, but in the dark he trusted the sitters' imaginations would do the work. And it would be gone, leaving only a damp sticky trace, by the time the lights went up.

Duncan thought that he was known to many as a card sharp and conjurer would be a hindrance, but belief in spiritualism was then so widespread and fervent in Glasgow society that few questioned whether the prodigies of his séances were real or faked.

He often began sittings by passing around the Cartesian devil in its jar. He told how he'd come across a treatise on the creation of a homunculus in his readings of alchemical works, one that disdained the wonted absurd esoteric recipes: take the root of a mandrake sprung from seed spilled by a man hanged, leave it weltering in a posset of curdled milk, honey, and goat's blood, and a dwarfish living human will finally grow therefrom; take a hollowed-out gourd, fill it with the sperm of a man, sew it into the womb of a horse, and allow the whole to fester, and from this putrefaction will spring a tiny person of incorporeal aspect, which, if fed daily on the Arcanum of human blood, after forty days has passed will gain solidity... No, this formula was far less recondite, and, in its simplicity, had about it an air of verity. So Duncan duly attempted it. That it was indeed a true method could be seen from the strange creature it bore. No, he didn't feel at liberty to divulge it. Were it to come into the hands of the unscrupulous, or irresponsible, the results could be most terrible.

Then, the mood set, Duncan would begin the séance. His rites took one of two forms, depending on the circumstances, his assessment of the credulity of the gathering, and his mood. If he was feeling cautious, he'd make use of the spirit cabinet. He'd request his host bind his hands tightly with rope, then enter the cabinet, have the curtain drawn behind him. Then he could communicate with the spirits hidden from leery peering. He'd free his hands from their bonds and retrieve, from a concealed compartment in the heel of his right shoe, a Jew's harp of unusual design, whose keening, most sitters would take for the cries of the anguished dead. When bolder he'd begin with the spirit cabinet, but then join his sitters at a table, channel in full view. He'd ask all to clasp their neighbours' hands, and, by a wile, a secret trick of mediums, keep one of his free. He could then manipulate his mechanisms, tip the table, snuff candles, scrape chalk down a slate, cause ladies' gloves to dance in the air, and also sprinkle the sherbet into his mouth.

Research was also key to the illusion of communication with the dead. Duncan pored over the obituaries every day, put it about that he'd pay serving staff from the households of Glasgow's great and good for any intimate details of their masters' lives, no matter how insignificant, ensured he knew all about the deceased relatives and friends of those likely to attend one of his séances.

It wasn't long before he'd risen to a position of eminence among Glasgow's mediums, was in great demand. He was shrewd and his fakery, subtle; his choice of spirit guide also played a part in his ascent, for there was something of a fad for rebellion among the aesthetic and decadent rich at that time. His lifestyle was one of flagrant debauchery by then.

But the period of his success was only to last a season. Not even a year passed between his quitting his booth on St Enoch Square and the last séance he conducted. It was held at the town house of a woman of noble lineage, a marchioness. This residence was one of a number of stolid buildings of reddish stone that crowned a hill in the city's West End. Before ringing the bell, Duncan stood looking at the prospect from the portico, of Kelvingrove Park and, beyond, the pall of smoke that hung over the Clyde Shipyards. He felt a pang of mingled rage and sorrow.

On being shown through to the dining room by a fawning butler, Duncan found there were twenty guests at the party that evening. Seven had expressed cynicism on the subject of communication with the dead and, on Duncan's arrival, were politely asked, by the marchioness, to absent themselves, go through to the drawing room.

That left thirteen to take part in the channelling. There was the marchioness herself, a plump dowager, who wore a shapeless floral-print dress, had strings of pearls around her neck, and whose sagging face was larded with powder; Douglas

Kilbride, a wealthy aristocrat and fanatical collector of antiquities; Joseph Lister, whose recent innovations in sterile
operating conditions were just then earning him the acclaim of
the medical community; Lady Alicia Hitchman, a young heiress,
whose large brown eyes, set in a face of unparalleled comeliness,
had been the cause of many duels between rivals for her affections; the inscrutable Mr Lodge, whose tales of travels in the Far
East, of encounters with tattooed savages, of bizarre flora and
fauna, man-eating pitcher plants, death worms, hulking apes,
had caused a sensation; Jacob Bridges, a young man who'd been
discovered ten years earlier in the Trossachs by a pig farmer,
apparently feral, gibbering and acting like a wild thing, and who,
having been taken in, tamed, and educated by a prominent
Glaswegian philanthropist, was at that time prized at dinner
parties for his callow, candid observations; Claire Turner, the
socialite, whose wit had snared many men, and whose skeins of
blackmail, though well-known, were too snarled to untangle, and
would provide her with a healthy income into her dotage;
Alexander 'Greek' Thomson, the famous architect, whose
favouring of the classical style had earned him his sobriquet, a
courteous, slightly deaf, elderly gentleman; Heather MacLellan,
widow of a wealthy mine-owner; Allan Pinkerton, the renowned
founder of America's first detective agency, who'd returned to
Glasgow, the city from which he hailed, for a brief sojourn
following the War of the Rebellion, a sullen, taciturn man, who
wore a full unkempt beard; Augustus Kellner, poet and petty
dissident; a man calling himself John Walker, a friend of
Kellner's, who wore a tousled periwig, ill-fitting clothes, and had
an alcoholic's florid skin and bloated features; and Rebecca
Graves, wife of wealthy liberal advocate Herbert Graves, who'd
turned to superstition on the untimely death of her son.

(Upon hearing the description of John Walker, Elliot
inexplicably grinned broadly.)

The séance began in the usual way with a round of introductions, then Duncan began his patter. He explained the spirits' reluctance to manifest themselves in bright light and the dangers of interfering either with himself, after he'd entered his trance, or with any ectoplasmic manifestation. Afterwards, he had one of the servants turn the gas lamps low, requested the group clasp hands. After urging calm, no matter what might take place, he closed his eyes, threw back his head. Ten minutes of tense silence followed, then, at what he judged the right moment, he began moaning, a low lamentation that mutated into half-formed words in English and French. He opened his lids, stared blankly up at the crystal chandelier hanging from the ceiling, began to speak in the accents of his control spirit.

'It seems that in death, as in life, I'm to have no peace. For what purpose have I been called forth today?'

The marchioness answered.

'We wish to speak with the spirits of the dear departed.'

'Is that so? There are a number of souls here who wish to make themselves known.'

'Yes?' Rebecca Graves asked, slightly frantic.

'But why should I offer you salve? Have I ever found an unguent to soothe this infernal itching?'

The persona Duncan had created for his guide was cantankerous; he'd realized pliancy would draw suspicion.

'It would be a great comfort for us to speak with those souls,' Heather MacLellan said, a slight break in her voice.

'Of that, I've no doubt,' Duncan replied.

In a way, he enjoyed these moments of cruelty. His hard childhood had left him with little empathy for the rich, those who'd always enjoyed every privilege, knew nothing of suffering.

'Is there anything we can do for you in return?' the marchioness asked.

This question allowed Duncan to indulge his subversive impulses with impunity.

'I would ask you to pledge to do what you can to improve the plight of the worker. Many have been cozened into exchanging fields for factories, lied to, misled. Though, as farm labourers, they broke their backs tilling and sowing, they were at least their own men, and worked in the health-giving air of the country. Now they have their backs broken for them on the wheels of dark mills, reap none of the fruits of their labours, toil for a pittance in mephitic pits. All whilst the owners cavort with Mammon. Beware the industrialist!

'Beware also your leaders! In the future, wars will not be fought nation against nation for political ends, but waged merely to fill the purses of the arms manufacturers. The poor will be sent to their deaths for naught but greed. Even you, rich as you are, will likely not be spared, for War in the industrial age will no longer be constrained to the battlefield, but will stalk abroad smiting at haphazard. Only the servile scientists will escape the fall of the axe, for they have placed their souls in hock for their lives, have pledged to develop the fell, havocking weapons of which the potentates dream.

'Beware the industrialist, beware your leaders, and give to your poor!'

Augustus Kellner sighed.

'That's good advice.'

'Life is unfair. Get over it or kill yourself,' said Jacob Bridges, in his curiously stilted, lilting intonation.

Putting her hand on the simpleton's shoulder, the marchioness said, gently, 'He's already dead, dear.'

There was shuffling, stifled titters, choked sniggers. Taking advantage, Duncan dredged his tongue with sherbet, swilled it, slavered and snorted froth, groaned. When he again had everyone's attention, he began to speak, 'A spirit demands to communicate with the company. A young man. With a birthmark on his upper-arm. Form of a cross.'

'Lucas, is that you?' Rebecca Graves asked, sobbing pitiably.

Duncan altered his voice, began to speak with an adolescent boy's cadences.

'Yes, Mother.'

'Oh, son, son. I miss you so much.'

'I miss you too, Mother. Are you well?'

'Oh, Lucas, I wish that I weren't. I wish I could soon be joining you.'

'You mustn't say things like that. We'll be together when God wills it.'

'My son, how are you?'

'Things here are wonderful, Mother. So many interesting people to talk to, no more pain. Do you remember those terrible headaches I used to have?'

'Yes, of course, my darling. Are they gone?'

'Completely, it's such a relief.'

'I'm so, so glad. Have you seen your grandmother?'

Here Duncan began to tip the table violently, then said, in his Marat voice, 'The young man has left us now. But there are other souls crowding in.'

Rebecca Graves wept, hunched over the table.

The séance went on and Duncan 'channelled' several more spirits: a former suitor of Lady Alicia Hitchman, killed in a duel; Charles MacLellan, Heather's plutocrat husband; Douglas Kilbride's former butler, but recently dead of consumption; and twin girls, victims of brutal murder, who were fabrications Duncan invoked to lend credence. When he felt it was time to end, he caused the tablecloth to float into the air with one of his devices, screamed, sat upright in his chair, cried out for the lamps to be turned up.

The participants then filed through to the drawing room, redolent of coffee, vintage port, fragrant cigars, joined the sceptics. A discussion about spiritualism and the occult was struck up. After an hour or so, Walker, by then very drunk, approached Duncan, perched on the arm of his chair, raised a glass, looked about the room, and proposed a toast to the medium. The other guests joined him in it. Then he leaned close, whispered conspiratorially, 'Impressive stuff, I must say. You had them eating out of your hand.'

Duncan's rejoinder was weak, 'It's the spirit-world that deserves the credit. I'm merely a conduit.'

'Don't worry, I don't intend to expose you. It's an artful hoax and you have my admiration. Besides, deep down almost everyone knows spiritualism's just flim-flam. They're just so desperate to believe. You're aiding them really, solacing them in their grief.'

Duncan snorted.

'No, I really believe that,' the strange Walker said.

'Well?'

'I was only wondering whether you'd be interested to see real evidence of the eldritch, proof there truly are more things in Heaven and Earth, so to speak.'

'What are you talking about?'

'And if the prospect of having the scales plucked from your eyes does not strike you as its own reward, I've also discovered wealth for the taking. If you're curious, meet me tomorrow at midnight, outside the main entrance to the Necropolis.'

Before Duncan could ask any further questions of the rum Walker, the marchioness interrupted their murmured conversation, 'Mister Walker, you appear to be monopolizing our guest. I'm sure everybody would like the opportunity to quiz him about his extraordinary gift.'

The Necropolis. Though conceived as a tribute to the city's esteemed dead, it had, by that time, less than half a century after its inauguration, fallen into neglect; its grounds were strewn with empty liquor bottles and encroached upon by slum dwellings, its monuments were graffiti-scarred; it had, in ignorance, been laid out on a cankered drumlin, in darker times the site of a fane consecrated to dire rites, was blighted.

Duncan, unknowing, was fond of the boneyard's silence, thinking it peaceful, not dread; he'd visited it often during the time he'd been living in filth in the Great Eastern Hotel and knew many of the tales of those buried there. From where he waited, at the Necropolis's wrought-iron main gates, Duncan could see the hotel to the south; lambent orange and red, lit from within by fires, it seemed a rough-hewn jack-o'-lantern.

The night was cold, and the sky, clear, though smog roiled in the streets and fog draped the cemetery. Elevated above the shroud by the column it stood on, the dour statue of John Knox, a leader of the Protestant Revolution, was silhouetted against a sickle moon; the clergyman hectored the city beneath with a sermon whose hard lessons were illustrated by passages drawn from the Bible he held in his hand.

The appointed hour passed and there was no sign of the strange Walker. Duncan began pacing back and forth. To the north, Glasgow Cathedral loured, its stonework soot blackened. Once, three years before, he'd gone inside, descended the stairs to the lower church, to the tomb dedicated to Saint Kentigern, also known as Mungo, founder of Glasgow. There he'd read a plaque which gave an account of one of Mungo's famous miracles; at the time, he'd been teaching himself his letters and had taken all opportunities to practice. The text on the panel told how an adulterous queen, Longoureth, presented to a young lover a ring given to her by her husband, King Rhydderch Hael. The king had been told about the affair by a servant, but trusted in his wife's fidelity. Not long after, though, he saw the band on the lover's finger and was consumed with jealousy. He conceived a plot to force his wife to own to her faithlessness. On a hunting trip with his rival, he got the younger man drunk, took the ring from his finger, threw it in the Clyde. Then, on his return, he demanded his wife present the ring to him, and, when she failed to do so, publicly denounced her, locked her up. But, while imprisoned, Longoureth managed to persuade one of her warders, a man smitten, to get a message to Bishop Mungo, begging shriving and aid. The man of God directed the besotted guard to go fishing in the Clyde and return with his first catch. When the warder reeled in his line, there was a sleek pink-bellied salmon flapping on the end of it. Mungo slit this fish open from gills to gut, found, in its stomach, the missing ring. The warder took it back to Longoureth and received who knows what reward for his pains (the account maintained decorous silence on this point). The queen then presented the ring to her husband, who had no choice but to publicly forgive her, pay penance for his accusation. Reading about it, Duncan had been struck by how easily Kentigern's 'miracle' could have been accomplished by deceit and sleight of hand.

Duncan had been waiting some time when Walker came skipping down the road, out of the sallow smother, dressed in motley, carrying a canvas bag, and grinning obscenely, his periwig askew.

'So glad you've come,' he slurred.

The man was a soused buffoon; there were no riches to be had, no revelations; Duncan wondered why he'd come.

'Sorry. A mistake. Think I'd better leave.'

'Nonsense. Don't get chicken-hearted on me. You probably just need a drink.'

Walker proffered a hip-flask, solid silver, ornate chasing, an antique, probably worth quite a bit. Shrugging, Duncan took it, sniffed its contents. Cognac, good quality. He tilted his head back, took a swig, savoured it before swallowing.

'So, will you come with me?' Walker asked.

Duncan shrugged.

'You said there were riches. Proof of the strange.'

'Beneath the knoll,' Walker gestured behind him. 'Do you know about the catacombs?'

'I know plans were made, but abandoned. It was unsafe or

so?'

'My dear sir, don't believe all you're told. Those plans were carried out. The place is riddled. As for unsafe, well...'

Walker scratched his scalp under his wig with long filthy nails, then went on.

'When the Necropolis was first opened there were entrances all over. But they were sealed up, that untruth you've heard put about, and that was that. But I've been down there.'

'What's it like?'

'There are tunnels, vaults filled with treasures. You see, before the catacombs were closed, a number of the great and good of the city of that time were buried there, some inhumed amid opulence, crypts crammed with luxuries, for all the world like Pharaohs, as if the pull of pagan rites was too strong at the last, and they abandoned religious scruples.'

He took out the hip flask again, had another pull from it.

'This is something I found down there. There's lots of other loot like it. Some of it's too unwieldy for me to carry alone and it's all fairly deep underground. The upper levels have already been plundered. But together we could make a good haul.'

Duncan nodded.

'Right.' It sounded unlikely, but perhaps there was something in it. 'What about this preternatural stuff?'

'Well... I must warn you, the place has a dread atmosphere, and strange things are said to have happened there. I've seen things too.'

'Oh, I'm not afraid of boggarts, or anything of that sort.'

'No. You're a man of reason,' Walker said, a mite sardonic. 'Good. But, still, I feel I must tell you the stories. It'd be on my conscience otherwise.'

He smirked.

'Fine. Get on with it then.'

'Of course.'

Walker doffed his periwig. Duncan glimpsed scabs, boils,

before it was slapped back again.

'So, burial in the catacombs proved very popular with nobs in the years after the Necropolis opened, even for many who'd also monuments or mausolea commissioned for the graveyard itself. The vaults were all soon taken, and a decision was made to dig out more. Miners, working to this purpose, hacking away with picks by oil lamp, broke through into some primeval warren. A crew of six was sent down to explore it. Only one was ever seen again, found several days later in the cellar of a house some miles distant, naked, gibbering, hair turned white as new-fallen snow. No sign of how he got there. The foreman, fearful of losing labour, had him committed to a lunatic asylum, put about the lie the others of the detail had blundered into a pit. But, the miners were anyway wary and the olden ways were blocked off.'

Walker paused, grimaced, before continuing.

'He's still there, that man, in the madhouse, still deranged. I've visited him. Feral, now very old, cowering, filthy, in the corner of his cell, whimpering, shrieking. His flesh is all over cankered.

'Anyhow, the works continued, but were plagued. Knockers tormented labourers, moved props. Strange howls and scrab-blings were heard, and lamps were, of a sudden, extinguished where all was still and the air, good. Then there was a cave-in. Thirty-seven men killed. The tunnels were abandoned altogether after that.

'These incidents have been forgotten by all, save a few with long memories, grey hair, wrinkled, sagging skin. Some of those grizzled ancients insist the tunnels broken into weren't delved by nature, but terrible elder beings, were outerlying passages of the regions of Agartha, those primeval borings said to riddle this spinning husk.

'I don't know what I believe about this myself, but I've heard scuffling and muttering down there, felt, at times, stalked. And I've *seen* things too.'

Walker stared at Duncan, eyes wide.

'Pah!' Duncan scoffed. 'If weird things do exist down there, I'd like to see them. But I don't believe it.'

'As you will. Still, I wanted to assuage my scruples, apprise you we may be in danger. I see you're a brave man, not to be discouraged, and esteem it nonsense, in any case. But, anyway, here is your opportunity to wash your hands of the venture.'

Walker folded his arms across his chest, regarded Duncan sly.

It was chill. Duncan rubbed his hands together.

Walker was a sot. If there were any riches to be found, it would be easy enough to cheat him of his share, perhaps even without violence.

'No, no. I'm undeterred.'

Walker grinned.

'Good. Follow me.'

He turned, and, producing a key, unlocked the Necropolis gates, went through, lurched away. Duncan followed, close on his heels. The two men went along a cobbled path, crossed the Bridge of Sighs, a bridge of lichen-starred masonry spanning a stream, the Molendinar Burn, that was, that night, in spate, seethed. On reaching the far side, Duncan looked up at the Necropolis knoll. The graveyard's trees had shed their leaves, and a drab mulch lay thick on the ground. But, as it had been wet, the place was still green, overgrown with weeds, moss, ivy, bramble, nettle.

Taking a track that climbed the hillside obliquely, the two men first passed, on their right, a squat, ugly monument commemorating the life of the physicist William Thomson, then, a little further on, a sculpture of Lieutenant-Colonel Alexander Hope Pattison, in military uniform and cloak. The effigy's right arm had been broken off at shoulder and wrist, and the severed hand nestled grotesquely in its fob pocket. Nearby was the cenotaph of the Lieutenant-Colonel's brother, the anatomist Granville Sharp Pattison. He was a rogue, to scandal and trouble what raw meat is to blowflies; he kept a loaded brace of antique dragoons' pistols on his desk always. In his youth, he'd consorted with resurrection men, but, unlike other surgeons forced to rely on the illicit trade in cadavers, had been quite brazen about it, and was finally indicted for body-snatching, though a 'not-proven' verdict was recorded. Then, in 1816, he was forced to flee to the US after an affair with the wife of a colleague became public. He lived dissolute in Philadelphia a few months, before moving to Baltimore, where he was known for toping and brawling. In 1822, he returned to Britain to take up a post at London University, but his teaching was so poor, indignant students rioted in his lectures, and he was sacked. After this, he left Albion, never to return, sailed back across the Atlantic and, after a time living in a doss house in Atlantic City, playing the pipes on the boardwalk for small change, his fortunes were revived when a former colleague spotted him and found him work at a university in New York. There he lived out his final years, an anatomy lecturer, known and beloved for his flamboyance.

Bearing left after they'd passed by the anatomist's cenotaph, Duncan and Walker trudged up a miry path, passing an ancient oak – bark scarred by the pocket-knives of young lovers – and rows of monuments – obelisks, Celtic crosses, draped urns. When they crested the hill, Walker turned, went over to a low parapet, looked down on the city sprawling beneath. Duncan crossed to join him. Most folk were abed, but a few lights glimmered here and there, in the less salubrious quarters, Duncan's haunts; he thought of buttocks, beaten livid by his fists, strewn with clusters of bright pox pustules, smiled. Near to where he and Walker stood, gazing out at the prospect, there was a very grand mausoleum, design modelled on a Templar church: the Monteath tomb. Under its porch, a group of drinkers huddled round a bad fire of newspaper and brushwood, passing a bottle of whisky between them. Monteath, born poor, had, after coming of age, joined the East India Company, and, by dint of diligence, risen to the rank of major. But still, his income would have been limited. Yet, when he returned to Glasgow from the subcontinent, he entered the city's high society, a man of great wealth. No one knows quite how the Major came by his fortune, but the story goes that, one day, while watching a Maharajah's procession, he chased after and recovered a stampeding elephant. In a howdah on the animal's back had been a casket of precious stones; Monteath claimed it had been lost, fallen into a river, but, had, in truth, secreted it somewhere to pick up later. Duncan suspected the truth was a mite more sordid.

Walker and Duncan turned away from the prospect, went on. Ahead was an odd monument, silvered by light from the crescent moon, a sculpted likeness of a proscenium arch. It had been erected in honour of renowned theatrical entrepreneur, John Henry Alexander, who suffered a long decline and finally passed after a hocus cry of fire at one of his playhouses kindled a panic and a trample for the exits that led to sixty-five deaths. Duncan knew him best as the pioneer of the Great Gun Trick, a bullet-catching illusion.

As they went by the grim stylite Knox's column, a darting fawn startled them; Duncan sought to curb tremors, Walker giggled. Then they walked on. Beyond the pillar were two sepulchres set a little apart from other monuments. One was squat, plain, had niches on either side of its entrance holding effigies: on the left, the Virgin, cradling the infant Christ, on the right, Mary Magdalene. Peering in, through the iron gate, Duncan saw, but dimly in the gloom, statues of a crowned woman, and, flanking her, two female angels at prayer.

But it was to the other tomb Walker led Duncan, a tomb of Moorish design, octagonal, with a domed roof, the final resting place of early travel writer, William Rae Wilson. Walker took out a key, unlocked the padlock securing the gate, pushed it open. Hinges shrieked. That trope (again). Though Gothic novels had already worn it out, Duncan, who'd not read any, jumped.

Walker giggled again. They went in. Three cartouches adorned the walls inside the mausoleum; they were water-stained, worn, their inscriptions, difficult to decipher, but Duncan could just make out the phrase, 'Thy Saints take pleasure in her stones and favour the dust thereof.'

'What?'

He said it aloud.

Walker turned to him, sneered.

The floor of the tomb was strewn with the leavings of opium eaters and louts: empty vials, empty bottles, lewd scrawls, among them a sketch of Zeus's possession, as a bull, of Europa, that, though crude, had an anatomical fidelity that made Duncan flush, jaded as he was. Sweeping the dross aside, Walker cleared off a trapdoor, then lifted it, let it crash open. A stink rose up. He took an oil lantern from his bag, lit its wick with a match, turned the flame up, held it over the hatch. By its glimmer, Duncan saw a deep shaft sunk into the knoll, rusty iron rungs bolted to the rock. Then Walker spoke, the first words to pass between the two men since they met at the gate.

'We're going to need another snifter. Steady our nerves.'

Duncan gulped down the brandy when it was passed to him. The boneyard at night had unnerved him. And now there was the stench wafting from the hatch. And a low snickering; he thought he could hear a low snickering rising with the fetor. He shook.

'I've changed my mind. I'm not interested in seeing these riches. In fact, I don't believe there are any to be had.'

'Oh, there are.'

'So you say, but...'

Walker seized Duncan's wrist in his bony grasp.

'Are you a coward?' he hissed.

'No.'

The drunk let go, was jovial again.

'Well, in that case...'

He gestured at the pit.

The two men clambered down into the stink and the murk. After a while, they reached the foot of the ladder. Before them was a low dank tunnel. They stumbled on in the half-light, Walker in front, Duncan following. Duncan used his handkerchief to cover his mouth and nose against the high, cloying stench, but still choked. Walker capered, gurned, whistled cracked reels. The passages they took sloped down.

'Where are the treasures? Why are we heading deeper?'

'I told you, the upper levels have already been pillaged.'

It grew warm, close, Duncan began to sweat. He paused to take off his heavy overcoat. As he fumbled with its buttons, Walker, standing a little way ahead, turned, sniggered.

'Lasciate ogne speranza,' he chanted.

Then he cackled, winked, plucked off his periwig, bowed low, pointed to his mangy pate.

'The bones of my skull never fused. Look.'

He prodded with his fingers, dug with dirty talons, peeled back a flap of scalp. There was a gape beneath. A little clear liquid seeped, but there was no blood. Duncan thought he saw maggots squirming in the brainpan, but then Walker stood, put his wig back on.

Duncan gagged.

Walker grinned at him, then opened the lantern, pinched out the flame.

When running his rigged card games, Duncan would sometimes play blindfold, claiming he could still best all-comers. A ruse; the blindfold would be tied by a plant, tied slightly askew, giving Duncan sight of the cards with one eye. Once, though, the plant, drunk, missed his cue, and someone else came up, tied the blindfold, tied it tight. That was a smothering dark, but the dark of the catacombs then was even starker; it was as if it hadn't been the light that had been put out, but Duncan's eyes.

There was no sound. He called out, frantic, began groping his way along the tunnel, not even sure if he was heading up, towards the ladder, or further into the ravelled passageways.

Then, after some time had passed, he saw a faint glow a little way off, made towards it. As he approached, though, it ebbed from him. He stumbled, staggered after it. Soon he was wrapped in a shroud of filmy spiders' webs. Then he struck his head on a jutting rock, laid open his brow. Blood ran into his eyes, stung.

He blundered onto a steep scree, his feet went from under him, and he slid, then dropped, landed hard on dank rock scattered with potsherds. The air knocked from his lungs, he lay there gasping, a landed fish. His ankle hurt; he gently prodded the joint; it was sprained, swelling. He felt round him, crawled about a bit. Then his fingers closed on something; it was cloth, greasy, an oil slicker; he reached into the pockets, turned up a candle stub and a single match. Striking the match against the sole of his boot, he lit the stub.

By the fitful flame, Duncan saw he was at one edge of a vast cavern. The far side and the ceiling were lost to gloom. The near wall was slick grey rock, starred with strange pale fungi. A little distance away, towards the centre of the cave, was what looked like a cromlech, two upright stones supporting a large slab. It wasn't potsherds strewing the floor, but bones, some old, yellowing, others stark white, with scraps of pink meat still clinging. Duncan saw, among them, the skulls of animals, the skulls of cattle, sheep, and swine, one he thought was a large dog's, or possibly a badger's, a stag's, with branching antlers, and what he guessed to be a crocodile's. But there were human skulls too. A great many human skulls.

Not far off was an entrance to a tunnel. Duncan staggered to his feet and hobbled towards it. But didn't get far before the flame went out. He limped on. Then heard a low gurgling close by.

'Who's there?'

There was silence a moment, then the blackness dinned in his ears: a tumult of snarls, gibbers, howls, sobs, yowls, yawps, yatters, yammers, pules, whickers, wails, shrieks, moans, groans...

He sensed lurkers in the dark, put out his hands to fend them off, felt cold yielding slimy flesh, rough scaly hide, matted greasy fur. Retching, he backed away. Then turned and ran, ankle pangs dulled by fear.

All Duncan could ever dig up of that flight were sherds, fragments. His right arm felt dull, leaden, as if touching the vile things had corrupted. There was a low narrow passage, chocked with clay; Duncan had to lie, squirm, kick, fight, dislocated his left wrist. Hordes of black rats. A flooded tunnel, frigid water that chilled his very bones. A fraught painful clamber up a chimney. The half-rotted carcass of some thing that could not, should not be. A rotten rickety plank crossing an abyssal chasm.

Then, much later, he ran out into the open air, from a mausoleum at the foot of Necropolis knoll, almost careering into a granite monument, a memorial to nineteen firemen who died when a blazing whisky bond they were dousing exploded. He was in great pain, his clothes were filthy and tattered.

Sitting calmly on a nearby gravestone, swinging his feet, drinking from his hipflask, was Walker.

'Where did you go?' he asked. Grinned, winked.

Duncan hurled himself at the sot, fists flailing, but he was weak, a wreck. Walker snickered, then struck out; a blow that, despite Walker's scrawny build, was brute, felled Duncan.

The antic sot then hopped down from the headstone, stood over Duncan, seemed to swell, blotted out the sky.

'He can't have entered that place, then,' Walker mused, prodding Duncan in the ribs with his boot. 'No constitution could stand that. Nevertheless, something happened, that much is clear.'

He peered down a moment longer, shrugged, then sauntered away, whistling a jaunty air.

Duncan waited till he'd gone, got unsteadily to his feet, limped off.

Over the next few dread-ridden days, Duncan's arm grew weaker, began to stink. He was forced, finally, to seek the counsel of a medic. The doctor diagnosed necrosis due to some form of blood poisoning, advised the only course was amputation. Duncan found a surgeon to perform the operation, then, following a hasty convalescence, went down one morning, early, to the docks, carrying a small bundle of clothes, and, as a sole memento of his life hitherto, the beautifully crafted glass eye from the Cartesian devil homunculus. He sought a ship sailing for North America that would hire him on, dislimbed though he was, perhaps a vessel needing to cast off urgently, or one engaged in an illicit trade. Fate, that had been so cruel to him, smiled on him that day, for it wasn't long before he found a craft to take him, a tea clipper whose captain was in a great hurry to get under way.

IX

I've been writing in a frenzy, frantic, but with only part of my brain: the rest listens for footfalls, scents for pipesmoke; I wait for the office door to be forced, splinter, the filing cabinet to topple.

A lone blowfly drowsily circles the bulb, on occasion blundering into it, singeing its wings. The light wavers now, dims; the fuel in the generator's reservoir is running low.

We've been without food several days, shared the last of our water yesterday morning. I'm feverish, tremble, my stomach is shrivelled, pangs. But the tribeswoman suffers the worse: she's weak, gaunt, the healthy dusk hue of her skin's faded wan, her dark lips are cracked, her tongue, black and swollen; she lies listless, stretched out on a pallet improvised from our outer clothing – we've stripped off, it's stifling down here. She's not acted as my scrivener for some time now. She's dying, and it's my fault; I'm heartsick. Though, I have to own, part of me envies her; I'd rather die of thirst and hunger than in the dread way I must.

My fate is sure, when it will come is not; my fervent hope is that I'm granted time to finish my narrative, to bring my tale to a meet end, and, to that end, I type fast, as fast as I can without the typebars jamming. But, though it's what I truly wish to tell, I weary of the central strand of my tale for the moment, and, try as I might, can't force myself to go on with it. So, for respite, of a kind, I'll now relate the tribeswoman's and my exploration of the Ark's hold, after we were first forced below decks. And it will enable you, my reader, to understand our terror, understand why we won't thread those ways without a light source, not even to seek water or food to lessen our sufferings.

If you recall, when the tribeswoman and I found ourselves at the foot of the companion stairs, having sought refuge from the natives' bombardment, I shone my torch about us and we saw we stood at one end of a long narrow corridor. It had walls of riveted steel plate, rubber matting lain on the floor, and a low ceiling made still lower by the ducts, conduits, and bundles of cables that ran along it. The air was stale, but draughts issuing from grilles set at intervals in a duct overhead stirred the dust hanging in the air, set the motes eddying; I guessed the ship's ventilation system had been long dormant, but re-activated by my opening the companion hatch.

We nerved ourselves up, the tribeswoman and I, then set off down the corridor. We soon came to a T-junction. Weary, we decided to pause, rest there a moment, sat down, slumped against the wall. Though I left the torch on, determined we shouldn't doze, we were drowsed by the heat, the stuffiness, and ended up sleeping a short time.

On waking, I found the tribeswoman with her head upon my shoulder, snoring. I roused her. We went on, choosing our direction on a whim.

After a while, turning a corner, I stepped on something yielding, greasy, skidded. A foul smell rose to my nostrils, I gagged. Shining the torch down at my foot, I saw I'd trodden on a mouldy ham hock. I can only assume the vessel's hold sealed when it sank, was sunk, or ran aground, and that this prevented corruption somehow. With the outer air admitted for the first time in millennia, decay had proceeded apace.

The ham had been rank, but going on we became aware of a stench far worse. We thought it a larder, hoped for some dried goods still fit for eating. There was also a low droning.

The stink and noise swelled with each step. Then, rounding a corner, we came on a steel door. I turned the handle, it opened, and I stood on the threshold, shone the torch in. By its beam we could see it *was* a larder, but a larder for maggots. It was a large cabin, chockfilled with moiling, thrumming blowflies, with row on row of bunkbeds, with, in each berth, a rotting, flyblown cadaver.

The sight of all that human carrion thicked our blood. We retched, backed away, turned, fled the way we'd come. Reaching the junction again, we paused, hunched, hands on knees, got our breath back, then pressed on.

After, we wandered the dismal ravelled guts of the freighter a long time, more and more horrored, more and more wretched. Those passageways were grisly with the putrefying dead. Some had apparently succumbed, panicked and agonized, to a fell contagion that swelled the head, made the eyes to bleed. The rest had died of savage violence. Most of the wounds appeared self-inflicted, though were so brutal that was hardly to be believed: in the galley we came across a young woman who'd opened her belly with a long knife, intestines, liver, womb tumbled out, and a man who'd hacked his neck almost through with a cleaver; elsewhere we saw those who'd seemingly smashed their own skulls butting walls. Others were not: we came across a few knots of corpses, folk who'd seeming killed each other in a queasy tangle of orgy and frenzied fray, of lust and bloodlust.

Then we found ourselves in a chamber where weird devices yammered, twittered, snickered, groaned, hissed, yowled, tutted. Some looked misbegotten creatures from the deepest abysses of the oceans, tangled in nets of fine copper wire; others, the glistering entrails of huge beasts set in blocks of amber; others still, granite menhirs or dolmen, graved with arcane runes. The sounds they made had the air of pleas, provocations, insinuations, imprecations, taunts, expressions of annoyance or anguish. We fled this room of machines, ran across an iron gantry suspended high in the air over a monstrous engine, that, beset with bile-green electrical components, bristling with wires and tubing, looked the partially decomposed carcass of some vile behemoth, then went through a vast stowage, where we slowed to a walk, chary lest we knock against one of the piles of crates beetling over our heads and topple it, less because we feared being crushed, than because the idea of those boxes breaking open and revealing their contents was dread.

Finally, as I've written, our torch failing, we discovered this office. And here, many weeks later, we remain, the light of the bulb, flickering, dim and dimming still, and the chirr of the generator that powers it our only palladia against the maddening darkness and silence beyond the door.

X

The aghast hush that fell on the gathering with the last words of Duncan's tale lasted some time, was only broken by the landlord of the Nightingale signalling last orders, tolling a bell. Then William got to his feet, went up to the bar, and returned with a round of malts and an earthenware jug on a tray. When he set Duncan's whisky before him, the butcher downed it at one swallow.

'Cheers,' he said, voice hoarse with the spirit's burn. 'That was kind, I needed that.'

After trickling a dash of water into my Scotch, I sipped it. The peaty savour was a balm. Feeling calmed, I turned to the Scot.

'Duncan,' I asked, 'how old are you?'

'I don't right know how to answer you. You see, I was born more than a century and a half ago, but haven't aged a day since... Well, since *then*.'

He took a long pull on his pipe, frowned.

'Well, in body, anyhow. In spirit I'm as weary as you might suppose.'

William shook his head. 'You swear?'

'Yes,' Duncan said, solemnly. 'I swear.'

'Jesus,' William muttered, then lit a cigarette. His hands shook.

Rashmi turned to the graphic designer. She was grey. 'Can I scrounge a smoke?'

William, smiling wan, passed her the packet. She took out a cigarette. Then he flicked the flint wheel of his lighter, sparked the flame, held it out to her. Once she'd the cigarette alight, she took two long draws, then, turning to Duncan, squinting at him through the smoke rising from her mouth, asked how he'd spent his long life.

He sat forward in his chair, cradling his stump in his left

hand.

'Well,' he began, 'after crossing the Atlantic, I settled in Boston. At first it was hard, for, with only one arm, I couldn't any longer perform sleight-of-hand magic, or run rigged card games, and no one would give me a job, for I'd no particular skills and was also, of course, unfitted for manual trades. I had to rely on charity for some weeks, slept rough. But I was lucky in the end, found employment in a shambles, and a bed in its workers' bunkhouse, taken pity on by the head slaughterman. I worked there several years. During that time, I learnt about meat.'

Here Duncan paused, made a chopping motion with his hand.

'But, then I started gambling again, got myself badly in the hole to some toughs, and desperate, tried stealing a side of pork to sell on. But I was caught. The slaughterman, in a rage over how I'd repaid his kindness, fired me, threw me out, but also smashed up my knees with a cast-iron killing mallet. It should've been a death sentence, being out on the street with ruined legs, but the broken bones healed weirdly fast. Scrabbling around for scraps to eat, though, I barely noticed.

'After another hard stretch, I was again fortunate, was saved from starving by a grifter who took me on as a shill, to help him work his card-sharping swindle. I was useful to him, for I could teach him the tricks I knew, even though I couldn't perform them myself. What's more, people seemed to take the honesty of a one-armed man for granted. But a couple of years later, after arrest and a spell in a labour camp, I gave that life up.'

William, Rashmi, Jane, and I sat listening closely to Duncan's narrative; Elliot, however, seeming to be paying scant attention, ran his fingers through his hair, stared down at his drink. Something in his manner then was familiar, but I couldn't place it.

'After being released,' Duncan went on, 'I travelled to Colorado, see if I couldn't get myself hired on at a mine. None would have me, though. I then spent some years stravaiging about the Old West, but I hated the relentless brutality of frontier life, eventually headed back east. I wound up in New York. Several terrible years followed. I was bedding down in doorways, beneath railway arches, begging and stealing what I could to keep hunger at bay. But, though I suffered dreadfully, I lived on. I was starting to get an inkling my hardiness was unnatural.'

Duncan paused, gingerly tamped the smouldering tobacco in his pipe with his thumb.

'One night I was set on by a drunken mob. An aged priest found me bleeding in a gutter, took me in, tended me. Before long I made a full recovery. I repaid the minister's kindness by staying with him, aiding him with those tasks he'd grown too weak for. And when he died, a few years later, I took over his ministry. I was happy a while. I knew by then there was definitely something uncanny about me. I didn't age, rarely got sick, injuries healed swift... But I hardly cared. Like I say, I was happy.

'Then I fell in love with one of my flock, a beautiful young woman who returned my affections, and we were married.'

Duncan rubbed his eyes with thumb and forefinger.

'But two years later, she died in childbirth. The baby itself was stillborn. The midwife wouldn't let me see it. She wouldn't tell me why, but I believe it was hideously deformed. I was distraught, spent months alternating long drinking bouts with days sunk in despondency when I'd remain in my bed.

'Then I read a newssheet in a bar, a story about the Klondike Gold Rush, about the hardships of the miners there. A few weeks later, I set out for the Yukon. My plan was to wander those frozen lands, offering succour where I could, preaching and ministering to those in need. I hoped it would help me bury my grief.

'You're probably wondering how, given everything, I'd retained my faith. But remember that, back then, religious conviction was much more widespread. I believed my trials punishment for my former dissipated lifestyle, thought I needed to atone by evangelizing, making myself a vehicle for God's message, thought God had made me undergo the horrors beneath the Necropolis to awaken me to the true faith and the awful things awaiting sinners, and kept me from ageing, made me hardy, so I could better spread his word. I'm ashamed now to recall the things I believed and the pious bollocks I spouted in those days.'

He gave a wry grin.

'I spent some years as an itinerant priest in Alaska and Canada after that. Met many fascinating folks during that time, stampeders, that's what we called gold rush prospectors back then, seeing as how they acted like spooked cattle, Indians, sorry, Native Americans, poets and writers, and rum fellows, as had wayward and cruel habits, who lived as if they were beyond the law's reach, which I suppose they were, man's law anyhow.

'I tried to impress on folk their faith in gold was misplaced, to urge kindness, but few listened, and dejection returned to me. My soul fell again into a pit. And, in the end, I overcame pious scruples, and cast myself into a canyon, a hundred miles or so east of Juneau.

'I struck the walls of the ravine as I fell, tumbled, then thudded down at the bottom. I blacked out. When I came to, I found I couldn't stir. I believe not one of my bones remained unbroken. My head was twisted at an unnatural angle, all I could see were my innards flung in loops on the rock. My belly had burst when I'd hit.'

Duncan paused, supped his beer.

'I lay for two days in that sun-shunned place, in agony the while, as the weird healing of my body took place, as bones knitted, skin healed.'

He shuddered.

'On the afternoon of the first day, I was fair scunnert when my guts slithered fast back inside me. It was repulsive, and a horrid sensation. After, though, I'd reason to be glad it happened so quick. That night a lone coyote came snuffling round. I dread to think what I'd have suffered if it had got its teeth into my entrails!'

Making his hand into a canine maw, Duncan snapped at the air, then grinned.

'When I felt strong enough, I headed for the nearest town, crawling and stumbling. When I reached the place, the name of it escapes me, I holed up in a cheap hotel room for a week. At the end of that time, I was hale once more.'

Raising his hand to his mouth, Duncan blew a fanfare through his fist.

'Step right up,' he said, in a carny barker voice. 'Step right up and witness the amazing, invincible Scotsman! Hurt him and his wounds will heal themselves before your very eyes!'

Duncan paused, drew breath, grew serious once more.

'Lying in that dim hotel room, I thought about Glasgow a lot, pined for my birthplace. When recovered, I returned east to New York, sought a berth on a ship bound for that fair city. I'd money to pay for the trip, I'd panned a bit of gold, so found one fairly swift. That was in 1906. I've stayed in Scotland ever since. Just change my name, job, friends, every few years. Easier to avoid attracting notice than you'd think.'

Duncan then sat back in his chair, took his pipe from his mouth, put it, still smouldering, down in an ashtray.

'Have you ever seen that man Walker again?' I asked.

'On my return to Glasgow, I spent the first few years seeking him out. But I've never seen him again. And I've never been back in the Necropolis. Even to see it from a distance raises a shudder. But that drunk. Here tonight. That's Walker, I'm sure of it.'

Just then, Elliot began to shuddering. I thought, for an instant, he was having a fit, then realized he was juddering with silent mirth. Duncan turned, looked at him, bemused.

'What? What is it?'

Elliot composed himself, wiped his eyes, took up Duncan's briar, smoked it. Duncan went to snatch it from him, but Elliot leaned back out of reach.

'I've always enjoyed a good pipe,' he said. 'Truly one of this world's greatest pleasures.'

Then, turning to the butcher, he smiled fondly, 'Ah, Duncan. You were my first success.'

'What do you mean? And give me back my pipe!'

Duncan reached out again to grab the pipe, but Elliot seized his hand, gripped it. I heard bones crack, Duncan yowled, then Elliot loosed his hold. Duncan drew back his hand, put it in the pit of his stump. I saw it was mangled, fingers crooked.

Casting a glance about to see if anyone had, hearing Duncan's howl, looked over, I saw that, though there were still a few drinkers in the public bar, we were alone in the saloon; even the rowdy birthday party had moved on.

Duncan puled.

'Hush, you idiot,' Elliot said. 'Listen. It's no easy matter to lure someone over the border. The border between this world and that black place. Most see only the way ahead, not what lies off to the side, can't see it, stay in their ruts. And, should someone whose blinkers are off be found, it's then easy to entice them too far from the road, to where they can't return from. If some part of them is already pledged to darkness they will be lost. Others will, of course, die of fright or lose their minds. It's been my experience that very few can see those dread hinterlands and return not too violently altered.'

We sat fraught, yet quiet, listening; awaiting a terrible revelation, but with no idea what it might prove to be.

'You're a curious incurious lot,' Elliot jested, fleering. 'Though actually, of course, in your case,' he gestured at me with the pipe's stem, 'inquisitiveness *was* your undoing. The rest of you were just unlucky, I set toils, drove you into them. Ah, but I'm forgetting you, Duncan. Avarice was your downfall. Anyway, how to goad you all now? I know.'

Elliot set down the pipe, began moaning. His face moiled, then his features became those of the old man who warned me about wolves that night in the Saracens Head, spoke to me again by Smithfields Market. Flesh boiled again, and he became a good-looking young man with a harelip. Then a hoary ancient, cheeks and forehead begrimed, matted beard, clouded, sightless eyes; an elderly woman, fleshy, piggy face, haughty air; and an old man, kindly air, red-raw skin stretched tight over his skull, lank thinning grey hair, dandruff. Then the pulp weltered a last time, and Elliot sat before us again, though a shade altered, eyes set deeper, baleful, teeth sharper, ears sticking out more, lower jaw lengthened, prognathous, complexion wan, now the flat grey hue of spoilt fish.

Jane opened her mouth to scream, but no sound came from her throat. The rest of us sat listless.

Elliot went on, tone veering between spite, glee, and bragging.

'Now I've your attention, I'll introduce myself. For a long time I thought I was a scion of a diresome house. Maybe. Or perhaps was a scholar who, prodigiously learned, but in worldly things callow, made a rash deal with an emissary of Satan. Or perchance was not cozened into that pact, but submitted to it voluntarily, was a diabolist who chanted some incantation from an age-yellowed grimoire while standing within a pentagram chalked on the floor. Or it was conceivable, I supposed that I was entirely innocent, that I was what I was simply because the hour of my birth had seen a powerful celestial conjunction. At other times I wondered if I wasn't the victim, willing or not, of dark forces, but was cursed by good for evil actions. That maybe I was even he who was the first farmer and the first murderer, who was execrated, condemned to wander the Earth till fire comes to cure it, calcine its clods.'

Here Jane whimpered.

'He who,' Elliot went on, taking no notice of her, 'should he attempt to cultivate the land again, will find his tillage turns fertile soil to fruitless dust, and whom no man may kill on pain of suffering vengeance seven times over. Yes, I thought that quite feasible, though, against it, there is no trace of a mark on me, not a mole, birthmark, or liver-spot whose shape could be construed as significant. Since that time, in any case, I've learned of another possible reason for my condition, so perhaps none of those surmises were correct. In any case, it's hardly important.'

Elliot stopped to take a breath, and William flicked a lit cigarette at his face. With his tongue, now long, thin, and darting, Elliot caught the cigarette midair, pulled it back to his lips, smoked it to the filter in one long draw. The ash did not drop, but hung, a withered finger. Then Elliot swallowed the butt and the burnt tobacco, before resuming speaking as if nothing had happened, the strange and now solemn accents of his voice rolling slowly on his auditors' ears like a peal of distant thunder. William, his hand trembling, reached into his pack for another cigarette.

'What *is* important is that, by curse, ritual, or chance, I have life without cease. It's a terrible anguish, for all I may have received it as a sought-after boon, something no ordinary man, oppressed by the certainty of death, could understand. For me, it'd be rapture to know the rattle in the throat that heralds the end.

'Of course, at first I might well have revelled in my immortality. I can recall that time only murkily, for it is many ages ago, but I seem to remember I devoted myself then to rare evil, unthinkable debauchery, dread cruelty. Thinking on that, maybe it's most likely, after all, I'm a son of Perdition, granted immortality by some Potentate of Shadow in exchange for a pledge to go through the world corrupting and bringing low. If, however, that is the case, the Enemy of Souls has long since lost interest in my deeds. It's possible, anyway, that my malevolence was born merely of perversity.

'How long I pursued unspeakable paths I can't say, but at some point, perhaps as an act of rebellion, but more probably simply bored of misdeeds, I turned to benevolence. This also, I discovered, didn't satisfy my yearning for sensation, for just as I hadn't felt remorse, or the pricks of conscience, I knew no pleasure in kindness. I knew my term would be endless and felt any deed of mine, good or ill, was as nothing in the balance sheet of eternal life, that, just as in games of chance the outcomes tend toward equilibrium, so my actions, foul or fair, were cancelled out by the conduct of past and future selves.

'I began seeking other diversions to palliate the appalling tedium of life everlasting. At some time during the years of relative ignorance in Europe following the Classical period, I learnt, from an ancient forbidden book, of places where this world abuts another, one dark and uncanny. The writer of that weird volume wrote of certain unfortunates, of whom he'd heard tell, who'd strayed across the threshold at one of the liminal sites, wandered awful tracts lost and forlorn for years before finding their way back to the mundane sphere once more. Many of those men were maddened, those who remained sane told of terrors beyond imagining.

'I wanted badly to gain entry to that strange realm. After searching for many decades, I found a way in. It's a dread place. One of the most disconcerting things about it is that it's never the same twice, sometimes lurid, grotesque, sometimes seemingly ordinary, but seething with menace. It's known by many names on this side of the veil, several of which will be familiar to you. I've only ever heard its denizens use but one word for it, a drawn-out guttural sound no human throat could give issue to. I call it Tartarus. You,' he then glared at each of us in turn, 'have but glimpsed its horrors. I abhor it, but have been compelled by some twisted part of me that seeks sensation and worse, to spend longer and longer there with each passing year. For at least three centuries now, I've spent more time in its umbral regions than in this world of light. And spending so much time down there has given me powers, powers that have alleviated some of my boredom.'

Elliot took up his pint, drained it, ate the dimpled glass jug it had been served in, crunching and swallowing, grinning the while. He squinted, winced, retched, then brought up and took from his mouth a small glass sculpture, very lifelike, very obscene, of William and Rashmi naked, fucking, set it down on the table, winked at William.

Rashmi looked shocked; William flushed, turned his head away.

Elliot swept the sculpture to the floor, where it smashed, then went on.

'When the Enlightenment was a waxing glimmer on the horizon, I made a strange discovery. I was in southern Ireland, and, having grown bored of the tiresome attentions of a young woman I'd seduced, brought to ruin, I sought to escape her by going to a Tartarean pit I knew of, which lay concealed beneath the cellars of an ancient and evil house situated in the midst of a barren moor about forty miles west of Ardrahan, and flinging myself in. But the girl followed and leapt in after me. We fell a long time, then our falls were broken by a flabby welter of bodies. Once my eyes had adjusted to the gloom, I saw we were in cavern filled with degenerate creatures, pallid, purblind, stinking, shit-streaked, and swinish, if with lingering, debased, loathsome, humanity. These beasts tussled, fornicated, gorged on their weak and dead in eerie silence, save the odd low chortle. I fought free, clambered up on to a ledge above the moil, sat watching, grinning, the girl's terror, her struggles; the vermin clutched, pawed at her, tore her garments, slobbered over her, and worse, so much worse, so much filth. She shrieked, pleaded at first, then mewled, and finally lay silent, still, staring. Then she managed to free herself, ran wailing. I chased after her, into a pitchy warren, and, though she was fear fleet, laid hold of her, knocked her out, carried her back to the everyday realm. It was too late, what she'd seen, undergone, had taken her sanity, and when she came to, she raved. I abandoned her.

'Then, on returning to that country, over a hundred years later, I heard tell of a bugbear, a legend, a banshee haunting a bleak tract of moorland, whose appearance was said to be an omen of death. The stories told she was ageless, could not be killed, had survived a close-range blast from a blunderbuss loaded with rusty nails, fragments of sheep bone, gravel; being run through by a pitchfork; being beaten senseless and cast into a flooded turlough. Hearing these rumours, I realized it was the same girl, that something had made her deathless, as I was. I'd never heard of such a thing before, but it seemed clear it was entering Tartarus that had done it. Which, of course, made me ponder my own state again…

'Anyhow, I got it into my head to try whether I could do what others had apparently failed to, bring death to her. I sought her out. She was living in a cave, in a tor, out on the barren heath. She was feral, naked, hair all tangled and wild. And she'd not aged. I caught her and throttled her, but she wouldn't die. I unsheathed the dirk I always carried about with me in those times, gored her with it, but, though blood welled, she lived on.'

Elliot sighed, puffed on the pipe, ran a hand through his hair.

'Well, irked, I again leapt into the pit, roamed Tartarus for several years looking for something to end that unnatural life. Many times I was tempted to give up, but persevered, knowing the laws of the place were such that, with intentions black as mine, I'd turn up the thing I was after in the end.

'And this proved true. I found it in a fane consecrated to dire rites. It lay between two black candles set in bone holders, on a stone altar draped with a blood-steeped cloth. A knife, short blade, plain wooden handle. Quite ordinary looking, but I knew straight away it was what I'd been seeking.

'Armed with this knife, I went back to the surface world, tracked down the young woman, ran her to ground, tried it on her. She died without a whimper, and my frustration was allayed.

'I pondered these events a long time. It seemed to me they hinted at a way to alleviate my torment, the immortality that dragged, left me listless. I've tried the knife on myself, by the way, but it brought no end, only pain. I'm not sure why.

'Revelation came one night after I'd been on a drunk in London, was lying on the banks of the Thames, swigging from a liquor bottle. I had, by then, by trial and error, ascertained that entering Tartarus ignites immortality in ordinary folk. Why, though, I've no idea. Perhaps some smouldering talisman is kindled to flame by its hideous atmosphere. But it had also, in all my trials, driven the poor unfortunate mad. It seemed it was impossible to witness the full horrors of that place without being crazed. But it occurred to me then that, were I able to trick people into following me into Tartarus, but prevent them from experiencing its true terrors, avoid maddening them, I'd have prey who couldn't die save by my hand, who, able to feel fear, would flee me, and whom I could pass the time hunting.'

Elliot peered about at us. Then sneered, knocked the ash and dottle from the briar, turned to Duncan.

'Baccy,' he demanded, holding out his hand.

Scowling, Duncan handed over his pouch, and Elliot set to refilling the pipe again. Once he'd done so, he sat back in his chair, lit a match, held the flame to the pipe's bowl, puffed till the tobacco was glowing red, giving off a drab fug. No one else moved; we sat aghast and quaking.

'As I've hinted,' Elliot went on, 'my first attempts to create such specimens were failures, sometimes striking ones. Indeed, one of my earliest botches has passed into legend. I spent most of 1680 living in Amsterdam, passed much of my time in drunkenness in squalid places frequented by sailors. One autumn day, I was drinking grog with an old tar when our talk turned to the matter of a ship, a brigantine, which had drawn my notice because it had been languishing in dock since the spring. My acquaintance explained that its captain, a Hendrik Van der Decken, was having trouble hiring on hands. According to gossip, on his last trip out, he'd claimed before the whole crew he'd rather be damned for all eternity, beat about the seas till the Last Judgement, than seek a safe harbour in a storm. The salts of Amsterdam town, a superstitious lot, were chary of signing on with a skipper who'd tempted fortune so.

'Van der Decken's rash declaration seemed to me a sign. I managed to get myself taken on as helmsman of the vessel, waited in Amsterdam till it had secured a full complement of crew, many of them desperate men. We got underway, I bided my time. Till, one fateful night during a tempest, when we drew near a fearsome whirlpool I knew of, off the Cape of Good Hope, which sucked vessels down into a sunless sea where kraken spawned. I steered for it. I hoped to be able to have the ship gyre on the brink of the loathsome pit without being swallowed, and awaken immortality in the sailors without exposing them to maddening horrors. But I was thwarted by the power of the maelstrom, and, though the brigantine survived intact, it was drawn down into that dread maw, and, by the time the vortex abated, spat us out, the captain and crew had seen things no men were ever meant to see, and were terror-crazed and useless to me. Without the wits to fly from pain or extinction, they'd have made poor quarries. Though they did afford me some entertainment. In their frantic state they were very suggestible, and I amused myself by, inspired by Van der Decken's foolhardy boast, instilling in them a peculiar horror of landfall.

'After I quit them, they sailed haphazard over the oceans for nearly a century, keeping to the open sea, afeared to approach any coastline. But then, tiring of the fables that had sprung up about them, irked by their renown, which far exceeded mine, though I courted infamy, I ended their miserable existences, sent their corpses, and their rotting vessel, to the bottom of the sea.'

Elliot drew musingly on the pipe several times, holding the smoke in his mouth, savouring it, before allowing it to spill from his lips. No one spoke. Till then, terrified and enthralled, I'd kept my eyes fixed on him, but at that moment I cast a glance round the Nightingale, saw that all was in darkness save our table, around which a greenish nimbus roiled. The landlord must have turfed out the other patrons, shut up for the night, and gone to bed; Elliot must have, by some arcane means, hid and muffled us.

'I've never known true infamy,' Elliot went on, 'though I've craved it from time to time. But some of those I've tried to make prey of over the years have been artists and writers who've gone on to depict the traumas I inflicted on them, if obliquely. Some of these works have become well-known, so I can claim to have inspired some notorious art. There was a Spanish painter, who saw Tartarus, and was there set upon by grotesquely outsized carrion birds. But he only saw that dark place briefly, did not become deathless, though the experience did leave him deaf. His attraction to dark and violent subjects ever after is testimony that the experience affected him deeply. Another of my victims was an English Romantic who could not see clearly enough to follow me, as his sight was bleared by swigs of nepenthes. Then there was an Irish priest, who, of a suspicious cast of mind, was wary of me, resisted my lures, though he was very poor, and I offered great riches. An American writer, a sot, whom, in the guise of a man named Reynolds, I succeeded in tempting, was too fuddled to tread in my steps, though he wished to and I believe my grubs wormed into his heart. A prolific French novelist, being of a scientific bent, was inquisitive and followed me, but was also supremely rational and chased away, in his mind, with false light, the shadows I showed him, and thereby avoided Tartarus's maw. Then there was an English poet, a Victorian, who, sensible and worldly, if nervy, dismissed his vision of Tartarus as a dream, though he wrote some remarkable verses on it. Another poet, another Frenchman, had already too much darkness in him, eating away at his soul, just as syphilis was eating away at his brain, and would, had I allowed him to accompany me as he desired, have been corrupted utterly, forever passed over to the other side. And there was yet another French poet, a prodigy, a native of Uruguay, who exalted me in bizarre lays, who, frustratingly, died young, before I could drag him down into dark hinterlands. That was in Paris, during the siege, and in that turbulent time, I also failed with another, this one a Belgian poet, who wrote, fittingly, under the pseudonym Hendrick Van der Decken. On the strength of his bizarre, cruel collection, *Cette terre clinkerisée*, he is considered, by the few who know it, one of the most imaginative and radical of the decadents. It is though, in truth, a relatively unembellished account of things I showed him. But immortality did not fasten upon him, perhaps because he was dull in many ways. He too died during the siege.

'One of the more irksome failures was my attempt to make a quarry of another American writer of strange tales, also a journalist, and a sardonic and brilliant wit. He laughed in my face, got away. But I'd my revenge, some years later, in Mexico. And then there was another Englishman, this one a mariner, who I nearly managed to drag into the pit on some lonesome isle in the South Pacific, but, of an imposing build, burly, if short, and trained in martial arts, he fought me off, the only person ever to have done so. He later wrote weird tales that made veiled allusion to what I put him through. He died in the Great War. Then came a London-based painter, who was hailed as an illustrator of genius in his youth, but who lived out his life in obscurity, in dank south-London basements, trying through various esoteric rituals to recreate that place I took him to in his youth. Mad, that one, so mad it would seem Tartarus spurned him. The dark portal I dragged him through can be found in a Smithfields back alley. It takes the form of a cunt.'

Elliot sighed, leaned back, and blew out a cloud of smoke. It hung weirdly in the air, and he sculpted it, using the pipe's stem, into the shape of a vulva. Then wafted it into the shadows.

'And there was a man, a stockbroker, born in Glasgow, but residing in Argentina, best remembered now as a translator of Latin American epics, but who also, after I'd shown him dread things, wrote two works of bleak horror. He found humankind dismaying enough, so Tartarus was no particular novelty to his blasted vision. There was another British expatriate, a headstrong Englishwoman who lived most of her life in Central America. I tormented her in a Madrid asylum, but, though the experience harrowed her at the time, her strength and anarchic intellect allowed her to transmute it into wonderful and strange art and literature. Less resilient was the American author who I next attempted to make quarry. Afterwards she suffered neuroses and depression, aggravated her mercurial personality with an addiction to prescription amphetamines, lived badly, and died young, though not without writing some remarkable fictions, which, though largely depicting the mundane, are suffused with Tartarean atmosphere. I believe it was her mix of frailty and brilliance that prevented the place from getting its hooks into her. Then there was another Englishman. He was inspecting a stretch of the Grand Union Canal, the preservation of Britain's waterways was his great cause, when I dragged him down to Tartarus through an opening beneath an ancient and terrible willow tree. He was cynical, wry, and shrugged off its horrors, but, ever after, wrote restrained, muted, but deeply strange tales. And there's one last, an American, still alive, whose fictions are the stuff of nightmares. The things I put him through in an abandoned Detroit tenement were sore vile and dread, but didn't seem to grip him. His outlook was altogether too bleak already.'[10]

Elliot paused scratched his nape.

'With these men and women, my efforts were in vain. And, though they were all in some way marked by the torments I put them through, they survived, returned to the mundane realm, lived a semblance of a life. More often, I've failed because I've been unable to shield my victims from deranging sights, and they've became helplessly frenzied, and either run raging deeper into the weird realm, and been lost forever, or returned from what they've seen, heard, and experienced, with bloodshot eyes, pierced eardrums, and feeble minds, as the Irish lass and the Dutch mariners did. Of these latter wretches most I've destroyed, for, though hunting down and murdering rank idiots is pretty humdrum, it offers a visceral thrill. Jane,' he said, turning to the author, and grinning hideously, baring his teeth, 'your husband is one of the former type, who, deranged, will roam Tartarean regions till the end of days. I now believe darkness already had its hooks in him before I got to him, some disturbing tomes he read in his youth. And,' he continued, addressing me, 'your friend Colin was one of the latter. I made away with him when I thought he might threaten my plans for you. I tortured him horribly, before stabbing him, throwing him off that cliff.'

I beat my palm with my fist. Jane slumped with her head on the table.

'Oh, and that bewigged maniac is another of those who returned, but too damaged, too crazed. I let him live because he has some moments of lucidity during which I can get him to aid me, but there's no point hunting him, he worships me, wouldn't run.

'I've failed many times. But only once have I been found out. Just recently, about a year ago, I hauled a minor horror writer into Tartarus through a hole in the floor of the toilets of a derelict boarded-up pub on Glasgow's South Side. He remained sane, but also, I'm sure, had that talisman awoken in him. But somehow, I can't work it out, he discovered what was planned for him, for you all, and also found out how to enter Tartarus, went in there of his own will, just a few days ago. I believe he hopes to thwart me, perhaps find a weapon to strike at me with when I come for him. But he's not come back out again. My guess is, this time, he's lost down there.[11]

'As I say, I've failed many times. But, with you,' he continued, stabbing a gnarled forefinger at each of us in turn, 'my success has been complete. You're not my only triumphs, though. Over the years I've created many other immortals of sound mind, men and women from all over this dismal orb. But you're the first to see me as I really am, the first to hear my history. I hope for more like gatherings, so I can strike terror into the hearts of all my victims, all those I've lured or dragged into Tartarus, and who've returned still able to fear.'

(I should write here, I've never, as far as I know, encountered any of Elliot's other sane victims, save those in the pub that night. Neither have I entered that awful otherworld again, never managed it on my own, though I've spent many centuries seeking out and poring over its dark lore. I can't understand why not, I've studied the rituals, know where portals are to be found. Unless it's that, terrified of what I might find there, I, without being conscious of it, have sabotaged my own efforts.)

Elliot sat back in his chair, repeated the trick with the smoke, though this time carved a death's head from the puff.

'For all of you here, I'm the sole bringer of death. Nothing can kill you, not sickness, not calamity, not your own hand, nor the hand of any save me. Only I, with the knife I spoke of, can bring about your ends. But I won't send you off peacefully. It will be harrowing. Do not doubt this, I've had aeons to whet my cruelty. So don't seek me out and prostrate yourself at my feet when immortality becomes unendurable. Fly from me, quail at my approach always. I'll seek you, I will hunt you down, and you will run. You, and those others like you, are to be my sport till the world's end.'

He looked round the table. We were all wan, cowered. He smirked, then a change came over him, the monstrous drained from his features, and he looked the good-humoured pensioner once more.

'Go from this place,' he sang, smiling, to the tune of an air that seemed familiar to me, but which I couldn't place, beating the pipe in time, like a conductor's baton. 'You've six months before I set out after you, use them to get as far from here as possible. Though you can't evade me forever, I hope some of you will be resourceful enough to keep me searching a good while.'

Then he winked.

With that, William, Rashmi, Jane, Duncan, and I leapt up from the table, knocking over chairs, leaving our copies of Verne's strange novel lying on the table, scrambled to leave the Nightingale. Chuckling to himself, Elliot sat, watched us. William reached the door first and, discovering it locked, took up a bar stool and smashed out one of the pub's etched glass windows. Then he clambered through, out into the night. The rest of us followed. Then we tore off in separate directions. You might be shocked by this, but terror had reduced us to frantic beasts, and brute instinct told us we'd be easier to track in a group than alone. Indeed, till I stumbled across William's body, I didn't see any of that company again.

XI

The thing I'd dreaded many ages has finally come to pass.

It was early this morning (or perhaps yesterday morning: it's night, has been so for a time, and I've no way of knowing whether or not the witching hour has yet passed). Just before dawn, or so I learnt a short while afterwards, when, on being toted, wrists and ankles bound with strong cord, up the Ark's companion steps and into the outer air, I saw the sun cresting the eastern skyline.

I was sitting at the desk in the cramped cabin below the Ark's decks, reading over the foregoing section of this narrative. The tribeswoman lay on her pallet, sleeping fitfully, gaunt, cheeks sunken and hectic. Indeed, we both were more parched and wasted than when I last described us; I doubted the tribeswoman had long to live, was astounded, actually, she'd held out as she had, awaited her death, felt sadness, though a sadness tinged with relief, relief her sufferings would end.

Then the door was thrown wide. A gibbous monster, swollen features, a hooked nose, stumbled in. Its movements were wooden, awkward. A life-sized Punch puppet.

I thought myself delirious at first, but then, when one wooden eyelid creaked shut and open, I realized it was Elliot wearing that guise to taunt and horror me. He was followed by a rabble of the local natives. They carried flaming brands, and their faces were smeared with woad; in the flickering torchlight, they looked gaudy fiends.

My heart pounded fit to burst.

I got to my feet, meaning to resist, but, enfeebled by hunger, thirst, the corrupt air of the hold, slumped to the floor. Lifting her head, the tribeswoman gazed blankly at the intruders, the sinews in her scrawny neck standing out like banjo strings. Then she coughed, spluttered, and bloody spittle spattered the front of her undershirt.

We were soon trussed up like capons for the spit.

'That's the way to do it!' Elliot jeered, shrill and reedy.

The rabble bore us up through the hold's tortuous ways, jostling us aloft, out onto the deck, and down the gangplank. Elliot loped along, a little way out in front, turning from time to time to beckon the tribe on, bark commands in their tongue.

Pulled up on the mudflats, a short way from the Ark, was a barge woven from rushes. The tribeswoman and I were loaded on board, her listless and unresisting, me struggling weakly. Then some of the natives got behind the boat, launched it. It wallowed as Elliot and six heavyset brutes embarked, but found an even keel once they'd settled, Elliot on his feet in the stern, at the tiller, and the tribesmen, having taken up paddles, kneeling in two rows on either side. Their first fierce strokes took us out to the centre of the estuary, then Elliot, pushing the helm from him, swung the prow upstream. At first the tribesmen, who sang a tuneless dirge in time to their strokes, struggled to paddle against the current, but they were burly, and the craft soon outstripped the mob walking along the bank. Elliot bellowed orders at his crew and stared ahead, on the lookout for snags. He, as Punch, was dwarfish, but his shadow, thrown by the low sun at his back, was spindly, stalked ahead. Sat in the bows, bound hand and foot, in undergarments soaked with brine, shivering in the early morning chill, I felt a pang of regret I'd never complete this text, that it would certainly be lost or destroyed and never read.

I think I must have blacked out a short time, for I can't recall the barge's landing. Then I was being hefted by two tribesmen across marshy ground towards a palisade of tall pine stakes, with a gate of another pale wood, perhaps maple or birch, all white as new ivory. Hide tents circled this stockade. The tribeswoman, in a faint, was being carried alongside me. As we neared the camp, I saw a number of ebon knobs mounted above the gate. I thought them finials in a different wood, set there to temper the pallor the façade. Drawing closer, though, I saw I'd been wrong: they were not ornaments, but warnings, a row of shrunken heads on spikes, leathery skin, sparse tufts sprouting from scalps, raw staring sockets, knife-slash mouths. I stared aghast.

Elliot, noting my gawking, gestured for the tribesmen to throw down my companion and me, then crossed over to where I lay, stood, his hooked nose beetling over me.

'I've found these brutes more tractable when the threat of bloody death hangs over them,' he said. 'Recognize that one over there?'

He pointed out the head on the far left. Though fresher, less shrivelled than the others, it was still sere, festering, and it took me a moment, but then I realized: it was the chieftain who'd not given me away, who'd let me escape.

'No doubt you feel a pang over that,' Elliot said, sneering.

I groaned, slammed my head against the earth.

It wasn't only remorse over the chieftain's fate that troubled me. I was sickened by how I'd thought of the tribe; I'd not, as Elliot had, sought to subjugate, but I'd too seen them as other and base, as not fully human.

Elliot, peering down at me, then said, 'Killing a few keeps the rest on their toes, you see.'

'King Stork,' I murmured.

'Huzzah, huzzah!' my captor crowed, then grinned. There were wooden teeth in that mouth, brown and higgledy-piggledy.

The tribeswoman started at Elliot's crow, opened her eyes. I don't know what strange ancestral dreams she was roused from, but she uttered then, weakly, barely a whisper, a word in the tongue of her ancient forebears, the language of this typescript: 'Help.' It panged me, but I could not. Then her eyelids fluttered closed once more.

Before long, I felt the tramp of feet in the ground. Then it could be heard, and chatter, and song. It was the rest of the tribe approaching. They reached us, halted. Then Elliot turned, threw open the gate of the stockade, and directed the men who'd borne me before to take me up again, heft me inside. They did so, though they seemed scared of entering the place, paled on passing through the gate, did not go far before they threw me down, fled. Elliot then entered the compound, started towards where I lay prone, face in the dirt, but stopped, and, turning back, stood staring at the tribe, who huddled a little distance off, as if afraid of drawing near the stockade, quailing under his gaze. Then he gave vent to a series of howls and grunts, a victory address perhaps, and slammed the gate closed. There was a moment's quiet, then a hushed counsel in the native's tongue, then grunts of exertion, blows, and the tribeswoman's feeble cries and moans.

'Don't leave her out there,' I croaked.

'Why not?' Elliot asked. 'It's none of my concern. I'm happy to let them exact their own vengeance. No doubt it'll lack subtlety, they're a barbarous lot. But I'm sure it'll be grim enough, if not as artful as your death'll be.'

I lifted my head to look up at him. He began capering about, clattering his wooden limbs, swiping his huge nose from side to side. Then he stopped, looked up, his eye caught by something. I followed his gaze, straining, cricking my neck, saw a lynx padding atop the stakes of the palisade. Reaching the end of the row of severed heads, the cat batted at the chieftain's with a paw, then began gnawing at it. Elliot frowned, then sent a long pink tongue whipping from between his wooden lips through the air, lassoed the lynx, pulled it down from the fence, and dragged it struggling and screeching across the ground towards him. As it neared, he got down on all fours. Then, when the cat was close, he loosed his tongue and pounced, took a hunk out of the lynx's belly with his wooden gnashers, slurped up its spilled guts. The creature yowled, then fell still. Elliot stood, kicked its bloody body away.

'That's the way to do it!' he yawped.

'W-w-w...' I stuttered.

Elliot cackled. 'Cat got your tongue?'

'W-why?'

'Why do anything?'

'What do you mean to do to me?'

'Wouldn't you like to know,' he jeered.

Then he paused, scratched his head before continuing.

'Actually, I'm not sure yet. I need more time. To be inspired. Most had something I could seize on. Made it easier. You saw the body of the young man, the heavy smoker from the gathering you arranged, I believe?'

I shuddered, nodded.

Elliot turned his eyes on me; set in Punch's outlandish face, they burned with mockery.

'Unless I just bore you to death. Though I suspect your tolerance for boredom outstrips my ability to inflict it...'

Then he squinted, scratched his head.

'What was he called?' he asked. 'The smoker.'

'I can't remember.'

'You too, eh? Yes, I forget names. Forgotten my own. Well, forget pretty much everything in truth. Save how to be cruel.'

Walking past me, he entered a log cabin. I watched, waited a while, but he didn't come back out. I tugged against my bonds, but it was futile, the knots held; I was enfeebled and had been tied tight.

I found that by squirming, turning my head this way and that, craning my neck, I was able to piece together, from glimpses, the space enclosed by the palisade. It is a rough square, with two small buildings at its heart: the cabin I'd seen Elliot go into (I persist in calling him Elliot for the sake of consistency), and a small roundhouse of open-faced flint with a limpet-shell slate roof. A curtain of dark heavy fabric hung in the entrance to the cabin and it was drawn most of the way across, but I could still glimpse the interior through the slight gap, and, from what I could see, an iron cot and a wooden table, I gathered the building Elliot's living quarters. The roundhouse's door is sturdy, pale wood, again maybe maple or birch, with a wavy grain, reinforced with iron battens, and was secured with a large antiquated padlock. The stone walls have an air of some age, are ivy garlanded, beset with mosses and lichens, but the door and the roof tiles are clearly new, though where Elliot got the materials, I can't think. Who built the roundhouse, and when it dates from, I've no idea, but it must have been its ruin that attracted Elliot to the site; as it's exposed, and near to mephitic marshland, I can see no other advantage to the place.

Within the compound the ground is hard-packed bare earth, with the impressions of many unshod feet. As the tribesmen who bore me had seemed scared to enter, and the rest of the natives loath to approach, this bewildered me. The tribe's fear did not; those impaled heads, with their wisps of hair, their leathery skin.

I lay there hoping against hope for a quick death.

I lay listless, eyes closed, turned to torpor by the sun, a while. Then Punch's grating, shrill voice startled me.

'You're the last, the very last, of my quarries, you know. The rest are dead. Slain.'

I looked up, squinted. Stark against the glare, I saw Punch's monstrous profile, hooked nose, jutting chin. Elliot leant over me, peered closer. Though his mouth was fixed in a cruel smirk, there was a hint of frailty in the set of Punch's features, that mollifying trace that allows the audience to laugh at his outrages. This I found grotesque; Elliot, I was sure, was without such weakness.

Turning my head, I stuck out my tongue. Elliot reached down, seized hold of the rope tying my ankles, started hauling me towards the roundhouse, lifting my feet high so my face dragged. The rough earth skinned my nose, my right cheek, my forehead.

'You should pride yourself on having evaded my clutches so long,' he said as he trudged, red-faced, breathless with exertion.

I sneered.

'Why? It wasn't difficult.'

Elliot let go my feet, stood with his palms in the small of his back, stretched out his crooked spine. Then he spat in the dust, stepped forward, kicked me in the head. All went black.

While out, I had an uncanny vision. In it, I perched on the top step of a large marble staircase that jutted bizarre from a barren grey waste girded round by sawtooth mountains. Dark clouds scudded across the sky, away to the west, as if driven before a gale, though I couldn't feel a breath of wind. Rents in the rack gave glimpses of a pale winter sun. A brass handrail, supported by marble balusters, ran down each side of the staircase. The lower ends were ornamented with intricate clockwork orreries whose planets and moons described eccentric orbits.

A lone horseman was crossing the plain towards me from the west, slumped forward in the saddle. With a knife far too large for the task, he was paring an apple, dried, withered, worm-eaten, mould-flecked. He wore a suit, a long wool overcoat, and a hat with a wide floppy brim, which he'd pulled down low over his eyes. He and his mount, a skittish starveling stallion, were so greyed by dust thrown up by the horse's splayed and bloody hooves, they seemed moulded from the stuff of the waste they passed through.

On reaching the staircase, the rider dismounted, tethered his horse by its reins to one of the orreries, put his knife into a pannier slung over the animal's flank, and sat down on one of the lower steps. Then he bit into the bad apple. I watched as he ate the fruit slowly, painstakingly, all of it, even the blackened core.

Then, getting to his feet, he crossed over to the stallion again, reached into the pannier, rummaged around, drew something out, concealed it in his coat. He turned, began climbing the stairs. As he did, he raised his head to look up at me under his hat brim. I saw it was the young chieftain whose act of kindness towards me had cost him his life. But his face was that of the severed head on the spike, not the living man, resembled the apple he'd just eaten, its skin puckered, rot-speckled, flesh-grub pocked, its orbits, hollow pits.

It was only when he reached the top of the stairs and stood over me, I realized how tall he was; he towered over me, blotted out the stars. I stood up, came only to his knees. He took out the thing he'd hidden in the folds of his coat. A fish of a kind I didn't recognize: big lumpy skull, flat wide tail, droopy barbels. It was putrid, reeked. Hunkering down, the chieftain shook it in my face, spattering me with stinking gleet from its mouth.

'I wanted to show you this,' he then said. 'Look here.'

He pointed out four appendages hanging, limp, from the dead fish.

'These are vestigial limbs, not inchoate ones. Do you see!' Suddenly he was shouting, and I was bowed over backwards, a sapling in the teeth of a storm. 'The creatures of the land are returning to the sea. Creation is in disarray!'

'What?' I asked. 'Isn't this the end of the world, anyway?'

He shook his head slowly.

'You don't understand,' he said, quiet once more. 'It was too much to hope you would, I suppose.'

He shook his head, weary, went back down to his horse, unhitched it, clambered into the saddle, rode off. I watched him crossing the plain, back the way he'd come. The sun hung low over the mountains in the west, and he and his mount cast a long scraggy shadow behind them, the shadow of some spindly monstrosity. Then the orb impaled itself on the peaks to the west, went down gushing blood, and the light grew dim, then gloomy, then dark. I stood, mute and motionless as a stone, in that utter black.

Then I was riding a tiger loping swift through the air, flat grey ocean below. I clung on with a fierce grip, hands buried in the beast's fur. Looking ahead, I saw we approached a range of vapour like a limitless cataract rolling silently into the sea from some immense and far-distant rampart in the heaven. When we were almost on this pallid veil, I came to. Just before, I saw a giant shrouded human form looming in the mist...

I found myself lying on my back, on dank earth, pain making an uproar in my skull, a glaring ray falling across my eyes. I turned my head out of the dazzle, looked about. I was in a circular cell with stone walls: the roundhouse. All was gloom save the bright sunlight spearing in through a gap where the door had been left ajar. Gyves were chained to the walls, and though they were new, gleamed, it occurred to me the place was probably originally built, at a time long past, as a lock-up.

Elliot hunkered in the dark near the door, breathing hard, glaring ireful. Seeing me stir, he grinned.

'Well, finally got you. The most cunning of all. Much more resourceful than you seemed. I thought you so unworldly.'

'But what of... the young man, the smoker?' I'd almost called him William. 'He held out nearly as long.'

'No. I found him centuries ago. Holed up beneath the ruins of London. In ancient sewage tunnels. I thought he might be my last remaining beguilement, so I toyed with him a good while before killing him.' Elliot smirked. 'I wondered if I'd been mistaken about you, thought perhaps eternity hadn't been wakened in your breast. If you hadn't come back here, I mightn't have ever realized you were still living.'

I cursed bitterly. Elliot cackled.

'Yearning for home wax too strong, did it?'

I cast him a sullen glance.

'Where've you been hiding all this time?'

I turned my head away from him, spat.

'No matter. Soon you'll be telling me everything for just an eyeblink free of pain.'

I was rattled, but shammed bravery, laughed, taunted him.

'You aren't frightening, you know. More... Ridiculous.'

His face clouded. He crossed over, taking a stubby knife with a wooden handle from a sheath hanging at his belt. I guessed it was the Tartarean blade he'd spoken of that night in the Nightingale, and hoped, enraged, he'd plunge it in me, finish me. But that wasn't to be, he was in command of his temper. Instead he used the knife to cut through my bonds, then, twisting his fingers in my hair, hauled me to my feet. I stood there tottering, reeling, queasy.

'Come on, you poltroon, you pigeon-hearted prick!' he bellowed.

I set my teeth, steeled myself. I'd provoke, stand still, unresisting, take the beating as well as I could, choke groans, whimpers. Elliot sparred at me a little, but then, realizing I wasn't going to put up a fight, belying the infirmity he'd shown before, picked me bodily up, hurled me to the floor. The air was driven from my lungs, I bit my tongue. Cowering away, I crawled backwards till I struck the wall, then slumped against it, struggled to get my breath back, the salt tang of blood in my mouth.

'Nowhere to run now, rat.'

He capered towards me, warbling a ditty in Punch's cracked, tuneless voice.

Right foll de riddle loll,
I know a craven soul.
He hid like a rat,
But I found him out,
And dragged him from his hole!

I lay down on my side, drew my knees to my chest, wrapped my head in my arms. Elliot vented his wrath. He pummelled, kicked, stomped.

'Hee, hee, hee. Weakling. You're pitiful!'

I drifted away once more.

When I came to this time, I found Elliot had clapped me in the roundhouse's manacles, wrists and ankles. The iron chafed, bit. I lay on the floor, up against the wall. The door was shut, but it wasn't too dark, chinks between the slates overhead and the stones of the walls let in slender blades of sunlight. These put me in mind of the ever-popular sword-cabinet illusion, which I've seen a number of conjurors perform in my time. If you don't know it, my reader, it's as it sounds: a cabinet, containing an assistant or volunteer, is run through with rapiers; the assistant or volunteer remains, of course, 'magically' unharmed. This recollection caused me to mull the nature of memory generally. It struck me that its ability to draw such apt analogies, the basis, I'd hazard, of all invention, swells with its hoard of reminiscences. Thinking this, a clammy dread threw its coils round me, for I realized, given the aeons he's lived for, even though his recall isn't suited to eternity, Elliot is doubtless horribly creative, is unlikely to fail to dream up some awful torment for me.

As I lay there, pondering my fate, the door opened, and Elliot entered, now in the guise he'd adopted for the gathering at the Nightingale, that genial old man. I wondered if this was his true or habitual form. I'd thought it would solace me for him to abandon the form of Punch, but I actually found this aspect even more disquieting, for it suggested benignity. Though it had hinted at a weakness alien to the stuff of Elliot's being, the hooknose's loathsome phizog had been truer to his antic evil.

Elliot was followed by a tribesman who carried a bulging sack. Elliot gestured and the tribesman emptied it out on the mud, left. I looked over at the heap: the tribeswoman's and my meagre things.

'There's nothing there that'll interest you,' I croaked.

But Elliot ignored me, began to go through the pile. He first spent some time scrutinizing the typewriter, turning it about in his hands. Then exclaimed, 'Ah!', nodded to himself, put it down, and began looking through the remaining stuff. It wasn't long before he came across this document. He riffled through its pages, looked perplexed, scratched his head. Then he arched his eyebrows, grinned, giggled nastily, put the document down, rubbed his hands together in glee.

I ranted then, begged him not to destroy my work. He turned to me, said, 'We'll see,' then took up my papers again, left the roundhouse, sniggering.

He left me alone some time. At first I lay still, tried to sleep, but the ground was too hard, the gyves strained, so I squirmed, sat up, leant against the wall. This took some time, fettered as I was. I was then a little easier in my body, and my mind was free to wander, and I was afflicted by terrible anxiety, terrified Elliot had taken my memoir away to burn it.

But, when he later returned, it appeared I'd been granted a reprieve; he held my tale in his hand.

'This isn't all that bad,' he said. 'I found it quite gripping, am dying to know how it ends.'

He chuckled.

'The tone is overwrought, though, and some of the writing stilted, mannered.'

I lifted my head from my chest, where it lolled, went to spit, but my mouth was too parched.

'Just a little constructive criticism,' he jeered. 'Anyway, don't worry, I'm not going to destroy it, much as it would hurt you, and give me pleasure. I've devised a more apt torture. I know you won't be able to resist continuing your narrative, whatever you have to suffer. Besides I'm itching to read your account of all that's happened today. You can get on with it straight away.'

'But I'm too weak to write now,' I said.

'Well then, you'll have something to drink and to eat. That should get your strength up.'

And that's why I've spent the last few hours in the roundhouse, seated at a small rickety wooden desk, composing the foregoing story of my capture. After Elliot had brought in the desk and chair, placed the things that clutter its surface there – my typewriter, an oil lamp to see by, a tin mug filled with water, and a dish containing salty scraps of bacon rind and stale crusts of bread – unlocked the shackles, and sat me down, he told me to write it as swiftly as I could, to call out for him once I was done. I'd no need to bring things to a fitting end, he said, as there'd be more to set down.

Then, before leaving, he tore my nails from the quick and flayed my fingers to the knuckles with a rusty paring knife. Typing is agony. But as he surmised, I've been driven to write on in spite of the pain. The typewriter is gory, I worry its mechanisms might become clotted, and these pages are covered with gruesome smears.[12] Yet, to me, the blood I've shed is the blood of a birthing, for as my life draws near its end, so inevitably does this tale, which is a record of it, and I feel proud I, whose aeonial existence has been so barren, will leave something entire behind me, that, despite its many faults, will endure, perhaps, and this is my greatest hope, to find a reader other than my murderer.

XII

When I'd finished writing the foregoing chapter, I called out as told, and Elliot came, took the pages and the oil lamp away, put me back in manacles.

Sat there in the gloom, I must have drifted asleep, for the next thing I knew, I woke with a start to a din. It was still dark, but whether I'd not drowsed long and it was the same night, or had slept the day away and it was the next, I've no way of knowing. The row was coming from outside. Exultant howling, drumming, the pounding of dancing feet. Through the chinks in the roundhouse walls, I could see fitful flaring.

A dread revel by firelight.

The raucous spree went on a time, then Elliot barked, and all fell silent. He yelled a bit in the natives' tongue, then there was the sound of a struggle, followed by a horrid shriek, a low terrified groan, a moan of pleasure from Elliot. I gagged on a foul stink. Then came rending, cracking, gasps, a blood reek. Then hammering, pleas, Elliot laughing. Followed by splintering wood, panicked flight, footfalls dying away. A lone whimpering. A wet thud and it ceased.

Then Elliot called out, 'I do love a good party, don't you?'

I kept quiet and still.

'These primitives really should thank me, you know. The things I'm showing them.'

Then the mewling came again.

'Well, I never...'

Elliot guffawed.

'How is he still alive?'

There was the noise of pissing, splashing, Elliot sighing. The puling became a scream, drawn out, agonized. There was the stench of acid and burning flesh. Then peace again. I sat in the dark, shivering, harrowed. But I was so tired sleep finally overcame me.

Sunlight streaming in through the roundhouse door roused me. Elliot stood before me, wry grin on his face.

'Sleep well?'

He was naked, his flesh daubed with dried blood. He had gory hunks of viscera on a string about his neck. Blowflies buzzed about him. In one hand held the account of my capture and, in the other, a metal bowl filled with an acrid stinking liquid, which he set on the floor before me.

'This is good,' he said, waving the pages in my face. 'I really liked the bit describing your strange dreams. I wonder what gave rise to them?'

'No idea,' I mumbled.

'No?' He shrugged. 'Out of interest, why did you name me Elliot?'

'On a whim.'

'Oh. I wouldn't have chosen it for myself.' He chuckled. 'For some reason though, it does have a sinister ring.'

He set down the typescript, then crouched, unlocked the manacles securing my wrists.

'Hold out your hands.'

I shook my head, kept my hands, which were raw, grisly, like things newborn, close to my chest. But Elliot grabbed my wrists, yanked, plunged my fingers into the bowl.

It was something like vitriol. Burned. Shreds of my flesh shrivelled, floated free, drifted, dissolved. Bone showed through in spots. I bit almost through my tongue, hissed.

Then Elliot let go, and I jerked my hands back.

'Still want you to be able to type,' he said.

'Fuck you,' I slurred, tongue ruined, mouth full of blood.

Elliot sneered, held his middle finger up to me. I watched as the nail lengthened, became a sharp curving talon. Then he slashed open my belly with it, hooked out my guts. Then he was

Punch again, bawling 'Sausages!', hauling out my innards, gobbling them down.

Woken by my keening, the natives sleeping off their awful frolic perhaps thought it the wail of a bizarre beast, brought into this world from some eldritch realm by the blood rite, so little did it resemble a human cry.

I blacked out again.

When I came to it was also light, but I'd guess, at the earliest, it was two days later, for my stomach wound, my fingers, and my tongue were nearly healed. Elliot stood over me again. He was washed and dressed, in a button-down shirt, cardigan, brown cords, tan brogues, looked benign again.

I shrank away.

'Just kill me,' I groaned.

Elliot smirked.

'Don't worry, death is coming to you, and soon. First, though, I want you to finish your tale. It wouldn't be complete, would it, if it didn't tell how I plan to snuff your life? And don't you think your readers would be curious to learn how the others who met that evening in the Nightingale died?'

I shrugged. Feigned unconcern.

He smirked down at me.

'Oh, and your tale wouldn't be complete without it telling of the fate of the young tribeswoman.'

I groaned, strained against the irons. If I could have clapped my hands over my ears I would.

'Well,' Elliot went on, ignoring me, 'last I saw of the natives, a few hours ago, they were leaving camp, dragging the woman's broken body with them. I think they were headed for the river. They've not come back as yet. Not sure what they were planning to do with her, but suspect she's dead by now. She was spared the direful sights of my ritual, left tied up outside, but I think the tribe have been taking out on her the vile things I subjected them to then.'

I sobbed. Elliot cuffed me hard on the ear.

'Shut up!'

I choked my misery, best I could.

'Right,' that devil went on. 'Shall I tell you how you're to die first, or save that for later? Begin with the tales of how I ended the lives of those you gathered in the pub that night?'

I shrugged.

Elliot scratched his chin, pondered.

'Hmm... Yes, I think I'll start with them. That way you'll be kept on tenterhooks. I won't bother telling how the young man you've called William Adams died. What you inferred from the state of his body was pretty much dead right. But let me describe how I killed the other two, the butcher and the author...'

Though I was in dread of provoking him, I was perplexed, so blurted out, 'What about the young woman, the one you didn't let tell her story?'

'Ah, yes,' he said, musingly. 'I'd all but forgotten her. I was wrong in her case, as I thought I might've been in yours. Immortality wasn't quickened in her, and I watched her age, sicken, and die.'

Elliot then went on to tell of the grisly deaths Duncan and Jane suffered at his hands. I can only stomach giving scant sketches of his gleeful, vicious, sordid, and ranting accounts.

Duncan was the first quarry Elliot tracked down, less than a year after the gathering in the Nightingale. It seems he found the idea of a hunted existence unbearable, for he made almost no attempt to evade capture, returned to Glasgow, merely shaved off his beard and dyed his hair, a very half-hearted effort to alter his appearance. Elliot, in a rage at being denied his sport, took the butcher then and there, locked him up, spent some time thinking up a cruel penalty. It took him a few days, but then he had it. He severed, with a cleaver, the three limbs the Scot still had, then stuffed him into a sack, lugged him into the catacombs beneath the Necropolis, chucked him into a sarcophagus in one of the lower crypts, left him there a very long time. Only once in a rare while, did Elliot go to him, to pour brackish water down his gullet and cram his mouth with putrid foodstuffs; thirst and hunger couldn't, obviously, kill him, but would, if only after months, bring on catalepsy and spare him torment, something Elliot wanted to avoid.

When Elliot finally lifted Duncan out of the stone cradle he'd lain in for centuries – on a pallet of bones, beneath a blanket of cobwebs – and lugged him up into the daylight, he was like an infant, weak, helpless, babbling. His brain had been wrecked by isolation, but not just isolation, for he'd not been always alone in the dark, had been dandled, caressed by dread olden things. But Elliot tended to him, succoured him, and, in the end, vigour, if not sanity, returned. Then, by sorcery, Elliot grafted on to his trunk arms and legs hacked from a drunken student.

After that Duncan was the ideal toady, trailed after Elliot, hung on his every word, did his bidding. Elliot initiated him into some perverse and bloody rites. Then, once he was corrupted utterly, inured to the foulest horrors, Elliot took him into the blackest regions of Tartarus. There they wallowed in depravity many years. On their return to the mundane realm, many years later, they roamed the globe degenerate and cruel. But, after a time, Elliot tired of Duncan, and, after making him swallow quicklime, burning out his innards, made away with him, cutting his throat with the knife brought back from the pit.

Jane's murder was far less drawn out, but equally grotesque. Several thousand years after the evening in the Nightingale, Elliot found her hiding in a cave in the Australian Outback. He showed her some of the terrifying avatars of that place, those beings that the Aboriginals had communed with in times long past. Then, assuming the form of her long-dead eldest son Peter, he raped and tortured her, then, taking on the guise of the hoary cripple from the Woolwich Foot Tunnel, stabbed her life out.

After he'd finished telling me how he'd ended Jane's life, Elliot paused, looked thoughtful.

'It occurs to me,' he said, 'there's one other killing you'll be interested to hear told. The Rastafarian, the cabbie, was, of course, another of my victims. I ran him to ground at about the time the cities were abandoned...'

Elliot found Clifton during a bitter winter, hiding out in a water tower on the edge of one of the world's most northerly cities, wrapped in many furs, but still blue-lipped, shivering, eking out a dwindling supply of kif. He then dragged him to an old butcher's shop, hacked off his arms and legs, ground them up, gutted him, made sausages with his looped bowels and minced limbs. Then fried them in a skillet with some onions, and sat before Clifton eating them, from time to time forcing morsels into his mouth.

Elliot paused, looked at me, smirked.

'He kept spitting them out though. Rastas don't eat meat, you know. Or didn't, rather. There can't be any left.'

He tugged his earlobe.

'To be honest, those sausages hadn't any savour, as I'd no herbs, spices, seasoning. Though they were better than what I ate of you the other day. Yuck! Anyhow, I quickly got bored of the whole thing, made away with the Rasta, goring him with my knife.'

He looked down at me.

'Well, what do you think of all that then?'

I turned my head from him.

'Eh? Don't fret, I've got something just as good in mind for you. Better even! You're my last, so I need to make the most of you. But all that talk of food's got me peckish. I'll just go have a bite before I tell you.'

He left. I sat sorrowing, afraid, waiting for him to return. He wasn't very long, came back capering, gleeful, chewing a last mouthful. He hawked up a glob of phlegm, spat it into his palm, anointed my brow. Then took out his knife, held it to my face.

'I've whetted and whetted the point of this knife,' he said, twisting it, digging it a little into my cheek. 'It's now keen enough to anatomize a flea. I mean to carve the whole of your tale into your flesh. In teeny tiny script. It'll be agony, and, done with this knife, the cuts will never heal, but I'll keep them shallow. You won't die. Then I'll bury you in salt, leave you a time, a long time. Perhaps I'll while the years away slaughtering the folk of this island. I don't know. But I'll dig you up in the end, go on with your harrowing...'

He then took the knife away from my cheek. It was only a shallow cut, but it hurt badly. The touch of the blade had burned.

Filled with dread and misery, I howled. But my cry was choked by a cackling that welled within me; where it came from, I don't know. Despair maybe. I cackled, sniggered, guffawed, quaked. Elliot looked vexed, fell silent.

I calmed, he remained lost in thought a bit.

'Of course,' he then said. 'That would be rapture for you. I should've known. Well, then, I'll go straight on to the next racking...'

I gazed listlessly at him, as he reeled off torments. I won't repeat them here, wish to put my death from my mind in this brief respite, and also don't want to bore you; the idea of being a living book of blood did slightly horror me, but Elliot's other plans for me are not imaginative, or particularly frightening, just tedious. I was wrong to think he'd be horribly creative. He's a dullard. It'll be painful, it'll be horrible, but I'm not scared, I look forward to the end. I just can't be bothered to write about it now. So, should anyone ever read these pages other than Elliot, as I hope (and there's a chance: Elliot's told me he won't destroy this typescript, that he wishes his cruelties to live on in its pages), should you, my chimerical reader, be summoned into existence

by my invocations, you'll have to cope with this one lacuna. I feel
I've been a constant narrator else.

'So,' Elliot said after. 'I'll allow you a short time, bring your tale
to an apt end. Then...'

Smirking, he unlocked the manacles, led me back to the desk,
the typewriter. He sat me down, crossed to the door, opened it,
started out. But then he paused, turned back.

'By the way, you know how you couldn't enter Tartarus?'

'Yes?'

'You might have had the rituals by rote, but did you realize
some of the steps weren't mental or spiritual operations, but
practical?'

'What do you mean?'

'You perhaps thought the injunction to purge, referred to
emptying the mind?'

'Yes?'

'Well it didn't. You can only enter that place by vomiting,
throwing up, scouring, shitting your guts out. You must literally
be an empty vessel. Anything in your alimentary tract, anything
at all, will stop you from crossing the threshold. Hence the traditional link between fasting and mystical experiences.'

I looked at him, shrugged.

He took his paring knife from a pocket, waved it in my face.

'Best keep that other knife sharp,' he snickered. 'Besides,
wouldn't want this not to heal. As you know, you'll need your
fingers for some of what I've in store.'

Then he grabbed my hands, flayed my fingers again, and left,
locking the door behind him.

So this really is it. I face death, stripped of all hope; till now there
remained a glimmer of reprieve: I felt I could maybe spin out my
tale till the end of the world came to spare me torture. But it's
over, my yarn's been drawn too thin, snapped, I've nothing more

to relate that can enthral. I'd written down all the best bits before the fiend caught me. That was foolish.

Omens foretell my end. Night fell, and for a time all was dark, but, a little while ago, I noticed a reddish taint to the light filtering in through the chinks in the walls and roof. Then heard Elliot yawp, gleeful, 'Bloodmoon!' Then a dog howled and howled and howled. And, not long since, several birds alighted on the slates overhead, talons scrabbling; from their raucous cawing I know them to be carrion crows.

It's only taken me an hour or so to write this, my last chapter. All the while, Elliot's been playing a dirge on a wheezing squeezebox. In a short time, I'll holler out to him, he'll take these sheets from me, and my drawn out, agonizing, if not very dread, death will follow. Therefore, my reader, if you exist, and I pray you do, this must be my farewell. I'm in no mood to make it a sentimental one, but I will say this, disburdening my mind onto these pages these last months has been a great consolation. And now I'll take my leave; I wish to spend some moments in this dank cell alone, in quiet reflection.

XIII

It seems I misread the portents, for I eluded death. I hope this gladdens you, my reader, but, while I cling to the faint hope you've been, and remain, captivated, I know it's more likely you've long since, wearied by its ravelled skeins, lost interest in my tale. I'd urge you to read on, though; things are drawing to a close, and it'd be foolish to have come this far only to quit now. But, if you are too fatigued, or simply prefer your endings bleak, stop here, don't go on, tell yourself I died a tragic harrowing death at Elliot's hand.

Still, I hope you will read on.

(I don't think *you're* bored, you, my *real* reader (and I couldn't have wished for a better), or, at least, am sure you, patient and hankering always for a happy outcome, *will* read on; I hope, though, you don't mind if I continue to write as if there may, unlikely as it seems, be others, and as if for someone who knows nothing of my tale, our tale; I want this account to stand on its own.)

When I left off writing at the end of the foregoing chapter, well over a year ago now, it was to sit quiet a short time, before calling to Elliot, let him know my work was done. I had my lull then hollered. Elliot's concertina wheezed silent, then, after a moment, he entered the roundhouse. After putting me back in shackles, he picked up the pages I'd left by the typewriter, waved them in my face.

'I'll take these away, read them,' he said, 'leave you alone to brood. When I come back it'll be to snuff your life. Slowly.'

While musing, I'd determined not to meet my end meekly, knowing Elliot wouldn't stint on cruelty just because I yielded without a fight. So I gobbed on his brogues. He looked down at the spittle mottling the leather, smirked at me, hit me in the mouth. Then, turning on his heel, he left the roundhouse without another word. I let my chin fall to my chest, drivelled blood down my vest.

Many hours passed. Night became day, day became night. I found solace and distraction pondering the lore of the Himalayan tribes I'd lived amid so long. Their holy folk taught that, through ritual, through the chanting of mantras to stop up the base orifices and prise open the bone sutures of the crown of the skull, the dying could attempt to ensure their immortal spirit passed into the realm of the gods. If, then, the correct path was taken through that land and the deities met on the way appeased with apt tributes, the spirit would be liberated from the wheel of being.

I give these ancient beliefs scant credence, yet then my reason found refuge in them, and when Elliot came back, he found me not raving, as he'd doubtless thought I'd be, but sat quiet in my chains. He held an oil lamp and my typescript, tied up with twine. He hung the lantern from a nail jutting from one of the beams of the roundhouse's roof, put the typescript down on the ground at my feet, then went out, returned a few moments later clutching a flint and steel striker. He held these things before me, but I just shrugged, their meaning lost on me; in my mind I wandered the plane of wonders of the Himalayans' faith.

I think Elliot was a mite irked I sat so placid. He cuffed me.

'Come on,' he said. 'Snap out of it. I've lots of fun planned for us.'

The slap brought me back, but, realizing I could perhaps provoke him, I didn't react, just smiled vacantly.

'By the way,' Elliot went on, 'you don't fool me. Writing as if I don't scare you, as if I'm just some grotesque pantomime villain to you. I know full well you're terrified.'

I shrugged again.

'No, I'm not.'

Elliot took out his knife, held it to my neck.

'I don't believe you. And if you're really not, you should be. Pah! Pretending you don't find what I've in store for you frightening... A bit irritating you didn't describe it in your account, you know.'

I shrugged a third time. Of course, seeking to vex, to provoke, to force, perhaps, some error, I'd dissembled, was continuing to dissemble. What Elliot had told he'd do to me was terrifying, dread, foul...

'Oh well,' he said. 'I've other stuff planned anyway.'

Then I had another idea, went on.

'No one who knows, as I do, your true origins *could* be scared.'

'What? What are you on about?'

'I've read a lot in my time. Dug up some fascinating manuscripts, lost and forbidden texts. In one, a late-medieval German tractate on ancient myth, I came across a reference to a Manichean account of Sumerian folklore.'

Elliot gave me a little nick on the ear with his knife. I flinched.

'So what?'

'Well, apparently the Sumerians told a story about a being moulded from elephant dung by men, given life to by sorcery, created and given to the gods, for them to slake their lusts on, in hopes it'd lessen the rapes of mortals, the unnatural pregnancies, the births of half-breed monsters. Of course it didn't work out that way. And the ill-used creature grew cruel. And then, one day, was turned loose by the gods, who'd tired of it...'

Elliot just laughed, but his right arm became a tentacle, whipped round my neck, throttled me, suckers biting. I passed out. But I think only for a short time. When I came round, Elliot was still crouched before me.

'And your attempt to gull me,' he said, sneering, 'make me think your fit of laughter was despairing, not rapturous, was pitiable. I saw straight through that. If you'd hoped you might trick me into graving your carcass after all, you were mistaken.'

(This I didn't understand, have since spent many hours

pondering. It seems Elliot really thought having my tale inscribed on my flesh would be bliss for me. Why, though, I'm not sure. Perhaps he suspected a desire to pass from this too, too solid flesh to the abstraction of language. If so, he misunderstood my motives for writing.)

'Perhaps I've double-bluffed you,' I said. 'Who can say?'

'Oh really?' He chuckled. 'Well then, how about this?'

And he grabbed my head, began carving my brow with the point of his knife, gripping it, by the blade, in his right hand. The cuts were shallow, but the pain, awful. He graved, 'PRIC', then, partway through the 'K', slipped, gashed the webbing between thumb and forefinger, dropped the knife, jumped back.

Cursing, wincing, he took a handkerchief from his breast pocket, wrapped it about his hand.

'Oh, you dolt!' he said, to himself. 'You shouldn't have let him get your goat. Idiot.'

He picked up his knife, walked over, stuck it into the jamb of the door. Then turned, loped towards me, kicked me in the stomach. But his run-up was faltering, and the blow, weak.

I laughed.

'Shit to shit, eh?'

He kicked me again; another puny blow.

'Is that the best you can do?'

'Oh, just shut up,' he sighed.

Then he undid the knot securing the string binding my account, began loosely crumpling the pages, piling them in front of me.[13]

'What are you doing? I said.

'Haven't you guessed?'

And then I realized. I couldn't pretend unconcern then, howled.

Elliot ignored me, looked down at his wound. Blood had soaked through his makeshift bandage, was beading on the cloth. Distractedly, he raised his hand to his mouth, put out his tongue, lapped at the gouts.

I broke down, begged. Elliot paid me no mind, just went on balling up the pages of my typescript. Realizing it was futile, I stilled my pleas, sat, looked on, dejected. Elliot worked slow, pausing often to cavort, sing coarse ditties. He belted out one crude song, telling of a woman's disappointment with an inept lover, with pointed emphasis.

It took him some time to build his fire. I felt hollow.

Then he'd finished, straightened up, stood grimacing, kneading the knotty ridge of his spine.

'Wretched backache's back.'

He grimaced, then squinted at me.

'All the fight's gone out of you, hasn't it? You got me a touch riled, I'll admit it. But I've still bested you.'

I looked away.

A high gloating gurgle broke from Elliot's lips. Looking down at his injured hand, he unwound his handkerchief, and, seeing the cut was still bleeding, retied it tighter. Then he left the hut, came back a few moments later carrying a metal stake and an iron mallet. He crossed over to me, put down the stake, hit me in the mouth with the hammer. I spluttered blood and tooth shards. He seized the fetters and hauled, hoicked me away from the wall, stretched me out, dropped my feet down just by the pile of crumpled sheets. Then he let go. I drew up my legs.

He sighed. 'Do you want me to break them?'

He pulled on the fetters again, again laid me out. This time I stayed still.

'Good. Now, I'm just going to secure your feet with this spike. Stop you flinching away.'

He turned, reached down for the stake. Just then, I saw, in the door of the roundhouse, a rawboned form stark against the gory light of the bloodmoon. Then the thing stepped forward into the lantern's wavering glow. A freak, human in form, but with a warty reddish hide, awful, staring eyes. I gasped. Elliot looked over his shoulder. The freak pounced, wrestled him, wrested the hammer from his grasp, struck out with it, hit him on the brow. Stunned, he staggered backward, toppled. The freak snatched up the stake, which he'd let fall, fell on him, held the spike's point over his sternum, drove it through his chest and into the ground with a blow from the hammer. Elliot thrashed; his heels drubbed the earth, his arms lashed the air. He shrieked.

I goggled. The freak turned from Elliot to me. I feigned death, closed my eyes, let me head loll, but it had seen me move, loped over, bent down, stared at me. I cowered away. Then, the freak reached up, clawed away some of the scabrous husk from its face, and I startled again; it was my amanuensis, the tribeswoman, caked head to foot in dried estuary mud.

She sighed.

'I feared he'd killed you already.'

My brain reeled. I gaped up at her, and bloody slobber ran from my mouth. She shuddered, threw down the mallet, reached out, took my head in her hands, looked at the mess Elliot had made of my forehead.

'Fuck. What's he done to you?'

Then, she went down on haunches, peered at me.

'Haven't you realized? I'm Rashmi.'

Elliot then bawled again. We turned, but he was still pinned by the spike.

'Rashmi,' I echoed.

'Well, I doubt it's my real name, I mean the one my parents gave me. But I've forgotten that anyway, just as you have yours. But, yes, I'm Rashmi.'

I knew straight away this was true. It explained several enigmas: that strange sense I'd had, more than once, that I recognized her; her hardiness; that she was able to type up my edited proofs, something which should have told me she knew the English language, but which I explained away with an absurd rationalization.

257

'Where are the keys?' she asked, pointing at the manacles.

'I don't know,' I said. 'He probably has them.'

I nodded towards where Elliot lay staked, snarling, writhing.

Rashmi went over, crouched, reached out warily, patted Elliot's trouser pockets. The right jingled, and she put her hand gingerly in. Elliot wriggled, mugged, oohed and aahed, licked his lips. Then lunged with his right hand. Rashmi had strayed too close, and he managed to grab her ankle. She tried to struggle free, but his grip was fierce. Then with his left hand he took hold of the end of the spike, started rocking it side to side, wincing and whimpering the while. Blood foamed up. I looked on, helpless. At first the stake held fast, but Elliot kept on, and it started to wiggle loose. He crowed, but his glee was hasty; Rashmi jerked her foot, and it would seem his injury panged, for he hissed, slackened his grip, and she was able to wrest her ankle free. Returning to me, she then picked up the mallet, went back over, felt again for the keys, this time fending Elliot's grabs off with swipes of the hammer. She finally hooked the ring the keys were on with her finger, took them from Elliot's pocket, then drove the spike again. He clenched his fists, threw back his head, his knuckles went white, the tendons in his neck stood out, taut, his eyes started from his head. He screamed.

Rashmi unlocked the gyves, then we crossed over to Elliot. He was tugging on the spike again, twisting it, trying to work it free once more. Rashmi smote his hands with the mallet; scowling he let them fall to his side. He seemed sore beat out, his eyes glassy. Then cunning sparked them, and he hollered something in the natives' tongue.

Rashmi waited till he'd finished, then said, 'Save your breath. They've fled, will be long gone by now.'

Elliot snorted. But his eyes fell dull again. Then, looking into them, I was shocked to see fear and pain there. It was as if I'd glimpsed a fish swimming in the depths of a turbid pool whose waters I'd been sure were hostile to life. But then this trace of human frailty fleeted away again.

'As soon as you run,' he sneered, 'I'll pull out this wretched spike, come after you.'

'No you won't,' Rashmi spat, 'because we're going to kill you.'

'How?' Elliot jeered, raising his eyebrows.

Rashmi grimaced.

But then I spat, 'With your knife!'

'Of course,' Rashmi said.

I pointed out the blade, and she handed me the hammer, crossed over to it, pulled it from the jamb.

Elliot looked up at me.

'I can't fathom it. As I told you, I watched her age and die.'

'What's that?' Rashmi asked, walking back over, feinting with the knife.

Elliot shook his head.

Then Rashmi went down on haunches beside him, held the blade in her fist, over his heart. She was about to stab down, when he put up his hands.

'First, a question.'

Rashmi shrugged.

'Go on. Just one.'

'I want to know how you tricked me. I watched you grow old and die. Yet, here you are.'

Rashmi looked puzzled a moment. Then nodded slow.

'I'd a twin sister.' She paused, seemingly lost in reflection then went on. 'After the evening, the evening of the gathering, I went straight to her, told her all.' Rashmi paused, grimaced. 'There was weeping and pleading. She was aghast, but she believed me!' Her voice wavered, she wiped her eyes. 'We were twins! We had that bond of trust. She came up with the plan.'

'What plan?' Elliot's eyes darted ire. His forehead had begun to purple.

I gibed at him.

'They fooled you, it seems.'

Rashmi, hunkered over Elliot's pinned frame, holding the blade, her skin crusted with red mud, looked the high priestess of some crude faith, about to take a life to appease some cruel deity.

'We left Edinburgh, went into hiding in the Highlands,' she went on, tears in her eyes. 'We spent a few, short years together, then my sister returned to the city, pretended to be me. We'd alienated our mother, much of our family, our father was dead, and she told our friends, who believed her to be me, that she'd died, a skiing accident I think, can't remember. We hoped you'd find her,' she glanced down at Elliot, 'see she'd aged, believe you'd failed. I didn't want her to take the risk, in case you tortured her, killed her anyway, but she was determined. We couldn't ever see each other again, it would have ruined everything. That was so hard for me.'

With sudden ferocity, she stabbed down. Blood welled, sluggish, dark.

Elliot groaned. Then fell still. There was a lull. Then Rashmi turned to me.

'It's over.'

I gave a wan smile.

Then Elliot brayed scornfully, 'You can't kill me! Did you really think that weapon could end the life of he who willed it into existence? You may have deceived me, but you can't best me.'

Rashmi drew out the dagger, chucked it into a dark corner of the roundhouse. A rat squeaked, scurried across the floor, out the door.

'Do you think, if I'd found some way of ending this, I wouldn't have taken it?'

'But it did hurt you before? ' I said. 'Didn't it? Weaken you?'

'Oh fuck off.'

Rashmi sighed, cuffed Elliot on the side of the head, then tore a strip of cloth from the hem of his shirt, wadded it up, stuffed it into his mouth. She got to her feet, left the roundhouse. I stood waiting for her to come back, hefting the mallet, looking warily down at Elliot. He winked, mumbled around the makeshift gag.

After a few minutes had passed, Rashmi came back clutching a rusty old hacksaw, shook it in my face.

'He made one of the tribesmen trade with him,' she said. 'This for the man's daughter. Gave him no choice. She wasn't seen again. Just a girl!'

Then Rashmi gestured down at Elliot, mimed sawing. As if she couldn't bear to give voice to what she meant us to do, as if doing so would defile her utterly. Elliot understood before I did, shrank back, and the weakness I'd seen in his eyes before came back, but again, for just an instant, replaced swift by the old fleer.

First I moved the pages of my typescript, so as to be out of the spray and spatter, then Rashmi and I set about our task. Without a word. How long we laboured, I can't say, it seemed a long, long time; horror bloats. Though the day was chill, the sweat ran from our brows. We took turns with the saw. Its wooden handle had snapped, leaving just a splintery stub, so we were forced to turn it about, grip it by the other end. Work was awkward. For me it was painful; my fingers were still healing, were still tender.

Soon we were sleeved in gore. At one point a dog came to the door, yapping, and I had to drive it off with the hammer. We shut the door then, wary of fiercer beasts being lured by the blood reek. Conditions inside the roundhouse worsened after that, forced us out into the bloodmoon's vile glow from time to time, retching. As we sawed, Elliot, for the most part, was flippant, chuckled round the gag, mugged, made faces. However, a few times, when the blade snagged, I saw that agony and fear creep into his eyes again; those moments harrowed.

Reader, I'm sorry to leave a gap your mind may plug with grisly things, but I can't bring myself to tell any more of the horrors of that work.

When we were done, Rashmi and I left the roundhouse to go look for something to carry Elliot's sundered parts in. We had a scout around the enclosure. The earth was churned, particularly about the gate, and the gate itself had been torn from its hinges, was in splinters on the mud. We found two satchels next to a woodpile behind the cabin, but they were not large enough for our purposes. I asked Rashmi if she thought there'd be anything in the natives' camp.

'No. In their haste, they left their tents, and some junk, but they took most of their stuff. Their packs will be gone.'

So we entered Elliot's living quarters. Weapons – daggers, swords, axes, clubs, and maces – and torture devices – wicked hooks, needles, thumbscrews, and other bizarre contraptions, whose appearance was dread, but whose use I couldn't hazard (though there's one I can put a name to; sewn onto one of its leather restraints was a scrap of cloth embroidered with the words 'Ouroboros Apparatus') – were heaped in the corners, strewn over the floor.

Looking round at the arms, Rashmi hawked and spat.

'We should've known to come in here to find something to cut the bastard up with.'

I nodded.

Though wanton in malice, it seems Elliot was in other ways ascetic: his bed was a pallet on the floor; he ate with a wooden spoon out of a plain wooden bowl; the only foodstuff to be found was a sack of meal; and the only sign of any pastime, other than cruelty, was the concertina I'd heard him play.

We came across a large carpet bag. We took it, went back to the roundhouse, started picking up butchered chunks of Elliot, stuffing them into it. No easy task; though severed, the limbs writhed, struggled. Seizing the head, I nearly dropped it, for its eyes moved still in their sockets, its jaws and lips worked. I believe it sought to speak, lopped and gagged though it was. We also took Elliot's knife, planning to unmake it.

Then I went and got those small satchels. Into one I put my typewriter, and into the other, after flattening out its pages, and binding them again with the string, my typescript. Then we set off. Feeling awful sullied, the first thing we did was go down to the river and wash.

XIV

By that thing we did, we've gained a reprieve (it's come at some cost to our ease, though; often, one or both of us will wake up in the dead of night, the hacking whoops of the rusty sawblade fading in our ears). We've no idea how long this lull will last, though we did our best to ensure it'll be a good while: left Elliot's limbs staked to the ground at the four corners of the island once known as Britain, for scavengers and burying beetles and maggots to get at; tore out his offal, cast it to a pack of feral dogs somewhere on the wild and wasted moors that can be found in the south-west of that land; chucked his gutted torso into the sea over the edge of the south-east coast's white cliffs; buried his head in that city once known as London. Perhaps we should have spread his pieces over a greater area, over the globe, but we couldn't bear to tote them too long, and were concerned they might, with time, put themselves back together again in the bag.

We were fortunate, our travels were not too wearisome, and done fairly swift, for, on the morning of the second day out from the stockade, we came across a herd of horses that turned out to be quite docile, tractable, that still had, it seemed, the servility of their long-ago forebears in their blood, and selected the two sturdiest to bear us. At first we made slow progress, our injuries kept us to an easy pace, but within a few days we were healed, then we drubbed our mounts' flanks with our heels, rode them hard, eager to get shot of our grisly burden.

You might wonder why we didn't throw Elliot's pieces into a fire, let them burn up, scatter the ashes. Well, this course did occur to us after a few days journeying, and we tried it, tossed one of his forearms onto a pile of blazing logs, but we found the thing did not burn well, healed even as the flames lapped at it. Also, it squirmed from the fire, and we had to prod at it with sticks to keep it there. But worse was the smell; it was so savoury, caused our mouths to water, even as we gagged on it. Then a pack of wolves scented it, came yipping out of the dark. We tried to fend them off with flaring brands grabbed from the fire, but, hunger whetted by the smell, they'd lost their wonted fear of folk and fire, and it went badly for us, and we were hurt. Then a big cat, with huge canines, slunk by, snatched the arm up, loped off. The wolves tore after, howling, and we, weak, sat, slumped. Once we'd our strength back, we went back to our horses, left, luckily, at a distance, tended to our wounds, settled down, taking turns to rest while the other kept watch.

We chanced across Elliot's forearm the following day, after a short ride. The big cat was not far off, dead, had choked on its own tongue, torn through at the root, swallowed. The arm was badly charred, but still moved, pulled itself along the ground with its fingers.

We didn't try burning any part of Elliot again after that.

I believe, then, we did the best we could. There's even a small chance it'll prove to have been not a provisional, but final measure; for, though Elliot will, given time, be whole once more, it's possible the end of the world will come first; the colours in the sky wax more lurid by the day.

Rashmi and I talked a lot during this time and the mute companionship of the previous months grew into true friendship.

(Here I should note, my companion, having grown fond of the name, has asked me to continue to call her Rashmi. Her name for me, Melmoth, is a jest of ours.)

We kept Elliot's head till the last. Half wondering if there mightn't be a kind of binding witchery in interring it there, and unable to shake the idea once we'd thought of it, we went to the spot where the Nightingale had, long, long ago, stood. At the dismal heart of that yew grove, we found William's bones, picked fleshless, gnawed, strewn about. Then, taking turns, we dug a deep pit with a spade we'd found on our travels, I forget where. It was hard work, there were lumps of concrete and tangled roots in the soil. When we were done, worn out, sweat-soaked, we opened the bag, took out Elliot's head. On the ride from the southwesternmost point of the island, once Land's End, where we'd left the right leg, it had managed to spit out the gag, and, as I picked it up, dropped it in the hole, it worked its jaws, tongue, lips, Elliot execrating us, I'd hazard, though, as there wasn't any sound bar the clacking of teeth, I can't be sure. While we shovelled dirt back into the pit on top of it, it continued, soundlessly, to jabber.

After we'd buried the head, Rashmi and I rode down to the Thames. The clattering of our horses' hooves on the few patches of paved road that remained raised clamorous echoes from the buildings' walls, and, at those times, it sounded as if a herd stampeded along with us. Reaching the river, we made camp, cooked up and feasted on some tasty victuals we'd been saving. It was a warm night, and, after eating, we sat on the worn remains of a concrete groyne, dangling our feet in the river, talking of our plans, something we'd been loath to do till then, lest we blight the undertaking. Overhead, wispy clouds scudded across the bright spatter of the constellations, the placid face of the moon. We talked of what we should do, where we should go. I extolled the many wonders of the Himalayas, their peace, for a time, in the end swayed Rashmi, who'd been pressing for somewhere warmer. We resolved to try mountain life a while, see how it suited us.

We set out the following day. Before leaving London, we raided the stacks of the British Library, took all the books we could carry.

Several weeks ago, following a long, arduous journey, we arrived at the foothills of that spiring range, began our ascent. After a few days' climb, we came across a cave, high above the treeline, that seemed an ideal place to dwell. We've made it homely, comfortable; pelts are strewn about the floor, there's a goat-hair pallet to sleep on. But it's also spare and simple, which is as we wish it; there's nothing by way of ornament, save Elliot's knife, hanging on the wall (we tried all we could think of to destroy it, but found it unbreakable, so have kept it as a trophy, memento, caution). It's quiet here, yet I doubt we'll find life dull; the prospect from the mouth of our cave, of hoar-capped peaks, calm tarns, swathes of dark firs below, clouds drifting by just overhead, fills us daily with awe, and there's drama in the scenes we've seen when out foraging or hunting: a raptor stooping on its prey, a hare, a young goat, a fish; a flight of cranes soaring overhead; a snow leopard stalking a herd of the sure-footed yak who graze the coarse grass of the steeps.

And, though this is a remote spot, where there are no local tribes and few travellers pass by, we won't be lonely, for we pleasure in each other's company, indeed have become lovers. And we won't be completely starved of other society, either. A few days ago we descended to the lower slopes, found a village where we could trade for essentials, iron cooking vessels, spears, rice, and were warmly welcomed by the folk there. They cooked a festival meal, gave us rice wine, played their shawms, singing bells, and tanpura, danced for us. We sat up late into the night, drinking, listening to the keening music. I plan to make myself a new banjo, join the band next time, for, with its eerie drone and brittle tone, I think it would harmonize well with the Tibetan instruments.

And so, overturning all portents, we seem to have found some repose.

Epilogue

A few things remain to be told, then my tale will be complete. Though they concern events whose protagonist was Rashmi, and not I, she's said she can't write of them herself; telling them once was harrowing enough and dredging them up a second time, in committing them to paper, would be too much, would be agony. And she says, and I think she's right, that setting something down is more gut-wringing than just saying it, for, while the spoken word is fleeting, the written, endures.

But she insists on my describing these happenings here. In part, this is because she believes when she reads my third-person accounts she'll be able to convince herself their main player was not her but another and put them behind her (I hope this proves true). She also has a further, much stranger reason, as will become clear.

One cold night, during our trek to the Himalayas, out on the great plains of central Europe, Rashmi and I were sat warming ourselves at a fire. We'd eaten a good dinner of venison stew and were swigging from a gourd of firewater we'd traded for cured buffalo with a tribe of nomads a few days before. A touch drunk, I asked Rashmi about some things I'd been burning to learn of, but which I'd not before brought up for fear of galling sores.

In response to my probing, she told me she'd been cast out by the tribe for killing a senior tribesman. This grizzled elder, who'd been leering lewd at her some weeks, entered her tent one night, soused on a potation brewed up from beetroot, staggering, cock in hand, and threw himself down, sprawled, writhed on her. Waking terrified, she grabbed her blade, held it to his neck, meaning to warn him off. But he flinched, and then his throat was cut, and the tribe, roused by his death rattle, finding Rashmi blood-drenched, went to attack her. So she fled, was just able to outpace them.

It was sheer chance she came across me the next day while I was bathing, she didn't even know I was alive, let alone nearby. Having spotted the Ark before, thought it might make a good place to hide, she'd come to look it over. She recognized me straight away, though she wondered, at first, if it mightn't perhaps be Elliot in my guise. But she decided to take the chance, thinking there could perhaps be safety in numbers, and, besides, unable to come up with any reason why he take on my appearance, supposed it unlikely. That I didn't attack her, and, after, let her go, all but confirmed it. That I seemed not to remember her, bemused, but she surmised my memory had simply fared worse than hers. Deciding it was best not to disclose who she was, she played the frightened native woman. That I was obtuse and misinterpreted her, irked. And she reckoned, after all, it might be dangerous for us to remain together. So she ran away, she hid in a spinney not far off. But when the natives discovered and bolted her, later that day, she made for the hulk once more, doubting there was anywhere else nearby she could hole up. She thought, vaguely, she might be able to drive me off. But she wasn't fleet enough, the natives caught up with her, and, as I've told, set about her. After I rescued her from the beating, she warmed to me, wondered whether we mightn't be better off together after all, decided to stay with me, but to continue shamming the tribeswoman.

That evening as we sat toping by the campfire on the plains, I also asked Rashmi about her later treatment at the hands of the clan, after Elliot left her to them. She told me it hadn't been much of an ordeal, the tribesfolk had been angry, but their ire had cooled, and they'd largely felt pity for her. If it hadn't been for their terror of Elliot, they'd have released her, she thought. She said they just beat her about a bit, then tied her up. While she was bound, some days, she was given water and fed. Occasionally one of her captors would kick her, but not hard; it was clear their hearts weren't in it.

She looked at me.

'There was some kind of terrible revel during that time, wasn't there?'

'Yes,' I said. 'I didn't see it, but I heard.' I shuddered. 'That was enough.'

Then, Rashmi went on, they decided to end it, dragged her out to the mud flats. There, the chieftain stabbed her in the heart with a ceremonial flint knife, and they threw her in a deep pit. She lay prone, while they buried her, then burrowed back to air, a long gruelling toil. When she finally rose out of the sludge, she spotted, by the faint glow of a fire, the natives' camp nearby, went to them to spook them; they fled howling into the night.

Then, after another gulp of the firewater, I asked Rashmi about the thing I had been most wary of broaching, but also was most curious over: the ruse her twin had contrived that took Elliot in. She sat quiet a moment, then shook her head, said, 'I didn't have a twin. Or any brothers or sisters at all. Was an only child.'

'What?'

She smiled, wan.

'Perhaps, it's time for you to hear, at last, my story, the one I went to the pub that night, so long ago, to tell. It doesn't give any answers itself, but... Well, you'll see.'

And so it was, sat by a fire, amid rolling plains, drunk on rotgut, with a bright sickle moon cutting swathes through the hazy cloud overhead, and large animals, perhaps buffalo, or bears, moving about in the girding darkness, I finally heard Rashmi's tale.

It was a weird tale, close kin to those told on that long-ago evening. Rashmi described how the year before the gathering in the Nightingale had been very hard for her. It had started well; she'd got a secretarial position at a successful firm of solicitors, found her own flat, moved, finally, out of her parents' house. But then it had turned ill. Her mother, who'd never been kind and was very traditional, was angered by her new independence, arranged a marriage for her to a friend of the family who lived in India, a much older man. Rashmi refused the match. There was weeping, yelling, handwringing. Rashmi was told she was bringing shame on the family. But she stood her ground. In the end, her mother and aunts disowned her.

Her father, though, supported her, took her side. But this caused a rift between her parents. There were some bad rows. Then her father died, a stroke. At his funeral there was a scene, and Rashmi was thrown out.

After that, Rashmi started going out a lot, drinking heavily, drugging, sleeping little. She stumbled blearily through those days. She didn't then, pick up it was odd, when, a few months later, she was called on her mobile one Saturday, by an old man, who gave his name as Joseph Curwen (like the rest in this text, this name is made up; Rashmi, having forgotten it, asked me to provide a fitting invention), who claimed to be a client of her firm. He said he'd been given her number by one of the partners, her boss. She didn't think it was strange, when, explaining he was housebound, following a fall, and needed to draft his will, he asked her to come, that afternoon, to his cottage, in the Trossachs, north of Glasgow, to witness it, deliver it back to the office. He said he'd cleared it with her boss. She didn't realize it bizarre he'd offer her a fair amount of money. Didn't notice the urging in his tone. Didn't think to ask her boss about it. He'd have told her he'd never heard of any Joseph Curwen, that he'd never give out her personal phone number, that he'd never have asked her to do something like that. Just thought of the fee Curwen had promised. Hoped she might also receive a cup of tea and a slice of cake for her trouble.

She did feel jitters when she drove out and found Curwen's cottage was isolated and set amid a large tract of pine forest, but she quelled them with a swig of gin after parking up.

She received the tea and cake she'd hankered after, but they were laced with a soporific. When she awoke from the blank slumbers the drug had cast her into, she found herself in a small dank chamber, the cottage's cellar, it turned out, bound to a stake, a pentagram chalked round her on the flagstones, black wax candles guttering at each of its five points. She'd been stripped of her clothes, and strange sigils had been daubed in red blood on her brown breasts, belly, and limbs. Snakes' skeletons, strung along lengths of string, swagged the walls, the bones phosphorus dipped and glowing eerily.

At first Rashmi thought the cellar otherwise empty, but then, her eyes adjusting to the dim light of the candles, she noticed, in a dark alcove on the other side of the chamber, a looming gaunt form. She took it, at first, for a statue, perhaps an idol, but then heard it moan, desolate and low, realized it was a living creature of some kind. She stifled a gasp. And, lurching from the nook, tottering upright, the beast burst into the fitful light, loped towards her. She glimpsed a rawboned demon, pallid cankered flesh, spindly limbs, a maw drivelling slobber, then the length of iron chain tethering it, attached to a studded leather collar round its neck, arrested its dart, choked and felled it. Yowling, it scrabbled back into its niche on all fours, back arched, spine jutting, the chain clattering on the flags. Rashmi's nostrils were mobbed by the fetor of rot.

Staring at the recess, every sinew taut with terror, Rashmi saw the creature's gnarled skull jut slowly, warily, as it craned its neck to peer at her. Most of its face was cast in shade by the pillar, but light fell on its right eye, a portion of tallowy forehead. It gazed at her for a long time, stock still. That eye was graven on Rashmi's mind. It was filled with terrible malice, had a palsied, drooping, upper lid, a white, jaundiced and laced with skeins of blood, like the smear of a pulped fecundated egg, and, set in this mess, a pitchy, speckled iris, a coal seam, glistering flecks of mica, with, at its heart, a sliver of pupil, blacker still, an abyssal fissure.

After a time, Rashmi, helpless with terror, pissed down her

legs, and the thing nodded its head, gurgled mirthful, lewd, then ducked back into the alcove, was still, silent again.

Once Rashmi had recovered from the bad shock, she tested her bonds. She found that, though they held firm, they'd not been tied quite tight enough, and, after several hours struggling, she was able to wriggle free. During this time the creature didn't come forth from the nook again. She heard shuffling and the clanking of chain every so often, though.

Then, when Curwen came in to sacrifice her, clutching a curved dagger and a grimoire, she, frantic, half-crazed, overpowered him, ran into the night, fled the gloom of the pines. A farmer, up early to milk his herd, saw her scampering, naked, across his field, caught up with her, gave her his coat, and took her back to his house to be looked after by his wife. When Rashmi had recovered a little, she told the couple her tale, leaving nothing out, though she painted the thing in the nook as a filthy starveling bestial man, for fear they might think her deranged. They were inclined to believe her, for there were rumours about eerie noises coming from the hermit's cottage and strange flickering lights seen in its windows at night, so called the police immediately. A WPC came to take Rashmi's statement, while officers were sent to investigate the old man's property. But, by the time they arrived at the cottage, he'd fled. The weird scene in the cellar confirmed Rashmi's account, though. Of course, the demon, or whatever it was, was also gone. When the police scoured the property after, they discovered human bone fragments mixed into the earth in the kitchen garden. The hermit had apparently ground up the bodies of many victims, perhaps, it was speculated, used the meal to feed the soil he grew his herbs in. And it was a strange lot of herbs.

By the time Rashmi finished telling me her story, she was shaking. I reached out to hold her, but she pushed me, gently, away.

'It's fine,' she said, hugging herself. 'It was a very long time ago. It's just, well, I've not thought about that night in millennia.'

She shuddered.

'I didn't want to relive it now, but...'

She paused, scratched her nose.

'But I think, somehow, if you record it, it'll warn me. So you must set it down, just as told.'

Drunk, I merely nodded absently. Then, reaching for the firewater, I stopped, my hand halfway to the gourd.

'Warn you?'

'Oh, I don't know.'

She picked up the gourd herself, took a draught from it, then held it arm's length, squinted at it.

'We're going to feel horrible in the morning, you know.'

'I know.'

She passed the drink to me, then sat silent a time, biting her lip.

'Well?' I prompted.

'I'm not really sure. All I know is, Elliot was convinced he saw me die. I think your narrative somehow, well...'

'What?'

'Hmm. I'll try my best to explain.'

She then told me that, throughout the terrifying night tied up in the cellar, she'd had a tenuous memory of having before read an account of the things she was undergoing. At the time, she gave it scant thought. And afterwards, when she pondered it, she put it down to that uncanny sense of having lived through something before, which isn't uncommon.

But when she looked over my typescript, after I'd taken her aboard the Ark, she'd had a strong recollection of having, some weeks prior to her horrific encounter with the evil diabolist, found it in a second-hand bookshop in London, during a trip she'd made to the capital, having bought it, the same typescript, though bound in cloth covers, having read it, closely, cover to cover. Yet, weirdly, at the same time she also felt certain she'd never seen it before.

When Elliot described watching her age and die, she'd had a sudden realization: she must, at some point, have split into two separate selves whose paths had forked. Therefore, while she'd agreed to go out to the diabolist's cottage, endured the terrors of his cellar, responded to my classified, attended the gathering in the Nightingale, and so on, her fetch, who'd read my account, had refused, never saw the horror beneath the mundane surface of things, lived out a normal life.

'I envy her so,' she said, shaking her head.

'I'm glad things have turned out as they have, though,' I said, hoping to cheer her.

'You know what bewilders me now?' she asked, ignoring me.

I shook my head.

'Well, you see, if I'd never read your story, I wouldn't have become immortal, couldn't have saved you from Elliot. But had I not rescued you, even allowing for Elliot's not, for some reason of his own, burning your typescript, and it slipping backwards through time so I could read it, you'd have never recorded my tale. Perhaps it's that very paradox that divided me.'

We both sat quiet awhile. My brain reeled.

'Anyhow,' Rashmi went on, eventually. 'I lied to Elliot, told him I'd had a twin because I didn't want him to suspect any of this. Not that I can make any sense of it.'

'I can't either. Though it isn't any stranger than anything else that's befallen us, is it?'

At that we fell silent, stared into the fire, lost in our thoughts. But, before long, our reveries were disturbed. One of the beasts whose lumbering in the dark we'd been hearing all evening blundered into our camp. It was not a bear or buffalo after all, but a huge primeval armadillo, with bone barding and a spiked club at the end of its tail. We leapt to our feet, seized up brands from the fire, backed away. But it meant us no harm, just cocked its lumpish skull to peer blearily at us with one moist yellow eye, then wrinkled its nose, waddled ponderously off.

We stared at each other a moment.

'Yes,' I said, peering off into the night. 'Creation *is* in disarray.'

Rashmi laughed.

'What?' I asked

'You! So serious.'

I squinted at her, started to open my mouth, but she leaned over, silenced me with a kiss.

And here, I bid you farewell, my reader. This is the end of my tale; against all odds, it's a mostly happy one.

Afterword

This will be hard going. It's been a very long time since I last used this typewriter. I have though, meanwhile, taken care of it, kept its mechanisms in good order: protected it from dust, grime, and damp with a cover made from the stomach membrane of a yak, a fine but impermeable stuff; kept it oiled; wiped it fairly often with a soft cloth. I felt sure, you see, I'd have cause to use it again, that some portentous event would compel me to again set its typebars clattering, jostling its ribbon against a sheet of paper clamped in its jaws. So what will make writing this afterword slow, laborious, is that my fingers, out of the habit of typing, are clumsy, halting, and my brain, long unused to composition, struggles to find the words needful. The inspiring prospect from the mouth of this cave, Rashmi's and my home a long time now, should help, though: we're in deep midwinter, so the steeps are swathed in unsullied snow, the tarn, frozen, glister, and the swathes of darkling pine are mottled with white. And, overhead, a grey canopy is breaking up to reveal a wan sun and sliver of moon hung in a sky strewn with bright motley stars, a sublime sight, for all it's an ill omen.

The end of things has been much longer coming than I thought; the signs I noted while writing the tale this will serve as an afterword to, were merely tokens of the onset of a drawn-out decay, not of looming havoc, the end of things; Rashmi and I have dwelt many centuries in the Himalayas since then. They've been mostly happy and peaceful. We've had only one real sorrow: though I soon overcame my impotence, it seems, whether for reasons eldritch or prosaic, I can't say, no children can come of our couplings. But I'm sure the last days are really upon us now, for the sun, after waxing till, several hundred years ago, it was a blazing ball of fire, forcing us to shelter in our cave some decades, has dwindled, is now sickly, faint, no brighter than the moon once was, and things grow cold and dark. So, soon, our long, long lives will cease (and we won't try, my reader, if you were wondering, to escape the Earth's end by running into that dread realm Elliot was so fond of; we've pledged never to enter it, though we now know how to, feel that to do so would be to forfeit something we're not prepared to give up.)

I've spent much time in the last few years, then, musing on the nature of things, now believe the world, the universe, every once in a great many ages, shrivels to a dead core, a dead core that then becomes the seed another cosmos sprouts from. Many have argued this, or something similar, at different times in Earth's history (though my formulation of the notion has, of course, been, in part, shaped by the beliefs of the folk of this mountain region). I don't reckon, though, as some thinkers of past ages have, that the cosmos is reborn to the same over again; Rashmi's uncanny feeling she was sundered, perhaps on reading this very document, had an eldritch twin who knew a life different from hers, has suggested something other to me. I reckon the Earth, on returning from cold and stasis, may sometimes have a slightly different history, and suppose the cause of any changes to be objects that survive the end and, lasting into the next cycle, set up eddies time's flow. Though the cosmos perhaps resists such shifts, those, in particular, that give rise to paradoxes, I'd suppose the possibility of transformation to remain. I've, then, become determined to somehow ensure the survival of this account of mine.

This region has always had its roving holy folk, known as weavers of spells, but in all the time I've lived here there's only been one who's seemed to me to possess any real power, a woman, once almost terrifyingly vital, latterly, at the end of a very long life, a withered crone, though still formidable. I've, myself, witnessed her bringing back to health men, women, and children seemingly beyond hope, rid a field of rice of fungal blight, and raise, by mumbling some words over a line scratched in the dirt, a weird barrier that kept a village from being swept away by an avalanche. Thinking on this last, I decided I'd speak to her about my typescript. I'd only met and talked with her a few times, but felt she might help me if I explained things to her. I thought, then, I'd track her down next spring, when Rashmi and I went down the mountain, lugging furs to trade for rice, iron arrowheads, and other things. But, hearing from a passing traveller the holy woman been taken badly sick, I asked Rashmi if we could go early. She was reluctant to travel in winter, but knowing the hardships of it could only hurt, not kill us, and half swayed by my ideas, agreed.

We left our cave a week ago then, went down to the foothills, and, in the first settlement we came across, made enquiries as to the whereabouts of the holy crone. We were told her illness had got even worse, that she'd returned to the village of her forebears to die. So we set out, in haste, for the place. Partway through our trek, the weather turned really bad, squalls, driving snow, very cold, and, as our way took us through a defile where the drifts were waist high, by the time we arrived we were sore weary, had painful chilblains on our hands and feet. It wasn't, then, till the following morning, when I was recovered, rested, warm, I sought out the witch.

Leaving Rashmi drowsing in the yurt we'd been offered for the night by a kind villager who'd taken pity on us, I made my way to the drystone and sod roundhouse where, I'd been told, the holy woman could be found. The storm had died, and it was eerie quiet; the snow and heavy cloud muffled.

Reaching the place I'd been directed to, I was let in, saw the witch lying on a heap of bearskins against the wall. I was sad to see she really was near death. Family, the brood of a sister, sat sunk in sorrow, were loath to let me speak to her. But hearing my voice, she called out in a reedy tone for them to bring me over. They did, but pleaded low that I not tax her waning strength too much.

She lay slumped, gaunt and wan, shivering in spite of the furs piled on her. She greeted me with a wave of her hand, then, suffering pangs, sat up, clawed at her coverings, moaned. I was moved to see her like that, asked if she couldn't be healed by either her own sorcery, or the remedies of others. But she shook her head slowly and, smiling feeble, told me the span she'd been allotted was drawing to a close, that she was well-prepared for the end.

She gestured for me to take a seat on a three-legged wooden stool drawn up by her pallet. We talked a short while about the weather, friends in common, then she told me of her worries about the cranes. The numbers flying over the range in autumn and spring had been dwindling every year, and hunters were now wary of shooting many down, lest their end be hastened. The flesh had been one of the staple foodstuffs of the Himalayan people's winter diet, so this caused much hunger and misery.

This served as a natural lead into the matter I wanted to broach. I told the holy woman how I believed the end of days drew near and outlined my notion of recurrence with shifts. Listening, she nodded sagely.

'In dreams,' she said, 'I've seen the world tumbling in the void, didn't know what this vision meant. But perhaps it's a sign the Earth, existence, is like that game we call, in these parts, Climb the Mountain, whose players take turns to roll a die, aiming to throw all scores in turn. Perhaps, slow, so slow, all possible histories are gone through.'

'Who, then, gambles with our lives?'

'I suspect but the Void, and its friends Desolation and Emptiness.'

As our talk was beginning to tire her, I thought it prudent to raise the subject of the warding incantation. At first she was bemused. Then, when she realized what I hoped to do, she looked sharply at me.

'I didn't take you for vain.'

'I'm not vain,' I protested, and pointed to my forehead, to the letters Elliot carved there, that have never quite healed, that I've lived with so long. 'I don't care about memorializing my life, my deeds. It's that, if my tale is found and read, it might impede, in the world that's to come, the evil of a creature who's brought misery to many.'

And I told her about Elliot, and his malice, his cruelty, about the things this typescript sets forth.

When I'd done, the witch said, her voice hoarse, 'That explains the things rumoured about you.'

She nodded to herself.

'Well, I *will* help you, best I can. Perhaps that's the true meaning of my dream, that I'm meant, with the last of my fading strength, to aid you in gambling with history.'

Taking one of her limp, burning hands in mine, I thanked her.

'Can I ask,' I said, 'how you'll do it? It is an old magic or a new?'

She laughed.

'I suppose I can trust you?'

I nodded.

'Well, I'll show you.'

And she reached beneath her bedding, took out some kind of gizmo. It was small, fitted into her palm, was made of metal, rusting in spots, had lights fluttering weakly down the side.

'It's that kind of magic,' she said, then she hid the device away again. 'Its secrets will die with me, for it can do terrible ill as well as good.'

I touched her hand.

'Of course.'

'There's something else,' she said. 'Another vision I've had. I thought it merely an ill fever dream before, but now...'

She broke off, spluttered. I started from the stool in concern, but she waved for me to sit back down, took up a rag, hawked, spat a dark clot into it. Then groaned, went on.

'In this dream, I saw a man without a head scrabbling at the earth. Beneath dark, gnarled branches.'

I shuddered.

At that moment, one of the holy woman's nephews came over, implored me not to keep her from sleep longer. The witch looked up at him.

'Thank you. I'll rest in a moment, but there's something I must explain to my friend first.'

I left the roundhouse a little after, clutching a large cloth bag. The witch had told me to put my typescript in it, seal it up, bring it back to her so she could cast a 'charm' on it. She urged me to haste. I found Rashmi breakfasting with some villagers, related to her what had passed, and we returned here. I sat down at my typewriter to compose this afterword, as soon as we arrived back.

So now it comes time to finally conclude this memoir. Once I've sealed this document in the sack the holy woman gave me, taken it to her to be 'enchanted', it may not be opened again, for to do so would break the 'spell'. When I asked her what I should do with it after, she told me it didn't really matter, but suggested I might bury it. After some thought, I've decided I'll leave it in the stacks of the British Library, beneath London's ruined streets; I feel that will be a fitting resting place.

Besides, we've another reason to go back to that desolated city. When I told Rashmi of the witch's second vision she suggested we return, with haste, to either prevent Elliot from putting himself back together again, or, if we should be too late, find him, attempt once more to best him.

'I don't,' she said, 'want to live in fear, in hiding, ever again, even for a moment.'

I agreed with her. Though we're sure the end of all things is coming, we wish the short time remaining to us to be as calm, as happy as it can be. We also feel we should attempt to prevent Elliot's fleeing the eschaton by going into Tartarus.

This, then, is truly the end of my story. Rashmi, I hope you'll forgive me if (while in my heart I inscribe it to you) I dedicate it to the hoped for, though doubtless chimeric reader who's been so faithful to me (who may, perhaps, be some version of you). Reader, if you do exist, you'll live on a new world, one sprouted from the germ of this frozen Earth. I'm sure it'll be a world where good and ill vie for dominance, just as they did on this; I urge you to thresh grain from chaff, plant and nurture the seeds, burn the husks.

But I've waxed sententious. I must now curtail these foolish ramblings, place this text in the sack the holy woman gave me. After that's done, Rashmi and I will climb to the peak of this mountain, spend some time gazing at the welkin's tapestry, telling each other stories of the things we see sketched in the weave, the tales of our own sidereal mythos, a common pastime of ours. Then, tomorrow, we'll leave behind this cave we've spent a long happy time in, and, after seeing the witch on her deathbed, will strike out for that place once known as London, on what, I think, may well be our final journey. Homeward bound once more.

Endnotes

1   This is one of three alterations to the typescript. The name of
    the book here has been blotted out by thick hatching, and in
    Peterkin's hand, just above, this title interpolated. *At the
    Mountains of Madness* is a 1931 novella by H.P. Lovecraft. It is
    not possible to make out the original reference, the heavy
    erasure has obliterated it.

2   Many of Peterkin's stories and novels feature minor
    characters who share his surname. But a note, in Peterkin's
    distinctive crabbed hand, in the margin of the typescript at
    this point, works against the reassuring interpretation. It
    reads: 'Coincidence? Or an obscure threat?'

3   Here Peterkin has scrawled, in the margin: 'A coincidence?'

4   Another of Peterkin's marginal notes: 'Never heard tell of
    this.'

5   By this text is written another note in Peterkin's hand. It is
    heavily underscored. It reads: 'This dates it!'

6   This is the second of Peterkin's changes to the typescript;
    again the original title is heavily crossed-out and illegible.
    The Sphinx of the Ice-Fields is a novel, of 1897, by Jules Verne
    (original French title, *Le Sphinx des glaces*). It is a sequel to
    and re-imagining of Edgar Allan Poe's *The Narrative of Arthur
    Gordon Pym of Nantucket* (1838), a novel Peterkin was fond of
    and whose title is interpolated in a similar fashion later in the
    typescript.

7   On this page is another of Peterkin's marginal jottings: 'Was
    a smoking ban not in force then? Whenever 'then' was?'

8   This is the third of Peterkin's changes to the typescript. His
    pen was, it seems, pressed against the page with excessive
    force while he hatched out the original title – the nib has
    perforated the paper in places. *The Narrative of Arthur Gordon
    Pym of Nantucket* is Edgar Allan Poe's novel of 1838. And

there is another marginal note on this page: 'Both Verne's and Lovecraft's formulations vitiate the horror of Poe's original conception.' It is underlined three times.

9   There is another of Peterkin's marginal notes here: 'Reading this again, I realize the notion gives a dreadful cast to things I've thought consoling.'

10 On the back of this page of the typescript, with clear reference to this roll of artists and writers, Peterkin has scrawled: 'Am I to be part of this illustrious company? To date my evil has been shabby, my imagination tame. But what might I be able to write now? And, am I one of the successes? Now an everliving quarry?'

11 In the margins here, Peterkin has written: 'Things will go differently this time.'

12 Daubs of some darkish matter do mark this chapter of the typescript and the one immediately following.

13 All of the pages of *The Wanderer* typescript up to and including chapter XII, are indeed creased, as if at some point they have been screwed up then smoothed out again.

Appendix I

Editor's Note on Peterkin's Emendations to the Text

After my second, and thorough, read through of *The Wanderer*, I passed it to Fiona G. Ment, to get her opinion. I told her I'd been fretting over the authorship and provenance, indicated to her those elements I thought uncanny. When she'd finished the typescript, she came back to me to say she was, herself, certain it was a work of fiction.[1] She'd come up with a thesis. The preponderance of evocations of the works of Edgar Allan Poe had started her thinking about their significance (though the text alludes to other works, largely in the Gothic tradition, references to Poe's corpus outnumber those to any other writer's).

Ment noted three things. First, the number of Poe allusions, in and of themselves, point to Peterkin as the author, for he was a Poe obsessive, had stated in interviews that it was reading 'The Mask of the Red Death' as a teenager that had infected him with the desire to write, had even composed two tales, 'Reynolds' (collected in *The Black Arts* (1999)), and 'Bottle Found in a MS.' (collected in *The Blood Cults of Bognor Regis and Other Weird Tales* (2003)), that fictionally account for Poe's lost last days.

Second, there are the references to Poe's tales 'The Angel of the Odd' and 'The Sphinx'. The first, a short story of 1844, describes the narrator's encounter, while in a drunken stupor, with the eponymous entity, a creature entirely composed of various alcohol receptacles and appurtenances, who announces, in heavy-accented tones, that he's the 'the genius who preside[s] over the contretemps of mankind, and whose business it [is] to bring about the odd accidents which are continually astonishing the skeptic.' The Angel has manifested before the narrator because he's scoffed at the likelihood of such strange and terrible coincidences after reading a report in a newspaper of a bizarre death which he believes 'a poor hoax.' The protagonist pays scant attention to the Angel, his contempt, after a time, driving the odd creature away. As a punishment, this avatar of chance then subjects the narrator to an increasingly absurd series of trials. The story superficially seems a warning to those who'd sneer at the weird, but this ostensible meaning is undercut by comic absurdity and the unreliability of its soused protagonist; its suggestion would, in fact, seem to be that the odd happenings arise, not from an eldritch cosmos, but from the idiotic imagination of the sottish narrator. And, taken with this reference, that the characters of *The Wanderer*'s inset tales are all drunk, or half-drunk at least, or drugged, or high when they have their dread experiences, intimates that much in the novel is intended to be delusion, or so Ment believed. In 'The Sphinx', a tale from two years later, the morbid narrator's vision from a window of a fearsome behemoth ponderously clambering up a distant hillside, taken to be a harbinger of his death, is revealed, by a clear-headed friend, to be accountable by his having seen a tiny moth climbing a gossamer thread hanging before the glass, and to have been a quirk of perspective. It's the story of the triumph of reason over the eldritch, and the mention of it another hint from the author of the typescript, according to Ment.

And third, and in her opinion, most conclusively, Ment felt that the allusions were pointing at Poe's well-known reputation as a hoaxer. Poe framed a number of his fictions, including 'MS. Found in a Bottle' and the novel, *The Narrative of Arthur Gordon Pym of Nantucket*, both referred to in *The Wanderer* (though the mention of *Arthur Gordon Pym* is one of Peterkin's later emendations), as true accounts, and, in 1844, published an article in the *New York Sun*, an account of a balloon trip across the Atlantic Ocean, that though presented as reportage, was a fiction. Ment suggested, therefore, that, in invoking Poe, the author of *The Wanderer*, whom she assumed to be Peterkin, was subtly drawing attention to the typescript's status as an invention.

At the time, I was convinced by her arguments, and *The Wanderer*'s grip on me slackened for a short while. But pondering the matter subsequently, I've grown unsure again. A number of things have eroded my peace, troubled me, in particular Peterkin's three alterations to the manuscript, the three book titles interpolated, *At the Mountains of Madness*, *The Sphinx of the Ice-Fields*, and *Arthur Gordon Pym*, and the strange jotting, stressed by being underscored three times, in the margin of the page on which the last change occurs, 'Both Verne's and Lovecraft's formulations vitiate the horror of Poe's original conception.'

As I noted in a footnote, Jules Verne's *The Sphinx of the Ice-Fields* is a sequel to *Arthur Gordon Pym*. It's also a rationalization of that work. It posits Poe's novel as a mostly true narrative, but either accounts for, by scientific principles, or rejects, as hallucinations, all the horrors and wonders of the American writer's imagination.

H.P. Lovecraft's *At the Mountains of Madness* is also, in some ways, a sequel to *Arthur Gordon Pym*; it contains references to Poe's novel, is likewise presented as a true account, a testimony, and takes from it the haunting call of the gigantic white birds of the polar regions seen by Pym, 'Tekeli-li!', which becomes, in Lovecraft's novel, the cry of the vile, terrible shoggoths the narrator's party find beneath the Antarctic wastes, a cry the shoggoths learnt from their old masters, the Elder Ones. Lovecraft's approach to the material differs significantly from Verne's, though. In *At the Mountains of Madness*, *Arthur Gordon Pym* is asserted to be a fabrication. It is one, though, that may have had its origins in Poe's reading of 'unsuspected and forbidden sources', notably, it's hinted, that dark book of Lovecraft's fabulation, the *Necronomicon* of the Mad Arab, Abdul Alhazred. Lovecraft subsumes Poe's tale into his nihilistic cosmology, which, though terrifying, has a certain coherence, a certain logic. This is perhaps because, for Lovecraft, the ludic chaos of Poe's fragmentary, incomplete, and amorphous text would have been insupportable; Lovecraft's real fear, as many commentators have noted, was of disorder; in his writings the approach of the monstrous and grotesque is often heralded by a Dionysian piping of flutes.

By inserting references to *Arthur Gordon Pym*, *The Sphinx of the Ice-Fields*, and *At the Mountains of Madness* into *The Wanderer* typescript, Peterkin was perhaps indicating to any reader perceptive and thorough enough that, just as Verne's scientistic approach and Lovecraft's alignment of the text with his relatively stable mythology, rather than ravelling out, just cut through the knots of Poe's enigma, so rationalizing or fabulous readings of *The Wanderer* are false, are simplifications. Perhaps he sought to indicate, clandestinely, he felt the document an authentic account of things that had really happened, or were to happen...

1   Fi remained convinced of this till her untimely death.

Appendix II

A Tale of Penury

Editor's Note

Not long after completing my first, slightly cursory, reading of *The Wanderer* typescript, while engaged in my second, more attentive, perusal, I was browsing the shelves of a second-hand bookshop in Stoke Newington and sighted a strange title inscribed, in gold, on the spine of a slim leather-bound hardback. This title was *Tales from the Land of Nod*. It drew my notice, resonated, because the Land of Nod is the place, in the Book of Genesis of the Hebrew Bible, to which Cain flees after the murder of his brother, and, 'nod' being the root of a Hebrew verb meaning 'to wander', the usual interpretation of the passage is that it implies Yahweh condemns Cain to wander the Earth for all time. The name of the author, Walter Waldegrave, was not known to me.

I bought the book, took it straight home to read. Its first few leaves are blank. They're followed by a frontispiece; an etching depicting an old man, with a matted beard, dressed in a cloak. He stands, hunched, leaning on a knotty staff, amid a barren, rocky landscape. Facing this illustration is the title page; the text printed there runs as follows:

Tales from the Land of Nod
Ten startling stories heard from the lips of men and
women of the Legion Lost
By Walter Waldegrave

There's no other information, no publisher's or printer's details, no publication date. On the leaf immediately following, there's an epigraph:

Him the Almighty Power
Hurld headlong flaming from th'Ethereal Skie
With hideous ruine and combustion down
To bottomless perdition.

This quotation is taken from lines 44-47 of Book I of *Paradise Lost*.

Tales from the Land of Nod is a very strange literary artefact. It contains ten episodes, which are presented as factual accounts. They relate encounters on the trail in some of the least hospitable places of the world, set across a period spanning the last few years of the nineteenth century and the first decades of the twentieth. They lack any overarching narrative; the only thing unifying the collection is the identity of the narrator, Waldegrave, who, of course, might be a fiction. They're written in an archaic, awkward style. The format of the episodes is familiar from supernatural and horror literature: a frame describes a meeting between Waldegrave and another individual, who then goes on to tell a yarn.

In the first nine tales the central story is presented to the reader in full. In the tenth, however, which has the rambling title, 'A Tale of Penury, Bloody Murder, Card-Sharping Swindles, Sham Séances, and the Realms of the Foul Olden Horrors that Prowl the Primeval Lightless Ways that Riddle the Earth: The Chilkoot Trail, 1897', it is withheld. This tale is an account of the first time a bizarre narrative was related to Waldegrave by someone he met on the road. It was this experience, so he writes, that gave him his craving for similar odd tales. The strange inset story is here left out because Waldegrave claims he promised never to recount it to another soul.

There are a number of eerie resemblances between the occurrences 'A Tale of Penury' sets forth and the events of Duncan's life as related in *The Wanderer*. Therefore, I present it here for the light it might shed on the nature of the typescript I found in Peterkin's apartment. It is, of course, possible, that Peterkin, having read *Tales from the Land of Nod*, borrowed from it, either as straightforward copying, or as part of a bizarre attempt to make *The Wanderer* seem a genuine account. But the more disturbing alternative remains, and I, for one, can't shake it.

A Tale of Penury, Bloody Murder, Card-Sharping Swindles, Sham Séances, and the Realms of the Foul Olden Horrors that Prowl the Primeval Lightless Ways that Riddle the Earth
The Chilkoot Trail, 1897

My fund of eldritch narratives (at least those I can tell without compromising my principles; it will become clear what I mean by this) is now exhausted, but I feel it important for me to relate how I first came by my mania for wandering the wild and barren places of the Earth seeking men of that strange band, the Legion Lost, striking up acquaintances with them, and asking them to recount for me their bizarre tales of woe and hardship. To this effect, I present the following – the story of my hearing the yarn that, like a drug, got me craving for others of its ilk. Sadly, though, as I promised I would not ever breathe or write one word of it, and will not go against my scruples on this point, this account will have a void at its heart, an absence.

The man who told me the tale forced me to make this pledge on learning I had literary ambitions; I call him Robert here, but, as I also swore not to reveal anything that might give away his identity – he was insistent about this, claiming that danger to him, and to myself, might result from my doing so – this name is a fabrication.

It was the autumn of '97. Young, foolish, and reckless with misery following the untimely death of my young wife, my first love, from cholera, the year before, I was lured by tales of Yukon Gold, and, along with tens of thousands of other poor venturesome sapskulls, outfitted myself in Seattle and secured a berth on a ship bound for Alaska. In doing so, I spent most of a legacy I had been bequeathed by a wealthy uncle. I disembarked at Skagway, the Alaskan port from which one could most easily make one's way to the gold fields in the vicinity of Dawson City. Before the rush, Skagway had been an outpost of the fur trade, a dismal place of churned mud and clapboard shacks, inhabited by a mere handful of brutish men who bludgeoned seals to scrape a living, but by then it was moiling with unscrupulous provisioners, whores, and crackbrained missionaries, all there to waylay, gull, and fleece the frantic, reckless, and easily duped stampeders who passed through. I myself tarried there a deal longer than I should have, mainly due to the ministrations of a pretty young moll named Laura, who looked something like my dead wife. It was only when I noticed the nights were waxing longer than the days, I realized I would have to light out if I was to make it over the mountains into Canada before winter set in and the notches became impassable. I paid a visit to the Tlingit camp just outside of town and took on three Indians to lug my food and equipment, then found a ferry prepared to take me over to Dyea, a small settlement at the head of the trail.

On the morning of the second day I reached the foot of the Golden Stairs, a set of steps cut yearly into the snow and ice of the steep slope that rose to the Chilkoot Pass. It was a cold and gray day, exceedingly cold and gray. At the foot of the steps was the Scales, a tent city, with a saloon and a couple of restaurants, that had sprung up round a Mountie checkpoint where packs were weighed to ensure all stampeders carried at least a ton of supplies, reckoned a year's worth – a measure put in place to prevent those bound for the gold fields from being driven to desperate acts of plunder against Canadian homesteaders by hunger and thirst. This stipulation meant that many, those too poor to afford to pay Indians to help them carry their load, had to make several trips between campsites lugging their provisions – the rigors of the route were too much for pack animals. The weight of my baggage was found to be sufficient, and I was allowed through the checkpoint with my bearers. There was a primitive horse-drawn tramway offering to haul loads up to the highest point of the trail, but the fees being charged were exorbitant, and besides, I preferred to trust my things to my reliable Indians, than to a ridiculous contraption.

I set out up the staircase, clinging to the guide rope, eyes narrowed against the sleet squalls that beset us, seekers of gold, guides, and pack bearers all. A great number of us, hooded against the bitter cold, trudged up the ice steps. We looked pilgrims bound for a shrine containing a precious relic – in a way, I suppose, this is exactly what the prospectors among us were, though it was to gold we pledged our devotions and made our supplications. Or perhaps it would be more accurate to say we resembled an order of flagellants, for if the man in front, fatigued, slowed, many would – the way being strait, and they, frantic to cross the ridge before nightfall when temperatures would plummet – drive him on by striking out with anything to hand. Lengths of hempen cord served as makeshift lashes, walking staffs and pickaxe, mattock, and shovel handles were used as goads. Or perhaps with our clothing ragged and our belongings bundled up on our backs, we looked more like bindlestiffs or hobos.

About halfway up the staircase, at the pass's famous false summit – a ridge that appears the highest point of the trail until reached, when a further steep climb can be seen beyond it – there was a ledge of rock beside the path offering respite from the arduous ascent. This shelf was narrow and beetled over the void, but a large number of bone-weary stampeders, careless of the bluff's edge, sprawled or milled about, querulously bemoaning the hardships of the trail, as if they walked it at the behest of some potentate, rather than of their own volition; the noise they made was similar to one commonly heard at dusk by the sea, that of a colony of gannets roosting. Standing in knots, talking low, the Indians looked askance at their employers, no doubt contemptuous of the bellyaching – that proud race had been climbing the trail for generations. Sitting down, I took off my hobnailed boots and thick socks, rubbed lard into my swollen, blistered, and chilblained feet.

This done, I looked about me. A man, who, seemingly oblivious to the commotion about him, stood gazing out at the prospect of snow-tonsured peaks, attracted my notice. His clothing marked him out – while we men under the spell of gold were clad alike in hooded furs and oil-slickers, and the natives were dressed in garments sewn from bearskin and deerhide, he wore a stained and torn military greatcoat, a thick woolen scarf, and a beaver hat with earflaps which were tied under his chin with string. His thick matted beard and the locks of hair curling from beneath his hat were speckled with gray, and his back was bowed, though the impression this conveyed of decrepitude was at odds with the suggestion of sinewy vigor there was about him. I could not reach a firm conclusion about his age, though, for his back was to me, and his face, mostly hidden. He carried only a small satchel, seemed to have no pack bearers, and I wondered how he had managed to get past the Mountie checkpoint. It appeared he found something enthralling in the scene before him; perhaps he perceived evidence of the Maker's workings even in that desolate place. I, too, looked out at the view, but it gave me no solace: I felt no numinous awe, saw only a harsh unforgiving landscape – I had lost my faith on losing my dear wife.

My musings were soon disturbed – a man a little distance away took off his footwear, as I had, and, discovering several of his toes grey, shriveled, threw a conniption fit.

The afflicted stampeder was a very small wiry man, with a face like the blade of a hatchet, honed to keenness by life's grind. His eyes were shrewd, his lank greasy blonde hair straggled down over his ears and nape, his incisors were prominent, and his beard was pale against his red chapped skin. In short, he was of the type of the luckless rat-like petty miscreant of innumerable popular novels. He was railing about his ill luck and cussing in gruff tones, casting about him with his gimlet eyes and fixing other wayfarers with his glare as if he blamed them for his suffering.

The rat's travelling companion stood by, looking down, dull, agape, at his friend's ruined feet. No two more dissimilar individuals could be imagined. By contrast to the rat, his fellow was tall, hulking, had hands like ham hocks, thick matted hair, a full grizzled beard. In fact, he resembled nothing so much as a bear. And, or so it appeared from the way his mouth was hanging open to catch the swirling flakes of snow, was something of a dolt.

After a few minutes, the rat's bawling began to roil some of the other stampeders. There were grumbles, then a brute yelled at him, called for him to hold his tongue, keep his head. The brute's nose was squashed flat against his face, probably a legacy of a life of brawling, and that, combined with his apparent irascibility, gave him the air of a pit dog.

'I won't take no orders from someone looks like the kind whose sister's also his daughter and his lover,' came the rat's jeering response.

The pit dog was bemused at first – it took him a while to unravel the insult. Then he snarled, drew a Bowie knife from a sheath at his belt.

'I'm goin' uh cut you open from crotch to craw, you stinkin' weasel,' he snarled, then bounded at the rat. The bear stepped into the pit dog's path, swatted him to the ground with one of his giant paws.

Men of the pit dog's party pulled blades and flew at the bear to avenge the insult. Most on the ledge gathered around, yawping; only the dignified Indian porters backed away, looked on the ruckus with disdain.

On hearing the uproar, the man in the tattered greatcoat turned away from the outlook. My conjectures as to his age were ended then – judging by his countenance, he was only a few years out of his youth, though his hoar-flecked hair and stoop, together with something I had not noticed before, that he had lost his right arm at the shoulder – his sleeve was pinned across his chest and flapped in the wind – gave him the air of one ravaged by a hard life and old beyond his span.

The fight on the ledge was reminiscent of a scene I had witnessed once in a pit in southern California, when they baited a grizzly with lions brought over from the Dark Continent. Just as the lions were no match for that bear, the pit dog's friends were no match for this. At the end of the brawl, the big fellow was still standing, panting through clenched teeth, and, though steeped in blood running from many shallow wounds to his arms and chest, barely hurt. His adversaries, however, had fared badly – lay strewn about nursing cracked ribs and broken heads. The rat sat looking smugly on, his frostbite, for the moment, forgotten.

That would have been the end, had not the pit dog, recovered from the blow that had knocked him down, sneaked up behind the bear, blade in hand, meaning, it seemed, to hamstring him. At that the one-armed man took a revolver from his greatcoat, leveled it at the pit dog, and shouted, 'Enough!'

His roar brought silence to the ledge.

'That's enough. Leave him be.'

Then, looking down, shaking his head, he said, as if to himself, 'Shameful animals.'

He seemed to have some inborn sway, for the pit dog and his injured comrades melted into the throng.

After putting his gun away, the one-armed man crossed over, knelt down beside the rat, and looking askance at him, began speaking in a low voice. Furtive, ashamed to be eavesdropping, but too curious to repress the urge, I drew closer, hoping to catch some of what was said. I overheard their introductions, learned the one-armed man was Robert, and the rat, Peter. Much of their subsequent conversation was lost to the wind's howl and the tumult of the other stampeders' complaining and talk, but I managed to make out that Robert was attempting to get Peter to abandon his hopes of making a fortune in the Yukon, and return to the Mountie camp where he could get his feet tended to. At first Peter was reluctant, but on being told he was otherwise certain to lose toes and struggle thenceforth to walk, he seemed, suddenly, to see the good sense in the course being advised him.

Robert then turned to the bear, sought to persuade him to help his companion back down the mountain. This loyal friend, after only a moment's pondering, agreed. His name, it transpired, was Paul; Robert smiled on hearing that. After putting his boots back on for him, Paul helped Peter to his feet. The two men then shambled off, Paul all but carrying Peter bodily under his arm.

I had been moved and surprised by Robert's bravery and kindness – such compassion being a rarity in those bitter climes – and went over to strike up a conversation. I expressed my admiration for the way he had acted. His stammered reply demonstrated humility, but also self-righteousness.

'I think most people would have done as I did, had they been able. That no one here did, is merely evidence of the way gold preys on these stampeders' minds. I, though, do not hunger after Earthly riches.'

I noticed a faint trace of Scots lingered in the man's accent, but he had clearly been in America some years, for it was almost buried.

We were having to shout to make ourselves heard above the clamor, and Robert suggested we take shelter from the noise behind a large rock at the far end of the ledge. I turned to ask my Indians to wait for me, then followed him behind the boulder. Once we were ensconced in its lee, I asked him what, if he was not a fortune seeker, he was doing out there in that hostile waste.

'I'm a preacher and it's my calling to succor those in bleak circumstances. Where better to do so? I came out here to help, where I can.'

I frowned at him.

'What's more,' he went on, 'I succumbed once to the enticements of fabled wealth, and it eases me some to comfort those who've likewise fallen prey.'

My admiration was fast souring, curdled by the rennet of Robert's priggish manner.

'That gold isn't fabled,' I said, belligerently. 'I've seen some of it with my own two eyes, back in California.'

'Was just a figure of speech is all. There is gold in some of the Klondike's creeks, as you say. May as well be fabled, though. Most of the claims are taken, and even if you were able to gang together with some others and stake yourself a place, you'd most likely be driven off by roughneck claim-jumpers before you'd even had a chance to thaw out a patch of earth to dig.'

'I can look out for myself.'

'Well, it's not just toughs you've got to look out for, there are outlandish-cruel men out there who get up to things as would freeze your blood quicker than a night out in the open at the pole.'

He struck a pose, with his arm held out before him, began declaiming, 'There are strange things done, in the midnight sun, by the men who moil for gold. The Arctic trails have their secret tales, that would make your blood run cold.'

Of course these verses are now familiar to me as the first lines of 'The Cremation of Sam McGee' by Robert W. Service, but back then they were novel, and that great poet of Yukon life, the 'Canadian Kipling', was yet to publish them. The only explanation I can think of, is that Robert must have encountered and discoursed with Service during his wanderings. Service hailed from Glasgow, as, I was later to discover, did Robert, and it is possible, had the two men met in the frozen Yukon, so far from the city on the banks of the Clyde, they might have struck up an acquaintance over reminiscences of that Dear Green Place.

'Also,' Robert continued, 'digging isn't as easy as you'd think. It's back-breaking labor. And even when you've got down to the gravel layer, chances are you'll find it isn't pay dirt and'll have to try delving elsewhere.'

'Oh, I think I'm doughty enough,' I said, sardonically.

'You'd be best off turning back now, reckoning whatever sum you've outlaid thus far lost through ill fate. You may have wasted money, but, as yet, you've risked and endured little. All the dangers and hardships lie ahead of you.'

He went on to evoke these for me, in a harangue filled with the lurid parlance of the evangelic pulpit. His description of the White Horse Rapids struck me particularly, it was so turgid, and I can recall it practically verbatim.

'At one point the river runs through a narrow gully, the Miles Canyon, then courses down a steeply shelving rock-strewn reach, known as the White Horse Rapids. This isn't far down the Yukon from the winter camps, you know. Yes, it *is* a right poetical name, isn't it? It's said they were christened by early pioneers who were reminded of the wind-tousled manes of hoary steeds by all the spume. You *suppose* it's dangerous? Well, you'd be right there, it's perhaps the most treacherous stretch of the whole river, and it's at no point along its course a calm waterway. A lot of rafts and poorly made barks have capsized or wrecked shooting the rapids, and this has resulted in the loss of provisions, and occasionally of life, for some have been dragged under by eddies, smothered by roily waters. Yet, many stampeders still tempt providence in spite of this, for they're a foolhardy breed. What's even more astounding is that there are alternative routes, land trails that are well-known, and fairly easy-going. They just take longer is all. Impatience? Brute avarice, I'd call it. Fittingly the roar of the rapids sounds as the tumult of the damned in Hell must, for those that have drowned there will, for their greed, have been cast down forthwith into the infernal lake of fire.'

Once he had concluded his catalogue of risks and adversities, Robert looked up at a skein of geese that was flying by, far overhead. He continued staring into the sky long after their silhouettes had been lost against a dark high mass of cloud moving in from the east. I said nothing, a little rattled, for I realized that, if the tone of Robert's disquisition had been risible, in tenor it was probably an accurate reflection of the hardships of the route. Then, after a time, his eyes still fixed on the heavens, he sighed.

'And you'd put yourself through all of this,' he said, 'for material gain, which God frowns upon.'

That irked me. I resented his Pharisaical stance on the, in my view, natural hankering after wealth.

'Thanks,' I blustered, 'but I'll take my chances, and go on. I'm not gutless.'

'I'm not impugning your pluck. Just warning you, is all. Doubtless you'll make it to Dawson City without coming to harm. But, like I say, when you get there you'll find local miners have taken all the gold-bearing creeks.'

Most of those who reached Dawson ended up living on the settlement's fringes in shanties built using broken-up river craft, disappointed, milling about town, biding their time while deciding how best to make the journey back south, Robert said. Furthermore, he claimed that, due to the huge incursion, disease was rife and the city now teetered on the brink of famine.

'Therefore, you may find you're able to do some good, if you're inclined to, and you insist on pressing on,' he continued. 'That's why I'm bound there. If so, you'll have the satisfaction of knowing you're lending a hand to a community in dire need, or rather two hands, which is more useful, when all's said and done, than just the one.'

He grinned, almost diffidently, plucked at his empty sleeve.

I was disarmed by Robert's joke at his own expense and began to wonder whether I had allowed my prejudice against preachers to fog my judgment. After all, for all his cant, Robert had only been trying to alert me to the trials he thought I would face. The thawing of my opinion was attended by a sudden onset of cold. Heavy snow began to fall from the black rack overhead, which now shrouded the entire sky. I looked round the corner of the rock behind which Robert and I had been conversing, and was perturbed to see one of my Indians sitting on the floor, clutching his head and shivering. I crossed over to find out what was wrong. It emerged he had taken very ill of a sudden. Concerned for him, the other Indians implored me to let him return to Skagway straightway. I could hardly refuse their earnest pleas, in any case it did not look like the sick man had the strength to take up his pack again. I was resigned, therefore, to abandoning some of my provisions, and was just about to sort out a pile of the least essential items to leave behind, when Robert approached, asked what was the matter. When I explained, he said, 'Well, as you know, I think it's foolhardy to go on at all, but since you're determined, and I'm going that way anyhow, I may as well help you out by toting what I can.'

I gratefully accepted this offer of aid, partly out of desperation, and partly because my glimpse of Robert's streak of self-deprecating humor had, as I say, endeared him slightly to me, given me to think he might be more pleasant company than I had hitherto thought, though I still considered him a prig. Thus, as a consequence of the vagaries of fate and a weak jest, I heard the story that fired the great obsession of my life.

We went on to the end of the trail – Robert, the two remaining Indians, and I – and, after a good day and a half's slog on from the top of the Chilkoot pass, reached Lake Bennett. During that time my dislike of Robert fast turned to regard, and my regard quickly burgeoned into friendship; he was, in truth, a congenial fellow – I discovered a good heart lay beneath his preachy vesture. And he too had recently lost his wife; this shared tragedy forged a bond between us.

On the shores of the frozen lake, towered over by hoar-dredged mountains and hemmed in by tenebrous pines, vast numbers of dun-colored tents, brindled here and there with snow, had sprouted up, like toadstools after heavy rain. As we walked down the path into the encampment we passed many men whipsawing logs into planks for boat-building; it looked wearisome work.

On reaching the camp, Robert suggested we take a stroll among the tents. Everywhere we walked he pointed out brutishness and squalor: men brawling, women smoking and spitting, children suffered to run underfoot, besmirched with filth. We saw one man hack another's ear clean from his skull with a Bowie knife, and a withered prostitute lifted her skirts to us.

It seemed the good were outnumbered by the low, the violent, the snarling, and the bestial. Whether I would have seen this, had Robert not directed my gaze to it, I do not know – possibly I might still have been bleary-eyed with dreams of making my fortune – but, whatever the case may be, I realized that, were there gold still in the Klondike, there would be a horrid scuffle over it, one I did not have the stomach for; scrabbling in the frozen earth with men such as the men in the camp on the shores of Lake Bennett was not for me, not even for a fortune the like of Hearst's.

Further, we learnt, from conversations overheard, that the ice had formed on the Yukon early that year, making the river impassable until the spring thaw, then at least four months off.

So I decided to return to Skagway, secure passage on a boat bound for a port further down the western seaboard. When I announced this intention to Robert, he said, if I would have him along, he would like to postpone his trip to Dawson City and accompany me. I was touched, told him I would be glad of his company. He then asked if I had any objection to going back by way of the White Pass Trail, and trying if we could do any good there. He explained that, though the route was less severe than the Chilkoot Trail, in some ways conditions on it were worse, largely because thieves and grifters preyed on wayfarers. I assented.

As it was getting late in the day by then, we decided we would have to spend one night there, in the camp, wait until the following morning to set out. First I dismissed my Indians, then spent most of the rest of the afternoon selling off my gear, save my tent, at the best price I could get, sadly still a bad loss. When I went to meet Robert, at the spot where we had pitched our tents, I found him talking to a young woman, looked like a wanton to me, and a boy who was not more than eight or so. As I came upon them, I heard the woman say, 'His c—ks——r father hit 'im so hard it jes' jumped outta his head.'

Then I noticed the boy was missing an eye, his right, the orbit a raw pit. Robert took the boy's chin, turned his head this way and that. The boy sniffled, but otherwise submitted to the examination.

'Looks, at least, like it's healed up nicely,' Robert then said. 'I am so sorry though.'

'All the other kids is mean to 'im now.'

'Look. I tell you what,' Robert said, taking, from his pocket, what I, at first, took to be a marble. 'You have this, boil it up, then pop it in. It should fit well, I reckon. It'll keep dirt from the socket, and the other children won't tease him anymore.'

I peered closer. It was a beautifully crafted glass eye. The mother took it, and she and her son scampered off. I greeted Robert, then asked him where he got the glass eye from.

'Ach,' he said. 'It's a long story.'

He would not be drawn on it. Then we went off to get ourselves a plate of beans before turning in.

The following morning, we set out, early, along the White Pass Trail.

I will not bore you with the details of that fatiguing and fretful journey. The route did not come to be known as the Dead Horse Trail for nothing – the frozen carcasses of horses, ponies, and mules strewed it; they lay on their backs, four legs stiff in the air like stovepipe hats, hides partially flayed by the wind, ribs poking through like the timbers of wrecked coracles. Our toils were, in small part, recompensed by the fact we aided some stampeders in straits, though we were unable to convince any of the idiocy of continuing into Canada.

Not long after gaining Skagway, I managed to talk the captain of a steamer, bound for Seattle, into taking me on. I tried to persuade Robert to likewise seek a working berth, but he said he preferred to stay on in the frozen North and continue his humanitarian enterprise, meant to head back down the trail once more, make it all the way to Dawson City this time. His eyes filled with sentimental tears when he talked of this duty, which, despite the high esteem I, by that stage, held him in, still irked a mite.

We spent our last evening together in a saloon – a seamy, noisy, sawdust-and-rotgut establishment typical of that place – drinking cheap whiskey (Robert's scruples did not extend to temperance). After a few glasses of the acrid liquor, an enigmatic phrase my friend had employed when we first met, and which I had hitherto forgotten, returned to me, prompting me to ask him a question.

'You mentioned before you were led astray by the lure of riches. What did you mean by that?'

'Do you believe there are things that, though beyond the ordinary ken of man, nevertheless mold our lives, weird forces at work?'

'No, I do not.'

'Neither did I once. Back then I would have scorned such notions, but now...'

'You have your belief. I'm not a religious man.'

I tried hard to keep the scorn from my tone, but Robert heard it, looked a touch wounded.

'It was not to God I adverted.'

He was silent a moment, then peered at me through the fug in that place.

'Will you permit me to tell a tale? It's true, and concerns things that befell me back when I was a rash youth.'

Given that Robert was still young, I thought this formulation queer, but ignored it.

'Of course. I enjoy hearing a yarn spun.'

Then, as we sat there, at the counter, staring into our tumblers like crones scrying for auguries, Robert told me a bizarre tale as would shock you and grume your blood, if only I could tell it, a tale set in Glasgow, Scotland, a tale of penury, bloody murder, card-sharping swindles, sham séances, and the realms of the foul olden horrors that prowl the primeval lightless ways that riddle the Earth. But to say any more would be to break my word for, as I wrote at the beginning of this account, I promised him then I would not ever divulge the story to another soul.

When he was through, my companion took a handkerchief from his pocket and wiped his brow. Though the fire in the saloon's grate had died right down, and a biting wind howled in through the open door, he was sweating profusely. At a loss for words, I murmured that I was sorry. He grinned and turned to me.

'Oh, it's not your fault.'

I had been filled with horror by what I had heard, so packed the bowl of my briar, lit the tobacco with a match taken from a pot on the bar, and took a calming draw.

'What did you do after?' I asked.

Robert took his own pipe from his shirt pocket.

'First, could I thieve some 'baccy from you?'

I assented, gladly. He took my pouch and set about filling and lighting his pipe, a deft feat one-handed.

Once he had it smoking nicely, stem clenched in his teeth at the corner of his mouth, he continued his tale. Following the awful caper, he told me, he had fled for North America. On his arrival in the New World after a rough but uneventful crossing of the Atlantic, he had settled in Boston, a town he chose on a mere whim. Many years followed, filled with a slew of tribulations – poverty, hardship, a spell in a labor camp, some time wandering the brutal Old West – before he finally wound up in New York, where he suffered a beating at the hands of a drunken mob and was taken in and nursed back to health by a preacher. Robert repaid this kindness by staying on, once recovered, and helping his rescuer, who was aged and doddery, if not doting, with his duties. When the minister died, a few years later, it was only natural that Robert take over his flock. He subsequently married a member of the congregation, a beautiful young woman, who returned his affections in spite of his being a cripple, but, as he had already told me, she died in childbirth two years after their wedding.

'The pain has not paled one bit, though it's been many months since I suffered the loss,' Robert concluded, biting his lip. 'When I heard of the Klondike Gold Rush and of the stampeders' hardships, I came out here to wander these frozen lands and offer succor where I could. I've found respite from my grief in ministering and preaching to those in need.'

Again, I said how sorry I was to hear tell of his woes. Smiling, he once more brushed my expressions of sympathy aside, suggested we eat. This proposal met with my favor, I realized then I was ravenous, my composure, and appetite, restored by pipe smoke. While we tucked into some poor fare brought out by the barkeep, it dawned on me that Robert's apparent youth could not be reconciled with his account of his life. I challenged him.

'It is of no consequence to me whether you choose to credit me or not,' he countered, with some asperity.

I glared at him, shook my head. The anger that had flared up died away, and he looked down at his food, said, in a tone of mollification, 'But I am grateful to you for listening. Each time I tell my tale, its burden grows lighter.'

I could not respond straightway, as I was chewing one of the lumps of tough, gristly meat that were swimming in the stew we had been brought (lamb on the menu, but I doubted this, particularly as I had seen the proprietor of the place buying a broken-down old mule from a stampeder only the day before). Once it was pappy enough to swallow, I replied, 'I'm sorry. It isn't that I didn't believe you. I was bemused is all.'

'As for that, all I can say is that I haven't, in my outward seeming, aged a day since... Since then. I don't expect you to believe that. I wouldn't myself if I didn't have proof of it every time I look in a glass.'

I nodded, turned the conversation to other topics, sensing it would be futile to press Robert further. I am, to this day, unsure whether the weird things he told me of were delusion, a mere pack of lies, or the entire truth. I quail to consider this last possibility...

We finished our food, then Robert proposed we share another bottle of whiskey before turning in. I agreed, he ordered it, and the barkeep brought it over. Robert poured us both a slug, then asked me what I thought I might do with myself on my return south.

'Well,' I said. 'I've always fancied trying my hand at writing. I might give that a go. Your story would make a great yarn, you know.'

I was half-joking, but he suddenly looked very stern. And that is when he made me take the vow.

Afterwards, his expression lightened.

'Otherwise, I wish you all the best with it,' he said. 'I hope you can understand?'

I nodded.

'Of course. It was crass of me to suggest it at all.'

We finished the bottle, chatting easily, then went back to our lodgings. I slept poorly that night, apprehensive about the voyage I was to embark on the following morning, disquieted by Robert's ghastly tale. Lying awake, on my bunk, I gazed up at the fly-specked ceiling, wondered how flies could breed in a country so grimly cold I could not picture a rotting carcass, even at the height of summer. Instead, I imagined them pouring forth, in a droning mass, from a crevice, high up in the mountains, a chasm that gave on to some vile alterior place.

The following morning was cold, blustery; ragged scraps of white cloud scudded overhead through an ashen sky. Robert accompanied me down to the docks. We said our farewells on the wharf, then I walked up the gangplank and boarded the steamer. As the vessel pulled out of the harbor I stood at the taffrail waving to my friend. His breath plumed in the cold air – it was as if his spirit had broken free of the hawsers mooring it to the flesh. I gazed at him until he was little more than a mote in my eye – a dark smut at the point where the yellowish daub of smoke belched from the ship's funnels and the churned wake converged – then turned away from the shore, went to report to the boatswain. He assigned me first watch at the bow. I was to keep a lookout for ice floes. Crossing the deck, I took up my position, leaning far out over the gunwale, holding onto the bowsprit to steady myself. For several hours I watched the hatchet prow cleave the sea. At one point I am sure I glimpsed a narwhal's tusk break the surface of the water.

I have never seen Robert again. But my encounter with him changed my life utterly. Unable to get his tale from my thoughts, barbed as it is by weird and sinister implications, I have spent a great deal of time, as this book is testament, seeking others like it. My motives are obscure, even to me. I think it is partly that I sought similar yarns in the hope that, discovering them all absurd lies or delusions, I would finally be able to dismiss Robert's as falsehood or madness. Too often, however, I have found a shred of truth in the stories told me, and have, over the course of my life, sewed these scraps into a patchwork of uncanny horror.

Acknowledgements

Peterkin (or whoever) dedicated *The Wanderer* to a 'hoped for, though doubtless chimeric, reader.' I would like to dedicate this book to Fi Ment, much missed, without whom it's likely the typescript would have never come to light.

Much of the work on this book was done as part of a PhD project. I'd like to thank my doctoral supervisors, Willy Maley and Andrew Radford, for their generous support and insightful critiques; the examiners of the resultant thesis, Rob Maslen and Adam Roberts, for astute and valuable feedback; and the Arts and Humanities Research Council for funding. Much gratitude to those who read this work and gave encouragement, comments, and editorial suggestions: William Curnow, Al Duncan, Susan Jarvis, James Machin, and Neil Stewart. Many thanks to Phil Jourdan for patience, enthusiasm, and hard work. Thanks to my family for all their support. And thanks, Sophie Tolhurst, for endless tolerance and kindness.

"There are many who dare not kill themselves for fear of what the neighbours will say," Cyril Connolly wrote, and we believe he was right.

Perfect Edge seeks books that take on the crippling fear of other people, the question of what's correct and normal, of how life works, of what art is.

Our authors disagree with each other; their styles vary as widely as their concerns. What matters is the will to create books that won't be easy to assimilate. We take risks, not for the sake of risk-taking, but for the things that might come out of it.